THE INK MASTER'S SILENCE

GLASS AND STEELE, #6

C.J. ARCHER

C.J. ARCHER

CHAPTER 1

LONDON, SPRING 1890

When events have not been going one's way for some time, it can take a period of adjustment before realizing all will be well. Finally, a week after his magic watch had been fixed, I allowed myself to believe Matt was going to live. He looked handsome and healthy in his full evening attire as he sat opposite me in the carriage. The lines of exhaustion had smoothed away, the color returned to his skin, and the spark to his eyes.

It was both thrilling and humbling to know that I had helped save him along with the doctor magician, Gabriel Seaford. Not only that, but Sheriff Payne was in prison. For the first time since arriving in England, Matt was free.

Almost.

There was only the marriage to his cousin Patience standing in his way of complete happiness. Sometimes, when he looked at me with love and affection, I didn't mind that we couldn't be together yet. I had his devotion, after all, and he had his health. We were fortunate in so many other ways; surely I could settle for being in his life in a minor capacity, if I could not be his wife.

But when I thought on it further, on the long future stretching before us and the prospect of spending it as mere friends, it shattered me.

"India? Are you listening to me?" he asked. "You're miles away."

"I'm right here, admiring how well you look tonight."

He hooked a finger inside his stiff collar and stretched his neck. "I loathe formal wear. This shirt is as hard as a plank of wood."

"Wishing you were back in the wilds of California, wearing leather chaps and a cowboy hat?"

"You've been reading too many dime novels. I knew it was a bad idea for Willie to lend you her copies."

"No chaps?"

"Only on special occasions." He leaned forward and rested his hands on my knees. The mischievous smile that was never far from his lips nowadays hinted of things to come…one day. "Like the one I just mentioned."

"Are you going to a costume ball?"

He sat back with a satisfied smirk. "I knew you weren't listening."

"So…you're not going to dress up as a cowboy?"

"I will if you want me to." His eyes positively sparkled.

I liked this side of Matt very much. It made the ache in my chest bearable.

"One day, and in private, just for you," he added. He leaned forward again and caught my hand in both of his. He pressed it to his lips, lightly kissing the knuckles through my glove. "I should warn you that in the mean time, I am going to seduce you."

"Is that so?" I whispered breathily. "And how do you plan on seducing me?"

"I can't tell you that or I'd spoil the fun."

I ought to remove my hand and tell him not to talk about seduction. We were neither married nor betrothed, and as far as his family and Patience were concerned, *they* were engaged to be married. But I didn't want to see the light fade from his eyes or a mask of polite civility slam into place. Nor did I want to admit there was any possible outcome other than the two of us being together. I didn't want to admit it even to myself. As far as we were concerned, there was a way out of his entanglement with his cousin. We just needed to find it.

If only Matt would tell me how his uncle could force him down the aisle. He continued to deny that there was a reason beyond his sense of cousinly duty, no matter how much I cajoled, begged, or argued with him. According to Matt, by publicly agreeing to the union, he was shielding Patience from gossip that might arise from Lord Cox ending their engagement due to her past indiscretions. Matt claimed he was saving her from a life of spinsterhood, and her sisters too since they would be tainted by association thanks to Patience's scandalous liaison.

I knew there was more to it, however. Matt went to great lengths to avoid answering me when I asked him directly if his uncle had threatened him. Those conversations inevitably led to him kissing me until my wits abandoned me and I forgot my resolve.

"Now that I have your attention, I wanted to tell you where I went today." The light from the passing streetlamps struck the left side of his face and cast the right side in shadow. Dark and fair, a gentleman and a rogue, happy and healthy yet never far from death. That was Matt.

"I hoped you would, in your own time," I said. Matt had been out most of the afternoon and had so far refused to tell me where he'd been.

"I didn't want to say in front of the others. They'd pepper me with relentless questions. I visited Lord Cox. He's in London on business."

My hopes rose. "And?"

He put up his hands and my heart dove again. "He is still refusing to take Patience back. The man has higher morals than most clergymen, and he's stubborn. He even seems to care for her and how the situation is affecting her, but not enough to change his mind."

"Caring isn't enough," I muttered. "Only love would do."

"I even sketched out her future for him and he still refused to relinquish. The man's a coward."

I was about to make excuses for Lord Cox but swallowed

my words. Matt was right. Lord Cox was a coward for not being prepared to protect Patience from gossip by marrying her.

"He thinks I'm going to step into the void and considers himself off the hook," Matt went on. "I told him he'd been taken in, just as my uncle intended. I informed Cox I wouldn't be marrying Patience but have not formally denied the arrangement for her sake. He seemed somewhat interested in that piece of news."

"But not enough to resume their engagement."

"No."

"So your visit was in vain," I said heavily.

"Not entirely. I did make him promise not to tell anyone what Payne told him about Patience's past. He agreed. He even seemed offended that I felt a need to extract that promise."

I scoffed. "Given the speculation swirling around their broken engagement and his cowardice, your lack of faith in him is understandable."

I only knew about such speculation because Miss Glass, Matt's aunt, had informed me every day. She seemed to want to make sure I knew why I was sacrificing my own future. I couldn't deny that it hurt that she thought Patience's happiness more important than mine, yet it was understandable that she'd support her niece over her companion.

"It's one thing off my mind, at least," Matt said. "And another nail in the coffin of my uncle's scheming. Her secret will remain safe, no matter what happens. Payne can't do anything from prison, and Cox will keep his silence."

I leveled my gaze with his but did not see hope in it. "Yet speculation as to why they ended their engagement will remain unless she's betrothed to you," I said, annoyance making my voice hard. "That's the excuse you're going to give me for not ending the charade now, isn't it?"

He looked out the window.

"Tell me, Matt. Tell me what Lord Rycroft is doing to force your hand."

The coach slowed to turn a corner. "I think we're here." He

picked his hat off the seat beside him and slapped it on his head. "Are you ready to see what Lord Coyle wants?"

I sighed. "You're infuriating."

He leaned forward and pressed his palms to the wall behind either side of my head. "And madly in love with you, India." His warm breath brushed my ear then his lips tickled me, sending a wave of tingles spreading through me. "Never forget that. Never forget that I will get out of this entanglement. I just need time to find Cox's weakness."

"You're going to blackmail him into marrying her?"

He pulled away to look at me. "You sound shocked."

"I suppose I thought you above underhanded tactics."

"I am going to do everything in my power to be released from this obligation, I promise you." He lightly kissed my nose, my chin, my throat above the pearl choker necklace Miss Glass had loaned me.

I struggled to maintain my train of thought. "Everything except tell me what your uncle has over you."

"Everything in my power." It was the closest he'd come to an admission that Lord Rycroft was indeed blackmailing him.

Lord Coyle's footman opened the carriage door and offered me his hand. Matt adjusted my shawl, skimming his thumb over my arm, and indicated I should exit.

It wasn't easy to concentrate as the footman escorted us inside. I was very aware of Matt's imposing presence at my side and the simmering desire between us. All of that fled, however, when I handed my shawl to a different footman in the entrance hall.

I stood in the very spot where I'd been attacked by Mr. Pitt, the apothecary, magician, and murderer of Dr. Hale. My watch had saved me then. Sheriff Payne broke that watch and it remained to be seen if the new one Matt bought me would do the same. I hoped I'd never need to find out.

"Are you all right?" Matt murmured, his hand at my back.

I nodded and followed the footman up the stairs to the drawing room, where Lord Coyle waited with three other gentlemen and a woman.

"Welcome, Miss Steele," Coyle said, bowing over my hand. "And Mr. Glass." The greeting was pleasant enough but brisk, almost dismissive. It confirmed that the invitation had been extended to Matt because I'd refused the earlier ones, and Lord Coyle assumed I'd accept if I came in Matt's company.

He was right, of course. The earl made me uncomfortable. I wasn't yet sure if he was friend or foe. I did know that he had a keen interest in all things magical. We'd seen his collection of objects infused with magic in the hidden room off the library. I assumed this evening was taking place in order to convince me to infuse a watch or clock with my magic so he could add it to his collection. I thought it harmless enough, but Matt wasn't so sure. He didn't want me to display my magical abilities, in any way, to anyone.

I agreed with him, to a certain extent, simply because I didn't want every craftsman in London asking me to use my extending spell on their own magic. Yet I wanted to live openly, without hiding what I was from the world and in fear of reprisal from the artless.

Lord Coyle introduced the other guests to us. Mr. and Mrs. Delancey were beyond middle age, like Coyle, and greeted me enthusiastically. Sir Charles Whittaker was younger, about forty, with streaks of gray through his hair. He was more reserved than the Delanceys but I liked that he gave my hand a firm shake. Usually men didn't shake my hand, and if they did, it was limp. It was a minor thing but important.

The third gentleman, Professor Nash, was a similar age to Sir Charles, with thinning hair and spectacles. He couldn't stop staring at me, even after introductions, and I felt quite uncomfortable as we sat.

The drawing room held few feminine touches. Understandable, considering Lord Coyle was a lifelong bachelor. Even the sofa had sturdy legs and was upholstered in burgundy velvet. There were no vases of flowers, no portraits of family members, and decorations consisted almost entirely of white marble busts of men I didn't recognize.

We spent a few short minutes in polite conversation that felt as though it were being carefully directed by Lord Coyle. I learned that the professor was an expert in history, but Coyle cut him off before he could tell me his particular field of study. Mr. Delancey was a banker, and going by the diamonds at his wife's throat, he was very successful. Sir Charles seemed to have no profession. Perhaps, like Lord Coyle, his income came from land holdings.

It was something of a relief when the butler informed us that dinner was served. The long table was made for larger parties than we seven, so we sat at one end. Miss Glass wouldn't have liked to see the women outnumbered by the men but the arrangement worked well enough. We were into the second course when I realized the footman refilled my glass at every opportunity. It was near impossible to tell how much I'd had to drink. I made a conscious effort to abstain for at least a while.

I eyed Matt, sitting opposite, wondering if he was being as careful. Considering his past battles with liquor, I suspected so. He seemed rather on edge, his gaze flitting between the other guests and our host. He rarely showed impatience, so that put *me* on edge. I wished Coyle would just get on with it and tell us why he'd invited me.

We had to wait for the final course of jellies, ice cream, French pastries and lemon water ice to learn the reason. Lord Coyle dismissed the servants and waited until the doors closed. It wasn't he who spoke first, however, but Mrs. Delancey.

"So you're a magician, Miss Steele," she said, as if it were normal to ask.

Beside her, Matt tensed. He did not speak, did not indicate in any way that I shouldn't answer in the affirmative, but I knew him well enough to know that he didn't want me to.

"What an odd question, Mrs. Delancey," I said with what I hoped was smooth indifference. I'd come prepared for this conversation and did not plan on giving anything away without first learning why I was here.

"Oh, it wasn't a question," Professor Nash said. "Lord Coyle has already told us that you are a magician. She was merely encouraging you to tell us more about your magic."

Mrs. Delancey touched the large diamond pendant at her throat as she laughed. "Nash has a habit of over-explaining things, Miss Steele. He's so incredibly clever that I think he believes we're all too stupid to understand subtlety."

The professor blushed and concentrated on his food.

"What is this all about, Coyle?" Matt demanded. "What rumors have you been spreading?"

"Truths, Mr. Glass," Lord Coyle said. "Not rumors. I've observed enough to know that Miss Steele is a magician. I want to assure you both that whatever you say here will not leave this room. My guests are not only discreet, they have an interest in keeping magic private."

"Why?" I asked.

"I'm a collector of magical objects, which you already know. The Delanceys and Sir Charles are also collectors. Our collections are unique, and that makes them valuable among our acquaintances. If magic becomes publicly known, our artifacts suddenly become commonplace. Everyone will want a magical object."

"Thereby increasing the value of your collection," Matt said. "Isn't that what you want?"

"Values won't increase. At the moment, only a select few can afford to obtain the objects from a small number of sources—known magicians. If the entire world is aware of magic, and magicians come out of the woodwork and sell their magic-infused wares, then prices will plummet. It's simple economics of supply and demand."

"Our collections will become worthless," Mr. Delancey added. "I haven't spent the last twenty years seeking out the rarest pieces for that to happen." He picked up his glass. "You understand my meaning, Miss Steele?"

"Perfectly," I said tightly. "As long as magicians fear discovery and backlash from the guilds, they'll remain in hiding and prices for their products will remain high. Your collections will retain their value. Essentially, you're trading on fear."

Mr. Delancey sipped his wine, his eyes glittering as he stared at me. We understood one another perfectly. His wife, however, pressed a hand to her chest as if to still a racing heart. "You make us sound quite avaricious. Let me assure you, that is not the case. It's not about the value of the objects, you see, but about their uniqueness. What is the point in a collection when objects are easy to find and purchase? All our friends belong to the club—"

"Club?" Matt pressed.

"Fellow collectors. It's not an official club, just an informal gathering of individuals who like to pass on information to one another about magical objects, where to buy them, that sort of thing. We are members." She indicated all of them except the professor. "If our collections become pointless, then our group becomes pointless, and our friendships will disintegrate. It's that which I value most, Miss Steele."

She might, but I didn't think the men in the room did, particularly her husband. "And what about you, Professor?" I asked. "You're not a member of this club?"

He pushed his spectacles up his nose. "No, but I am well aware of it. Lord Coyle approached me a year ago and told me all about it. I've given lectures at some of their meetings."

"On what topic?" Matt asked.

"The history of magic. It's my specialty."

"Which university teaches the history of magic?"

The professor chuckled. "I am a professor of history at University College here in London. As far as the university is concerned, I specialize in medieval studies, but my real passion is magic."

I must have stared rather stupidly at him, because he smiled sympathetically at me.

"You probably have some questions, Miss Steele," he said.

I had quite a few, but I bit my tongue. Matt was right to be cautious. We knew nothing about these people.

"Very few outside the collectors' club know about my specialty," the professor went on. "I don't want to be ridiculed any more than you do."

"It's not ridicule that worries us," Matt said darkly. "Are you a magician, Professor?"

"No, but my grandfather was. He could manipulate iron but

not to any great extent. He could bend it a little, shape a small piece into something else, but his magic was relatively weak. Magic in my family ended with him, but my interest in it is strong. I've spent my life researching it and have traveled extensively in search of original texts that mention magic."

"And what has your research taught you?" I asked.

"A great many things, but mostly I've come to the conclusion that magical powers have diminished to such an extent that it's almost useless. Nowadays, magicians can perform a few simple tricks, but in the past, magic could alter reality. Objects could be manipulated into something else entirely. Perhaps magic even changed the course of history."

A mapmaker apprentice had once told me stories of sketched rivers flowing off magical maps into real life. My own grandfather believed that ancient disasters, miracles and myths that seemed impossible could be explained by the use of magic. I did not tell the professor any of that.

"Such magic appears to be lost forever, thanks to the dilution of bloodlines," the professor said.

"Except, perhaps, in a select few," Lord Coyle added. "You, for example, Miss Steele, can make a watch save your life."

"No, sir. You're mistaken, "I said. "A watch is an inanimate object. I cannot make it do anything."

He leaned forward and placed his meaty fists on the table, either side of his plate. "Your watch saved you downstairs in my entrance hall, Miss Steele. I saw it with my own eyes. "

There was no defending myself. He had seen it, and I could think of no excuses. Lord Coyle knew it too. He stroked his drooping white moustache with his thumb and forefinger, not quite hiding his smirk.

"Are you trying to tell us that those old stories are true?" Matt asked Nash.

"Were true, Mr. Glass," the professor said. "As far as I am aware, only a few magicians possessed that sort of power. Even then, it's not known whether they possessed it because they came from unbroken magical lineages or their magic was different to that practiced by humble craftsmen."

I came from unbroken magical lineages, according to Chronos, my grandfather. But these people couldn't possibly know that. Could they?

"Tell me about the powerful magicians," I said to Professor Nash.

"From what I can gather," he said, "they could create new spells from existing ones because they possessed the language of magic. From those new spells, all manner of things could be created or affected."

"Miracles," Mr. Delancey pronounced with all the authority of a preacher. "Or the appearance of them."

I got the feeling they were all watching me very closely to gauge my reaction. Lord Coyle had told them what I was capable of, but they didn't realize I had limited knowledge of the extent of my own power. I knew as much as they did—that I could make a watch run on time, fix almost any timepiece, and extend the length of another's magic. I did not know how I made watches and clocks fly off the shelves to save me.

"India doesn't have that kind of power," Matt said. "Did you think she did? Is that why she's here?"

Mrs. Delancey waved a hand that happened to be holding her glass. Some wine sloshed over the rim. "Not at all. We're delighted to meet her. We hoped she could speak a spell into Mr. Delancey's watch to add it to our collection, that's all. As Professor Nash says, powerful magic has probably died out. No one expects someone as ordinary as Miss Steele to be a spell caster."

"She is *not* ordinary," Matt said.

"Oh, of course not. She's quite lovely, just not...special." She laughed.

The men did not. "Spell caster is the name I gave those rare magicians," Professor Nash said. "They seemed to be the only ones who possessed full knowledge of the language of magic."

"The language has disappeared?" I asked.

"I haven't been able to find any sources that explain it thoroughly, only second and third hand descriptions. The particulars seem to have been passed down orally until such time as magicians were persecuted. Then it either went so deeply underground that only a select few maintained knowledge of the language, or it was forgotten altogether. Of course, most individual magicians know a simple spell, but that's all. The rules of the language, its construction, are gone."

The room fell silent. With the courses finished, the gentlemen would usually retreat to the smoking room, and Mrs. Delancey and I would return to the drawing room to wait for them, but our host didn't get up. He sat at the head of the table, watching me, as did the other guests. Only Matt's gaze focused in a different direction.

"I understand why the Delanceys, Sir Charles and Lord Coyle want to keep magic a secret," he said to Nash, "but why do you, Professor?"

"I don't particularly care one way or another," he said. "On the one hand, perhaps public acceptance of magicians will encourage them into the open, perhaps even a spell caster. That excites me. But my studies in medieval history have proved to me that when the majority feel threatened by the minority, the minority always loses. I'm afraid magicians would simply be persecuted more openly rather than in the few select cases we've experienced so far. That frightens me. I don't want to see that happen any more than you do, Mr. Glass. My grandfather may have passed years ago, but I do know other magicians. I'd like them to remain safe."

Matt nodded, happy with the answer. "Then you will agree that Oscar Barratt's enthusiasm for writing about magic in *The Weekly Gazette* should be curtailed."

They all murmured their agreement or nodded. I kept my mouth shut. I wasn't entirely sure what I wanted. Or, more precisely, I *wanted* peaceful integration, but it was no more possible than unicorns. As Professor Nash said, magicians would most likely still be persecuted if they were publicly acknowledged.

"How do you propose we do that, Mr. Glass?" Lord Coyle asked. "I don't know *The Weekly Gazette's* owners."

"And they don't bank with me," Mr. Delancey said.

Sir Charles shook his head and the professor shrugged.

"Mr. Force's articles in *The City Review* are doing a serviceable job of refuting Barratt's claims," Sir Charles said. "We could encourage him to write more."

"It's not enough," Lord Coyle said. "Barratt is clever and fearless. Every time Force states one thing, Barratt states another. Besides, the public believes Barratt, and belief is a powerful thing."

Mrs. Delancey rose and refilled her own glass from the bottle the footman had left on the sideboard. "We need to discredit him," she said. "We must expose him as a fraudster, and his claims as hoaxes dreamed up to sell more copies of that rag."

"How do we do that, my dear?" her husband asked.

She had no answer. No one did.

"Could someone not threaten Mr. Barratt?" she eventually said. "Accost him in a dark alley and order him to retract everything."

I stared at her.

"He wouldn't be harmed," she went on. "Just threatened. How do you say it in the slums? Roughened?"

"I am not from the slums," I bit off.

"It's not Barratt we need to stop," Sir Charles said. "It's his editor. He has the real power at that paper."

"Baggley," Matt filled in. "An old fellow. I don't think it needs to be said, but I'll say it anyway, I do not condone violence or the threat of violence."

Mrs. Delancey pouted.

"Of course, of course," Mr. Delancey said. "No one here does. But I disagree with you, Sir Charles. Baggley may be able to stop Barratt from writing his poisonous articles for the *Gazette,* but Barratt could easily go elsewhere. A number of papers would welcome him. His articles are extremely popular. I think it's him we have to stop."

"Unless someone comes up with a non-violent way to stop him, this conversation is pointless," I said hotly. I was no friend to Oscar Barratt anymore, after he published more information in his articles than I'd liked, but this sort of talk could become dangerous. I didn't think these men had the same morals as Matt. I wouldn't put it past them to threaten Oscar—or worse.

"Are any of you magicians?" Matt asked.

"My father was a wool magician," Mr. Delancey said. "But I am not."

"It's how his family made their money," Mrs. Delancey said. "They manufactured woolen garments. My husband sold the business after his father's death and bought a floundering merchant bank. It's now one of the most successful banks in the city."

"And you, Lord Coyle, Sir Charles?" Matt asked.

"Not me," Coyle said.

"Nor me," Sir Charles added. "Magic is unique to the trades class. You won't find many magicians among our circle for that reason."

Mrs. Delancey told her husband to hand me his watch. He unhooked the chain and passed it to me. "Will you, Miss Steele?" he asked.

"She will not," Matt growled. "This is absurd. She's not a magician."

"Don't treat us as fools, Glass," Lord Coyle said. "It's hardly a secret that her magic is powerful enough that her watch can save her. We also know that she combined her magic with that of a doctor to extend your life."

I sucked in a breath. He could only have known that if he'd spoken to Sheriff Payne. No one else who'd been there that day would have told him. If Coyle was associating with Payne then I didn't trust him at all.

Matt glared at Coyle, his fingers stroking the stem of his wine glass. I thought he might pick it up and throw it at our host, but he remained outwardly calm. Perhaps too calm.

"You ought to know that the sheriff is mad," I said quickly. "Don't believe him. Witnesses at his trial will refute every outrageous claim." The trial hadn't started yet. The sooner it did, the better. If Payne was saying things in prison, he needed to be stopped before the rumors took flight.

Lord Coyle dismissed my speech with a lazy lift of his hand. He didn't even bother addressing it. It was rather insulting.

The entire evening had become quite upsetting; added to which, I still wasn't entirely sure why I'd been invited. I didn't for a moment think it was because Mrs. Delancey wanted me to infuse magic into her husband's watch. That watch now sat on the table between us, its chain coiled on the white tablecloth like a snake.

I caught Matt's eye and jerked my head ever so slightly.

"If you'll excuse us, we're leaving," he said, rising.

All the gentlemen rose as I stood.

"But you haven't used your magic on my husband's watch," Mrs. Delancey whined.

I thanked our host and managed polite goodbyes to the other guests. Matt offered me his arm and went to open the door only for it to open from the other side. The butler entered and whispered something in Lord Coyle's ear. Matt and I made our exit but Lord Coyle summoned us back.

"Something has happened which will interest you." Coyle looked to Sir Charles. "It seems someone else thought as you do, Whittaker. Mr. Baggley, editor of *The Weekly Gazette*, has been murdered."

CHAPTER 2

"What did you eat?" Duke asked the moment Matt and I set foot in the drawing room. He, Willie and Cyclops had waited up for us, although Cyclops looked drowsy.

Willie set down her cards. "*That's* your first question?"

Duke shrugged. "I'm hungry."

"The food was delicious and plentiful," I told him. "The wine superb, although there was rather too much of it for me."

Willie gave a knowing nod. "You don't hold your liquor well, India, it's true. Ain't your fault. You just need more experience."

"What did Coyle want?" Cyclops asked.

"I'm not entirely sure," I said. "Perhaps just to introduce us to his friends."

Matt offered to pour me a drink but I declined. He sat down without pouring himself one either. "I think he wanted to gauge our reactions to Professor Nash's claims," he said.

We told them about the other guests, the collectors' club, and the professor's interest in the history of magic. Twice I had to explain the lost language of magic and how spell casters used it to create new spells.

"But *you* know the language, India," Willie said. "So do other magicians."

"We only know a few words. There are probably thousands

more. According to Nash, those magicians knew how to string the words together to make new spells, just like writers and storytellers have done for centuries with the English language."

"Nash also thinks they were powerful magicians with unbroken lineages," Matt said.

They all looked at me.

"I am not a spell caster," I said. "I'm doubtful they even existed. Nash is only guessing, after all. He has no proof, only his own interpretations of some old texts. He said so himself." I picked up Willie's cards and pushed her entire stack of matchsticks into the middle.

"Not that much!" She pulled them back again.

"They're matchsticks, Willie," Duke said with a roll of his eyes. "We ain't playing for diamonds."

"I don't like losing to you."

I sat again and looked at Matt. I was so used to seeing him exhausted at this time of the evening that I almost ordered him to bed. Instead, I smiled, although my mood wasn't as buoyant as it had been before dinner. The news about poor Mr. Baggley unnerved me. I told the others what Coyle's butler had reported just before we left.

"Murdered!" Cyclops's one eye squinted. "How?"

"Shot from behind," Matt said.

"Shot!" Willie cried. "From what distance?"

"The butler didn't know," Matt said wryly.

"Then how'd he know Baggley was shot?"

It was a good question. According to the butler, Baggley had died mere hours earlier from a gunshot wound to the head. He'd been working late at the *Gazette's* office on Lower Mire Lane but the butler couldn't say if anyone else had been present or if someone had been arrested. But how had he known about the murder in the first place?

"Coyle must have spies," Matt said.

"At the *Gazette*?" I asked.

"All over the city, but particularly at the *Gazette's* offices now. You heard him tonight, India. He and his friends don't like Barratt's articles. I wouldn't put it past him to have paid an employee to report who meets with Barratt, what he and Baggley discuss, that sort of thing. Coyle will be looking for any way to sabotage Barratt and the paper."

"Like murder the editor?" Duke said.

"You think him capable?" Cyclops asked.

Matt looked to me. "India?"

He was allowing me to express my opinion before him, in an attempt to boost my confidence. I'd been quite hopeless at judging character in the past, having made some terrible choices in my friendships, but I liked to think I was getting better. For instance, I trusted the people in that room implicitly.

"Yes," I said. "I think he is capable."

"So do I. He has the resources to pay someone to do it, so he can look innocent, and he's ruthless enough to want to protect his collection's value."

I shivered. Lord Coyle could have orchestrated a murder while dining with us. Surely his ruthlessness didn't extend that far. Yet I couldn't shake the thought.

"To be fair," Matt went on, "any number of people must want the articles to end. The other guests there tonight, for example, Abercrombie and the guild masters, and even a few magicians who want to remain anonymous."

"That's the thing, though," I said. "They wanted the *articles* to end, so why not kill *Barratt*? Killing Baggley probably won't change anything. The newspaper will still go out weekly, and Barratt's articles will still be included. They are popular enough that a new editor won't stop them."

It was the conclusion we had all come to over dinner, and I saw no reason to alter my opinion. To end the articles, one had to stop Oscar Barratt, not Baggley.

"Maybe it has nothing to do with the paper," Duke said. "Maybe it were personal."

"I'll see what I can learn tomorrow," Matt said. "Cyclops, you look done in. You haven't stopped yawning since we got home."

"I've been fixing the convent roof," he said, turning a flinty glare onto Duke and Willie. "Without help."

"We helped," Willie protested. "Holding the ladder requires two of us on account of you being so heavy."

"We thought it would be good for you to work alone up there," Duke added. "Physical work tires you so you don't have time to think about Catherine Mason."

"What does she have to do with anything?" Cyclops growled.

"You have been thinking about her a lot lately," Willie told him. "And it's making you sad that you can't be together."

"We're doing you a favor," Duke added.

Cyclops pushed to his feet. "You can't talk, Willie. You been thinking a lot about your lover lately, too. Your face has been as long as an old nag's."

"She ain't my lover no more." Willie slid all of her matchsticks into the middle of the table. "Let's get this game over. I want to go to bed."

She and Cyclops glared at one another while Duke showed his hand then gleefully raked in all the matchsticks.

"The three of you need to blow off some steam," Matt said, clamping a hand on Cyclops's shoulder. "The convent roof is finished, isn't it? Why not go out tomorrow? See the sights of London. Visit a museum. Have a picnic in Hyde Park."

The three of them looked at him as if he were mad.

"Or enjoy a drink at a pub," I said.

They agreed on that and went to bed in happier spirits.

* * *

I THOUGHT we should visit Oscar Barratt to find out more about Mr. Baggley's death, but Matt disagreed. He claimed it was because Detective Inspector Brockwell would know more, but I suspected it was simply because he didn't like Oscar. I doubted Brockwell would tell us anything. He was a stickler for following protocol.

I was both right and wrong. He was more informative than I expected when he finally invited us into his office after making us wait for twenty-three minutes. His willingness probably had a lot to do with experiencing danger together the day Sheriff

Payne was arrested. It was surprising how life and death situations could bring people closer.

"I don't think his murder has anything to do with the articles about magic that have appeared in *The Weekly Gazette*," he said in his precise, clipped manner of speaking. "Tea, Miss Steele?"

"Oh, er, no, thank you," I said.

"Nor for me," Matt added. He smiled one of his charming smiles.

It only made Brockwell shift uncomfortably in his chair and concentrate on the papers spread before him. I rolled my eyes at Matt. He glowered and crossed his arms. I knew he thought Brockwell was interested in me in *that* way, but I'd dispelled that notion. Or so I thought. It would seem he was still jealous. I found I couldn't be disappointed about that.

"Why don't you think his murder has anything to do with magic?" I asked.

Brockwell flipped through some papers. When he found the one he wanted, he drew it out and placed it on top of the pile. He shaped the pile until it was a perfect stack again. "If I wanted to stop the articles, I'd kill Barratt, not Baggley."

"That seems to be a common opinion," Matt said. "I'm not entirely sure it's a good enough reason to dismiss the theory based on the little we know, however."

"Was he alone in the office at the time?" I asked.

"Barratt was with him," Brockwell said. "They were discussing story ideas. Barratt had got up to retrieve notes from the desk, leaving Baggley alone. He heard a gunshot and ran out, only to find Baggley slumped over his desk and the killer nowhere to be seen. The front door was not locked. Anyone could have walked in off the street."

"Is Barratt under suspicion?" Matt asked.

"Matt!" I cried.

He shrugged. "He was alone with Baggley, and there are no other witnesses. He'd be my prime suspect."

"He is a suspect," Brockwell said.

Matt seemed satisfied, but I got the feeling Brockwell was keeping something from us.

"Who else?" I asked.

"I'm not at liberty to say, Miss Steele. I am sorry." He smiled gently. I smiled back, hoping it would soften his stance a little. But I wasn't a charmer and Brockwell wasn't the sort of man who could be charmed.

"Did you find the murder weapon?" Matt asked, breaking the silence.

"No," Brockwell said.

"Any witnesses?"

"I am not at liberty to say."

"Did the killer leave behind any evidence?"

"Again, I am not at liberty to say."

"Don't make me go over your head, Inspector."

Brockwell clasped his hands on the paper stack. "Since this case does not involve you, Commissioner Munro is unlikely to give you the answers you seek."

Matt stood and buttoned up his jacket. "Are you quite sure it doesn't involve us?" He offered me his arm and went to escort me out.

"Before you go," Brockwell said, once again searching through his papers. "I have an update on Sheriff Payne's trial. The prosecutor wants it to go ahead soon."

"The sooner the better," I said.

"Quite. Payne has been telling the other inmates that he saw you and Mr. Seaford bring Mr. Glass back to life using magic. In light of the public's interest in magic, it won't take long for the newspapermen to get wind of it. The sooner the trial is, the less opportunity for them to hear him spout his maliciousness."

Again, Matt went to escort me out. We thanked Brockwell as he walked us to the door.

He touched my elbow. "Good day, Miss Steele. My door will remain open to you during this difficult time of Payne's trial."

"And to me?" Matt asked.

Brockwell merely huffed.

"You shouldn't tease him," I said as we headed back through the Scotland Yard building. "He could have made life far more difficult for us. Besides, I thought you liked him. You like how methodical and thorough he is."

"True," Matt said. "But I don't like him flirting with you."

"That was hardly flirting. He was merely being a good policeman, offering me support. He probably assumed you didn't need it, since you're big and strong and quite capable of looking after yourself, now that you're healthy."

"Trust me, India, that was flirting."

"I suppose I should trust you since you are the expert."

His eyes narrowed and I grinned.

"And you can't blame him for flirting when he thinks *our* relationship is purely a working one," I added.

"As soon as I am free, he'll be the first I tell. Until then, I will exercise my right to scowl, glower and glare at him when he flirts with you."

Matt deposited me at home but climbed back into the carriage after assisting me out. He refused to tell me where he was going but promised to inform me later. It was most infuriating.

Miss Glass was the only one at home and she was glad to see me. "It's been so dull here all morning," she said with a pout. "Come and read to me, India."

I read a few pages of her book aloud but stopped when I realized she wasn't listening. She stared out the window, her neck craned to see the street.

"Are you expecting someone?" I asked.

"Just Beatrice."

"Alone or with her daughters?" I could manage one of the Glass women, but all four would be a trial. I suspected they would welcome my excuses anyway and prefer that I wasn't around. Patience in particular would feel awkward. She knew how Matt and I felt about one another.

Miss Glass turned back to me. "We're going to discuss wedding arrangements."

I closed the book and put it down. "I see."

"She wants to put an announcement in the papers, but I asked her to wait. It hasn't been all that long since the announcement of Patience's marriage to Lord Cox, and another so soon would be vulgar."

"I see," I said again.

"Matthew has also asked that we wait."

I lifted my gaze to hers. "Did he say why?"

"There's no need for him to explain. I know why. He plans on convincing Lord Cox to take her back."

"Lord Cox won't give in," I told her.

"No. He won't. He's far too proud." She rested her hand over mine. "This will be a difficult time for you, my dear, but I will help you through it. One day, you will thank me. You both will. You and Matthew are not right for one another—"

I surged to my feet. "How do you know?"

Her fingers recoiled. "I have experience in matters of the heart."

I wanted to tell her that she couldn't possibly have the same sort of experience, since she was alone, without love. But I did not. I couldn't stoop that low, not even in the heat of the moment.

"You may look at me and think of me only as a spinster," she said, guessing my thoughts. "But I was in love, once, and he was terribly unsuitable. I didn't know it at the time, but I later learned he was trying to trap me into marriage. Penelope saved me by stealing him from me."

It took me a moment to piece together the threads of her story. Penelope had once been her friend, but they'd become bitter enemies many years ago. This must be why. "Then shouldn't you thank Penelope for stealing him if he was that type of character?"

"She still stole him, India. Friends do not do that to one another. Besides, she didn't know he was a rogue at the time. She got rid of him almost as soon as she'd won him. She was never in love with him. She simply wanted to see if she could take him from me."

"That's hardly the same as our situation. I am not trying to trap Matt. I love him. I'd marry him if he were a pauper. I would hope you knew me well enough to believe that."

She sighed and turned to the window again but her gaze became dreamy. "I do miss him. I miss him very much."

For a moment I thought she was talking about the man who'd tried to trap her, but realized she was probably talking about Matt's father, her brother, Harry. Her mind often slipped into the past when confronted with conflict in the present, and her beloved brother featured regularly.

I sat again and picked up the book. Whether she listened or not, it didn't matter. Reading passed the time until the mail arrived. A letter came for me from Patience, of all people.

I set it aside and read the message from Lady Rycroft to Miss Glass first. "She says she won't be coming today after all."

"Good." Miss Glass declared. "It means she agrees to delay the announcement."

That was something, at least. A delay meant more time to convince Lord Cox. Although I hadn't a clue how we were going to do that.

"What is in your letter?" Miss Glass asked, picking it up. "It's from Patience. You can't ignore her forever."

I rather thought I could, but I took it anyway. "She apologizes," I said, scanning the page. "She hopes I will one day be able to forgive her."

"If it's forgiveness she wants, she ought to marry someone else."

I shook my head. "You are so contrary, Miss Glass. You want her to marry Matt. I thought you'd be telling me *I* ought to forgive *her*, or that there is nothing to forgive."

"Of course there's something to forgive. She's taking away my nephew. The household will never be the same again."

I blinked at her, not quite sure if I understood correctly. She thought *she* was the injured party in this arrangement, not me. I'd always assumed the upper classes were a selfish lot, and now I had confirmation. I wasn't sure whether to laugh, cry, or call her out. In the end, I said nothing. She was an elderly woman, used to thinking of no one but herself. Pointing out her selfishness would achieve nothing but discord between us, and despite everything, I was fond of her.

She patted my knee. "I don't think he should marry you, India, but that doesn't mean I want him to marry Patience. She'll do, I suppose. She's not as nasty or vacuous as her sisters. Anyway, you and I will still have one another, so something good will come of this. We'll muddle along well enough. Once we move into the big house on the estate, we can have the entire west wing to ourselves. We won't even have to see Patience if we don't want to."

It was impossible to tell if she was joking, serious, or had lost her mind. "I think you need to rest."

She touched the white curls at her temple. "Am I rambling again?"

I steered her up the stairs and settled her for a nap on the bed. I asked Bristow to serve me a light luncheon in the sitting room, since I was alone, but Duke, Cyclops and Willie returned in time. He brought in enough ribbon sandwiches for all of us.

Duke devoured two before my second bite.

"Slow down," Willie scolded him. "You'll give yourself a belly ache."

"I need to build my strength," he said around a mouthful.

"Are you doing more work at the convent after all?" I asked him.

"We ain't been to the convent," Cyclops said, picking up a sandwich in each hand. He inspected them both before deciding on the right one. He shoved the entire thing in his mouth.

"For his strength," Duke told me with a wink.

I set my sandwich down on the plate. "Will someone tell me what's going on?"

Willie and Cyclops exchanged glances. Duke ignored me in favor of his next sandwich.

"Tell me now or I'll fling that clock at you."

"All right," Willie said with a glance at the door. "But you got to promise not to tell Matt."

"I can't do that."

"Then we ain't telling you."

Clearly they were up to something that Matt wouldn't approve of, and I probably wouldn't either. It only piqued my curiosity more. "Very well," I said. "I won't tell him, but don't expect me to lie for you, either."

They all nodded. "We're going to a fight tonight," Willie said. "Bare knuckles. Last man standing is the winner."

"Go on," I hedged.

"Duke and Cyclops are contenders."

"Are you mad?" I cried. "You'll be hurt."

None of them seemed to think that a problem. "A few bruises," Cyclops said.

"A cut lip, maybe," Duke added with a shrug.

Willie grinned. "It'll be an improvement."

Both men grinned back.

They were definitely mad. This seemed to constitute entertainment for them. "I know you're from the Wild West, where things are, well, wild, but this is barbaric. No wonder you don't want Matt to know. He'll insist you stay home."

"He ain't our keeper," Willie shot back. "We can tell him if we want to, and he can't do nothing about it."

We both knew she wouldn't tell him. None of them would. Matt may not be able to stop them, but he could certainly spoil their evening by going with them and watching over them like a mother hen.

"We've been spoiling for a fight," Duke said. "You heard us last night. We're at each other all the time. Nothing exciting's happened for a whole week and we're bored. We need to release our frustration."

"By getting pounded?"

"We don't plan on getting pounded as much as our opponents," Cyclops said, his eye gleaming.

"I expected better from you, Cyclops. You have a gentle nature. These two are ruffians at heart."

Cyclops's face fell.

"He's a man, India," Duke said, not offended by my comment. "A man who's denied the woman he wants. This is the best thing for him, right now."

Cyclops looked away. I couldn't argue with him; I knew all about that kind of frustration.

"And what about your frustrations, Willie?" I asked. "Or are you going to tell me you've thrown your hat in the ring too?"

"Don't worry about me," she said. "I'll be ringside. Watching a fight is just as good for relieving frustrations as throwing the punches. Besides, they'll need me to make sure it's a fair fight. You should come, India."

"No," Duke and Cyclops both said. "Matt won't like it," Duke added.

"It ain't Matt's choice. It's India's. She's a free woman."

"A *respectable* woman," Cyclops said. "She don't want to see blood spilled, do you, India?"

"Not in the name of sport," I said. "Thank you for the invitation, Willie, but I decline."

"Fine, but you'll miss seeing a lot of bare, masculine chests." She winked.

Matt arrived home for a late luncheon, and finally informed us where he'd been. "I visited Payne in prison. That's why I didn't want you to come, India."

"You could have told me beforehand," I said.

"You would have insisted on coming."

He had a point. "Why did you want to see him?"

"Aye, why did you?" Cyclops asked. "I thought you'd never want to see his face again."

"Lord Coyle knew about India and Gabe Seaford saving my life," Matt said. "His other dinner guests also knew. I wanted to find out if someone had been to see Payne or if Payne was talking too much. If the former, then the information is relatively contained. If the latter, we might have a problem if the newspapers get wind of it before the trial."

"And?" Duke prompted. "Which was it?"

"According to the guard at the front desk, Payne had one visitor last week. The same guard was on duty at the time but couldn't remember the visitor's appearance. He said the man's toff accent stood out, however. The visitor register listed the man's name as Smith. The signature was unreadable."

"Smith?" Willie snorted.

"And what about Payne?" I asked. "What did he tell you?"

"I wasn't allowed to see him, being a key witness and an injured party. Speaking with him wasn't my primary intention anyway. I got the information I needed from the register and guard."

"Do you think Lord Coyle was his visitor?"

"Most likely."

"You going to confront him?" Cyclops asked.

"Want me to bring my Colt?" Willie added.

"There's no need to confront anyone," Matt said. "Coyle is allowed to visit Payne. At least he has an interest in keeping the information to his own circle of friends."

"But why did he want to know what happened that day?" I asked. "Why did he need to know about my magic and Gabe's?"

No one had a good answer to those questions.

* * *

I NOTICED CYCLOPS, Duke and Willie sneak away from the house after lunch and followed them to the mews. Cyclops was already in the process of rolling up his sleeves when I confronted them in the stables.

"What are you doing?" I asked.

Willie wheeled around. "What are *you* doing here? Go back to the house or Matt will come looking for you."

"We're just practicing," Duke told me, hanging his waistcoat on a hook.

"Keep Matt away." Willie shooed me and I retraced my steps back to the house.

A visitor had arrived in my short absence, one whom I wasn't sure I was pleased to see. Oscar Barratt always seemed to bring bad news with him. He'd tricked me in the past, telling me he'd be careful not to divulge too much about magic in his articles, yet he'd crossed that line anyway. The problem was, he thought the line was in one place and I thought it in another. Both of us being magicians, however, meant we also had a certain understanding of the other and the same wish—to see magicians openly able to practice their magic.

This duality made our relationship complicated.

He sat on the sofa with Matt opposite. Neither looked like they wanted to be in the same room as the other. My entry was met with expressions of relief.

"India," Oscar said. "I'm glad you're here. I wanted to speak to you both." He sat again and wiped the palm of his hand on his trouser leg. The uncertain smile he'd given me upon entry withered beneath Matt's glare.

"This saves us a journey," Matt said to Oscar. "We wanted to ask you about Mr. Baggley's murder."

"It's a terrible business." Oscar leaned forward and rested his elbows on his knees. He dragged a shaking hand through his hair.

This called for tea. I tugged the bell pull and asked Bristow for refreshments.

"Are you all right, Oscar?" I asked as I sat again.

Oscar nodded and leaned back with a heavy sigh. "I'm still coming to terms with what happened. Baggley was a good man and a fine editor. He leaves behind a wife and two adult children. He'll be missed."

"We heard you were there when he was shot," Matt said.

"You've been speaking to the police? I'm not surprised. Yes, I was there."

"Did you see anyone else?"

"No, but I thought I heard the front door shut as someone left. I ran out but saw no one on the street."

It was a narrow lane and the office was close to Fleet Street, with a number of lanes coming off it. Fleeing the scene would be easy if the killer was fleet of foot.

"Do you know who may have wanted Baggley dead?" Matt asked. "Has he enemies or been threatened lately?"

"That's the thing." Oscar scrubbed a hand over his goatee beard. "*He* hadn't been threatened, but *I* have. By a magician"

CHAPTER 3

Oscar handed several pieces of paper to Matt and I got up to read them over his shoulder. The words were formed using cut out newsprint letters pasted onto the paper. The short, deadly messages were addressed to Oscar and urged him to cease writing the magic articles or he'd be forcefully stopped.

"Crude," Matt said.

"Unoriginal," Oscar said. "Touch the paper, India."

I fingered a sheaf. "It's warm."

Matt held one of the pieces of paper to the light coming through the window. "The quality is exceptional. It's light in weight yet feels thick. It doesn't let much light through."

"Paper magic," Oscar said.

"Do you know any paper magicians?" Matt asked.

"No."

"Did they arrive in envelopes?"

Oscar shook his head. "Slipped under the office door. One has been delivered every night for five nights."

Bristow brought in a tray and left again. I poured the tea and handed a cup to Oscar. "We are very sorry about Mr. Baggley," I said gently. "He seemed like a good man."

He clasped the saucer in both hands and stared into the cup.

"He was my mentor, my friend, colleague... I was closer to him than I am to my own family."

Matt inspected the notes closely, turning them over, holding them to the light again, then spreading them out on the floor. "They have a pattern," he said, standing to get the best perspective. "The words are different but the sentence structure is the same. They were most likely written by the same person."

"Every word is spelled correctly," I said, standing beside him, teacup in hand.

"There are grammatical errors." Oscar pointed to the lack of a comma in two of the letters and the incorrect use of effect. "It should be 'Your irresponsible articles affect good people' not effect."

"So we can eliminate a writer or editor," Matt said.

"Unless the mistakes were deliberate to obscure his or her identity," I said.

Oscar sighed and slumped into the chair. "Too many suspects."

He was right. How could we narrow it down?

"Has anyone threatened you to your face?" I asked. "Or put their name to a letter ordering you to stop?"

"My brother, for one." Oscar's brother was an ink magician, like Oscar, and ran the family ink manufacturing business. It was enormously successful, and the family had grown quite wealthy, although Oscar preferred to make his own way in London, unaided by his brother. "Isaac made his point very clear."

"Surely he didn't threaten you," I said.

"Only to cut off my allowance, which I don't touch anyway. It all goes to our sister, who needs it more than me. Isaac threw her out five years ago when she chose a husband he didn't approve of."

"Abercrombie is a suspect," Matt added. "We know he's against your articles."

"He isn't the only guild master who made it clear I've been irresponsible," Oscar said. "A man known as Tucker, from the Carpenter's Guild, made a scene only two days ago. He had to be forcibly removed from the office after shouting all sorts of foul things."

"What about the editor and writer from *The City Review?*" I asked. "Mr. Force has been writing a number of articles refuting yours with the assistance of Abercrombie."

"True."

"I wouldn't be so sure," Matt said. "*The City Review's* circulation has likely increased too as a result of the tit-for-tat. Mr. Force and his editor are probably privately pleased."

"But *The Review* is a paper for businessmen," I said. "And businessmen want to protect their enterprises."

"Their *artless* enterprises," Oscar added. He scooted forward on the sofa and wagged his finger. "What about the *Review's* owners? On the one hand, they may be pleased with the increased circulation, if it has indeed increased. But on the other, they're so desperate for me to stop, they're devoting several inches of their front page to refuting my claims. I think they should definitely be suspects."

"It's quite a leap from owning a rival newspaper to killing someone," Matt said. "And why kill you if they're combatting your revelations through their own pieces?"

"Frustration because it's not working? The average people believe *me,* Mr. Glass, not the conservative *Review.*" Oscar drummed his fingers on his knee and nodded, over and over. He seemed to find it difficult to sit still. "Let me ask around. I'll find out who owns the paper."

We had a number of suspects then, if Lord Coyle and his dinner guests were included. With such little evidence, it would be tough to narrow it down. "The problem with someone from the guilds or *The City Review* being a suspect is that this paper was made by a magician," I said. "It's very unlikely a guild master will be a magician."

"It could be coincidence," Oscar said. "The killer could have unwittingly purchased the paper from a paper magician."

"It's worth speaking to the Stationers' Guild," Matt said. "A magician may belong to the company. We've seen it before."

"The Stationers' Guild is for printers and publishers," Oscar said. "Not paper manufacturers. I don't think they have their own company. There is a close relationship between the Stationers' Guild and paper manufacturers, though. It's worth following up."

"Is there anything more you can tell us?" I asked. "Anything at all?"

"I don't think so." He lifted one shoulder and winced. It was his injured shoulder from when he'd been shot some weeks ago. It would seem someone had intended to shoot him again, and Baggley had been shot by mistake.

"Do you often work late?" Matt asked.

"Yes."

"Is that common knowledge?"

"The other staff know. My brother knows. I'm often the only one there at night."

"What about Baggley?"

"He rarely works as late as I do. He has a wife, whereas I have no one to go home to." He gave me a flat smile. "Yet another reason why I think I was the intended victim."

"But you look nothing like Baggley," I said. "He's older and shorter. No one would confuse the two of you."

"Unless the killer hadn't seen Barratt before," Matt said.

"Even if he had, he could have made a mistake," Oscar said. "Mr. Baggley was seated, his back to the entrance, his head probably bowed over his work. I'd left him only moments before. Seeing only one man there, the killer assumed it was me."

Matt got up again and paced around the messages spread on the floor. "It won't be hard to find out who manufactures the best quality paper in the city. We'll begin with the Stationers' Guild."

"This may not have come from a large factory," I said. "The person who wrote those messages wants to stop magic from being revealed to the world. Any *magician* who wants that will not be manufacturing a quality magical product at a prominent factory. They'll be hiding away." I hated to think that a magician was behind the threats to Oscar, and the murder, but we couldn't discount any possibility.

"A number of magicians are scared now," Matt said, watching Oscar closely. "They've been safely in hiding, still producing good products, and now their secret is revealed, and possibly their identities, putting them in danger. No one can blame them for being scared of persecution."

"They should band together and fight their persecutors," Oscar declared. "There is nothing to be gained from hiding. And anyway, they wouldn't want to kill me but rather the people persecuting them. The artless."

Matt grunted. "Are you quite sure about that?"

Oscar swallowed.

"Well," I said quickly, "at least we have a direction, now. We'll try to find the source of this paper."

"And I'll see who owns *The City Review*," Oscar added. "I still think it's a worthwhile avenue to follow, Glass, even if you don't." He stood and thanked us. "I'll get started today."

"Wait," Matt said, as Oscar made to exit the drawing room. "Before we decide whether to take on this case, I want to ask you something."

"We haven't decided to take it on?" I asked.

Oscar frowned. "I thought we'd put our differences aside, Glass. Finding the killer is important to both of us, no matter if you think I'm doing the right thing or not."

"That may be true, but I want to know why you want our help. The police are working to find the killer. You should take these messages to Detective Inspector Brockwell and let him hunt for the author."

"He's artless."

"He believes in magic now," I said.

"I'd still prefer to have a magician involved in the investigation. Your unique perspective will help find the killer." He suddenly leaned forward and clasped my hand. "I only want you to do this if you promise to be careful, India. If anything happened to you..." He went to lift my hand, perhaps to kiss it, but changed his mind and let go. He flicked a glance in Matt's direction.

Matt scowled.

"Will you investigate?" Oscar pressed.

"Of course," I said.

"Until and unless it becomes dangerous," Matt added.

Oscar put out his hand. "I appreciate it, Glass."

Matt shook his hand, and a moment of shared understanding seemed to pass between them, but I couldn't decipher it. "Be careful," Matt said. "If you were the intended victim, the killer may try again once he learns he got the wrong man."

"Thank you for the warning. Fortunately, the office is crawling with police at the moment."

After Oscar left, Matt suggested I join him in his study to discuss our investigation. "What do you think?" I asked as he shut the door. "Could the bullet have been meant for him and not Baggley? Oh!"

He took me by the hand, and with another at my waist, waltzed me across the floor to his desk where he proceeded to kiss my neck.

I giggled. "Matt, stop. This is most improper."

"That's why I closed the door," he murmured against the sensitive flesh below my ear.

I clasped his face between my hands and marveled at the smokiness of his gaze, the lazy set of his mouth. "If we're going to be improper, we might as well kiss thoroughly."

He grinned. And then he pulled me even closer.

I dug my hands through his hair and pressed against his body, relishing the hardness and masculinity, and wondering when I'd get to see it.

That moment of thought opened a crack for the doubts to creep in. As far as some people were concerned, Matt was betrothed to another woman. While neither he nor I thought of him as Patience's intended, his family thought otherwise. Did that make this wrong? I wasn't sure, but it was difficult to dislodge that doubt.

I broke the kiss and couldn't meet his gaze.

"India," he purred. "I know what you're thinking." When I didn't look at him, he touched my chin. "Stop worrying about it. I will not marry her. I'm marrying you."

"Yes, but..." I shook my head. We'd had this discussion too many times already. "Let's make a list of suspects."

He sighed then sat at his desk. He wrote Lord Coyle's name at the top of the list, followed by the names of his dinner guests. Abercrombie came next, and we made a note that all guild members and masters were suspects. Matt added Mr. Gibbons at the bottom.

"But he's an old man," I said.

"He confronted Barratt at the *Gazette's* office. He might be angry enough to kill."

Angry and sad. Mr. Gibbons had lost his grandson, a cartography magician, because of the jealous members of the Mapmaker's Guild. He wanted to keep magic a secret to stop others from facing similar retaliation. Members from both the magician and artless camps wanted Oscar silenced. It was a very large and tangled puzzle we needed to solve.

"Write down Isaac Barratt," I said.

"Surely Oscar's own brother wouldn't try to kill him," Matt said, dipping his pen in the ink.

"Write it anyway." I leaned over his shoulder to watch, but he didn't write.

He caught my arm and drew me down for another kiss. It was swifter but just as effective as the deeper kiss. This time he drew away first. He growled and looked down at the ink splotch on the paper.

"This is hell," he muttered.

I looped my arms around his neck from behind and kissed the top of his head. "I know," I said on a sigh. "I know."

* * *

WE VISITED THE STATIONERS' Hall in Ludgate Hill only to find the guild master was not in. The porter asked us to return the following day and made an appointment in the register. He was quite amenable. Clearly Mr. Abercrombie of the Watchmakers' Guild hadn't warned every staff member of every guild hall about us.

Matt dined at Lord Cox's gentleman's club that evening, so Miss Glass decided to have a light supper with me in her private sitting room. We chatted easily enough, although a tense undercurrent was never too far away anymore. I wasn't entirely sure if she felt it too or whether I was the only one aware of it. She carried most of the conversation and thankfully didn't mention Patience or weddings once. She did talk about Matt's obligations as the future baron of Rycroft, however.

"That's why I'm so pleased he is dining out tonight at a club," she said, swirling her soup with a spoon. "He needs to make more contacts in London. That's how gentlemen get ahead, you know, by making friends with the *right* sort."

I tried to tune her out, as I usually did, but this time I couldn't. Perhaps it was the frustration of my thwarted passion, or perhaps it was simply that I'd reached the end of my rope. Her snobbishness stretched my nerves so thin they were in danger of snapping.

"Of course, I don't expect you to understand, India," she went on. "You're a lovely girl, but your family are from a different world to his. Your father had to rely only on his own skill, but Matt *must* make the right connections."

I dropped my soup spoon into the near empty bowl. "Miss Glass," I said hotly, "I don't know whether you are implying that my father had no friends or Matt has no skills, but neither is true. What I do know is that you are yet again telling me that Matt and I are not suited, that I am beneath him. Again, neither is true. We are well suited, and I am not beneath anyone." I stood, pushing my chair back so hard that it almost toppled. "I may not be the sort of wife you would like Matt to have, but I happen to think I'd be a worthy choice. He must think so too, because he has asked me to marry him when he sorts out the debacle with Patience."

Her lips pinched so hard they turned white. "That is hardly my fault. My brother is forcing them to marry, not me. I don't think they're suited very well either."

"You would still rather he married someone who is not me.

As long as you want that, we will be at odds." I shoved the chair forward. "I think it's time you found another companion."

She patted the lace collar at her throat. "India, my dear, it wasn't my intention to upset you."

"Well, you have."

"Then I must apologize and beg your forgiveness."

"I cannot forgive your prejudices. Not this time."

I stormed off, determined not to glance back. I was afraid that if I did, I'd see a frail, lonely woman trying to make sense of the changes happening around her while clinging to her traditional values. She wanted a nephew who followed tradition, but Matt wasn't like that.

I only hoped she would understand and accept it before she lost his love and respect. She was already well on the way to losing mine.

My temper cooled enough to send her maid, Polly Picket, up to her room to keep her company. It hadn't cooled enough to sit quietly on my own in my room, however. I found Willie in her bedroom, getting ready for their evening out. She studied her reflection in the mirror then, with a pout, undid her necktie.

"I need your help," I told her.

"With what?" she asked, retying the tie.

"With choosing an outfit for tonight."

Her gaze met mine in the reflection. "Where're you going?"

"To watch Cyclops and Duke fight. I need some entertainment to take my mind off...everything."

She grinned. "I know exactly what you should wear."

* * *

WILLIE HAD INSISTED I wear my dark gray-green day dress with its matching military style jacket and perky hat. It was more suited to an afternoon calling on friends, rather than a night at a disreputable tavern, and I'd questioned her reasoning.

"*That's* why," Willie said when we reached the back of the taproom.

I'd been so busy making sure my hem didn't touch the sticky

floor that I'd taken no notice of the other patrons. The taproom was crowded with drinkers, lining up at the polished bar, and all stools were occupied. Serving girls carried trays aloft, and they eyed us with as much curiosity as the men. I felt my face heat at the attention and kept close to Willie, Cyclops and Duke.

"I don't understand," I whispered. "Why are they looking at us?"

"You, not us," she said. "They think you're a toff, come to watch the fighting."

"If I were a well-heeled lady, I'd be wearing jewels and a fine gown, not this simple day dress, as nice as it is."

"You're a *sensible* well-heeled lady. You ain't stupid enough to flash your pretty rocks and invite light fingers. Trust me, India. If you want to fit in, you got to look like a tavern wench, a whore, or a lady who likes to ogle male flesh."

What had I got myself into?

"What about you?" I asked. "Why aren't you dressed like me? You're a woman too."

Duke snorted as he opened a door for us. Willie thumped him in the stomach as she passed, but he only winked at her. "Got to hit harder than that," he said cheerfully. "I'm made of iron."

"Aye, and up here too." She tapped her temple and skipped aside as he pretended to lunge at her. She fell against a barrel lined up with several others along a corridor. Duke let out a whoop of laughter, earning himself a scowl from Willie.

A man as big as Cyclops stood at the top of a narrow stone staircase, guarding a door. A flickering candle in a wall nook by his head cast his left side in shadow and made the scars on his right stand out. He looked each of us over, raising a single brow upon seeing me. It was Cyclops he addressed, however.

"You fighting?" he asked.

"Me and my friend," Cyclops drawled.

"You can't wear that." The guard nodded at Cyclops's eye patch. Cyclops merely nodded.

The guard let us past then shut the door. The air became cooler as we followed the steps down to a cellar. Despite the barrels and crates pushed to one side of the large space, it felt like a tomb, with its low vaulted ceiling and stone walls and floor. I shivered and wished I'd brought a shawl.

At least two dozen men were already there, mingling or hailing the serving woman as she passed between them. She stuffed the coins into her pockets and easily fended off the wandering hands of the men with a joke and a smile. None tried again, perhaps because there were as many thuggish guards stationed around the room's perimeter as there were patrons.

Cyclops and Duke spoke to a man who pointed to the far side of the room. He ogled me as I passed and licked his lips. I wished I had a clock heavy enough to protect me if necessary, since I wasn't sure if my new watch could.

Duke and Cyclops spoke with another man for some time. He stood back, studied them, and nodded before writing something down in his notebook. He indicated they should join two others standing by the wall.

"Come on," Willie said to me. "They're all set. Let's get a place at the front. Somewhere we'll be covered in sweat and blood by the end of the night."

"Perhaps somewhere in the second row will suffice," I said weakly.

She shot me a grin over her shoulder. "Getting cold feet already, India?"

"I just like this dress without stains." And I could imagine Matt's reaction when he saw me splattered in blood. I hoped we'd be home before him.

Willie stopped at a line drawn in chalk on the floor. I realized it was connected to other lines to form a square. "The ring," Willie explained when I asked.

"Shouldn't there be ropes around it?"

"In official fights for proper boxers. This one's just for local lads to test themselves and earn a few shillings."

"They're not fighting using Queensbury's rules then."

"Nope." She rubbed her hands together. "Makes it more fun."

And more dangerous.

The crowd tripled in size over the next fifteen minutes. I had to guess the time that passed because I didn't want to pull my new watch from my reticule and risk catching the eye of a pick pocket. I already pegged one skinny youth as the light fingered type as he slipped between the patrons. I didn't see him steal anything, but once the fights began and the ale flowed, he'd be at an advantage.

More spectators crowded into the room, and I could no longer see the door or Cyclops and Duke. Almost all of the patrons were men, but I was surprised to see two other women, both of whom were clearly ladies dressing plainly for the occasion. They sported the unmistakable stiff-backs and condescending air of the upper classes. No plain gowns could hide that. One even pressed a handkerchief to her nose. She removed it to speak to her companion, a gentleman with an oiled moustache and double chins.

Like the rest of us, the party of four had to stand. They positioned themselves at the front to get the best view, earning mutters and eye-rolls from the people they'd displaced. I wondered if the presence of ladies dampened tempers, however, as none looked prepared to start a fight over it.

An announcer took to the ring and demanded our attention for the parade of contestants. Two young men emerged through the crowd first, both of them far too slight to be of any real threat to Duke or Cyclops. They received some jeers but mostly whistles and applause. Some even placed bets on them with the roaming bookmakers. Another four fighters were introduced before Duke came out, his chest bare, his skin oiled. Willie folded her arms and made a great show of admiring him. He faced her and flexed his muscles. I got the feeling he was enjoying himself.

"This here's someone special," the announcer shouted above the murmurs of the crowd as they sized up Duke's potential. "You prob'ly heard of him—Wild Bill Hickok, all the way from the American West!"

"Christ," Willie muttered with a shake of her head. "Don't they know he's dead?"

Apparently not, going by the cheers.

"Last but certainly not least, ladies and gen'lemen," the announcer called, "we have Cyclops, the one-eyed giant!"

Cyclops came out without his eye patch. The crowd gasped and oohed. Some surged forward to get a better look. He bore their ogling with his usual good grace, but I wanted to order them to move back and stop staring at the lumpy, jagged scar pulling his eyelid closed.

"Haven't you seen a scar before?" I snapped at the man next to me.

He either paid me no mind or simply didn't hear me. The announcer called the first fight, and the crowd swamped the bookmakers. Willie linked her arm with mine, perhaps worried we'd be separated.

"Don't look," she said, "but someone's watching you."

"Who?"

"Gen'leman at nine o'clock."

I glanced in that direction just as the gentleman turned away. He disappeared through the crowd, but not before I recognized him. "His name's Sir Charles Whittacker. We met him at Lord Coyle's dinner. Did he see me?"

"He was looking at you direct." She craned her neck but Sir Charles was gone. "The man's rude if he ain't going to speak to you."

"Perhaps he's embarrassed to be seen at a bare knuckle fight. Or he thinks I'll be embarrassed to be seen here."

"Don't you English get offended when an acquaintance snubs you?"

I ignored her and scanned the faces again, but there were so many people now that he could still be in the cellar and I wouldn't spot him.

The crowd closed in as the two thin lads entered the ring. They paced around, getting the other's measure, but it took too long for the spectators. Calls to "Fight!" or "Go on!" reverberated off the walls.

Finally, the taller lad threw a punch. It missed, opening a gap for his opponent to strike. The blow hit the lad in the stomach, and a follow-up smashed into his cheek. He stumbled back into the crowd behind him and was promptly pushed into the ring again to face another round of blows. Two of his punches managed to hit their mark but they had little effect in slowing down his opponent. Despite his shorter, slighter build, he was strong, quick and clearly experienced. The tall boxer finally fell under the barrage of punches, and landed hard on the floor. Blood streamed from his nose and his lip sported a cut. Bruises already bloomed on his torso and jaw. Thankfully he got up and walked away after the announcer declared the fight over.

I breathed a sigh of relief but my heart still hammered in my chest. Watching two strangers fight for money was the oddest sensation. I didn't want to watch, yet I felt compelled to do so, and I found myself praying none would be seriously hurt.

I was caught up in the action in front of me and didn't notice someone come up behind me until his silky voice murmured in my ear.

"Enjoying yourself?"

CHAPTER 4

I jumped, my nerves shredded, and rounded on Matt. "What are you doing here?"

Beside me, Willie put up her hands in surrender. "India wanted to come. I couldn't say no, could I?"

Matt ignored her. His gaze burrowed into me. "I'm here because you're here, India."

"I'm allowed to come and watch a fight if I want to," I said.

"I know."

"There are even other women here."

"I can see that."

"Some would call this type of sport vulgar, and me too for watching it, but I don't care."

"Right."

"I am not a slave to the opinion of others," I went on.

"Good."

"If there's one thing my magic has taught me, it's that I can only be the person I am. That may not suit everyone but so be it."

His face had gone from scowling to confused with each declaration I made. "India, is something the matter?"

"I've come to enjoy the fighting, and that's what I plan to do. If you don't like it, you can go back to your gentleman's club and associate with less vulgar people. I'm staying here."

He looked to Willie. She shrugged so he turned back to me. "I only wanted to be with you. Being home alone holds no appeal."

"Oh," I muttered. "It's nice to see you too."

"How did you know we were here?" Willie asked.

"Bristow told me," he said. "He must have heard you discussing it."

Willie looked toward the ring as a cry erupted. "Or Wild Bill Hickok or Cyclops the giant told him."

"Hickok?" Matt followed her gaze to see Duke enter the ring with another opponent. One corner of Matt's mouth lifted. "This should be interesting."

To my surprise, he had no qualms watching his friend fight. Duke's opponent was taller, his reach longer, but Duke looked as if he were made of bricks and he was surprisingly quick. He easily accounted for the other man, which caused the crowd to jeer. They wanted a closer fight.

They didn't get it in Cyclops's bout, either. He knocked his opponent out without receiving a single blow in return. The final bout had better satisfy the spectators' thirst for blood or there might be trouble. During a pause in the fighting, two boys wiped the blood and sweat off the floor. The serving women were also busy, selling tankards of ale to spectators.

"Did you speak with Lord Cox?" I asked Matt during the lull.

"I did. He's refusing to give in."

"Did you find his weakness?" Willie asked.

His gaze slid to hers. "Not yet..."

"Then you gotta look in different places. You want to find dirt, you got to play in the mud."

"I'm not sure how muddy I need to get."

"The muddiest." I thought she was going to leave it at that, but after a moment, she added, "If you want to beat these folk then you got to think like them. I ain't never been rich, but I seen how they work, and it ain't all above board. They use each other to get ahead and trade in dirty secrets to get what they want."

They made connections, just like Miss Glass had suggested.

"They're not all like that," Matt growled at her. "The problem with Lord Cox is he's very much above board. He appears to be so clean that nothing sticks to him."

"So you have looked, eh?" She nudged him with her elbow. "Good for you, Matt."

He sighed and sidled closer to me. "I'll find a way, India."

"But it'll take time," I said heavily.

He said nothing; he merely tucked my hand into his and twined his fingers with mine. We stood like that, our linked hands partly hidden by my skirts, and watched the remainder of the fights. It was the most unromantic setting for a very romantic moment.

As each opponent was eliminated, it became clear that Cyclops and Duke were to fight one another in the final bout. Willie was delighted and went to place a wager with the bookmaker, but Matt caught her arm.

"Are you sure you want to do that?" he asked.

She snatched her arm free. "Don't nursemaid me, Matt. I'm a grown woman, and I can spend my tin how I like."

"I'm just looking out for you the way you've looked out for me over the years. I don't want you to regret betting too much."

Her shoulders slumped, and I knew he'd won her over. She settled her stance, folded her arms, and waited for the fight to start.

"I don't think I can watch this," I said over the roar of the crowd as Duke and Cyclops entered the ring.

"We can leave if you like," Matt said.

I shook my head. "What if we're needed to help carry them out?"

"It won't get that bad."

I was determined not to watch, but I couldn't help myself. I followed the fight as eagerly as any of the other spectators, although not quite as eagerly as the two ladies. They seemed to have picked different favorites. One cheered every time Duke struck a blow, and the other clapped her hands and licked her lips whenever one of Cyclops's punches connected.

The fight was fair—perhaps too fair, going by the jeers of the crowd who wanted to see more blood and harder punches. Even

I could see that neither Duke nor Cyclops intended to hurt the other. The crowd grew more restless as the fight wore on, shouting at the boxers and calling them cowards and all sorts of other names.

"Glad I didn't place a wager if they're going to fight like princesses," Willie said with a shake of her head.

"Willie!" I scolded. "Do you want them to hurt one another?"

"I want to see a fair fight."

"Why don't they stop it and just leave?" I asked.

"Are you mad? The crowd'll kill 'em. They want to see blood spilled, even if they have to do it themselves."

I pulled a face and inched closer to Matt.

"Do you want to leave?" he asked me again.

"Not without Duke and Cyclops."

"They can take care of themselves."

Even as he said it, Duke fell to the floor from one of Cyclops's punches. He did not get up.

I gasped. "Duke!"

Both Matt and Willie stopped me from running into the ring. "He's fine," Willie said.

"We have to leave," Matt said, taking my hand. "Now."

He led me through the crowd, baying at Duke, ordering him to get up and finish the fight. Some accused them of cheating by throwing the bout. The guards peeled away from their positions along the walls and made their presence known with cracks of their knuckles.

The announcer with the booming voice called for calm but the crowd would have none of it. Some demanded their bets be refunded, others suggested the previous fighters be brought back to fight against Duke and Cyclops, four against two.

"Shouldn't we wait for them?" I said to Matt when we reached the staircase. To my surprise, Willie had followed us. I thought she'd want to stay to see if Duke and Cyclops were all right.

"They'll be fine," Matt said. "There's a back entrance."

"How do you know?"

"We've been here before, when we first arrived in London."

"They fought then too?"

"They thought about it and scouted for alternative exits in case they decided to and this happened."

Willie urged us to hurry up the steps. "Someone's going to pull a knife soon, and it'll get nasty in here. I got my Colt but I don't want to use it."

"How considerate of you," I said wryly.

"There're too many witnesses."

The taproom was almost empty of patrons since most were downstairs watching the fights. We hurried outside, where the air was dense and motionless, and it was only a little cooler than it had been in the cellar. It must have rained while we were inside as the cobbles were slick. I was glad for Matt's steadying hand as we walked briskly along the street.

Running footsteps pounded down the laneway behind us but it was only Duke and Cyclops, still shirtless, grinning from ear to ear. They caught up to us and accepted congratulatory slaps on the back from Willie.

"Did you see Cyclops's upper cut on that big man?" she said, smiling. "He went down like a smooth bourbon."

Duke slung his arm around her shoulders and kissed her temple. "What about me, eh? Did you see my right hook?"

"Aye, I saw it. I also saw you quit when you came up against the one-eyed giant." She punched Cyclops's arm as he positioned the patch over his eye.

"Ouch," he said.

"Big baby."

Duke chuckled. "If I didn't quit, we'd kill each other. We decided before we went out that it'd be me, on account of it being more believable for the shorter man to lose to the bigger. I don't mind. I ain't proud, 'specially since *we* all know I can beat him in a fight if I were willing to hurt him."

It was Cyclops's turn to chuckle in deep, resonant waves. He clapped Duke on the shoulder. "And I'm the queen of England."

Duke shrugged him off and put on his shirt and waistcoat. "Guess we'll never know now, will we?"

"If I find you two have been fighting in the mews, I'll dock your pay and inform both my aunt and Miss Mason," Matt said. "One will lecture you and the other will fawn over you, Cyclops, until you have to admit you have feelings for her."

Cyclops grunted. Duke and Willie laughed. "Don't tell the Mason girl," Duke said to Matt. "Tell your cousin, Charity. She won't fawn, she'll tie him to a bed and call it nursing."

Willie *whooped* and put her arm around Duke. They both laughed until their eyes watered.

"You two've got the brains of five year-olds," Cyclops said with a shake of his head and a smile.

Despite the brutal scenes we'd left behind, it was a pleasant walk back to Mayfair. It was a novelty to walk through the city at this time of night. Although the moon hid behind the clouds, the lamps glowed softly, casting enough light to show us the way and allow me to steal a glimpse of Matt's strong, healthy profile. We held hands, another novelty. It was thrilling to be able to show one another affection in public, even if that public only consisted of our friends. They didn't think less of us and, for almost half an hour, we all talked and laughed together. It felt so right, so wonderful.

I let his hand go when we reached the house. Being home erased the magic of the evening. Matt tried to rekindle some of that magic by kissing me in the corridor outside my room. He pressed against me, palm flat to the closed door near my head, and melted me with a blazing hot kiss.

A kiss that he suddenly broke off with a groan. "Damn it," he murmured, head lowered. "Damn this."

* * *

We returned to the Stationers' Hall the following morning to keep our appointment with Mr. Sweeney, the guild master. Unlike his porter, Mr. Sweeney had clearly been warned about us. His refusal to let us into his office proved that.

"Kindly leave the premises without a fuss," he said, his upper lip trembling as if he were on the verge of crying.

"We only want to ask you a few questions," Matt said.

"You've spoken to Mr. Abercrombie about us, haven't you?" I asked.

Mr. Sweeney folded one hand over the other in front of him and shot a speaking glance at the exit behind us. His lip continued to twitch in what must be a nervous tic. "I don't want to use force, but I'll have the porter round up some local thugs if you don't go immediately."

"There's no need for threats," Matt said gently. He was twice Mr. Sweeney's size and could have easily employed intimidation tactics if he wished, but he kept at a distance. "Since you have already cast the first stone, I am going to tell you how this will play out. Either you let us into your office so we can have a civilized discussion, or we will ask our questions out here where anyone can overhear them. Since our questions are of a magical nature, I suspect you'll want them to remain private."

It would seem he was going to threaten after all. It yielded the desired result. Mr. Sweeney took one glance at the approaching man pushing a cartload of books along the corridor and ushered us inside his office.

"You shouldn't use that word around here," he hissed as he shut the door. "Ever since those ridiculous articles appeared in *The Weekly Gazette*, the members have been on edge. Nobody knows who to trust anymore."

"Why should anyone not be trusted?" I asked. "If one or more of your members turn out to be magicians, what of it? They are still the same people."

He looked at me through two very blue eyes. His age was indeterminate. He was slender and short, with straight brown hair and smooth skin. There was not a wrinkle or whisker in sight. "You would say that, Miss Steele. I hear you are a watch magician."

"No doubt Mr. Abercrombie told you that I'm trying to ruin his business and that of all watchmakers."

His gaze shifted away.

"Let me assure you," I said, "I do not make or sell timepieces, nor do I have any intention of doing so. I have good friends in the trade and don't want to see their business suffer because of me."

"How noble of you." He smiled tightly. "Can you say the same about every other magician? What if there is a bookbinder magician? He could ruin me. He could ruin all of the good, honorable members of our organization."

I sat on the chair opposite him, even though he had not invited me. "By creating books that never fall apart? How diabolical."

He folded one hand over the other and settled them on his desk in a very deliberate and slow act. "I will not support magic businesses, in any shape."

"Then you'll want to answer our questions," Matt said.

Mr. Sweeney frowned, and his lip started twitching again. He wasn't expecting us to turn the tables on him. "What questions?"

Matt took out a piece of paper from his pocket. It was a blank section cut from Oscar's threatening letter. "Do you know who made this?"

"It's paper, Mr. Glass," Mr. Sweeney said. "You can't possibly expect me to determine who made it simply by looking at it."

Matt placed the paper on the desk. "Then touch it."

Mr. Sweeney picked up the paper, fingered it, turned it over, held it up to the light then sniffed it. "It's good quality paper."

"Do you know who manufactured it?" Matt asked.

"Why do you want to know?"

"It was made by a magician," I said.

He dropped the paper. It fluttered onto the desk then slipped off altogether. He wiped his fingers on his trouser leg. "How do you know?"

"I just do. Who made it, Mr. Sweeney?"

He held up a finger. "Why do you want to know who the magician is? So you can reward him? Recruit him for some magical scheme you're concocting?"

I sighed. This was hopeless. We should have used false names.

Matt, who'd remained standing, slowly skirted the desk and stood over Mr. Sweeney. Mr. Sweeney leaned back. His upper lip resumed trembling. "Contrary to rumors spread by Mr. Abercrombie, Miss Steele is not an evil mastermind determined to take over the world, one trade at a time."

I pressed my lips together to keep my smile from breaking free. Fortunately Mr. Sweeney didn't look my way, and Matt managed to keep a straight face.

"There's no watermark," Mr. Sweeney said, pointing to the paper on the floor.

"But it's very distinctive paper. You know who made it."

"I do but...I still don't understand why you need his name."

Matt moved and Mr. Sweeney scooted back in his chair. Matt bent and picked up the piece of paper. He returned it to his pocket and rejoined me on the other side of the desk.

"An acquaintance is being blackmailed," Matt said. "The threatening letters were sent using this paper."

"I see." Mr. Sweeney folded his hands on the desk again. "You think the magician's paper was used by the blackmailer? Or the magician *is* the blackmailer?"

Matt said nothing.

"There's no identifying markings on the paper," Mr. Sweeney said.

"The name," Matt ordered.

Mr. Sweeney's lip twitched. He bit it but it didn't stop. "His name is Melville Hendry."

"How well do you know him?"

"Not at all well, as it turns out. I didn't know he was a magician until those articles came out. He told me then." His thumb rubbed the knuckles of his other hand. "We've hardly spoken since."

"Is he the sort of person who would blackmail someone by sending threatening letters?"

Mr. Sweeney studied his folded hands as the thumb continued its slow slide across his knuckle. "A few weeks ago my answer would have been certainly not." He pulled the inkstand closer and plucked out the pen. "This is where you can find him. He's always there, either in the shop, the workshop, or in the rooms upstairs."

Mr. Sweeney insisted on seeing us to the front door, no doubt to make sure I didn't perform a magic feat on the guild's hall clock to slow it down.

* * *

WE WENT DIRECTLY to the Smithfield address of Mr. Melville Hendry. Just as Mr. Sweeney said, the paper magician was there, working in the small workshop located behind his even smaller shop. We heard the *thump thump* of machinery before we saw the man himself. Despite our repeated ringing of the counter bell, he did not appear, so we pushed open the door at the back of the shop.

The noise came from a large hammer-like device that repeatedly pounded pulp in a vat of liquid. A middle-aged man with thick gray hair slicked back from his high forehead stood over a rectangular wooden mold on a long counter top, talking to himself in low tones I couldn't hear over the machine. Behind him, dozens of rectangles of paper in varying stages of drying hung from washing lines. They were all pristine white and looked smooth. The room didn't smell of anything much, and that gave me the answer we needed. Melville Hendry must be a paper magician. To turn the pulp white, bleach would need to be added to the process, and its distinctive odor would linger. A paper magician didn't need to use chemicals.

"Mr. Hendry?" Matt asked.

The man jumped, startled. He pressed a hand to his chest and offered a shaky smile. "I am sorry. I didn't hear you." He moved away from the counter and the machine slowed to a halt. He must have been operating it with a foot pedal. "How may I help you?"

"My name is Mr. Matthew Glass, and this is Miss Steele. You have some fine paper in your shop, Mr. Hendry. Very fine."

Mr. Hendry indicated we should return to the shopfront ahead of him. "I pride myself on my work, Mr. Glass. I produce everything on these premises. My small operation allows me to give particular attention to every individual commission." He indicated the examples of invitations and calling cards displayed in a glass cabinet. They looked thick and smooth, with the lettering in gold, silver or black. There were other examples of his work too, including books opened to particular pages to show off the quality of the paper. He encouraged us to touch the blank sheaves stacked on the counter as well as the posters glued to the wall.

"Very fine indeed," Matt said, passing a piece of paper to me.

It felt warm. I touched another piece and it too held magical warmth. I smiled at Matt.

"Dare I ask if you wish to announce a happy event to your friends?" Mr. Hendry asked. "I don't write the text but I know a fine calligrapher who uses only the best quality ink from a superior English ink manufacturer."

"Would that be Barratt's?" Matt asked.

"You've heard of them?"

"In passing. The family members are ink magicians."

Mr. Hendry's eyes widened. His mouth worked but no sound came out.

"It's all right," I told him. "I am a horology magician, and we know you're a paper magician."

Mr. Hendry stroked his hair at his ear, as if he were tucking it back, although not a single well-oiled strand strayed from its place. "Steele. I think I know your name."

"Oscar Barratt's articles in *The Weekly Gazette* have mentioned my grandfather. Mr. Barratt belongs to the Barratt family you just spoke of."

"But you already knew that," Matt said. "Didn't you, Mr. Hendry?"

Mr. Hendry locked the front door and flipped over the sign to say CLOSED. He glanced at the street through the window before finally responding. "What do you want?"

Matt removed the piece of paper from his inside jacket pocket and handed it to Mr. Hendry. "Did you make this? And don't try to tell us that all paper looks and feels alike. We know it doesn't. This paper has been infused with magic."

Mr. Hendry rubbed the piece between his thumb and forefinger but barely looked at it before handing it back to Matt. "It's mine, but I suppose you already guessed that. How did you know to come here?"

"Your name was given to us by your friend, Mr. Sweeney."

Mr. Hendry's shoulders slumped and his spine lost some of its rigidity. "He no longer considers himself my friend. I'm sure he told you that too, since he seems to want to make it widely known."

"Because he doesn't want to associate with a magician?" I asked gently.

He gave a slight nod. "I should never have confided in him, but he asked me directly after reading an article written by that bloody fool, Barratt. I couldn't lie to Patrick's face."

"You were very good friends."

Another nod and he moved away to rearrange the stack of papers on the counter, hiding his face from us.

"Perhaps you'll be friends again one day," I said. "Once this blows over and he realizes you're not a threat to his business or that of the other Stationers' Guild members."

"That's what I don't understand. I'm a paper magician, Miss Steele, not a binder. I'm not even sure what kind of magician would be a threat to his publishing business."

"Leather or cloth?" I suggested. "For the book covers? Glue magic?"

"Did he ever use your paper in the books produced by his company?" Matt asked.

"My operation is too small. His supplies are manufactured by a paper mill in Norfolk."

"Did he ever use your paper for more personal items?"

"I made all his personal calling cards, note paper and letterhead." He set the stack of papers down and bowed his head. "After I admitted to being a magician, he said he was going to throw them all out and advise all of his friends to do so too. He was so *angry* with me. I still don't understand why. It's not my fault I'm a magician any more than it's his fault he has blue eyes."

"Perhaps he'll understand in time," I said. "Knowing that magicians exist is still quite new to most folk, and it's very strange. Everyone is adjusting, and on edge, but I do believe it will calm down and things will return to normal."

"As long as no one takes it upon themselves to persecute magicians," Matt added stiffly.

"And no magicians try to use their magic to steal business from their artless rivals." I thought that the more likely scenario than persecution, but Matt would not agree. "To whom did you sell that particular paper?" I asked Mr. Hendry.

"Why?" he said carefully.

"It was used to send threatening letters to Oscar Barratt, the journalist. The author ordered him to stop publishing his articles."

Mr. Hendry stroked his hair again then dropped his hand suddenly and met my gaze. "I don't know who bought that particular sheaf. My customers are generally from the upper echelons of society and wouldn't stoop to such a tactic. Now, if you don't mind, I have work to attend to."

"Come now, Mr. Hendry. I think you know," Matt said, in that way he had of sounding like a friend yet demanding an answer.

"I don't! I swear to you! I sell so much blank paper, it's impossible to track."

"Do you keep records?"

"Not specific enough to identify who purchased a particular sheet or sheets. That's absurd, Mr. Glass. Why do you want to know, anyway? What does it matter if someone sent that Barratt fellow threatening letters? Good on him, I say. I hope it works and Barratt realizes his mistake. He is, after all, a magician too. His brother must be furious. His customers will abandon him if they believe magic is a form of cheating, which it seems so many artless do. Magicians operating on a smaller scale, like myself, will tend to escape notice, thankfully. I may lose a few customers who suspect, but not enough to cause me difficulty."

"Except when friends abandon you," Matt said.

Mr. Hendry glanced away. "I ask again, why do you want to know who is sending Mr. Barratt threatening letters? What does it matter to the two of you?"

"Mr. Baggley is dead."

"Who?"

"The *Gazette's* editor."

Mr. Hendry's brows shot up. "The editor? Not Barratt?"

"Does that surprise you?"

"Barratt seems to have quickly gained some enemies."

"Threatening letters would imply as much," Matt agreed, tucking the paper back in his pocket. "It's possible the killer mistook Baggley for Barratt."

"Or perhaps this Mr. Baggley had enemies too. Was he a magician?"

"No," I said.

He stroked his hair at his ear again. "Is there anything else? I have to get back to my work." He scuttled about the shop, flicking dust off the counter and adjusting a stack of cards, all the while watching us from beneath lowered lashes until we finally left.

"Do you think *he* sent the letters?" I asked Matt as we settled into the carriage.

"Perhaps. Anything's possible, at this point, but if he did, I would expect him to throw suspicion onto someone else by giving us the name of one of his customers."

"Perhaps he's too honorable."

"He did give us a clue." His lips curved into a curious smile. "He mentioned that his clients were from the upper echelons, and we know some wealthy and titled persons who like to collect magical things."

I smiled too. "Those same people dislike Barratt's articles and wanted him to stop writing them. Shall we visit Lord Coyle first?"

"Directly after lunch."

* * *

My friend Catherine Mason was at the house when we arrived. I invited her to stay for luncheon, and she eagerly accepted, even though I couldn't guarantee that Cyclops would be back from the convent where he and the others had decided to do some final repairs after all.

"That's perfectly all right, India," she said cheerfully. "I don't mind seeing you and Matt. I mean, I'm happy to see you. *That's* why I came." I wouldn't have believed her even if she hadn't blushed.

I hooked my arm through hers and led her into the dining room ahead of Matt and Miss Glass. We were just getting seated when Cyclops, Duke and Willie arrived. Cyclops paused inside the door to the dining room upon seeing Catherine. His one eye took in her appearance from her blonde hair to her slender fingers. I could swear I saw heat in it.

"Apologies, Miss Mason," he said. "If we'd known you'd be here, we'd have changed."

"Bah," Willie said, pulling out a chair. "*You* might have, but I wouldn't."

Miss Glass clicked her tongue.

Willie waggled her fingers. "We did wash up."

"India would have changed, wouldn't you, my dear?" Miss Glass said. "You're such a good girl like that."

"I didn't change," I told her.

"But you would have, if you were working all day."

"India? Work out of doors?" Willie snorted. "She's too lily fingered for real work." Willie winked at me, and I rolled my eyes.

Miss Glass leapt to my defense. "She's a very hard worker, as well you know, Willemina. Apologize at once."

Willie picked a chicken leg off the platter using her fingers. "Why should I?"

"It's all right," I said.

"Willie," Cyclops hissed from across the table. "We have a guest."

"So?"

"So use your cutlery."

"Please don't on my account," Catherine said, sounding amused. "I have brothers. I'm used to cutlery being an afterthought."

"Brothers," Duke said with emphasis, "not sisters. I know it ain't easy to tell, but Willie here's a woman."

Willie used her fork to stab a boiled potato and add it to her plate. "And Duke's a quitter."

"Don't listen to her. I only quit the—" He clapped his mouth shut.

"Quit the what?" Miss Glass asked.

Willie sat back with a grin. "He and Cyclops quit riding horses because they fell off. That's why they both got them bruises and cuts."

"You fell off a horse?" Catherine asked Cyclops.

"Both of you?" Miss Glass said.

Catherine glanced between the three but made no further comment. Miss Glass, however, gave them a lecture on riding sensibly in the city. We all regretted Willie's white lie by the end.

Peter the footman brought in lemon ices in glass bowls to complete our luncheon and we subsequently retreated to the drawing room. Miss Glass stopped me before we entered, however. I found I couldn't quite look her in the eye. I was far too aware of my last words to her the night before. I'd been harsh, but I would not back down from my position. I would not allow her to talk me into remaining as her companion.

"Will you come to my room, India?" she asked. "I have a little surprise for you."

"Perhaps later," I said. "I'd like to spend time with Catherine while she's here."

"She doesn't need you as much as I need you. Come to my room so I can give you your gift."

I extricated my arm from her grasp. "Thank you, Miss Glass, but I don't want any gifts. I won't change my mind. You and I don't see eye to eye on one very important matter and unless that changes, I don't think I can serve as your companion."

She touched the hair at the nape of her neck as she stared into the middle distance. "Veronica, have you seen Harry?" she asked weakly.

I sighed. Her turns may be a result of her inability to cope with the conversation at hand, but this time it seemed a little *too* convenient.

"India? Aunt? Are you coming?" Matt asked, rejoining us.

"She's suffering from one of her episodes," I said, eyeing her carefully. "I was about to fetch Polly."

"I'll take her upstairs."

I watched them go, my heart feeling heavier than I expected, and entered the drawing room to a charged silence. Only Willie looked pleased. Duke seemed curious, while Cyclops avoided Catherine's hard glare.

"I was just telling Nate that I fell off a horse once," Catherine said to me. "My injuries did not look like his. I also have brothers who used to get into all sorts of scrapes. A punch in the mouth would split a lip like that."

"Ah," was all I said.

"Why is everyone lying to me?"

"I didn't lie," Cyclops said. "I would never lie to you. To anyone."

"Then why won't you admit that you two have been fighting? I don't understand why you feel as though you must hide the fact from me."

Cyclops shrugged his big shoulders and appealed to me. I'd never seen him look so lost. He didn't want Catherine to think poorly of him, yet he also didn't want to encourage her feelings. It was a delicate balance, one that I wasn't sure I could successfully navigate, either.

"He didn't want you to worry about him," I told her. "That's all."

Catherine's face colored. She looked down at her lap. "Oh. Well, thank you. *Is* there something to worry about?"

"Nope," Willie said. "Cyclops beat all his opponents."

"Except me," Duke added. "I gave him that cut lip and more than a few bruises you can't see unless he lifts his shirt."

Cyclops's gaze drilled into Duke. Duke grinned back.

"But why were you two fighting?" Catherine asked. "Did you have a disagreement?"

"It were just for a lark," Duke said. "Sometimes we fight to blow away the cobwebs."

"Is it a common form of entertainment in America?"

"Aye," Willie nodded. "Cyclops is dang good at it. Duke, too."

Duke puffed out his chest. "It weren't nothing to worry about, Miss Mason. His face is as pretty as it always were."

Catherine laughed. "So I see."

Cyclops laughed too, but I could see he was nervous discussing the topic with her. He took the opportunity of the lull to change it and told her about our latest investigation. Matt returned but hardly spoke a word until Catherine left and we were alone in the carriage on the way to Lord Coyle's house.

"Aunt Letitia says you threatened to leave," he said, suddenly scooping both my hands in his. "I know the situation is difficult for both of us, but I thought you agreed to stay at the house."

"Matt—"

"I *will* convince Lord Cox to take Patience back. I *will* find a way, India."

"Matt—"

"Please, don't leave yet," he murmured against my knuckles.

"She didn't explain properly," I said, touching his cheek then pulling away. "I didn't threaten to leave the house, only stop being her companion. It wasn't merely a threat, either. I can't be her companion anymore. Not while she's so against you and me being together."

He sat back too and sighed. "What did she say?"

"You know how she can be."

"Condescending?"

"She's a woman of her station, Matt. I don't blame her, not really, but I can't listen to her tell me she likes me in one breath and then tell me I'm not good enough for you in the next. She's a hypocrite. What's more, I think she knows it."

"Then you did the right thing."

"Do you think so? I was worried you wouldn't agree." She was, after all, the only member of his English family he liked, and she was elderly and in need of company. I thought he might see it as my duty as his future wife to put up with her.

"Of course I agree. India, I won't allow anyone to tell you you're not worthy. Not even her. If anything, it's the other way around. If she knew my past, she'd be surprised any sensible woman would want me."

I smiled. "Thank you, Matt. And don't worry. I'll always be kind to her, no matter what. I just won't take her on walks or go shopping with her. Polly will have to keep her company."

"Then Aunt will change her mind, soon enough. Polly's a nice girl but Aunt prefers someone with a little more conversation. I'll talk to her this evening."

"Don't do that. It makes me look like I ran to you with my problem. Like you say, she needs time."

The question was, how much time?

CHAPTER 5

Lord Coyle took a very long time to come down the stairs after his footman went to fetch him from his study. By the look of his sleepy eyes, I wondered if we'd woken him from a midday nap rather than interrupting him at work.

He greeted me enthusiastically—Matt less so—and invited us into the library. It was the same room that harbored the secret storeroom for his magical objects.

"Have you come to donate something to my collection, Miss Steele?" he asked, settling his wide frame into a deep leather armchair. He offered Matt a cigar but Matt refused.

"No," I said. "Is that why you asked me to dine with you?"

"Not at all. I simply wished to get to know you. My friends were eager to meet you too." He plucked a cigar from the box and plugged it into his mouth. "Magicians are not easy to find in this city," he said, clamping his lips around the cigar.

And yet it felt as though magicians were coming out of the woodwork lately. I was finding them everywhere. Then again, it was easy for me to identify them through their work now that I knew what magic heat felt like.

"Who supplies you with your personal stationery?" Matt asked.

"Odd question." Lord Coyle shook the match to extinguish it and sucked on the cigar. "Why do you ask?"

"Have you heard of a supplier by the name of Hendry?"

"No. Why would—? Ah." He pointed the cigar at Matt. "He's a magician, isn't he? Well, well. I'll add him to my list."

"You keep a list of magicians?" I asked.

"Of course. Names, addresses and magical ability. We share contacts with other collectors. This Hendry fellow must have been lying low to remain undiscovered."

My name would be on that list. I felt rather sick about it, although I couldn't say why. I felt even sicker that we'd just given Lord Coyle another name to add to it.

"I'll have to ask my butler who supplies my paper." Lord Coyle rang the small bell on the table beside the cigar box and a moment later, the butler entered. "Where do you order my stationery?" Coyle asked him.

"From Hendry's in Smithfield, my lord."

Lord Coyle waited until the butler shut the door on his way out and turned to Matt. "Well, well. It seems I can add the letterhead to my collection. How remarkable. Another magical object was right under my nose, and I didn't know it." He looked to the clock on the mantel but didn't ask me to use my magic on it, and I didn't offer.

"Can you tell us where to find the other guests who dined with us here that evening?" I asked. "Mr. Glass is thinking of hosting a dinner party and would like to invite them."

Lord Coyle's bushy eyebrows rose. "Of course. I'm surprised. I didn't think you enjoyed yourselves."

"Perhaps we just need to get to know them better."

He grunted. "Keep your friends close and your enemies closer, eh?"

Enemies?

He called his butler back with a ring of the bell and asked him to copy the addresses from the book on his desk.

We passed the next few minutes by discussing Matt's family. Lord Coyle knew Lord Rycroft, but they weren't close, and he'd never met any other Glasses. Indeed, he seemed quite disinterested in the conversation. He glanced frequently at the clock yet didn't ask me to use magic on it. If he did, I wasn't sure how I would answer.

The butler soon returned, thankfully, and we rose to leave.

"Just a moment." Lord Coyle heaved himself out of the chair. The effort brought on a coughing fit that turned his face puce. "Why do you want to know the name of my stationer?" he managed to splutter.

"Someone sent threatening letters to Oscar Barratt at *The Weekly Gazette*," Matt said. "Someone who wanted him to stop writing his articles. *You've* admitted to wanting him to stop."

"You think I'd send threats by mail?" Lord Coyle chuckled a throaty, phlegmy chuckle. "Think again, Mr. Glass."

"My mistake," Matt simply said.

"Does this have something to do with the editor's death?"

"Barratt received the letters, not Baggley."

Lord Coyle said nothing, and I wondered if he'd also concluded that the wrong man had been shot.

The butler saw us out, and Matt gave instructions to our driver to take us to Mr. and Mrs. Delancey's house, only a few streets away.

"I don't believe Coyle sent the letters to Barratt," Matt said once we were seated in the carriage.

I agreed. "I cannot imagine him hiding behind anonymous threats."

"We'll cross him off our list of suspects."

"Excellent. It has shrunk from hundreds to hundreds minus one. If we continue to eliminate suspects at this rate, we'll have our killer by the turn of the century."

"We'll get there, India. At least we're not directly affected by the murder, this time."

That was something to be thankful for.

The Delanceys were not at home, so we traveled to University College on Gower Street where Professor Nash had a room tucked away in a wing far from the main building. We had to ask directions from three students before finding one who knew Professor Nash and where to find him.

"Apologies for the humbleness of my abode," Nash said with an embarrassed glance at the bed.

It was made but the covers sported creases from where he must have been lying moments ago. A book lay open on the bedside table next to a candle melted down to its stub. The desk positioned by the north-facing window was covered with books and the room smelled stale.

"We're glad to find you here," I said. "We thought you might be lecturing."

"Not until this afternoon." He pushed his glasses up his nose and gave me a thorough inspection. He must have liked what he saw because he fussed over me, suggesting I sit on the only chair and clearing a space on the desk. "I can't offer you tea, I'm afraid, but I do have water and wine."

"I'm fine, thank you."

"As am I," Matt said pointedly.

Professor Nash didn't even glance Matt's way. "I'm thrilled you're here, Miss Steele. I was hoping you'd want to talk to me away from the others. I imagine it must be intimidating being the object of their obsession."

"Obsession?" I repeated.

Matt stiffened. "They have not made any demands of her."

Nash looked at Matt properly for the first time. "They will. That sort are used to getting what they want. They're probably biding their time. Am I right in thinking you would refuse to perform magic for them?"

"She is not a performing monkey," Matt growled.

Nash stepped away, hands to his chest. "No, no, that's not what I meant, sir. I simply mean that she is a powerful magician, and Coyle has told them, and me, about her watch saving her. I suspect they want to see that happen again with their own eyes. They'll probably ask you to donate the piece to their collections too, Miss Steele. I'd hazard they'd even auction it among themselves, the highest bidder to keep it. That's what happens with their rarest pieces, so Coyle told me."

"The watch wouldn't work for anyone else," I said. "Only me."

"They may *know* that, but I think they *believe* otherwise.

Anyway, an item from the famed Miss India Steele will be an asset to their collection nevertheless."

I laughed. "Famed?"

He peered over his spectacles at me. "Yes, Miss Steele. Among those who are aware of magic, and have spoken to that jailed sheriff, you are known as the most powerful."

I stared at him.

"You don't believe that nonsense Payne is spouting, do you?" Matt scoffed. "The man's mad. It'll be proven so in court."

Nash stared back at me, and I got the distinct feeling he was studying me as a scientist would an insect under a microscope, watching for my reaction. I tried to keep my face blank.

"According to my studies," Nash said, rifling through the books on the table in front of me. "You are not the first time-piece magician to extend the magic of other magicians." He found the book and flipped through the pages. He stopped at a page with a sketch of a man dressed in seventeenth century clothing standing beside a rudimentary clock. The scene appeared to take place at a smith's forge where another man sat, sword in hand. "This drawing is thought to be of two magicians combining their magic. The clock magician is probably extending the life of the swordsmith's magic."

"Or it could be a drawing of two men who are not magicians," Matt said. "It's not clear."

"Devices for telling the time were very new when this was drawn," Professor Nash went on. "While spells to manipulate wood or metal were very old by the seventeenth century, clock and watch magic was in its infancy. Those magicians were probably still experimenting with how to put the magic words together effectively at this point" He indicated the drawing. "It was also at a time when magic use was declining. That decline has persisted to this day. Then, as now, magicians were afraid for their lives and went into hiding. Unfortunately, that meant the complicated spells became lost, because they weren't passed on to the younger generations. It also meant magicians from different crafts didn't share spells. New spells were rarely created and even more rarely combined. This is one of the latest depictions of the combining of spells across disciplines. Even rarer is the notion of time magic being combined with medical magic. I'd never heard the like of it until I spoke to Lord Coyle. He told me about the experiment your grandfather and Dr. Millroy performed twenty-seven years ago. It was such a mad notion to me at the time, that I admit I laughed at him." He began pacing back and forth, his hands at his back, his eyes huge behind his glasses. "The idea grew on me, however, and then when he told me Sheriff Payne's story, well, I had to visit him and find out for myself."

"It was *you*," I said. "*You* visited him in prison."

"Lord Coyle told me you would not speak about it, even if I asked nicely and even if he offered you money."

"He wanted to *buy* information from her!" Matt crossed his arms and muttered, "Damn him."

"I don't think I am the only one who visited Payne," Nash said. "I know Coyle did. There are probably others from the club too."

I groaned. No matter how many of us refuted Payne's claims in the trial now, Coyle and his ilk wouldn't believe us. I only hoped the public never found out.

Matt rested a hand on my shoulder and gently squeezed. "As long as the general populace believe us, nothing should come of Payne's claims. It's the mob mentality that must be curbed before it gathers momentum. Coyle and his friends seem keen to keep magic quiet and exclusive."

"Quite right, Mr. Glass." Professor Nash passed the book to me. "You may borrow this. It'll help you understand the history of your power."

"Thank you," I said, clutching it.

"Did you have any specific questions to ask me?"

"We want to know where you buy your paper from," Matt said.

"My paper?" Nash pushed his glasses up his nose. "What has this got to do with Miss Steele's magic?"

"Nothing."

"Oh." Nash sounded disappointed. "The university supplies me with notepaper."

"What about personal stationery?"

"Monogrammed letterhead and calling cards are not items a humble professor can afford. Why? What is this about?"

Matt and I glanced at one another. An understanding passed between us and Matt said, "Someone sent threatening letters using magic-infused paper to Oscar Barratt at *The Weekly Gazette's* offices. We'd like to find out who."

"Barratt, not Baggley? How strange that Baggley was the one to die, then. I assume the two things are linked?"

"It would be quite a coincidence if they aren't," I said.

Nash nodded slowly as he thought. "Why are you two investigating and not the police?"

"The police don't think the threats and the crime are linked." Even as I said it, I wondered if we should have taken Oscar's word for that. "Mr. Barratt asked us to help, since we have experience in investigating crimes related to magic."

"Do you know of any paper magicians?" Matt asked.

Nash shook his head.

"Thank you for your time." Matt put out a hand to assist me to my feet.

I took it and tucked the book under my arm. "Thank you for the reading material, Professor. I'll return it to you as soon as possible."

"Keep it as long as you want." He clicked his heels together and bowed. "My door is always open to you, Miss Steele. I will endeavor to answer any questions you have."

"He paid you rather too much attention," Matt said as we made our way back through the hallowed halls of the university. "There were times I felt as though he forgot I was even there."

"It's understandable, since he thinks I'm a powerful magician," I said, lowering my voice. "He hasn't had the opportunity to study any before. Not that I think I'm powerful, you understand, only that he does."

"He is not going to study you, India. You are not some mediocre history professor's project."

"Mediocre? That's a little harsh, isn't it?"

"If he were more important, he would be given better rooms in a better part of the university. He's at the back end of the campus in a tiny room. He may not be mediocre, but the university thinks he is."

I did see his point. Not only had we walked down several long corridors, and up and down quite a few flights of stairs, but we'd also crossed a quadrangle and a lawn where several students lounged in the sunshine, and we hadn't even reached the main building on Gower Street yet. I was beginning to feel sorry for Professor Nash. His interest in me seemed harmless enough.

We drove to Sir Charles Whittaker's Hammersmith residence next. The bachelor lived in a handsome row house with white bay window frames and a small front garden. He wasn't a gentleman of means then, living off family land holdings as I'd assumed. Unlike the large mansion of Lord Coyle, and the impressive five level townhouse of the Delanceys, he did not have a butler or footman. The housekeeper answered the door and informed us that he was not at home.

We were about to leave when Sir Charles himself approached on foot along the pavement. He paused at the gate, surprised to see us, before inviting us to stay for tea. The sitting room furniture was elegant yet simple, neither too masculine nor too feminine, and the decoration was kept to a minimum, which I expected from a bachelor of his age. His pinstripe suit, with the crisp handkerchief poking out of the pocket of the jacket, was also elegantly simple.

"What is it you do, Sir Charles?" Matt asked.

"I'm an advisor."

"Whom do you advise?"

Sir Charles crossed his legs and flicked imaginary dust off his trousers. "The royal family."

"How interesting," I said. "What do you advise them on?"

"I'm sorry, Miss Steele, but I am not at liberty to say. Her Majesty prefers such things to remain private. I hope you understand."

"Oh. Of course." Whatever he did, it was enough to earn him a knighthood.

The housekeeper brought in tea and buttery biscuits that tasted as delicious as they looked.

Matt got straight to the point as soon as she left. "Someone has been sending Oscar Barratt of *The Weekly Gazette* threatening letters. He asked us to find out who."

Sir Charles's eyebrows rose ever higher with each sentence. "Probably wise, considering what happened to Baggley. What does it have to do with me, though?"

"The paper used was made by a magician named Hendry. He has a workshop in Smithfield. Does the name ring a bell with you?"

"No. Should it?"

"Who makes your personal stationery?"

"A local man by the name of Woodley." Sir Charles frowned. "Are you accusing me of being the author of the letters?"

"You wanted Barratt stopped."

Sir Charles set down his teacup with a clatter. "I did not send anyone threatening letters. I may not want Barratt writing those articles, but I wouldn't bother with a written threat. That sort of thing is ineffective, in my experience."

"What method would you employ?" Matt asked.

Sir Charles picked up his cup again and sipped.

"May I see one of your calling cards?" I asked.

Sir Charles pulled a small silver case from his inside jacket pocket. He flipped open the lid and picked out a card, which he handed to me. His name was printed in black ink on the thick cream paper. Neither the card nor the ink felt warm. I handed it back and shook my head at Matt.

"I suppose you're asking to see the stationery of all members of the collectors' club," Sir Charles said.

"Only those we met at Lord Coyle's dinner at this point," I said. "We have several other lines of inquiry to follow up too."

Sir Charles smiled. "You sound like a seasoned detective, Miss Steele. Lord Coyle tells me you two have solved other crimes together. You're gaining quite a reputation for yourselves."

"It's why Oscar Barratt came to us with his problem."

"Could it also be because you're a powerful magician?"

"Is she?" Matt stood and buttoned his jacket. "Lord Coyle seems to be basing his theory on the gossip spread by a prisoner who resents me. Has it occurred to you that Payne might be trying to get his revenge by making life difficult for Miss Steele?"

"You're right," Sir Charles said. "I do apologize. I don't appreciate gossip and innuendo either. Unless I personally see Miss Steele extend someone's life, I will assume her powers are as ordinary as every other magician's. Do you accept my apology, Miss Steele?"

"Of course," I said.

He put out his hand to assist me to stand. "I hope to see you again. I understand you're reluctant to talk about your magic with strangers, but I hope you will realize, in time, that no one in the club wishes you harm. We are merely curious about magic, as none of us have the ability ourselves. We are all quite dull." He chuckled.

"I don't think the artless are dull," I said. "But thank you."

He walked us to the front door and we were about to leave when I remembered something. "Did you enjoy the fights the other night?"

He blinked. "Pardon?"

"The fights at the tavern. I was there with my friends and saw you."

He shook his head. "I'm afraid you have the wrong man. I don't watch fighting for amusement. I find it rather unpleasant." He held the door open wider. "Good day, Miss Steele, Mr. Glass."

"That's odd," I said to Matt as we drove off. "It was definitely him I saw."

"Perhaps he's embarrassed to admit he likes to watch illegal bare knuckle fighting. It's not the most gentlemanly of sports."

"True. And he does strike me as rather a debonair gent who'd be particular about getting blood on his nice suit."

Matt smiled. "Not like my friends. I seem to have trouble keeping them away from blood sports. Willie in particular has an affinity for it."

"She's quite the ring leader when it comes to leading the other two astray. I know why Duke does whatever she wants, but I thought Cyclops would back down before the fights started."

"He needed the distraction. He's more interested in Catherine than he likes to admit, even to himself." Matt watched me through half lowered lids and I got the feeling he had more to say.

"Go on," I urged.

"If I don't find something for them to do, they're going to grow more restless. If they grow too bored, they'll either pester me to return to America, or they'll want to compete in more bare knuckle fights. Since Duke and Cyclops are averse to beating each other up for sport, they'll run out of taverns soon enough."

"Are you saying *you* want to return to America?" I wasn't sure how I felt about that. I wanted to be with Matt, and I would travel to the ends of the earth if needs be. But my grandfather was in London, and everything I knew was there too.

"No," he said. "Just that I need to give them something to do."

"Then let's start delegating before they kill one another."

* * *

MATT BROUGHT me breakfast in the morning before I was fully awake. He promised that none of the servants saw him enter my room, but since they would have prepared the tray, I thought the fact irrelevant. I wasn't sure whether I minded or not. I should. It was terribly scandalous to have a man in my room at such an hour, but it was also a small way of showing the world we planned to be together.

I sat up in bed and he handed me the tray. "What's happened?" I asked upon seeing his grim face.

He opened the curtains then removed the newspaper he'd

tucked under his arm. It was opened to the announcements page. I groaned as I read the short paragraph he pointed to.

> Lord and Lady Rycroft are delighted to announce the engagement of their eldest daughter Patience Glass to the heir of the Rycroft title, Matthew Glass of Mayfair.

CHAPTER 6

"So. It's official." I lowered the paper with a shaking hand. How had it come to this? The entanglement with Patience had seemed a little unreal up until now. I never doubted Matt, not really. I always thought he would find a way out of it. Now it was splashed in bold type in the most prestigious newspaper of the city, it was very real indeed.

Matt sat on the bed near my knee and closed his hand over mine. "My uncle assured me he would give me more time to convince Lord Cox." His fingers tightened. "I'll have it out with him this morning."

"What will you do?"

He said nothing. I wouldn't put it past him to punch his uncle. He'd threatened it before, and looking at him now, his chest rising and falling with his seething breaths, he was in the right frame of mind to do something rash.

"Don't," I said, my eyes burning with tears. "The more you anger him, the less likely he'll be to let you out of the arrangement."

"He was never holding out hope for Cox to change his mind," he bit off. "I know that, now. I was a fool for trusting him. Damn it."

I sidled closer and put my arms around him. I rested my head on his shoulder and felt him relax a little. "What do we do now? Keep trying to convince Lord Cox?"

He kissed the top of my head and tucked me under his chin. "He's not going to give in."

"Then what? Backing out of the engagement would embarrass Patience now that it's been made public. She already suffered after Lord Cox withdrew his suit."

"I know," he said heavily. "I can't end it, anyway."

I pulled back to look at him. He avoided my gaze. "Tell me, Matt. Tell me what he has over you. Together, we might be able to think of a way out."

He didn't speak for a long time, and I thought he was thinking up a lie to placate me. But when he spoke, I knew it wasn't a lie. "He told me if I didn't agree to the union, he would inform the home secretary about your magic. They're friends."

"The home secretary?" I murmured. When it came to the country's safety, only the prime minister was higher. "But…what would he do if he found out about my magic?"

Matt swept the hair off my forehead. "I don't know. That's the problem, India, I just don't know. He might treat it as a joke, or he might lock you up."

"Or he might have me studied."

He nodded. "If you can think of a way out of this arrangement without angering my uncle, I'm all ears."

I slumped against him and plucked the fabric of his shirt. "We could run away together. Let's go to America after all."

"It'll be an admission of guilt, and the home secretary will believe my uncle. You'll never be able to return here."

"So you do agree to do it? Even if it means hurting Patience and destroying her chances of a good marriage?" And that of her sisters, I might have said, but didn't want to add more burdens to his conscience. He already knew anyway.

He traced the line of my jaw with light, gentle fingers. "I'm not marrying her, India. Only you."

I pressed my lips to his in a light, feathery kiss then snuggled into his warm body with a sigh. "As much as I want to be with you, Matt, and as angry as I am at her for going along with this scheme, I don't want to ruin Patience's life." She desperately wanted to get away from her parents and sisters, and she saw marriage as her only way out. Without a skill or trade to fall back on, it probably was. But if Matt abandoned her so soon after Lord Cox had, no man would want her. She was already too old for most gentlemen to consider her, and she was too shy to easily attract beaus. Two broken engagements would bury her.

"I'll speak with her alone," Matt said. "If Lord Cox won't change his mind, perhaps she'll change hers and refuse me."

I doubted it, but I didn't say so. He needed to cling to some hope, just as much as I did. The problem was, I couldn't see a way out that didn't involve us running away and her being unhappy for the rest of her life.

* * *

MATT PROWLED from one side of the drawing room to the other while the rest of us sat and watched, helpless. "He said he wouldn't announce it yet," Matt growled to no one in particular. "He broke his promise to me."

"Did *she* make a promise?" Miss Glass asked. "Did my sister-in-law say she wouldn't announce it so soon?" It was difficult to gauge her feelings from her cool gaze, her outward calmness, but the steeliness of her question suggested she wasn't entirely ambivalent.

Matt stopped short. "Aunt Beatrice made no such promise."

"Then *she* is to blame for this." Miss Glass picked up the newspaper only to throw it down on the table again. It skidded off and fell on the floor. "You must speak to her, Matthew. You must tell her that you and Richard had an understanding. She shouldn't be allowed to get away with this gross mishandling of the situation."

Matt began pacing again. "It won't change anything. What's done is done."

Cyclops picked up the newspaper and placed it on the table. "So what are you going to do?"

Matt stopped again and his gaze met mine. "I couldn't say." He didn't need to tell me more. The situation had reached the crisis we'd discussed. It was time to make plans to leave England.

Willie, Cyclops and Duke seemed to reach the same understanding. Everyone's focus shifted to Miss Glass. Thankfully, she seemed unaware. I didn't want her reaching the same conclusion. Not yet. We had not discussed where she fitted into our plans, and now that I thought about it, I knew there was no easy solution. She wouldn't want to leave England, yet we couldn't leave her with her horrid relatives.

"I don't understand why Lord Cox is being so obstinate," she said with a shake of her head. "He seemed to enjoy Patience's company and didn't mind her timidity. Indeed, he seemed to like that she wasn't as brash as her sisters."

"He can't look past her indiscretion," I said.

"He feels as though he was taken in by her and her parents," Matt added. "He thinks the timidity you speak of, Aunt, was merely a ruse to secure him."

"The man's an ass," Willie said. "Most of 'em are, excepting you three. If you ask me, she's well rid of him if he ain't got the b—"

"Willie," Matt snapped.

She sniffed and crossed her arms. "He's an ass," she said again.

Miss Glass sighed and excused herself. She looked upset, and I rose instinctively to go with her. She paused at the door, but when she saw me sit down again, her chin lowered and she left.

"So when are we leaving?" Willie asked Matt once Miss Glass was out of earshot.

Matt's gaze connected with mine.

"For Patience's sake, we should tell her today that you cannot marry her," I said.

"Matt *has* told her," Willie whined.

"But she knows Lord Rycroft has something over him and will use it to force his hand. Patience thinks it's enough. She doesn't know it's not."

"We can't tell her," Matt said, finally taking a seat beside me on the sofa. "She'll tell my uncle, and he'll follow through with his threat. We have to leave before he finds out."

"You can send her a letter," Duke said.

"The coward's way," Matt muttered.

"You can't risk anything else. The gov'ment won't want India leaving the country."

"First of all, we don't know that Patience will tell her father immediately," I said. "Second of all, you're overstating my worth to any government. Thirdly, you are assuming the authorities will believe Lord Rycroft. So far, they have not commented on Oscar's articles. For all we know, the home secretary will laugh him out of the office."

"Or he won't," Cyclops intoned. "It ain't worth the risk. I agree with Matt and Duke. You can't tell Patience, or anyone else, when we're leaving. I know it ain't fair to her, but you got to think of yourself now. Don't play games with your freedom, India. When it's gone, it's mighty difficult to get it back again."

I swallowed. He was right. But I had one ace up my sleeve. "I have an idea. If it doesn't work, then we make plans to leave England in secret. If it does, then hopefully Lord Cox will change his mind and we can stay after all."

Willie gave another snort. "You going to blackmail him?"

"We have nothing to blackmail him with," Matt said.

"We're going to invite them both to dine here," I said. "Just the two of them, and neither will know the other is coming."

Willie snorted. "I want to be in the room when they realize it's a trick."

"It's not a trick," I retorted. "Merely a…"

"A matchmaking service," Duke finished for me. "Like them marriage brokers. Back in the old days, they arranged matches between men from the west and women from the eastern states."

Willie rolled her eyes. "It ain't like that at all, Duke. It won't work."

"You just ain't romantic."

"An arranged marriage ain't romantic. It's a prison sentence."

"It might work," I said. "At a suitable point in the evening, the rest of us will leave them alone. If Miss Glass is right, and Lord

Cox does truly like Patience, then perhaps he'll reconsider after spending more time with her."

Matt nodded thoughtfully. "It's likely they were never left alone much. If he gets to know her, he might fall in love with her."

"Or he might flee in the other direction," Willie said. "Well, it's true," she added when Duke admonished her. "She's as dull as mud."

"She's not," I said. "I like her better than her sisters. At least I did before she refused to defy her parents and set Matt free."

Matt took my hand. "It's a good idea, and I see no other way at the moment. I'll arrange it."

I gave him a flat smile. It was the best I could offer.

"And if it don't work?" Willie asked.

"Let's give it a chance before we make plans," Matt said.

She sighed. "I suppose I can wait. What about you two?" she asked Duke and Cyclops. "You want to go home soon, don't you?"

I wasn't surprised when Cyclops gave a non-committal shrug. Returning to America meant returning to danger, with his past employer still hunting him. He also had feelings for Catherine, even though he denied them. I was surprised to see Duke hesitate, however.

Willie muttered something under her breath that I didn't hear and pushed to her feet. "I'm going out for some air."

"I've got something for the three of you to do," Matt told them. "I want Mr. Hendry, the paper magician, Mr. Sweeney, the Stationers' Guild master, and Abercrombie watched. Decide which of you follows which man."

"You think Abercrombie is involved in Baggley's murder?" Cyclops asked.

"I wouldn't put it past him to have his finger in this pie."

The three of them left with flasks of whiskey and a pie in their pocket to eat cold for luncheon. If nothing else, it was something for them to do now that the convent's roof was fixed.

"Where are you going?" I asked Matt when I saw him asking Bristow to fetch his coat.

"To speak with my aunt and uncle," he said. "We had an agreement."

"It's too late to change anything now. Whatever you say to them will fall on deaf ears. Let them think you've accepted the situation. That way they won't anticipate our counter-move. Now go and write the invitations to Patience and Lord Cox."

He lightly kissed my forehead. "You're far more pragmatic than I."

He wrote the invitations in his study before handing them to Peter the footman to post. We'd decided the following night would allow Mrs. Potter the time she needed to prepare special dishes. Matt then informed his aunt of the plan and swore her to secrecy. We briefly considered not telling her at all but decided we had to. She would be joining us for dinner, after all.

I waited for Matt in the entrance hall, gloves in hand, ready to leave to call on the Delanceys. He joined me with his aunt in tow and watched on as she pressed something into my hand.

"I wanted to give you this, India," she said. "It will look very fetching on that jacket."

I opened my hand to see a silver brooch in the shape of a honeyeater. A small amethyst brightened the bird's eye.

"Shall I pin it on you?" she asked.

"I can't accept this," I said. "You shouldn't be buying me things, Miss Glass."

"I didn't buy it. It's one of my own, but I no longer wear it. It's for a younger woman, and the blue looks nicer on you than me, anyway."

I pushed it back into her hand. "It's not right to accept it if I am no longer your companion."

"Come now, India, let's set aside our differences and be friends again."

"Some things cannot be set aside. We will only argue again, and that's not how I want to spend my days. Do you?"

She clasped the brooch to her chest. "Matthew? Will you talk to her?"

"I agree with her decision," he said gently. "This is too important to the both of us to sweep aside. Can I fetch Polly to keep you company today? We have to go out."

She pulled a face. "Polly is so dull. I want India. Her conversation is much more lively."

"Polly will have to do until I employ someone else to be your companion."

"I don't want a stranger. I want India."

"I'd rather that too," I told her. "But we can't agree on an important matter, and both of us will end up miserable. I won't back down on this, Miss Glass."

"Nor will I," Matt said. "You need to accept that India and I will marry."

"It's too late, Matthew," she said, her voice frail. "The announcement has been published. I am sorry it happened this way. Really, I am. But nothing can be done now. The dinner won't achieve what you want. Lord Cox is far too proud and Patience is simply not that appealing. You'll be married to her within weeks and that's that."

Bristow fetched Polly just as a hack pulled up outside. Our own carriage had not yet arrived from the mews, and we were not expecting visitors. The long legged form of Oscar Barratt stepped out and trotted up to the front door.

We ushered him in out of the drizzle and Matt took his coat. His aunt, still waiting for Polly, clicked her tongue at her nephew performing a servant's task.

We waited for Polly to collect Miss Glass and for Bristow to return. Matt asked him to bring tea into the library, but Oscar insisted he couldn't stay.

"I needed to tell you something in person," he said as Matt shut the library door behind him. "Two things, actually. First of all, I discovered who owns *The City Review*."

"I'm still not convinced it matters," Matt said. "The owners don't want you to stop writing your articles for the *Gazette*. They're good for business."

"Not that good. From my inquiries, I've deduced that the *Review* isn't getting any more circulation than it was before. I'm persisting with my theory that the owners are men of business who would rather see magicians suppressed to maintain the successes of their own companies. They're powerful men of commerce. They won't stand idly by while magicians take over."

"Go on," Matt said. "Who owns *The City Review*?"

"A consortium of three bankers. The main investor in the consortium is an extremely wealthy man by the name of Delancey."

"Delancey!" Matt and I both cried. "We dined with him at Lord Coyle's recently," I added.

"We were just on our way to see him," Matt said. "Like the rest of Coyle's collector friends, he and his wife want to keep magic a secret. That already made them suspects in the shooting."

"But it does rather fly against your theory that all businessmen want to persecute magicians," I said to Oscar. "Delancey doesn't want to harm us. He is actually fascinated by magic and values magical objects. He's not afraid of us."

"Not when you were hiding away, performing magic in secret," Oscar said. "But things have changed, and businessmen like Delancey want to return to the status quo."

"Not by killing you, surely."

He didn't respond.

"We'll talk to him," Matt said. "Even if he isn't the killer, he might know something."

Oscar agreed. "The other thing to note is that he's not highly educated. His father came from humble beginnings before making the family fortune in the wool trade. He didn't believe his son required higher learning. We already suspect the author of the letters is not well educated in the traditional sense, and Delancey fits that profile."

"His grammar errors," I noted, not sure that I agreed. Mr. Delancey certainly sounded like he was from the upper classes, but I supposed the accent could have been affected over the years to fit in with the powerful men around him, like Lord Coyle.

"There's one other thing," Oscar said, scrubbing his short goatee. "Someone visited my office on the day of the murder and asked after me. He was told I was not in but would be working late."

"Was he told you would be alone?"

Oscar shook his head. "It may or may not be the killer, but I thought it worth mentioning."

"Do you have a description of the man?" Matt asked.

"Slender build, thinning fair hair, glasses. He had a quiet manner of speaking, sounded educated and his clothing was a little shabby. He left on foot."

"It could be Professor Nash," I said to Matt.

"Do the police know about the visitor?" Matt asked Oscar.

"Yes, but they have probably dismissed it as unimportant, since they don't believe I am the target." Oscar rubbed his hand over his eyes and down his face. He sighed heavily. "Will you confront the professor?"

"I have someone watching him now. We'll consider what to do next."

"How are you coping, Oscar?" I asked gently. "You look worn out."

He offered me a smile that fell flat. "I admit that I'm worried."

"Then you shouldn't have come here," Matt said. "For the sake of my family and friends, as well as your own."

"No one followed me," Oscar said. "I made sure of that. Besides, I'm not in any danger in broad daylight, and I needed to get out of the house and away from the office too."

"I imagine it would drive you mad to be cooped up all the time," I said.

"I can manage that. I always have something to read or write. I had to get out because those are the two places my brother knows where to find me, and he has a rather persistent nature when it comes to ordering his little brother about."

"Your brother is in London?" Matt asked. "Why didn't you tell us?"

"Because he's not a suspect, Glass. An irritant and a bore, yes, but he's not trying to kill me. We're brothers, for God's sake."

Later, when we were alone in the carriage, Matt said,

"Everyone is a suspect. Being family doesn't exclude his brother. My grandfather wanted to kill me."

While I hated to admit it, he had a point. Family members made the most dangerous enemies.

* * *

Being a Saturday morning, Mr. and Mrs. Delancey were at home. Their Belgravia house echoed Lord Coyle's in many ways, although it didn't face Belgrave Square and was painted all white. The red door made a bold statement and the entrance hall was equally bold with its pink marble floor and staircase. The footman invited us to wait in the drawing room, where the eclectic nature of Mrs. Delancey's style reigned in the deep red wallpaper, pale blue upholstery, the gold piping on the cushions, and gold tassels on the curtains.

She swanned in, all toothy smiles and a warm welcome. "What a thrill it is to have you in my humble home, Miss Steele." She indicated we should sit, and she too sat, only to spring up again. She went to lift a clock set onto an onyx base off the mantel but, finding it too heavy, put it down again. "What do you think of this piece? Is it not very fine? My husband bought it only last week from an auction at Marlcombe House. A very unfortunate business, being forced to sell one's treasured possessions. I'm sure Lady Marlcombe would be happy to know the clock looks well on our mantel. Would you like to touch it, Miss Steele?"

I blinked rather stupidly at her. "That isn't how my magic works," I said.

She laughed musically. "I know. I thought you might like to feel it anyway. Come on. Up you get." That smile of hers never wavered, and I felt I ought to reward her for her effort.

I flipped open the clock's glass case and ran my thumb along the brass minute hand. It was warm.

She clapped her hands. "Marvelous!"

"What is it, India?" Matt asked, coming up behind me.

"It's warm," I told him, inspecting the clock. It was old,

perhaps fifty years or more, and beautifully made. "Would you mind turning it, Matt? I want to see the maker's mark on the back."

"No need," Mrs. Delancey said, sounding smug. "It has your grandfather's mark. Lady Marlcombe says she bought it off a man who bought it from your grandfather's shop, many years ago."

Matt turned it and I traced my finger over the engraving. Chronos had made this, all those years ago. Or perhaps it was my grandmother's hands that had crafted the fine piece. She'd been a horology magician too, and more dedicated to the work of watch and clockmaker than her husband. I wanted to ask Chronos and was tempted to visit him. It could be for the last time.

"That's why you bought it," I said. "You saw the mark and assumed it held magic."

"We wanted it for our collection," Mrs. Delancey said. "When we learned about your family history in horology magic, we decided to find something a Steele had worked on. Your shop had closed, but we didn't want to buy anything from it anyway. What if we purchased something that artless man had worked on instead?"

Eddie Hardacre, also known as Jack Sweet, hadn't worked on much, by all accounts. The shop and all its contents would most likely become mine again soon. Matt's lawyer was working on the legalities, but with Eddie guilty of duplicity and other crimes, and my grandfather still alive, it would surely belong to my family again soon. I hoped I would still be in London to see it transferred back to Chronos's name.

"Why do you not keep your collection locked away like Lord Coyle?" Matt asked.

"Because we want our guests to admire our things," Mr. Delancey said from the doorway. "Otherwise, what is the point of owning them?" He entered and greeted us as warmly as his wife had.

"You're not like Lord Coyle in that respect." I indicated the clock. "Do you tell people it was made by a magician?"

"No. At least, we haven't yet." He looked at Mrs. Delancey. "My wife would like to, but I think it unwise."

"Because of your position in commerce?" Matt asked.

The butler pushed in a wheeled table with a silver tray and teapot. He left discreetly, and Mrs. Delancey filled the dainty Wedgewood cups. Her smile had slipped but it widened again as she handed me a cup and saucer.

"Mr. Delancey?" Matt prompted. "Are you worried how your magic collection will be perceived by your friends? I assume they won't look too kindly upon someone who appreciates the very thing they believe will put them out of business."

Mrs. Delancey took a very long sip of tea and avoided looking at us. Her husband, however, met Matt's gaze with his own steady one.

"I think it's wise to keep the unique nature of our collection to ourselves, for now," Mr. Delancey said.

"If it became known that you do collect magical objects, your friends would abandon you. Some would even grow angry and accuse you of supporting their business rivals."

Mrs. Delancey whimpered in protest.

"Our friends will always be our friends, Mr. Glass," Mr. Delancey said coolly. "But my colleagues and business partners might take a different view. Because of that, I think it's wise to keep quiet on the topic of magic. My wife agrees with me, don't you, my dear?"

She nodded quickly and sipped again. I suspected the topic was much discussed in the household, and her wishes had been overruled by her husband. I had to agree with him. They were better off not mentioning magic to anyone in the current climate, particularly to powerful businessmen who traded in the very goods competing with magical objects.

"Speaking of maintaining silence, that's why we're here," Matt said. "You're part owner of *The City Review*."

"What of it?"

"*The City Review* is involved in a war of words with Oscar Barratt and *The Weekly Gazette* over the existence of magic."

"I may be owner, but I have no influence over what is published."

Matt scoffed. "No one believes that."

I glared at him; we were guests in the Delanceys' house. But Matt paid me no mind, and I shouldn't expect him to. He wasn't a man who held his tongue simply because it was the gentlemanly thing to do.

Mr. Delancey set down his tea untouched. "I think it wise to let the two newspapers fight it out. The *Gazette* and Barratt need to be challenged by a respected source. If not, then the truth will be more widely accepted and we've just discussed why that would be bad, Mr. Glass, not to mention we want to maintain the value of our collections through their exclusiveness. What of *you,* Glass? Where do you stand on magic being openly discussed as a result of Barratt's articles?"

"I'll keep my opinions on the matter to myself," Matt said.

"Miss Steele?"

"As will I," I said.

Mr. Delancey smiled tightly. "Do I detect some discord between you? I can see why you would side with Mr. Barratt, Miss Steele, but I wasn't sure where you fell on the matter, Glass. I admit that the other evening at Coyle's I thought you two were...together. However, my wife informed me this morning that an announcement has appeared in *The Times*. Congratulations on your engagement to your cousin."

"Congratulations," Mrs. Delancey echoed. "How lovely."

Matt did not thank her. He didn't correct them and tell them he wasn't marrying Patience, either. "The reason we came here was to ask where you buy your personal stationery."

"Why?" Mr. Delancey asked at the same moment his wife said, "Hendry's. He does very fine work."

"Why?" Mr. Delancey asked again.

"Someone has been sending threatening letters to Oscar Barratt at the *Gazette's* office, ordering him to stop writing his articles. The letters were sent on paper made by a magician named Hendry."

Mrs. Delancey gasped. "I knew it! I knew his card stock was

too good to be made by an artless." She clapped her hands. "I pride myself on my good taste."

Her husband wasn't as excited by the revelation but he was equally interested. "Are you implying that *we* sent those threatening letters?" he asked. "And, by extension, are you also implying that we would harm Barratt if he didn't stop writing for the *Gazette*?"

Matt stared coolly at him.

Mr. Delancey went quite still, and I suspected he was thinking through the implications of Matt's suggestion. It didn't take long for him to come to the same conclusion as we had. "You think Barratt was the intended victim, not the editor. Don't you?"

Mrs. Delancey took a few moments to connect the facts, but when she did, she set her teacup down with a loud *clank* and pressed a hand to her chest. "It...it wasn't us. We didn't send those letters, did we, darling? Nor did we kill that poor editor. Tell them, Ferdinand."

"It's all right, my dear. Of course we didn't kill anyone. How could we, when we were dining at Coyle's when it happened? Mr. Glass and Miss Steele were there themselves."

It was a very good point, but he could have paid someone to kill for him. A rich banker like Delancey didn't need to get his own hands dirty. I didn't voice my theory, and nor did Matt.

"Besides," Mr. Delancey went on, "why would I kill Barratt when the articles in *The City Review* are doing a serviceable job of discrediting him?"

"Perhaps 'serviceable' doesn't bring fast enough results for you."

"Neither I nor my wife killed that editor, Mr. Glass. Kindly refrain from insinuating as much or we cannot be friends. And I would dearly like to remain friends with Miss Steele and, by extension, yourself."

The two men exchanged stiff nods, and Mrs. Delancey looked pleased they'd come to an agreement.

"You are our friend, aren't you, Miss Steele?" she said. "Please say that you are."

I nodded.

"Excellent. And of course we can't be suspects, can we? You dined with us at Lord Coyle's. I suppose that also means the other guests are innocent too. That's fortunate for Lord Coyle and Sir Charles Whittaker."

"Why?" Matt asked.

She waved a hand. "They've become quite secretive of late. Before you arrived that night, they spoke in whispers in the corner. Sometimes those whispers became quite loud and heated. I caught your name, Miss Steele, but I couldn't tell you in what context they spoke about you." Her smile was as eager as ever but the spark in her eyes caught me by surprise.

We made our excuses and directed our driver to continue on to Lord Coyle's house next. "Mrs. Delancey isn't as silly as she tries to make us believe," I said, watching the Delanceys' butler close the front door as we drove off.

"It's her husband I don't trust," Matt said. "He's too smooth. He had an answer for everything and never seemed particularly ruffled."

"If that was a reason to arrest someone then you'd be in prison."

"Some things ruffle me. Aunt Beatrice's action, for one. My uncle's blackmail, for another." He leaned forward and rested his hands on my knees. "Not being with you."

I swallowed past the lump rising up my throat and didn't respond, nor give him any sign of encouragement. It was dangerous being alone and intimate in the confines of the carriage. Matt was not a free man, and if we were seen, it would not go well for him with his family.

* * *

LORD COYLE DISMISSED our questions about his whispered exchange with Sir Charles Whittaker. "It was merely a discussion about whether we should invite you to meet our other collector friends," he said. "He wanted you to give a lecture on your magic, and I said it was too soon. Not only would you say no, it might jeopardize the trust we've begun to develop." He tapped his pipe on the edge of the table then bit down on the stem. "I couldn't risk that."

"You are quite right, sir," I said. "I would have refused."

"As to the trust," Matt said darkly, "I think you're overstating your relationship with India, somewhat. We trust no one with such a deep interest in magic."

Lord Coyle pointed his pipe at Matt. "You may not, Mr. Glass, but allow Miss Steele to make up her own mind. You are not, after all, her husband. I see from this morning's announcement that you never will be. It seems I was quite wrong about you two, and Miss Steele means nothing more to you than the doctor magician who saved your life. I apologize for my error."

Matt's jaw hardened, and I almost expected to see steam rise from his nostrils. I'd never seen him put in his place like that before. The worst of it was, we could not correct Lord Coyle. Not when the announcement of his engagement to Patience was in black and white.

"Or was my first assumption correct?" Lord Coyle's moustache lifted with his curious smile. "I am quite a good judge of character. You two act like a young couple in love. Miss Steele's blush would confirm it."

I dipped my head.

"Do you have a point, Coyle?" Matt growled.

"I have an offer to make you, one that could see you freed from your obligations to your cousin."

I sucked in a breath. "Go on. Tell us, sir, I beg you."

Matt put up a finger. "What do you mean by *offer*?" he asked carefully.

Lord Coyle puffed on his pipe then removed it from his mouth. "Patience Glass was engaged to Lord Cox, but something made him withdraw the offer suddenly. Am I right?"

Neither Matt nor I confirmed or denied his statement. Lord Coyle went on regardless.

"What if I told you I have a piece of information you can use to convince Cox to change his mind and take your cousin off your hands, Glass?"

CHAPTER 7

My heart thudded. This was what we needed, what we'd been hoping for, desperately searching for. Despite Matt's digging, he'd come up with nothing with which to blackmail Lord Cox. Clearly he wasn't as devious or as well connected as Lord Coyle.

"Tell us," I urged. "What do you know about him?" I felt a little sick for asking. There would be no turning back from this, yet I couldn't help myself. I wanted to know. I was desperate to know.

Lord Coyle blew out a puff of smoke. It mushroomed above the pipe, obscuring the lower half of his face, leaving only his eyes. The beady orbs shone.

"Forgive me, Miss Steele, but the information I have is not something a gentleman willingly passes on, particularly when the object of the information is another gentleman, and a well-respected one at that."

"Tell us!"

Matt rested a hand on my shoulder. "You want something in exchange," he said flatly.

Coyle pointed his pipe at Matt. "I knew you'd understand, Glass. Yes, I want something in return. Something from Miss Steele."

I should have expected it. Matt had, but I'd stupidly believed Lord Coyle wanted to help us. "What do you want from me?"

"Let's leave that open, for now. The favor shall be called in at a later date of my choosing."

"No," Matt said. "Let's leave, India."

I rose slowly, my gaze lowered. I couldn't look Matt in eye. If I did, he might see my uncertainty.

"My offer will remain open," Lord Coyle said. "Good day to you both."

Matt and I didn't speak on the way to University College. For my part, I didn't want him seeing that I wished Lord Coyle had told us what he knew about Lord Cox. I couldn't gauge if Matt remained quiet for the same reason. His face remained dark and distant as he stared out the window at the dismal view.

The campus seemed empty of students thanks to the drizzle, and only a handful of staff walked swiftly between the shelter of the buildings. The slate gray clouds shrouded the imposing structures and seemed to suit my somber mood. I couldn't shake Lord Coyle's offer from my mind, no matter how much I tried to focus on the task at hand.

Professor Nash was in residence. As with our last visit, he apologized for the sparse and slightly disheveled state of his room before inviting us in.

"Do you have questions about magic, Miss Steele?" At my blank look, he added, "After reading the book I gave you."

"I haven't read it yet. We're here for another reason."

Matt got straight to the point. "You visited the office of *The Weekly Gazette* on the day the editor was shot. You asked to speak with Oscar Barratt and were informed that he would be back later that night."

"What of it?"

"If Barratt was the target, as the threatening letters suggest," Matt forged on, "then that makes you a suspect."

Nash's throat worked with his swallows. "Are you accusing me of killing that man? Simply because I asked after someone else?"

"It's not an unreasonable connection to make."

"It is!" His voice pitched high. He cleared his throat and tried again. "You're leaping to wild conclusions, Mr. Glass. Yes, I was there, and I asked to see Mr. Barratt, only to be told he wasn't in but would be working later that night. Perhaps you think that makes me guilty, but I beg to differ. I have nothing against Mr. Barratt and his articles. While I do think he should be cautious and not name names, I actually was going to encourage him to continue writing. I didn't want to admit to it earlier. I was afraid you'd think me selfish, since my reasons are entirely that. I was going to offer him my expertise to flesh out the history of magic for his articles."

"That might endanger *you*," I said.

"I'd ask him to give me a false name or simply call me an anonymous source. If it looked as if the academic community was interested in the topic, and there turned out to be no danger, then I'd ask him to reveal my name. I could get more work out of it, Miss Steele. I could be courted by the dean of history in this very establishment. Oxford or Cambridge might come calling. You cannot deny me the chance of a better living."

"We're not," Matt said. "But understand our point of view. Your enquiry, coming on the day of Baggley's death, is suspicious. You are the only person who knew Barratt would be working late in the office."

"I am not! There was another man in the reception room at the *Gazette*. I assumed he was waiting for someone, but he left when I did. He heard the entire exchange between myself and the office boy."

"What did the man look like?"

"About my age, slender with gray hair and a high forehead."

It sounded like Melville Hendry, the paper magician.

"There was another odd thing," Nash said. "I think the lad I spoke to was wrong about Barratt not being in the office at the time. I've never met him, but I saw two men arguing through one of the windows as I left. I paid them no mind until one of them shouted the other's name. He called him Oscar. I should have returned then, but it's possible there are two Oscars working at *The Gazette*."

"Did you see the man called Oscar?" Matt asked.

"He was handsome, about your age, with a goatee beard."

It sounded like Oscar Barratt. "And the other man?" I asked. "What did he look like?"

"A lot like the first man. They must have been related."

Oscar's brother, Isaac. It had to be.

* * *

OSCAR WAS in a meeting when we arrived at the *Gazette's* office so we left a message that we would return the next morning. Matt and I ate a late luncheon together and spent the remainder of the day in the library. It was the one room Miss Glass rarely entered, although if she really wanted to find us, she would come looking.

Fortunately we were not disturbed and were able to draw up our long list of suspects in peace. We made notes beside each name, but the right side of the page still looked woefully empty by the time we finished.

"What do you want to do now?" I asked, stabbing the pen into the holder.

"Wait for Cyclops, Duke and Willie to report back," Matt said.

"And in the meantime?"

He drew in a measured breath and let it out slowly. "We'll discuss how to direct the dinner tomorrow night."

"We should discuss Lord Coyle's offer."

"We're not accepting it, India, and that's final."

"But it's exactly what we've been looking for. I know it feels somewhat sordid to stoop to blackmail, but if the dinner doesn't work, we have no other plan to fall back on."

"My reluctance has nothing to do with the nature of blackmail. I'm prepared to use anything in our arsenal to have Cox reconsider, but Coyle's price is too high."

I pushed to my feet. "Too high? You put a value on us being together?"

"When it comes to your safety, yes," he said, also rising.

"He probably only wants me to infuse a clock with magic."

"If that's all he wanted, he would have already asked. Make no mistake, he wants more."

"How do you know?"

He tilted his head to the side and arched his brows.

"Good lord, Matt, you're attributing villainy without evidence."

He grasped my arms and gently shook me. "And you're attributing innocence without evidence. I've known powerful men in my time, and many of them have reached those heights because of their less than innocent machinations. I know you want to believe that everyone is good, and that's one reason why I love you."

"So I am merely a naive girl."

"That's not what I said."

"You didn't have to." I tried to pull away, but he refused to let go. He drew me close and pressed his forehead to mine. "I don't want to argue with you, India. But I'm not giving in on this. I don't trust Coyle, not when it comes to your life or freedom."

"That's the entire point," I said, pushing away. "*You* think my life and freedom are at stake, based on no evidence whatsoever. Am I not allowed an opinion?"

"Of course you are. And you've voiced it. But my instincts are rarely wrong."

"I see," I said crisply. "And mine usually are."

"India," he purred.

I moved to the table and picked up the book Professor Nash had given me. I'd left it there the day before. "I'm going to read in my room."

"Let's not part like this," he said. "I won't be able to concentrate."

I barked out a laugh.

"I won't be able to sleep or eat either."

I spun around to tell him how ridiculous he was being, only to find him standing a mere few inches away, a smile toying with his lips. I tried resisting those lips for several seconds, but I gave up and went to kiss him instead. I stopped short as guilt settled in.

"You're too charming for your own good," I said. "Or perhaps you're too charming for *my* good."

He brushed his fingers down my cheek. "I plan to be *very* good for you, India. Very good indeed." He nuzzled my throat, nipping the sensitive skin, making me giggle. Despite the guilt, despite my conviction not to kiss him, I found I couldn't push him away.

The door behind me suddenly opened and Bristow made an odd gurgling sound. Matt and I sprang apart, but the butler had already seen us. So had the man standing behind him—Abercrombie.

"Does your intended know you're already deceiving her?" Abercrombie asked in that supercilious voice of his. "Does her father?"

Matt dismissed Bristow but did not invite Abercrombie into the library. "Is there a point to your visit?"

Abercrombie's slick moustache twitched with his excitement at catching us *in flagrante*. "Order your people to stay away from me and my friends. Don't try to deny it, Glass. I saw your one-eyed thug outside my shop then again as I walked to an appointment. As if that isn't enough, I also saw one of your other friends watching the Stationers' Hall. What is it you want from us? What do you think we guild masters have done this time?"

"I'm sure your friend, Mr. Sweeney, told you about the threatening letters written on paper infused with magic," Matt said.

Abercrombie wrinkled his long, equine nose. "He did. They were sent to that irresponsible journalist at the *Gazette*. Perhaps if he'd heeded the warnings, the editor would still be alive."

"Perhaps the two things aren't linked."

Abercrombie made a scoffing sound in the back of his throat. "If you believe that, you're a fool."

Matt straightened to his full height. "Do you know anything about the letters? Or about the shooter?"

Abercrombie's lips pursed. "Of course not."

"Won't Barratt's death help your cause? You want him stopped. What better way to do that than kill him?"

"If I was prepared to kill someone to keep magic hidden, I would have shot Miss Steele a long time ago. The fact I haven't is testimony to my good character."

Matt folded his arms and moved to fill the doorway so that I could no longer see Abercrombie properly, nor he me. I suspected Matt was giving the Watchmakers' Guild master one of his scowls, going by the way Abercrombie loudly cleared his throat.

A moment later, the front door opened and closed. Abercrombie was gone.

"He does have a point," I said. "He could have killed me before now to suppress magic."

"And incriminate himself as the main suspect?" Matt shook his head. He remained in the doorway, his body rigid as he stared in the direction Abercrombie had gone.

I touched his shoulder and urged him to look at me. "Do you think he'll tell your uncle that he saw us kissing?"

"He will." Matt suddenly scooped me into his arms. "So we might as well do it again."

* * *

"Sorry he caught me spying," Cyclops said as we sat in the library after dinner.

"It's the eye patch," Duke said. "It's too distinctive."

"It ain't just the eye patch."

Matt handed Cyclops a glass of brandy. "It's my fault. Abercrombie knows all of you. I shouldn't have sent you to watch him. Did you see where he went before he caught you?"

"He was in his shop most of the day then went to visit Sweeney at the Stationers' Guild Hall." Cyclops nodded at Duke. "We stayed separate so as not to attract attention, but seems we did anyway."

"Sweeney was at his factory most of the day," Duke said. "He went out for lunch at a chop house, where he met with three other fellows. All of 'em wore good suits. I think they were stationers. Their conversation was all about using new technology for printing, buying and selling equipment, and staff issues."

"Did they discuss paper magic?" I asked.

Duke shook his head. "Sweeney did tell 'em not to use that Hendry fellow for their personal stationery, but he told 'em it was because his work's gone inferior. He never mentioned magic."

Willie grunted. "Why's he got to do that to a fellow? It ain't like Hendry's magic can ruin *him*. They ain't in the same trade."

"Then where did Sweeney go?" Matt asked Duke.

"To the Stationers' Hall. A short while later, I saw Abercrombie and Cyclops. Abercrombie spotted me on his way in. The porter came out and told me to get going. I moved around the corner and stayed there until I saw Abercrombie leave. Not long after, Sweeney went back to his factory and then went home about five. He lives in a real nice place out in Highgate with a big garden. According to one of the maids, he lives alone and spends most of his time at work nowadays."

"Thanks, Duke." Matt turned to Willie. "And Hendry?"

She shrugged. "He was inside all day, then went out and got himself a pie from a pie man's cart about five. He ate it as he walked back. I could just make out the sound of his machines operating out back until seven, but the shop remained closed."

"Did he have many customers throughout the day?"

"Only a dozen or so. Want me to follow them again tomorrow?"

Matt shook his head. "Watch Sweeney. Cyclops, watch Hendry."

"You want me on Abercrombie?" Duke asked. "He knows me."

"He knows all of you. Forget Abercrombie, for now. I want you watching Lord Cox."

Duke frowned. "You already tried to find something on him. He's as clean as a new dime."

"It's worth trying again. Everyone has a past they'd prefer to keep hidden."

"Not me," Duke said. "My life's an open book. Everyone can read it."

"Nobody wants to," Willie said with a snicker.

"Do you have reason to suspect Cox of something?" Cyclops asked Matt.

Matt swirled his glass, watching the brandy coat the sides. I thought he wouldn't answer, but eventually he said, "Lord Coyle does."

"What?" Willie asked.

"He wouldn't say."

"Why not?"

"He wants something from India in return, only he wouldn't say what or when he'd call in the favor." Matt lifted his heavy gaze to me. "I don't like those terms and rejected the offer."

"So you should," Willie said. "Ain't nobody would agree to that."

"But if it gets you out of the arrangement with Patience, the price might be worth it," Duke said.

Cyclops agreed. "What would he ask for in return, anyway? If it means you and India can be together—"

Matt slammed the empty glass down on the table. "Don't you think I've thought of that? The decision is made, and it's final. We're not accepting his help. But it does mean Cox has something in his past that he can be blackmailed over. I want to find out what it is."

"Get your lawyer onto it," Willie said.

"I've already written to him."

"I doubt he can help," I said. "Whatever the secret is, very few people must know about it or you'd have uncovered it already. Coyle is well connected, Matt. He probably has spies in every club."

Matt sat back and ran his finger slowly over his top lip. "That's precisely why I don't trust him." He wagged his finger at each of his friends. "Before you three tell India that I used spies in America, I'd like to point out that the information I gathered was used by the law to catch criminals. The information Coyle gathers is used to blackmail."

Willie got up and poured herself another drink from the sideboard. "Honest men don't get what they want, Matt. You got to be devious too, or you'll never get rid of Patience. Look at Cyclops."

Cyclops straightened. "What about me?"

"You tried to warn your boss at the mine that the shaft supports were inferior, then he blamed you when the supports collapsed."

"I can live with being honest," Cyclops said. "My conscience is clear."

"We ain't talking about consciences. We're talking about winning and losing."

"Ain't no such thing in life."

"Don't be a dang fool. Course there is." Willie pointed her glass at Cyclops. "You can't walk free in Nevada, and maybe other states where your boss got the law on his side. If it weren't for Matt, you'd be in jail or dead."

"You calling me a loser, Willie?" Cyclops shook his head. "Then you don't know nothing. I got good friends right here under this roof. And look at this place I get to live in. Ain't too many folk back home can say they ever been in a house this fine, let alone sleep in a soft bed in their own room. I'm lucky, Willie, and I count my blessings every day I'm alive. You should too, instead of wallowing in self-pity."

"Self-pity?" Willie snorted. "Me? Ha! What have I got to feel sorry for?" She drank the contents of her glass, gulping loudly.

Duke and Cyclops exchanged glances. "You been acting like a coyote with a thorn in its paw ever since—"

"Duke," I snapped, shaking my head at him.

Duke closed his mouth and bowed his head. He was right, of course, and Willie had been acting oddly ever since her lover ended their arrangement. She only showed that kind of moroseness when she drank too much, however.

I gently pried the glass from her fingers when she went to refill it. "How about a game of poker?" I asked.

She wrinkled her nose. "Playing for matchsticks? No thanks. Ain't my idea of fun. How about we go fighting again? There's a private bout at the Kingsman's Arms tonight."

"Not me," Cyclops said.

"Afraid what Catherine Mason will think?"

"No," he said sullenly. "She already thinks I'm a thug."

"She doesn't," I said.

He crossed his arms and sank into the chair.

"I ain't fighting either," Duke said. "My ribs are still sore from the last time."

"You didn't protect your chest." Willie put up her fists, keeping her elbows together in front of her chest. "Like this."

"I ain't going," Duke said again.

"So what'll we do tonight? It's only eight."

Duke picked up Miss Glass's novel and opened it to the first page. "I'm reading."

Willie tipped her head back and laughed. "Don't strain an eyeball. I'm going to have me a good time."

"I'll go with her," Cyclops said, rising. "She shouldn't be on her own in this mood."

Duke sighed and closed the book. "I'll go too."

"Both of you can stay here," Matt said. "You've looked after her enough while I was ill. It's my turn now."

"She's a grown woman," I said. "She doesn't need a nursemaid."

The three of them just looked at me.

"On the other hand, it'll do her good to spend some time with you, Matt," I added.

Duke, Cyclops and I decided to play poker. We heard the front door open and close as Matt and Willie went out during our first round. The men were probably right; Willie did need company. She seemed irritable tonight, more so than usual.

"Did Willie receive mail today?" I asked Bristow when he brought in a pot of chocolate for us before he retired for the evening.

"No, miss," he said.

"That's the problem," Duke told me after Bristow left. "Willie ain't getting any response to her letters."

"She's still writing them?"

"Not for a few days now, but she's still hoping for a reply to her older ones." He studied his cards for a long time without discarding any. "If she found someone else, she might cheer up."

"You volunteering for the position?" Cyclops asked with a wry smile.

"No. We ain't never going to be together. I know that, now. We're better just being friends."

I set down my cards and touched Duke's arm. "I am sorry. I know how you feel about her."

"Don't be sorry. And what I felt for her is in the past. We've both changed since coming here." He finally discarded two cards.

Cyclops dealt him two replacements. "You think she'd want someone else so soon after that nurse?"

"Maybe. Problem is, I don't know what sort of person she likes anymore. It used to be simple."

Cyclops grunted. "That's because it used to be men."

"The pool's a lot bigger now." Duke removed three matchsticks from his pile and neatly laid them out, side by side.

"That's all you're betting?" Cyclops counted out eight matches from his own pile.

I also counted eight, and Duke matched the number. We all showed our hands. Duke's two pair beat us both. He chuckled as he raked in his winnings.

"You got to learn to bluff, India," he told me.

"I'm terrible at poker," I said. "Can we play a nice English game for once? Something that doesn't entirely come down to luck?"

"Poker ain't about luck."

"It's about who can lie best," Cyclops added. "You and me are too honest, India. That's why Willie's so good at it."

"Matt's good too, and he's no liar." Even as I said it, I knew how wrong that statement was. Matt was an excellent liar. He could get people he disliked eating out of his hand with just a few words and a smile. He'd infiltrated outlaw gangs back in America to gain information. Here in England, he'd pretended to be someone he wasn't on numerous occasions.

"Maybe one of us should speak to her nurse friend," Duke

said, picking up the thread of Willie's relationships again. He and Cyclops looked at me.

"You want me to do it?" I asked.

"Even if you can't convince her to see Willie again," Duke went on, "you can see what kind of person she is. It'll help us find someone new."

I picked up the pot and filled each cup with the rich liquid chocolate. I breathed deeply, drawing the heady scent into my lungs. "I don't think it's a good idea to try and play matchmaker when there's a very good chance we'll be leaving London soon."

A gasp from the direction of the doorway had me spinning around in my chair, spilling chocolate on the table. Miss Glass stood there, her hand pressed to her stomach, her eyes huge.

"Leaving?" she asked, voice trembling. "Who…who is leaving?"

CHAPTER 8

I tried to steer Miss Glass to a nearby chair, but she shooed me away.

"Answer me, India," she demanded.

"No one is leaving yet," I said.

"Yet," she repeated. "I see."

I appealed to Duke and Cyclops but they suddenly became very interested in their cards. "Come and sit down. I'll pour you a brandy."

She accepted my assistance and the glass when I handed it to her, but she didn't sip. Her gaze became distant, and I worried she'd slipped into the past to take refuge again from the present.

"Is this because of the announcement in *The Times*?" she asked, proving me wrong.

"I think you should wait for Matt to return and speak to him."

She held my gaze. "I'm asking you, India."

I sat beside her on the sofa with a sigh. I couldn't lie to her, even though lying might be the best thing to do if her mind couldn't cope with the truth. "What I am about to tell you is told in absolute confidence. You cannot repeat it to anyone, especially not to your brother and sister-in-law. Do you promise not to tattle?"

"I am not a common gossip, India."

I sucked in a breath and summoned some patience. "Matt and I have decided to leave England if we cannot break the engagement with Patience any other way."

She lowered her head and studied the contents of the glass cradled in her lap. After a moment, she drank.

"There is still a chance Lord Cox will change his mind after spending time with her at tomorrow night's dinner," I said.

She shook her head. "He won't."

"Then we'll make arrangements to leave. Patience will be told in a letter, as gently as possible, but…I'm afraid she'll be deeply hurt."

Miss Glass set aside the glass. "I didn't think either of you were so cowardly."

"There is no other way."

"A gentleman ought to face his responsibilities—"

"Marrying Patience is *not* Matt's responsibility. Her happiness is not his responsibility."

"He is her cousin. He'll be head of the family when Richard dies."

"You are being unfair, Miss Glass. You place far too much on Matt's shoulders, and do not tell me that it's how things are done with your lot. Perhaps if Matt was brought up here, he would think differently, but he is not the sort of man who believes marrying a woman he doesn't love will make her happy. Even if we had never met, he wouldn't do it. They are completely unsuited to one another and would end up miserable. Patience will realize that, in time."

I waited for her to disagree but she did not. "What about me?" she asked weakly. "What will I do?"

"Well," I said carefully, "Matt could set you up with a new companion here, in this house, if you like."

"I don't want a new companion. I want you, India."

"Despite everything? Despite our disagreement now?"

"We are not disagreeing."

I almost smiled. I wasn't entirely sure what we were doing either.

She blinked big eyes at me. "Where will you go?"

"We haven't discussed a destination. Perhaps America, or Europe. Matt has properties there, and I've always wanted to see the continent. Cyclops can't return to America," I said, looking over my shoulder at him.

Miss Glass plucked the brandy tumbler off the table and stared into it. "Patience might never recover from the rejection," she said, switching topic again. "It'll stain her for the rest of her life."

I buried my face in my hands. "I know," I mumbled into them. "But if we stay and Matt marries her, *we* will be unhappy for the rest of our lives." I scrubbed my hands down my face then looked at her again. "Your brother has forced this onto everyone. If you want to blame someone, blame him. Matt and I will not be manipulated by him. Or by anyone else."

I strode across the room, only to pause in the doorway. Miss Glass looked small and frail sitting on the sofa clutching the glass of brandy. She looked even smaller when Cyclops sat down beside her. I left them. Perhaps he could say something to convince her that Matt and I were doing the right thing.

Then perhaps he could convince me, because I suddenly thought leaving England was a very bad idea.

* * *

I INFORMED Matt of my conversation with Miss Glass over breakfast. Cyclops and Duke joined us, but Miss Glass and Willie had not yet risen.

"Did she have one of her turns?" Matt asked as he sat next to me, a plate in one hand and coffee cup in the other.

"No, surprisingly. Was she all right after I left?" I asked Cyclops and Duke.

"She was fine," Cyclops said, adding more bacon to his already full plate. "She's worried about her future. She don't want to live with her brother again."

"She won't," Matt said.

"I suggested you would employ a companion for her," I told Matt. "But she didn't like that idea."

Duke pointed his butter knife at me. "That's because she wants you, India."

"I'd be happy to remain as her companion—if she agreed to Matt and me being together."

Matt placed his hand over my arm and squeezed. "She'll come around."

"Hopefully soon. It's not long until the wedding." A matter of three weeks, in fact, since they were keeping the same date that was set for Patience's wedding to Lord Cox.

Duke glanced at the door then leaned forward. "How'd it go with Willie last night?" he whispered loudly.

"Fine," Matt said. "Willie got drunk."

"Did she talk to you about..." He waved the butter knife around. "About that nurse?"

"We talked about her, among other things."

"Did she cry?"

Matt met his gaze. "I won't tell you what we discussed in confidence. What I can tell you is that Willie needs time before she falls in love again. So no matchmaking. Understand?"

Duke held the knife up in surrender. "Matchmaking's a woman's job."

I laughed. "That's not what you said last night."

He glared at me, and I smiled into my cup.

* * *

We went our separate ways after church, with Matt and I heading to Oscar's residence. He rented rooms on the second floor of an old house within walking distance of *The Weekly Gazette's* office on Lower Mire Lane. His landlady opened the door only wide enough to peek through and demanded we state our business before letting us in. I could only make out the middle two inches of her face through the gap.

"Is Oscar Barratt at home?" Matt asked.

"He might be or he might not be," she said.

"We're glad to see you're being cautious," I told her. "He must have warned you that his life is in danger."

"Who are you and what do you want?"

"My name is India Steele. This is Mr. Glass. We're friends of Mr. Barratt's."

She opened the door wider. "He told me you can enter if you came calling. He's upstairs with his brother."

We were about to head up the staircase when there was a loud crash above our heads. Matt ran up, taking the stairs three at a time. I picked up my skirts and raced after him.

"Stay here," I told the landlady. "Keep guarding the door."

By the time I reached Oscar's sitting room, Matt held a man from behind, rendering his arms useless. Oscar lay sprawled on the floor, the pieces of a broken table around him. He rubbed his jaw.

"Get up, coward," the man in Matt's grip snarled. "Get up and face me like a man."

I went to Oscar's side and assisted him. Once he was on his feet, I glanced at his assailant and gasped. It had to be Isaac Barratt, Oscar's brother. He was a little shorter than Oscar, and more solidly built, but had the same shade of dark brown hair and eyes. Although they both sported sharp cheekbones and a strong jaw, their features were arranged a little differently so that Oscar was the more handsome of the two.

"Are you all right?" I asked Oscar.

He stretched his neck and adjusted his tie. "Yes, thank you. You can let him go, Glass. He took me by surprise, this time, and my shoulder is not yet fully recovered, but I can usually best my brother."

"You make it sound like you do this sort of thing a lot," I said.

He glared at Isaac. "We used to, for fun."

Matt slowly released Isaac. As soon as he was completely free, Isaac lunged at Oscar. Matt grabbed him again and jerked him backward. Isaac lost his balance and would have fallen if Matt hadn't held onto him.

"It seems our discussion will have to take place like this," Matt said, not letting go.

Isaac held up his hands. "You can release me. I can see I won't get anywhere with Oscar's thug in the room."

"Thug?" Matt echoed. "And here I thought everyone took me for a gentleman, these days."

I glared at Matt. Now wasn't the time for jokes.

He released Isaac again and this time Isaac didn't try to hit his brother. Oscar, however, didn't relax his stance. I thought that wise, since Isaac looked as if the slightest provocation would entice him into another fit of violence.

Matt held out his hand to Isaac. "My name is Matthew Glass, and this is Miss Steele. I assume you're Isaac Barratt."

Isaac scanned Matt from head to toe then stretched his neck out of his collar in the same way Oscar had. He finally shook Matt's hand.

"I suppose there's no need to ask what this is about," Matt said.

"Actually, you'd be surprised," Oscar sneered.

I looked from one snarling brother to the other. "This isn't about you writing those articles and naming yourself as an ink magician?"

"Of course it is." Isaac snatched his coat off the back of an armchair near the window. We stood in a small sitting room. A door led to an adjoining bedchamber. The bed was unmade, with Oscar's half-eaten breakfast on the table beside it.

"Is that so?" Oscar said with icy calmness. "Then why the months of cold silences *before* I left, before I ever thought about revealing magic through the papers? Why turn our friends against me?"

"Can you not forget that? I won, Oscar."

Oscar snorted. "You don't really believe that. Not deep down. She chose *me*, but she married you because you inherited the business."

Isaac puffed out his chest. "She married me because I treat her better than you ever did."

"Is she still in love with me? Is that why you hate me?"

"I don't hate you. You're my brother." It sounded automatic, like something Isaac had repeated so many times it simply fell from his lips.

"You tried to punch me! Of course you hate me."

Isaac marched toward the door, but Matt blocked his path. "We need to speak to you both," Matt said.

Isaac sighed. "About what?"

"We're investigating the death of Mr. Baggley, the editor of *The Weekly Gazette*."

"Oscar tells me *he* was the intended target," Isaac said. "Do you believe that?"

"We haven't ruled anything out at this point."

"Am I a suspect?"

"Don't be ridiculous," Oscar said. "You're my brother. No matter how much we fight, you're not going to try to kill me."

Isaac watched Oscar from beneath lowered lashes. Oscar swallowed and took a step back.

"We spoke to the man who came looking for you at the office on the day of the murder," Matt said to Oscar. "He claims he didn't return later and shoot Baggley."

"Of course he'd say that." Oscar inspected the damaged table. Finding its damaged legs unable to support it, he lay it down again. "He's hardly going to tell you the truth."

"He's a professor of history," I said. "He has a keen interest in the history of magic and wanted to offer his expertise for your articles."

Oscar looked up. "What's his name?"

"I'll tell you later."

Oscar's gaze slid to his brother. "Isaac isn't a killer. A fool, a crow and a...a word I won't use in front of a lady. But he's not a killer, India."

"Don't tell him the name in front of me," Isaac said. "I don't care to know it. If the professor dies in suspicious circumstances, I don't want to be the prime suspect in both murders."

"You're not the prime suspect in Baggley's."

"But I'm certainly *a* suspect, aren't I?" Isaac asked Matt.

Matt didn't respond.

"There was another man who came to see you that day and overheard the staff member tell the professor that you were working late," I said.

"Do you know who?" Oscar asked.

"We're going to question him now."

Isaac tried to step around Matt, but Matt moved to block the exit again. "You were seen arguing with your brother that day. Was it about the articles Oscar has been writing?"

"What do you think?" Isaac snarled. "He has no idea what harm he has caused me and my family back home. He swans around the city, doing as he pleases, and meanwhile we suffer the consequences. I lost customers because he told the whole bloody world that he's an ink magician, and now they all think I am too."

"You are," Oscar said lightly. "And don't exaggerate. The entire world doesn't know. The *Gazette's* a London paper."

Isaac bared his teeth but he thought better of lunging at his brother again, probably because Matt was standing very close. "There are people who want magicians to fade into the background, Oscar. A lot of them are very powerful, and they will do whatever it takes to protect their businesses. This is not a game. Lives are at stake, as you well know after the murder of your editor."

Oscar had the decency to look chastised.

"If you did this to get revenge on Cecilia and me—"

"Don't be absurd," Oscar barked. "I was never in love with her. She was in love with me, and going by your overreaction, she probably still is."

"Overreaction?" Isaac grunted as he put on his jacket. "I'm leaving. I can't stand listening to your narcissistic drivel."

"Go. I don't want to see you anymore. And don't expect a warm welcome next time. I'll instruct my landlady not to let you in."

"She can't keep me out. Or anyone else, for that matter."

"Is that a threat, Isaac?"

"Take it any way you like."

Oscar shook his head. "Our parents would turn in their graves if—"

"Do *not* presume to know what they'd think." Isaac marched out of the room, slamming the door behind him.

I didn't know what to say, so I picked a book off the floor and placed it on a chair. It must have been on the table that had ended up bearing the brunt of their argument. Oscar picked up part of a table leg.

"He brings destruction wherever he goes," he said, inspecting the splintered end.

"Is that a literary quote?" I asked.

One corner of his mouth lifted. "It's something I overheard him say to Cecilia once, after they fought about me and how she...how she had feelings for me. She claimed she no longer did, but..." He lifted a shoulder in a shrug. "I left the next day. It was better for everyone."

"If it helps, I think you did the right thing."

Someone knocked on the door, and Matt answered it. Detective Inspector Brockwell stood there.

"Miss Steele, what a pleasant surprise," he said. "But, may I ask, what are you both doing here?"

"Investigating the threatening letters sent to Mr. Barratt," Matt said stiffly.

"Since you wouldn't do it," Oscar chimed in.

"That wasn't my response, sir, and well you know it," Brockwell said, clipping off each consonant with brutal precision to convey his point. "I will investigate the letters as a separate matter, in due course. The murder is taking up all my time and much of Scotland Yard's resources. As I said to you, when you first brought the letters to my attention, I don't think you were the shooter's intended target instead of Mr. Baggley."

"Then why you are here?"

"I need to account for the movements of the main suspects during the day and evening of the murder."

Oscar recoiled. "*I'm* a suspect?"

Brockwell clapped his hands behind his back and lifted his chin. He almost looked noble, but his scruffy sideburns and crumpled shirt collar let him down. "You and Mr. Isaac Barratt were overheard arguing on the day of the murder in the *Gazette's* office. It's my understanding the argument was about the magic articles you wrote."

"My brother is against revealing magic to the world. What of it?"

"How did the argument end?"

"As they always do, with him storming out."

"What are you getting at, Inspector?" I asked.

"I am sorry, Miss Steele, but I can't divulge that at this point. I hope you understand." His gaze lifted to Matt's as Matt moved closer to me. Brockwell turned back to Oscar. "Where can I find your brother, sir?"

"You just missed him." Oscar indicated the broken table. "As you can see, we argued."

"He has a violent streak?"

Oscar frowned. "Are you accusing my brother of Baggley's murder?"

Brockwell glared back. "Where is he staying, Mr. Barratt?"

"You *are* accusing him." Oscar squeezed the bridge of his nose with his thumb and forefinger. "Christ, man, he's a fool, not a killer. Why would he kill Baggley to stop the articles, anyway? Why not me? I am the writer. I can take the articles anywhere."

"Can you? Have you tried?"

Oscar's frown deepened. "No, but...but I've helped the *Gazette's* circulation."

"And created enemies for yourself, the paper, and the editor." Brockwell paced the room, taking in the broken table, the unmade bed in the adjoining room, the half-eaten breakfast. Was he looking for evidence that Isaac Barratt was staying with his brother? "I am not a newspaperman. I don't pretend to know these things, but if I were an editor of a different newspaper, I wouldn't touch your inciting articles. Not for all the circulation figures in the world."

"The newspaper world is grateful you are not a newspaperman then." Oscar indicated the door. "If you're going to accuse Isaac or me, kindly leave. I have nothing more to say. Even if I knew where my brother was staying, I wouldn't tell you. He's not a murderer."

"Of course you'd defend him." Brockwell held up a finger when Oscar protested. "Wouldn't it make sense for your brother to kill your editor and not you? After all, it's much easier to murder a stranger than a family member."

Oscar marched to the door and jerked it wide open. "Get out."

Brockwell gave him a tight smile. "As you wish. Good day. Good day to you too, Miss Steele." To Matt he said, "I see from the announcement in *The Times* that congratulations are in order."

Matt hesitated then gave a curt nod.

Brockwell took my hand and bowed over it. "If I need to speak to you again, where will I find you?"

"I am still residing at number sixteen Park Street," I said.

Brockwell hesitated. "That is...unexpected."

Matt stood on the other side of the open door to Oscar, indicating Brockwell should leave.

"I wish you the best of luck in your marriage, sir," Brockwell said to Matt.

"Marriage?" Oscar blinked at me.

"Not to Miss Steele. Mr. Glass is engaged to his cousin, the daughter of Lord Rycroft."

Oscar's lips parted then a hesitant smile touched his lips. "Is that so? Congratulations, Glass." The smile stretched with each second that Matt didn't respond.

Brockwell stepped closer to me and lowered his voice. "I admit to being taken by surprise, Miss Steele. I pride myself on my observational skills, and I thought there was something more than a professional relationship between you and Mr. Glass. It seems I was wrong. I apologize for my assumption."

"No apology necessary," I muttered, unable to meet his gaze.

"Perhaps I can call upon you—"

"Didn't you say you were leaving, Brockwell?" Matt prompted.

Oscar opened the door wider. "Good day, Inspector."

Brockwell bowed to me again then left without another word.

"I'm also taken by surprise by this announcement," Oscar said, rejoining me.

I bit my lip, wanting to tell him the truth but knowing I couldn't. For now, everyone must believe Matt was marrying Patience.

Matt, however, must have had enough. When Oscar took my hand and kissed the back of it, he said, "You of all people should know not to believe everything you read in the papers, Barratt."

Oscar dropped my hand as if it burned.

"Be careful, Barratt," Matt growled, his voice low. "Your life is still in danger."

Oscar swallowed.

Matt offered me his arm and escorted me out. He gave our coachman orders to drive to Hendry's Smithfield paper shop and settled opposite me in the cabin.

"They're circling like vultures now they think you're available," he grumbled.

I fought to keep a straight face. This wasn't a laughing matter, although I did like that he was jealous. "I believe vultures eat the scraps left behind by predators. Are you calling me your leftovers, Matt?"

"Don't tease me, India. I can't see the lighter side at the moment."

I changed seats to sit beside him and closed both my hands around his arm. The muscle flexed then relaxed. "We'll be able to tell them I am not available soon."

"Not soon enough."

* * *

Hendry's paper shop was closed on Sundays, as were all the shops along the Smithfield strip. The street was quiet, almost entirely devoid of life, since many of the shopkeepers lived above or behind their shops. Two couples strolled by, and three children played on the pavement. I spotted a man lounging against a wall a little further along, but I couldn't see his face beneath his lowered hat brim. I knew it was Cyclops from his size.

The door to Mr. Hendry's shop was unlocked, even though

the sign read closed. Matt called out and Hendry emerged from the rear workshop, his sleeves rolled up to the elbows.

"What do you want now?" he said on a sigh.

"Why were you asking for Oscar Barratt at *The Weekly Gazette's* office on the day Baggley was killed?" Matt asked.

Mr. Hendry bristled. "Who says I was?"

"There are witnesses."

"It's none of your affair, and I don't have to answer you.

"At this point in time, the police don't suspect you," Matt went on. "They aren't aware that the threatening letters to Barratt were written on magic paper. We'd be happy to assist them, however, and you can answer their questions instead."

Mr. Hendry rearranged three small parcels on the counter that looked as if they were ready to be sent to customers in the morning.

"It won't look good for you if you don't answer," I said gently. "We know you overheard a *Gazette* employee tell another man that Oscar Barratt would be working late. Did you return that evening to speak with him?"

"I went nowhere near the *Gazette's* office that night." He moved on to a stack of invitations at the counter's end and ensured it was square. "I admit that I was there during the day. I wanted to reason with Mr. Barratt. He needs to know that his articles are putting people like me in jeopardy. I'm losing friends because of him." His voice rose, along with the color in his cheeks.

I touched his arm. "Perhaps those friends weren't worth having if they're abandoning you now."

Mr. Hendry snorted. "It's different for you. You don't work in your magic trade."

"And Mr. Sweeney doesn't work in yours."

His gaze sharpened. "Yet he refuses to speak to me now."

"And he's turning others against you," Matt added.

Hendry fidgeted with the stack of invitations again. The act seemed to soothe him, just as touching watches soothed me.

"I understand," I said gently.

He sniffed. "No, Miss Steele, you don't."

I looked to Matt, hoping he could say something to cheer the poor man up.

"Did you return to the *Gazette's* office that night?" Matt asked again. It would seem his sour mood had lingered, and his charm had abandoned him.

"I already told you I didn't."

"Why didn't you? You wanted to speak to Barratt, and you knew he was going to be there."

"I didn't go back!"

"Where were you?" Matt pressed.

"Here," Mr. Hendry grumbled. "All night."

"Can anyone confirm that?"

"That's none of your business!"

He stripped off the top invitation from the pile and threw it at Matt, murmuring something under his breath that I couldn't quite hear. The paper clipped Matt below the ear and fluttered to the floor.

"You're bleeding," I said, going to Matt's side.

He touched the small cut, smearing the drop of blood. He looked to Mr. Hendry. "You have more than one magic trick."

Mr. Hendry backed away, hands extended as if warning us not to get too close. "I...I'm sorry. I shouldn't have done that."

I picked the invitation off the floor and ran my hands over the blank back. It was hot. "You turned it into a weapon," I murmured.

"I...I said I was sorry."

"Death by paper cut," Matt said wryly as he wiped the rest of the blood off his neck with his handkerchief.

"How did you do it?" I asked Mr. Hendry. "What words did you say?"

He shook his head quickly. "I won't tell you."

"But that spell...you know two, don't you? One to improve the quality of your paper, the other to fling the paper."

His eyes widened as he backed into the counter. "Don't tell anyone. It's been years since I used that spell. If people think I can hurt them with paper, they'll come for me. I won't be safe."

"No one will harm you, Mr. Hendry, and I won't tell anyone

what happened here. Can you make the paper move *without* a spell?"

"India!" Matt gave his head a slight shake. "We should go."

"Can you make paper move without a spell?" I said again.

Mr. Hendry shook his head. "You should leave now."

"If you think of anything that exonerates you, let us know," Matt said.

Mr. Hendry turned wild eyes onto Matt. "I didn't kill that man! Please, you must believe me."

We left and the door slammed closed behind us. The lock tumbled.

"Are you mad, India?" Matt said when we were alone in the carriage.

"His paper turned into a weapon for him. It's the same as my watch." I clutched my reticule tighter, feeling the shape of my new, untested watch inside.

"Don't ask him that question again," Matt said. "He'll want to know why you're asking, and that'll reveal too much."

He was right. I needed to be careful. Yet knowing that didn't diminish my need to learn more about my power. I doubted Mr. Hendry could teach me, however, and that made questioning him further a pointless exercise.

I nodded and he finally sat back with a sigh.

"Do you think he lied about not returning to the *Gazette's* office that night to speak to Barratt?" I asked.

"It's hard to say. He grew angry when I pressured him, which is suspicious."

"Angry enough to give you a paper cut."

He smirked as he touched the cut beneath his ear. "I wonder if he could have flung all of those sheets of paper at me at once."

It was a sobering thought. One paper cut wasn't enough to distract Matt, but hundreds certainly would.

"I'll have Cyclops continue to watch him," he said as we drove past Cyclops. He tugged on his hat brim in deference but made no other sign that he knew us.

"He's very conspicuous," I said. "Perhaps you should get Duke to do it instead."

"I need him watching Cox. Cyclops *is* too conspicuous, and I can't have Cox getting suspicious."

"Just until this investigation is finished."

"My priority is finding Cox's weakness, not this investigation." His iciness invited no argument, and I offered none.

Matt had to summon his charms upon our return home, however. Gabe Seaford was waiting for us, and he was one man we both wanted to stay on friendly terms with. The magical doctor may be needed to save Matt's life again one day. We all hoped that day would not be soon.

"What a lovely surprise," I said, accepting his kiss on my cheek. "I must admit, we weren't expecting to see you."

Gabe shook Matt's hand and glanced at Miss Glass. He looked uncertain, and she graciously left the room, even though she knew what Gabe had done to save Matt. He seemed to relax a little once she was gone.

"I see you've already had tea," I said, sitting on the sofa.

"Miss Glass took good care of me," he said. "Your aunt is very kind, Matt, and appears to be in good health, considering her age."

Matt smiled. "Don't let her hear you discuss her age or she won't serve you tea anymore."

Gabe laughed.

"Speaking of her health," Matt said. "She sometimes has turns where her mind seems to slip into the past. It usually happens when she's upset. Can anything be done for her?"

"How long do the turns last?"

"A few minutes."

"Then I wouldn't worry too much. Short-term memory loss is quite common in the elderly, unfortunately. And what about you? You look well."

"I feel fine, entirely back to normal. Thank you again, Gabe. You're a miracle worker."

"And we will be forever in your debt," I added. "It was good of you to call on Matt."

"I read the announcement of your engagement in *The Times*."

Matt's face clouded. He looked away.

Gabe looked from Matt to me then back to Matt. "Is something wrong?"

"No," I said quickly.

"So the announcement wasn't a mistake?"

I searched for the right response, but could think of none. Matt didn't say a word. The silence stretched painfully until I could no longer stand it.

"More tea, Gabe?"

"No, thank you." He frowned and glanced between us again. "I've upset you both. I'm sorry, I'd better go."

We saw him out and watched him walk along Park Street to the corner. "That was nice of him to come and see if you're feeling all right," I said, returning inside.

Matt led the way to the library and held the door open for me. "I doubt that's why he was here."

"Then why?"

"He saw the announcement in *The Times*, assumed you were free, and came to ask you to the theater tonight or something similar."

I laughed. "Good lord, Matt. Before I met you, Eddie was my only beau. Now you see them everywhere. I haven't changed. I'm hardly going to attract four times more gentlemen callers now than before."

"You have changed. You just don't see it." He closed the door and circled his arms around my waist from behind. "You're more confident in yourself," he murmured in my ear, "and that confidence makes you desirable."

I pulled away, too aware of him and not trusting my reaction being so close to him.

"And for another, you're not very good at seeing what is right in front of your nose." He kissed the tip of my nose. "It wouldn't surprise me if you had more men interested in you before Eddie than you think."

I rolled my eyes, and was about to say something, when someone knocked on the library door. Bristow entered upon Matt's command.

"Lord and Lady Rycroft are here, sir. They wish to speak with you in the sitting room. Alone."

Matt took my hand. "They can say whatever they want in front of you, India."

I shook my head. "It'll be better for everyone if I stay away."

He nodded but didn't look too pleased to be facing the lions without me.

I headed for the stairs while he opened the door to the sitting room and closed it again. I met Miss Glass on the way down and informed her that Lord and Lady Rycroft wanted to be alone with Matt to talk.

"Alone? Tosh! This will be about the wedding and that concerns the entire family. Come along, India. You ought to be there too."

"Me? Why?"

"Because it concerns you too, whether they like it or not. You and Matthew have chosen a particular path, now you must face the consequences together." She pointed at the sitting room door. "In there are two of the consequences."

Cold dread pressed down on me. "Do not tell them our plans to leave, Miss Glass. I beg you."

She grabbed my hand and pulled me toward the sitting room door. I closed my eyes and prayed I only had to fight two lions, not three.

CHAPTER 9

"What is *she* doing here?" The grooves around Lady Rycroft's mouth deepened in distaste, as if she tasted something vile. "She is not invited."

Lord Rycroft watched me through eyes narrowed to slits within the rolls of fat. He left the talking to his wife.

"Letitia, take your companion away," Lady Rycroft said with a dismissive wave of her hand.

"She is not my companion anymore," Miss Glass said, taking a seat on the sofa. "India lives here and has as much right to know what is being said on the topic of Matthew's marriage as I do."

"A right?" Lady Rycroft spluttered. "Richard, did you hear that?"

Lord Rycroft had not sat down, and he now straightened, pushing out his chest and stomach to strain the jacket's seams. "What right does she have?"

"You know full well," Matt said, also standing. "I agree with Aunt Letitia. India should stay if she wants to."

I felt obliged to remain now, with them all making such a fuss. Besides, I couldn't let the Rycrofts win. I suspected that was what Miss Glass had counted on when she'd dragged me into the sitting room. The question was, why did she want me there at all?

"You might as well stay," Miss Glass said to me. "Matthew's going to tell you everything that was said later anyway."

Lady Rycroft clicked her tongue and refused to look at me.

"For God's sake, Letitia," Lord Rycroft muttered, slapping his hands together behind his back. "Why do you have to make everything so difficult? Why can't you do as you're told, for once?"

"I used to always do what I was told," his sister said with all her regal bearing on display. "Now that I live with Matthew, I don't have to. I am free. Unlike your daughters."

"Patience can have all the freedom she desires once she is also under Matthew's care," Lady Rycroft said. "I'm sure that's why she's so attracted to the notion of marrying him in the first place."

Her husband frowned. "He's a fine prospect for her, better than a girl like her can hope for. A union between them will also make her a baroness, one day, and mean she won't ever have to leave Rycroft Hall if she doesn't want to."

"She will want to be far away while you both live there," Miss Glass said.

"Matthew can put a very fine roof over her head, and those of her sisters. Patience understands that and won't let emotions rule her choices. She's a good, *obedient* girl."

"Congratulations on raising a dog, Richard," Miss Glass bit off.

He rolled his eyes.

"As to emotions, you're wrong," Miss Glass went on. "She is very much choosing Matthew due to her desire to be free of you. Not only does he present Patience with her best means of escape, he is her *only* means."

"Enough, Letitia! You've made your point."

"Do not raise your voice in my house," Matt said, quietly ominous. "State your business. I want the afternoon free to look forward to dinner with my future bride." He spoke directly to his uncle. He didn't blink and didn't look in the least like a man preparing to break his promise. I didn't know what it cost him, but I knew he was determined to convince his uncle he was prepared to go through with the arrangement. He had to succeed, for my sake.

Lady Rycroft clicked her tongue again as I took a seat beside Miss Glass. "Let's get this over with. We've come to discuss the wedding plans."

"I'll discuss them with Patience tonight," Matt said.

"It'll be in two weeks."

"Two!" I blurted out.

Lady Rycroft presented her shoulder to me. "We brought it forward. Invitations are being printed now."

My heart lurched. It was all so final.

"Since you insisted on staying, Miss Steele, you will not be spared what I have to say next," Lady Rycroft went on.

"There is nothing you can say that I have not anticipated," I said.

"Matthew, *she* must go. She cannot live here any longer."

"This is India's home," he said. "She's not leaving."

"Don't be absurd. It is highly improper."

"For God's sake man," Lord Rycroft muttered. "Keep your mistress separate—"

"India is not my mistress," Matt snapped.

Lady Rycroft choked in disgust. "You were seen kissing in front of the servants!"

So Abercrombie had reported what he'd seen after all. I was not surprised, although I couldn't hide my embarrassment as heat spread over my face. I wanted to sink into the sofa and hide.

Lady Rycroft gave me a smug smile. "My daughter doesn't deserve to be publicly humiliated by her fiancé."

"She doesn't deserve any of this treatment, Aunt, yet she is forced down this path," Matt said. "We both are. That is your doing, not mine."

Lady Rycroft's spine stiffened. "You think it fair that she share her new home with her husband's whore?"

Matt marched to the door. His features were set like stone, his eyes hard. "Leave. Both of you."

The Rycrofts looked at one another, uncertain. I hardly dared to breathe. Matt opened his mouth to speak but Miss Glass got in first.

"Your vulgarity does you no credit, Beatrice. India is a thoroughly decent girl. She is also my companion. It is *my* choice whether she stays or goes."

I bit my tongue. Now was not the time to correct her.

Lady Rycroft snorted. "You are a fool, Letitia. You always have been."

"I asked you both to leave," Matt said stiffly. "Don't force me to act in an ungentlemanly manner."

Lord Rycroft spluttered a protest while his wife gripped the chair arms as if that would anchor her if Matt decided to throw her out. She did not meet anyone's gaze, however, and her loud swallow was telling. She didn't know whether he was bluffing or not. Matt's poker experience was proving to be useful.

"Come, my dear," Lord Rycroft said. "We're wasting our time in this debauched house." He must have been worried Matt would manhandle them out, as he'd once done to Lord Rycroft in his own home.

"If it is so debauched, end the engagement," Matt said.

"And ruin Patience's happiness?" Lady Rycroft asked. "Ruin her one and only chance to marry well?" She stood and managed to look down her nose at him, even though he was taller. "You really don't know your own people very well, do you?"

"You may be my family, but you are *not* my people."

She lifted her chin. "My daughter is a naive, impressionable girl. I expect you to behave as a gentleman would tonight."

"Beatrice!" Miss Glass cried. "Matthew is always the perfect gentleman."

Lady Rycroft's narrowed gaze flicked to me. She wrinkled her nose.

"I won't do anything to jeopardize Patience's reputation or safety," Matt assured his aunt and uncle. "I merely wish to get to know her better, but you can be assured, we will not be left alone. I will not seduce her."

"They most certainly will not be left alone together," Miss

Glass chimed in. "Matthew may not seduce Patience, but one cannot say the same of the opposite."

"Letitia!" her brother barked. "That's enough."

Miss Glass smoothed her hands down her skirt. "Well, she does have a certain reputation."

Lord Rycroft's nostrils flared. His chest heaved with each breath. He indicated to his wife to walk out ahead of him.

She paused as she passed Matt. "And your..." Lady Rycroft jerked her head in my direction. "Will she be dining with you?"

"Of course," Matt said.

"No," I said. "I have other arrangements."

The corners of Matt's eyes tightened. "I want tonight to go well," was all he said to his aunt. "As you're fully aware, I have a deep interest in making sure the marriage goes ahead as planned."

"Do not think to attempt to change Patience's mind," Lord Rycroft said. "If you do, it won't go well for you."

Matt's flat smile was hard. "You have my word that I won't attempt anything of the kind."

Bristow escorted them out, and Matt closed the door. He crouched in front of me and took my hand in both of his. He didn't say anything. He didn't need to. Anger and helplessness swirled in his eyes.

I briefly cupped his jaw to reassure him they couldn't hurt me with their words then let go. I was too aware of Miss Glass's presence.

Not that she was watching us. She stood at the sideboard and poured herself a sherry from the decanter. The sight was one I had not seen before. She always waited for the men or a servant to pour her a drink.

"Beatrice does not deserve the title of lady," she said into her glass. "She's as vulgar as a navvy."

Matt indicated her glass. "Isn't it a little early for you to be drinking?"

"I'm making an exception today. I should have had one *before* they arrived." She sipped then sipped again. "Pour one for India too. I'm sure she needs a strong drink."

I shook my head at Matt. He poured himself a glass, however. "Thank you for not saying anything to them about us leaving," I said to Miss Glass.

"I don't want you to go," she said without facing me. "I don't want either of you to leave England. And I don't want you to stop being my companion, India. If that means trying to get Lord Cox to change his mind, then I will do my bit tonight at dinner."

"Thank you, Aunt," Matt said. "We're going to need all the help we can get."

"I meant what I said earlier," I told them both. "I won't be dining with you."

"You're integral to the plan," Matt said.

"Thank you, but I'm not."

He lowered the glass. "I can't do it without you, India. You're just as well equipped at convincing Lord Cox of Patience's charms as I am. You'll probably be better at it."

I doubted that, but I did appreciate his encouragement.

"I agree with India," Miss Glass said. "Hear me out, Matthew. Patience needs to be at her best. She'll be ruffled enough as it is when she sees Lord Cox, and India's presence will only make her feel more inadequate. Indeed, with India present, there's a danger Lord Cox will admire her more."

"I hardly think so," I said.

"I'm going to be honest with him," Matt told his aunt. "I'm going to tell him that I wish to marry India and that he is free to pursue Patience."

"Good lord, are you mad?" Miss Glass said.

"You can't do that," I agreed. "You ought to pretend nothing is wrong. That's why I won't be there. He'll guess there's something between us if he sees us together."

Miss Glass set down her half-empty glass and began to pace the room. "You must act as if nothing is wrong, Matthew. Show Patience due regard, but do not gush. Do not let Lord Cox think you love her. The lack of affection between you will give him hope. But do take pains to acknowledge her good points, just in case he is blind to them. If you can't think of any, make something up."

I left them to their strategizing. There was no point in my participation. I spent the rest of the afternoon in the library reading and was joined by Willie, Duke and Cyclops after they returned from their daily tasks. Matt also joined us when his aunt went to dress for dinner.

"Did Cox get up to anything?" he asked Duke.

"He met with his bank just before noon," Duke said. "He ate luncheon at his club and conducted some business with a Lord Carsmere."

"What kind of business?"

"He bought a carriage from him. According to the club's staff, Cox plans to be in London more. He's putting on more permanent staff at his townhouse and is redecorating. He'd only hired a carriage when he visited the city before, but the purchase means he's got one all the time now. He bought a growler."

"He still needs two horses to pull it," Cyclops added.

"Ain't nothing you can blackmail him with from that," Willie said with a sigh.

"What about you two?" I asked Willie and Cyclops.

"You were Hendry's only visitors," Cyclops said. "He didn't go anywhere or receive any callers."

"And Sweeney didn't do anything suspicious either," Willie said. "He went to church and then went home where he worked in his study, so his staff said. He only stepped out to take a turn about the garden. Seems gardening is his leisure. He picked flowers, tidied up some of the beds and generally poked about."

"Did he attend church with anyone?" Matt asked.

She shook her head. "He's a loner."

"Did he receive any messages?" I asked. "Perhaps he and Abercrombie are communicating in writing."

Willie shook her head.

Mr. Sweeney had a lonely existence indeed. Mr. Hendry, too. How sad that their friendship lay in tatters. They could have been company for one another on the one day of the week when married men spent time with their families.

"You ain't ready for your dinner yet," Willie told Matt. "Go on. Off you go."

"What about all of you?" he asked. "Where will you dine tonight?"

"There's a chop house in Soho that does a fine roast," Cyclops said.

"Will it be open on a Sunday evening?"

"We'll find something else if it ain't."

"India?" Matt asked. "Will you go with them?"

"I don't feel like dining out," I said.

"I'll leave the doors ajar in both the dining room and drawing room if you want to listen in."

"Matt!"

One corner of his mouth lifted. "You might as well. I'm going to tell you everything later anyway."

"It would still be a low thing to do."

"Don't be so prissy, India," Willie scolded. "Just don't get caught."

"So what will you do?" Matt asked as I rose to go.

"I'll eat in my room tonight."

I informed the kitchen that I'd like something sent to my room later before going to visit Miss Glass. Polly was helping her select jewelry to go with her outfit.

"Do come in, India," Miss Glass said. "We need your advice." She pointed at the two sets of earrings laid out on the dressing table. "Pearl drops or silver and garnets?"

"Pearls."

"But they hurt my ears after an hour."

"Then the silver and garnets."

"Excellent choice. You always do know what's best." She indicated to Polly to put the pearl earrings away. "And what about my hair, India?"

"Curls at the crown are very fashionable now," I said, making something up.

Polly gave me a sideways glance.

"See what you can do, Polly," Miss Glass said, sitting at her dressing table. "I am glad you're here to keep me company,

India. Your wise counsel and cheerful nature are always appreciated."

Poor Polly. Sometimes Miss Glass didn't realize how much her words could sting. "I'm not staying," I said.

Miss Glass swung around to face me, causing Polly to lose the strand of hair she'd begun to arrange. "But I insist!"

"Miss Glass," I said carefully, "I am not your companion, remember?"

She turned back to the mirror. "You're still insisting on leaving me? Forever?"

I glanced at Polly but she gave no indication that she was listening. Still, I did not want her to know our plans to leave England. No one else must know.

"I am hardly leaving you when I continue to live here," I said.

Miss Glass blinked sadly at me.

I sighed. "I came to thank you for not mentioning our plan to Lord and Lady Rycroft. I know you don't like lying to them."

"Withholding the truth is not a lie, India." She met my gaze in the mirror's reflection. "Well, not quite." Her eyes shone and I got the feeling she was enjoying tricking her brother and sister-in-law.

"Enjoy the evening," I told her.

"Wait." She opened the dressing table drawer and removed the small red box containing the pearl earrings Polly had just put away. "You take them, India. I can't wear them anymore."

"No, thank you. It wouldn't be appropriate for me to accept your gifts now that I am no longer your companion." I turned to go, not at all sure I should have rejected the earrings.

* * *

I WISHED Matt had never told me he'd leave the doors open so I could listen in on the conversations. It was torture to remain in my room knowing that I could eavesdrop—and with his blessing, too. But it wasn't fair on either Lord Cox or Patience.

On the other hand, nothing about this situation was fair.

I set aside the book I'd been attempting to read and headed

downstairs. It was no small thing that both Lord Cox and Patience were still here at all. We'd considered the possibility that either or both of them would storm out after seeing the other.

However, they were still in the dining room, the third course of pastries, creams and jellies before them. Bristow and Peter stood aside, waiting for orders, and I got my first glimpse of Lord Cox. He was short with a narrow face and slightly protruding front teeth. If I hadn't known he was much older than Patience, I wouldn't have guessed from his soft face and full head of blond hair. He had friendly eyes too as he smiled at something Matt said.

Smiling was definitely a good sign. My heart lifted. If there'd been awkwardness when he first saw Patience, it had vanished. Good food and an abundance of wine had a way of disarming a tense situation.

I watched for several minutes through the gap. Matt did most of the talking, but he engaged Patience and Lord Cox as much as possible, drawing them out with questions and getting them to talk about themselves. His aunt sat in silence, and it was difficult to tell if her mind had drifted off.

"Have you attended the races, Glass?" Lord Cox asked Matt. "Horses are something of an interest of mine."

"I like horses," Matt said. "They get me from A to B."

Lord Cox chuckled. "They get a jockey from A to B very quickly at Ascot."

"His lordship owns a stable," Patience said. "He has some very fine animals. They're quite successful up north."

"You like horses?" Matt asked her. "I had no idea."

"Oh yes. I don't so much enjoy the racing, but I do enjoy riding and taking care of them."

"You're a very nurturing girl," Miss Glass chimed in, no doubt for the benefit of Lord Cox who was, by all accounts, looking for a wife to be a mother to his four children.

"Women shouldn't take care of horses," Matt said. "Particularly ladies." He shrugged an apology at Patience.

She looked down at her uneaten jelly. "Of course."

Lord Cox watched the exchange over the rim of his wine glass but did not offer an opinion.

"You must forgive my nephew," Miss Glass said to Lord Cox. "He's quite set in his ways, particularly where women are concerned."

I bit my lip. That last part was laying it on a little thick. Surely Lord Cox would see through her act.

"I expected an American to be more enlightened," Lord Cox said, setting down the glass.

"My father was upper class English," Matt said with a laugh and a shrug. "Make of that what you will."

Lord Cox merely grunted and finished his pastry.

Matt continued to manipulate the conversation throughout the meal, being effortlessly charming yet not all that subtle. Just when I thought Lord Cox realized what was happening, Matt steered the discussion to financial matters. Patience could no longer contribute. After a mere minute, Miss Glass suggested it was time for the gentlemen and ladies to separate.

I rushed off and hid in the shadows. Neither Miss Glass nor Patience saw me as they passed by, but I suspected Matt knew I was there. He stared for long seconds in my direction until Lord Cox struck up a conversation.

I followed them to the smoking room. Matt made sure to leave the door ajar, and I took up a position where I could both see and hear. I thought perhaps the men wouldn't stay long, but they chatted for ten minutes before Lord Cox suddenly asked something I was not expecting.

"Why don't you want to marry her?"

Matt was rendered speechless, something which happened only on rare occasions.

"Come now, Glass, I can see what you're trying to do. You want me to take her off your hands."

"I care about my cousin's wellbeing and happiness," Matt said.

"But you don't want to marry her."

Matt sighed. "Patience is a sweet, good natured girl. She deserves to be happy and to marry a man who loves her, or who will at least learn to appreciate her many qualities. I am not that man."

Lord Cox swirled the liquid in his glass as he considered this. "Why not?"

"I am in love with someone else."

His lordship stopped swirling and regarded Matt with some sympathy. "I see. And why aren't you marrying her instead?"

"It's complicated."

"I have time."

Matt scrubbed a hand over his jaw. "My uncle and aunt want their eldest daughter to marry."

"For obvious reasons," Cox said darkly.

"I am the only candidate they could manipulate, given the short timeframe."

Lord Cox's gaze sharpened. He nodded slowly. I suspected he knew exactly what Matt was trying to say. "I'm sorry to hear it," he said. "For your sake as well as Patience's. I don't think she'll be happy with you."

"How sorry?"

"Not that sorry."

Matt shifted his weight in the chair. "She would be happier with you than with me. You're very suited to one another."

Lord Cox grunted into his glass. "Being suited is not a reason to marry someone."

"It is where I come from."

Lord Cox spread his arms wide. "Welcome to England." I suspected he was a little drunk and more than a little annoyed. Whether with Matt or Patience I couldn't say.

Matt took both glasses and refilled them. He offered Lord Cox one of Willie's cigars but was refused. Matt inspected the box, perhaps considering taking up the habit. In the end, he simply filled both glasses higher than the regulatory two fingers.

Matt handed him the glass but didn't let go. "I'm asking you as a gentleman to reconsider."

"I can't. I have thought about it, but..." Lord Cox squeezed the bridge of his nose. "It's impossible. Her reputation is in tatters."

"That will be forgotten, in time."

He jerked his head up. "And what of *my* reputation?" he snapped. "I cannot afford to marry someone with a tainted past."

Matt paused. "Patience made one mistake—"

"It only requires one."

"And she wasn't married at the time."

Lord Cox set down the tumbler. "I like you, Glass, and I like her, so please do not ask me again. I won't change my mind. I'm sorry but if you need to get out of this arrangement, you'll have to find someone else to take her off your hands."

"There isn't time!"

I heard footsteps on the stairs, and I quickly moved away from the door. Patience appeared at the top of the staircase, a little out of breath.

"India! There you are." She glanced at the door to the smoking room. Only a fool wouldn't realize what I was doing. She had the good grace not to mention it, however. "I've been looking for you. I thought you'd gone out."

I wished I had now. I felt utterly stupid standing there. My guilt must be written all over my face. I couldn't even look at her.

"I need to speak to you," she said, glancing back down the stairs.

"Where's Miss Glass?"

"Drawing room." She took my arm and pulled me into the shadows. "I know what you and Matt are trying to do tonight." Again, she glanced toward the smoking room. "I also know it won't work. Lord Cox is a very proud man. He wouldn't stoop to being with someone like me." Her face twisted as she fought, and won, to hold back the tears.

The poor girl. She was in turmoil over this too. It was easy for Matt and I to forget that at the heart of this saga was someone who just wanted to settle down and marry a good man. I couldn't blame her for agreeing to her parents' scheme.

I took her hands in mine. "There is nothing wrong with you, Patience. Never think that. You are a fine, lovely girl."

"I'm plain and simple."

"You're nothing of the sort." While she was no beauty, I thought her prettier than her two sisters. Perhaps that was more to do with their ugly character than their faces. "Lord Cox ought to be pleased to have you as his wife."

"But he's not pleased. Is he?" She pulled away from me. "I heard about you and Matt kissing in front of everyone."

I sighed. "Not everyone."

"It doesn't matter. India, this marriage is going to take place. No one is more sorry than me that it has to be this way."

"I doubt that," I said, my voice hard.

She stiffened. "The situation cannot be reversed. Lord Cox won't change his mind, and my life will be ruined if I don't marry someone. My sisters' lives too."

I folded my arms against the chill racing across my skin.

"I know Matt can't get out of it," she added, quieter. "I know my father has found a way to convince him to go through with this, despite what Matt feels for you." Her eyes welled with tears and her lip wobbled. Even if she didn't love Matt, it must be hard to know that the man she was about to marry loved another. "You have to leave, India. You can't live here anymore. You're ruining everything."

My throat closed as my heart swelled. I looked away, no longer able to face her.

"This situation cannot go on like this," she spluttered through her tears. "It simply cannot."

I nodded. She was right. It couldn't.

CHAPTER 10

Matt visited my room briefly after the guests left but he had nothing to report that I had not already heard. "We have two weeks," he said. "I'll speak with the others and see who wants to leave with us. Then I'll book our passage to France." He gave me a sad smile as he stroked my cheek with his knuckles. "We'll save the goodbyes until the last possible moment."

"What about Miss Glass?"

He blew out a measured breath. "She'll live here, of course. I'll ask her if she has a new companion in mind. If not, I'll place an advertisement. I'd like to see that settled before we leave." He kissed my forehead and bade me goodnight.

* * *

THE FOLLOWING MORNING, he repeated what had transpired for Willie, Cyclops and Duke's sakes. Miss Glass did not join us for breakfast, but that wasn't unusual. The trio greeted Matt's account with silence. Cyclops pushed his plate away, having only eaten half his breakfast. He'd never done that before.

"Someone say something," I said. "What do the three of you plan to do? Come with us or stay?"

"Ain't nothing for me here no more," Willie said. "I'll come with you. Duke?"

"Aye." But Duke didn't sound entirely convinced.

We all turned to Cyclops. "It's for the best," he mumbled.

"Not necessarily," I said. "Catherine—"

"Don't, India. Please. Just...don't." He got up and left.

I closed my eyes until I felt Matt's hand cover mine. I opened them to see him smiling sympathetically at me.

"Want me to book passage for five?" Duke asked. "Or will your aunt be coming with us?"

"Course she will," Willie said. "She can't stay here on her own. Her brother and sister-in-law'll give her no peace."

Matt studied his plate. "She's too old to leave. Her mind..." He shook his head. "Book passage for five, leaving next Saturday. A week before the wedding should give them enough time to inform the guests."

"Including today, that's only five full days to complete our investigation," I said. "What if we haven't solved the murder by then?"

"We'll leave it in Brockwell's capable hands."

"Speaking of which," Willie said. "Hendry and Sweeney met last night."

"How do you know?"

"The chop house closed early so we had nothing to do. We wandered about until I decided we should watch Hendry and Sweeney again. We split up, only to come together at Sweeney's house when Hendry called on him."

I sat up straighter. "What happened?"

"They argued."

"Made a ruckus," Duke chimed in.

"Punches were thrown?" I asked.

"More like slaps." Duke chuckled. "Sweeney ended up on his ass. Hendry felt bad and tried to help him up but Sweeney weren't having none of it. Hendry stormed out after that."

"What did they argue about?" Matt asked.

"Couldn't hear," Willie said. "Sweeney's staff didn't, either. Most had gone to bed."

I looked at Matt. "Shall we visit Sweeney or Hendry?"

"Hendry," he said. "If he was angry enough to go to Sweeney's home to confront him, perhaps he's angry enough to talk."

I checked on Miss Glass before Matt and I headed out for the day. She was still in bed, pleading an aching head. "I'll ask Polly to bring you a tonic," I said. "Do you require anything else?"

"Your company, India."

"I'm going out with Matt. We have some new information in the murder investigation."

She touched her handkerchief to her forehead and whimpered. "Is that more important than me?"

"You'll be fine, Miss Glass, and you'll have Polly for company."

She sniffed.

I sat on the bed and adjusted the pillows at her back to make her more comfortable. "Matt will speak with you later today about finding a new companion. If you have some time, perhaps you can make a list of suitable women of your acquaintance. You must know someone in need of employment. Someone you can get along with."

"I already do. You."

I sighed. "The situation has come to a head. Lord Cox made it clear last night that he would not give in."

She turned her face away and closed her eyes.

"I spoke with Patience," I went on. "She also made it clear that she will not set Matt free."

"Then you're leaving me," she whispered into her handkerchief. "All of you will be leaving."

My heart pinched. I tried to think of something to say but only lies would ease her distress and I couldn't lie to her about something so important. I touched her shoulder. "Think of an acquaintance who'd make a suitable companion."

I went in search of Polly then informed Matt that I was ready. It was somewhat of a relief to leave the house. The air had become oppressive. Even the servants seemed to sense something was amiss, judging by their long faces. I hoped they hadn't guessed that we would leave. Not yet. We couldn't afford for

Lord Rycroft to hear of our plans. At least there would be a place for all the servants here when we were gone, serving Miss Glass and her new companion. It would be awful to have to let them go too.

Mr. Hendry wasn't happy to see us at his shop, but nothing short of physically throwing us out would make us leave. He wasn't such a fool as to try.

"We only want answers to our questions," Matt said.

"Honest answers," I added. "You were seen arguing with Mr. Sweeney last night at his house."

Mr. Hendry's face fell. "How...how do you know that?"

"What did you argue about?"

Mr. Hendry rested a hand on the stack of paper on the end of the counter.

"Leave the paper," Matt growled.

His fingers recoiled. "I wasn't going to use it against you." He tucked his hands behind his back. "Why must you persist with these bloody questions? I am innocent. I've done nothing wrong. I can't help it if my paper was used to send malicious letters to that journalist."

"Tell us who bought the paper and we'll leave you alone," Matt said.

"I told you, I don't know."

"We don't believe you."

Mr. Hendry swallowed and looked away.

"If you won't tell us that, tell us what you and Sweeney argued about."

Mr. Hendry shook his head.

Matt slammed his fist on the counter, and both Mr. Hendry and I jumped. "There isn't time for these damned games! Tell us!"

"It was a personal matter," Mr. Hendry spat. "Forgive me, but I don't see the need to splash my private affairs about. They are none of your business."

"If it relates to the investigation, it is very much our business." All of Matt's pent-up frustration came out clear as day in his razor sharp tone. Mr. Hendry probably assumed it was directed at him. I felt no need to tell him otherwise.

"Here." Mr. Hendry swiveled the ledger around and stabbed a finger at the open page. "Look at my records. If you can link any of these sales to the paper that was used to send the letters, then go and arrest the customer. It would be a miracle if you can."

"We don't need a miracle," I said, glancing over the page. "We just need a name we recognize." I flipped back through the pages to the previous week. Each entry listed the customer's name, address, and details of the order, followed by the quantity and price.

"The paper could have been bought some time ago," Mr. Hendry said.

"This ledger is for the current month," Matt said. "What about last month?"

Mr. Hendry muttered something under his breath then rounded the counter. He pulled out a ledger from the low shelf on the back wall, only to frown at it. "These are out of order." He pulled out a second one then went very still.

"What is it?" I asked.

Mr. Hendry spun round and clutched the ledger to his chest. "Nothing. Everything's as it should be. Here." He held out the ledger.

Matt rounded the counter and ignored the book. "Step aside."

Mr. Hendry shook his head.

Matt nudged him and the much slighter Hendry stumbled. Matt bent and reached into the gap left by the removal of the ledgers. He pulled out a gun.

I gasped. Mr. Hendry's shoulders slumped.

"Is this yours?" Matt asked.

Mr. Hendry nibbled his lower lip.

"Is it yours?" Matt demanded. "If it is, it won't look good for you if this turns out to be the murder weapon."

Mr. Hendry's eyes widened. "It's not mine. Please, sir, you must believe me. I've never seen that gun in my life. I don't own anything like it. I wouldn't even know how to use it."

"If it isn't yours, why did you try to hide it from us?" I asked.

"Because I knew you'd jump to the obvious conclusion—that I used it to kill that editor. I was afraid you'd tell the police." He put down the ledgers and grasped Matt's arm. "I didn't hurt anyone. I swear to you. I don't know how that gun came to be here."

"Someone must have left it," Matt said. "Who else has been behind this counter since the murder?"

"Only me."

"You are often in your workshop. You might not see or hear anyone out here." Matt checked the gun's cylinder. Finding it empty of bullets, he pocketed it in his inside jacket pocket.

Mr. Hendry stared at Matt's jacket as if he could see through it to the weapon. He shook his head slowly, over and over. "Who would do such a thing?" he murmured.

"Someone who knows your paper was used to send those threatening letters to Barratt," I said.

"Someone who wants you to take the blame," Matt added. "Could it be Sweeney?"

Mr. Hendry blinked rapidly. "No," he said quite firmly. "He's my friend. Despite everything, he wouldn't do this."

"Are you sure?" I asked gently. "You've had a falling out. You've argued, quite violently."

He barked a brittle laugh. "Miss Steele, if you had seen our fight, you wouldn't call it violent. Neither of us is capable of really hurting the other. Trust me. This is not Patrick Sweeney's doing."

"That isn't for you to decide," Matt said. He patted his jacket. "I'll take this to Scotland Yard. Detective Inspector Brockwell will be able to tell if it's the same type of weapon that was used to shoot Baggley."

"Don't tell him where you found it. Please, sir, I beg you."

"I have to tell him. I'll also tell him everything else we know, including the argument you were overheard having last night with Sweeney. We'll let the police decide if it's relevant or not."

Mr. Hendry clutched Matt's sleeves. "He'll jump to the wrong conclusion! I don't want Patrick to endure this sort of questioning. He's got enough on his plate."

"Why do you still care what happens to him?" Matt asked.

"Because we'll be friends again when everything settles

down, once he sees that I won't use my magic against him, or he won't lose anything from the magic of others."

"He must know that already," I said. "He runs a publishing company, not a paper manufacturing business, or ink. I don't see how his business will suffer from magicians."

Mr. Hendry merely lifted a shoulder. He looked somewhat lost and very much out of his depth. Finding that gun had rattled him. I believed him when he said it wasn't his.

I came around the counter and inspected the shelf. I moved the ledgers aside and searched for anything else behind them. Nothing. "It must have been placed here in the last few days, since the murder. Think about the people you've seen in your shop, Mr. Hendry. People who didn't buy anything. Perhaps they acted oddly or were nervous."

He frowned at the shelf. "Wait. There was someone." He wagged a finger at me. "You're right, Miss Steele, someone did come on Friday. I didn't realize anyone was in here until I came out quite by chance. He did not ring the bell or call out, as most customers do. I saw him as he was about to leave. I asked if he required anything and he simply shook his head and left. That in itself is a little strange, but something else just occurred to me. He glanced at that shelf, right at the spot where I found the gun."

"Describe him," Matt said.

"Respectably dressed in a good suit. Slim build with a longish nose." His brow creased in thought. "No beard but his moustache was well oiled. Oh, and I saw a pince-nez poking out of his pocket."

"Abercrombie!" I cried.

"Who?" Mr. Hendry asked.

"Mr. Abercrombie, the master of the Watchmaker's Guild."

"Why would he have a gun?" Mr. Hendry looked at the shelf. "And why did he hide it here?"

I looked to Matt but his face was unreadable. "Thank you for your time, Mr. Hendry," he said.

"Will you still take the gun to Scotland Yard?" Mr. Hendry asked.

"I have to. You can expect a visit from Detective Inspector

Brockwell if the gun is the same type of weapon that was used in the murder."

"He won't learn anything more than I've already told you."

We left and directed the driver to Abercrombie's Fine Watches and Clocks shop on Oxford Street. He would most likely be there on a Monday morning rather than at the guild hall, and he certainly wouldn't be home. According to gossip, between the two Mrs. Abercrombies—his wife and mother—his house was no sanctuary.

"You have a determined look in your eye," I said to Matt.

"I don't like unfinished business. I want to resolve this before we leave."

I wasn't sure that five days was long enough to find the murderer and visit friends I wanted to see before leaving, not to mention pack and complete all the other tasks that needed to be done before going away. I'd never been away before, not even on holiday. Shopkeepers couldn't afford time off.

The buildings we passed changed from the small Smithfield shops with their displays crammed into narrow windows, to the grander premises of Soho that fitted more wares into big bay windows. I knew every watchmaker we passed, every street and lane. I had fond memories strolling through Hyde Park as a child with my mother. Matt had bought me sweets from that confectioner, and we'd run together down that lane to get away from a mob. My mother had bought warm buns from this baker; a ribbon for my birthday from that haberdasher. My parents were buried in this city. My grandfather still lived here. I must say goodbye to him.

But how could I say goodbye to my city? My home?

I wasn't like Matt. He was used to roaming across Europe, moving house every few years and learning a new language, new ways. He'd even found his feet and thrived in America, a country so alien to what he was used to in his childhood. And in England, he was every bit the gentleman of means. He was able to cut through cultural differences with humor and charm.

I wasn't like that. I had roots here, and those roots wrapped around the very foundations of the city. It was going to hurt like the devil to sever them.

Mr. Abercrombie spotted us the moment we entered his shop. He liked to walk around the floor, greeting customers in person and watching his staff to see that they said the right thing and did not try to steal his wares.

"Get out," he hissed. "You're not welcome here."

"What will you do?" Matt asked. "Throw us out? Call the constables? You do remember how well that went for you last time, don't you?"

Abercrombie's nostrils flared. "State your business and leave."

"Have you visited Mr. Hendry recently?" Matt asked.

"Who?"

"Don't pretend you don't know who I mean. Hendry, the paper magician. Have you visited him?"

Abercrombie glanced around then directed us to follow him to an adjoining workshop. He turned to the two men wearing leather aprons and ordered them to leave.

They exited through a back door to the laneway without closing the housings of the clocks on which they were working. I sat at the bench and peered at the innards of the domed skeleton clock. Some of its parts were laid out on the bench while others had been put back, albeit incorrectly.

"Don't mention the word magic near my customers," Abercrombie said to Matt.

"Have you visited the paper maker known as Hendry?" Matt asked again.

"No. Why would I? I don't even know who he is."

"Stop lying."

Abercrombie took a step back, away from Matt. He swallowed. "I...I do know who he is, but I haven't been to his shop."

Matt took a step forward. "Another lie."

Abercrombie backed away. "All right, I have been there, but not recently. That's the truth, Mr. Glass. Now, if you don't mind, I have work to do." He glanced at me as I rearranged the parts already in the clock. "What are you doing?"

"A favor," I said, picking up a spring from the bench. "Not

that you deserve it. I'm fixing this clock for you, free of charge. Let me guess, it's been a problem piece? Your employee hasn't been able to fix it?"

He stared at me, his mouth opening and closing.

"The words you're looking for are thank you," Matt said.

I flashed a smile at Mr. Abercrombie. "You're welcome. Now, I've done you a favor, so please do us one and answer Matt's questions."

"I did! I have!" Abercrombie swallowed heavily. "I have not been to Hendry's shop in at least a week. I have no reason to go there. The man's a traitor to his profession, and he's proven to be a terrible friend to those who trusted him."

"Do stop making offensive accusations," I said. "Or I'll do something to this clock so that you'll never be able to fix it."

He snatched the clock and hugged it to his chest. "Why do you want to know about Hendry? Is this to do with Mr. Baggley's murder?" He gasped. "Is Hendry the murderer?"

"According to Hendry, you were there mere days ago," Matt said.

"That's a lie!"

Matt opened his jacket just enough for Abercrombie to see the gun.

Abercrombie slid to the side along the bench's edge, as far as he could go to get away from Matt. "D—don't shoot."

"It's not loaded," Matt said.

"For goodness sake, we're not here to shoot you," I told him. "This gun was found in Mr. Hendry's shop."

"So?" Abercrombie shrugged. "What has that got to do with me?"

"It was not there before you visited him, but it was there afterward."

"That's a lie!"

"He saw you on the wrong side of the counter," Matt added.

"Another lie! You can't believe someone like him!"

"Because he's a magician?" I asked idly.

His Adam's apple bobbed with his loud swallow. "Go. Get out, and take that weapon with you."

We did leave but did not climb into our waiting carriage. Matt leaned against it and stared through the shop window at Abercrombie as he greeted another customer. Abercrombie caught him watching and hurried out of view.

"We need to find out if he went to Hendry's on Friday," Matt said.

"He should have been here most of the day." I had an idea and indicated Matt should follow me.

He smirked. "Where are you taking me?"

"To the lane behind the shop."

He sighed theatrically. "I don't particularly want to be ravished in a lane outside Abercrombie's shop."

"I'll be gentle with you." I grabbed his hand and dragged him along.

We entered the lane but he grasped me by the waist before we got too far. He kissed me lightly on the lips. "Glad to see you still have your sense of humor, India. You looked unhappy on the way here."

"I could say the same about you."

"Not unhappy, only thoughtful. How could I be unhappy when I am mere days away from running away with you?" He kissed me again. It was passionate and fierce, desperate and hungry, and over far too quickly. "So what's your plan?"

"I am stooping to blackmail," I said, taking his hand again. "Watch and learn how an expert does it."

He laughed softly.

I opened the door leading from the lane to the workshop behind Abercrombie's shop. The two men sat at the bench. The younger one, a man about my age, stared at the clock he'd been working on, a deep frown in place. He placed the clock to his ear, frowned again, then shook it.

"Don't do that," I said, opening the door wide.

He almost dropped the clock. "Sir! Miss! You shouldn't be here. You'll find service through there." He pointed to the door leading to the shop.

"We're not here to buy anything," I said. "We're here for information. Do you work here on Fridays?"

"Yes."

The other repairer, an older man, put down the clock he'd been inspecting. "What's this about?"

I ignored him. "Was Mr. Abercrombie here all day on Friday?" I asked.

"Why?" both men said.

I turned to the older man. "Would you mind waiting outside in the lane for a moment?"

When he looked as if he would dig his heels in, Matt stepped forward and drew himself up to his full height. "Do as she asks, please. Otherwise…" He patted his jacket where the gun was tucked away inside.

Both men gulped. The older one dutifully let himself out without a glance back.

"What do you want from me?" the younger man squeaked.

I picked up the skeleton clock. "This is a lovely piece. Quite complicated, though. Did you find it difficult to fix?"

"I—I… That is…"

"I fixed it for you a few minutes ago."

He stared at the clock, ticking away to a comforting rhythm. "How?"

"That's not important," Matt said before I could answer. Was he worried I'd tell this man I was a magician?

"Now," I said, "unless you want me to inform Mr. Abercrombie that your work is sub-standard, I'd answer my friend's questions." I stepped back to allow Matt to take the stage.

"Did Abercrombie leave the shop last Friday?" he asked.

"I can't recall," the man said. "That's the truth! He might have left. He comes and goes. I don't always know when he's gone out, neither. He doesn't inform us of his movements."

Damnation. I thought I'd been so clever too by blackmailing him into answering.

"He did receive a visitor that day," he went on. "He came back here with a man and they talked."

"Can you describe the man?"

"I can do better than that. I can give you a name. Mr. Abercrombie called him Mr. Sweeney. He's been here quite a bit, lately. Mr. Abercrombie always sends me and Jack outside when they want to talk, so I don't know what they're saying."

We questioned him a little further but he couldn't tell us more. We thanked him and went to leave, but he called me back.

"You won't tell him about this, will you?" He indicated the clock. "Only I'm still learning the trade, and I make mistakes sometimes. Jack helps me fix 'em before Mr. Abercrombie finds out." He lifted his trouser leg to reveal a wooden leg and foot tucked into his shoe. "I used to be a blacksmith but had to give it up after the accident. Can't get this thing too close to the fire."

I groaned. I felt awful for putting him through the inquisition. "Don't worry. Your secret is safe."

Matt placed a hand at my lower back and steered me toward the door. We passed Jack and hurried along the lane to the carriage. Matt directed our driver to take us to Scotland Yard.

"It's time to hand the gun over," Matt said, settling on the seat.

"We didn't learn much," I said with a huff. "We don't know if Abercrombie put the gun in Hendry's shop. We don't even know if he visited Hendry that day. We only have Hendry's word for it."

"Why would he lie?"

Matt had a point, and I couldn't give him an answer. Hendry didn't even know Abercrombie, although his friend Sweeney certainly did.

"Do you think Sweeney and Abercrombie are plotting something?" I asked.

"Hard to say. They might merely be discussing the newspaper articles and how to counter the influence of *The Weekly Gazette*."

"Or they might be doing something more sinister." I tipped my head back against the wall and stared at the ceiling. Finding no inspiration there, I looked at Matt again. The view was infinitely more inspiring. "I can't quite see why they would want to kill Oscar. If Abercrombie was the murdering kind, he would have killed me, a direct threat to his business—or so he thinks. And the counter articles that Mr. Force is writing in *The City Review* are doing a serviceable job, for now. And Sweeney doesn't have any interests in businesses that are in direct competition with magical trades. His only objection to magic so far seems to be a moral one."

Matt grunted. "Righteous indignation has been the motive behind some of the worst crimes in history."

It was hard to argue with him on that score.

* * *

WE CAUGHT Brockwell before he entered the new Scotland Yard building. He sent the constable accompanying him ahead and joined us for a walk along Victoria Embankment. It would have been a pleasant stroll on the river's edge if not for the subject matter of our discussion.

"I cannot give you any information about my investigation," Brockwell began. "This case doesn't involve you, and if you want my advice, you'll not assist Mr. Barratt to find who sent him those letters. I will get to it in due course, and your investigation may muddy the waters in the mean time."

"You're mistaken," Matt said, matching Brockwell's no-nonsense tone. "We've got some evidence for you." He pushed back his jacket to show Brockwell the gun.

"Mr. Glass!"

"It was found at Hendry's paper shop in Smithfield."

Brockwell put a hand out to stop Matt from walking on. Two ladies strolled by and Brockwell indicated we should move closer to the wall, out of the path of pedestrians. They exchanged the gun from Matt's jacket to Brockwell's, and both men leaned their elbows on the wall. They looked like two friends passing the time by watching the boats on the Thames.

"Tell me everything you know," Brockwell said.

Matt told him about Hendry, his paper magic, and the suspects who used his paper—or at least those we knew about. "We went to question him about an argument he was overheard having with Sweeney when he stumbled upon this gun, tucked away behind some ledgers on a shelf in his shop."

"Stumbled upon?" Brockwell prompted.

"He seemed as surprised as we were to see it."

"Is that your interpretation of Hendry's reaction, Miss Steele?"

"It is," I said. "The only person he could think of who might have been behind the counter and planted the gun there since the murder is Abercrombie."

Brockwell turned back to the river. "I see. And I assume you called on him too."

"Of course," Matt said.

Brockwell sighed. "Did you not consider, Mr. Glass, that you would be putting Miss Steele in danger by such an action?"

"If I thought that likely, I would not have taken her." Matt's icy tone sent a chill down my spine. Brockwell seemed unaffected.

"I wasn't in any danger in broad daylight in view of witnesses," I said.

Brockwell clasped his hands and dangled them over the wall. "What did you learn from Abercrombie?"

"Nothing of use," Matt said. "He denied visiting Hendry."

"Naturally."

Matt's jaw hardened. "We did discover that he has been in regular contact with Sweeney."

"Understandable. They're both guild masters. I'm sure they want to share information to combat Mr. Barratt's articles. I strongly advise you not to confront Mr. Sweeney about these meetings."

Matt leaned his elbows on the wall again. "You may *advise* all you want, Inspector."

Brockwell steepled his fingers and drummed his fingertips together. "Leave this to the police, Mr. Glass. For Miss Steele's sake."

"We have no plans to confront him," I said quickly, taking up a position on Brockwell's other side.

He turned his back to Matt and faced me. "I'm pleased to hear it, Miss Steele. You're a sensible woman. Very sensible indeed." He smiled warmly.

I smiled back until I caught Matt scowling.

"Keep us abreast of your discoveries," Matt said. "I want to know whether that gun could have been used to kill Baggley."

Brockwell grunted a laugh. "I'm afraid I won't be doing that."

"I gave it to you on good faith," Matt ground out through clenched teeth. "The least you can do is keep me informed."

"The least I can do is find the killer. If I require any more information from you, rest assured you will hear from me."

Matt shook his head. "I don't believe this. After we helped you capture Payne. After all we did for you."

Brockwell shrugged an apology, which only seemed to rile Matt more. I scrambled to think of something to say to defuse the situation, but I could think of nothing. I considered dragging Matt off instead. In the end, it was Brockwell who dragged me away, in a manner of speaking.

"Excuse us, Mr. Glass, I wish to steal Miss Steele for a moment." He chuckled at his pun.

Matt arched his brows, but Brockwell didn't notice. He took my arm and led me further along the wall, where Matt could not overhear. He stepped into my line of sight so that I couldn't even see Matt anymore.

"Mr. Glass is intent on finding the killer," Brockwell said.

"Is that such a bad thing, Inspector?"

"Not at all, if he were a policeman or if this murder case involved him in a personal way, as the case with Payne did. But...do you not worry that he is too driven?"

"What do you mean?"

He glanced over his shoulder. "He is exposing you to dangerous people. We already know that Mr. Abercrombie dislikes you because of your magic, so why would Mr. Glass take you along when he questioned him about the gun? You are, after all, only his assistant. Your presence wasn't necessary."

I stiffened. "Actually, I'm more of a partner. We solve the crimes together."

He didn't seem to hear me and rolled on like a boulder hurtling down a hill. "If you were Glass's paramour, I would understand it even less. I suppose that, because you are not, he doesn't see the harm he's exposing you to."

"No one has harmed me in Matt's presence. He can take care of us both."

"Even so, it only proves to me he does not care for you. Of course, I comprehended the situation after reading the announcement of his engagement, but before that..." His lips flattened. "I thought you were more than Mr. Glass's assistant, but I am happy to be wrong." He took my hand in both of his. I was so shocked, I didn't pull away at first. "I know you perhaps have some lingering feelings for him, but, if I may be so bold, I ask you to be careful. Don't follow him blindly. He doesn't care for you. Not enough."

I snatched my hand away. "Do not presume, Inspector. You don't know the full story." I strode off to the carriage, not waiting for Matt.

He climbed in after me. "What did he want?"

"To urge me not to blindly follow you into dangerous situations."

"Is that all?"

"All?" I echoed. "What were you expecting him to say?"

"I thought he'd invite you to the theater." The corner of his mouth lifted in a wry smile. "It seems I don't have to worry too much, after all."

"About Brockwell?" I smiled, despite myself. "No, you don't need to worry about him."

"I admit I grew even more worried when he called you sensible. What woman can resist a man who showers her with compliments of that caliber?"

I fluttered my eyelashes. "You should take a leaf out of the inspector's book, Matt. He does know how to treat a lady."

"Is that so? Do I have to challenge him to a duel to win your hand?"

"It'll come as quite a surprise if you do. He thinks you're marrying Patience and that I am merely your assistant."

His smile slipped and the shutters came down. He turned to look out the window. I swallowed hard and looked the other way.

CHAPTER 11

Matt didn't join me for luncheon so I went looking for him. I had a niggling concern that he would heed Brockwell's warning and leave me out of the investigation. I eventually found him mucking out one of the stable stalls. Duke sat on a bale of hay not far away, his booted foot propped up on a water trough. Cyclops leaned against a wall, his ankles and arms crossed.

"Where's the stable boy?" I asked, checking the second stall. Both horses shared it while Matt cleaned out the other.

He straightened and leaned on the broom. He looked far too handsome for his own good, dressed in a working man's trousers, his shirt open at the collar with the sleeves rolled up. Sweat dampened his brow and made the shirt cling to his muscular frame. I eventually dragged my gaze up to his face, only to find a wicked gleam in his eye as he watched me.

"You look hot, India," he said. "Perhaps you should take a seat."

"It is rather warm in here."

Duke shifted aside, and I sat on the hay bale next to him.

"The stable boy came down with a fever," Matt said, returning to his chore.

"We were about to help," Duke said.

"After we eat," Cyclops added.

"And give him our report." Duke cleared his throat. "I've just come from Hendry's paper shop. Willie's still watching him in case he gets more visitors."

"More?" Matt prompted, once again pausing. "Customers?"

"I don't think so. Ordinary customers came and went, but these two separate callers received special treatment. He escorted them to the door when it came time for them to leave. He was angry with 'em. His first caller was a man. Hendry called him Professor."

"Nash!" I said. "How intriguing. And his other visitor?"

"I thought she was just a customer when I saw her carriage pull up," Duke went on. "I took no notice of her until she left and Hendry slammed the door in her face."

"Did he call her by name?" Matt asked.

"No, but her carriage had this symbol painted on the door." He plucked a piece of paper from his pocket and handed it to me.

"It's Rotherby Bank's symbol," I said, studying Duke's drawing of a hawk's head in profile surrounded by a wreath of leaves.

"Delancey's bank," Matt said. "Hendry's caller must have been Mrs. Delancey. You say he argued with her?"

"Not argued, just made sure she left his shop and scowled a lot. That man's angry, Matt. He's real angry."

I folded up the piece of paper. "So would you be if you lost friends over Oscar's articles. I consider myself fortunate that I have good friends who look beyond my magic."

Cyclops pushed off from the wall and hefted a bale of hay in his arms. "If his friends are scared of him now, they weren't never his friends in the first place."

"Amen." Duke nudged me with his elbow. "You're the sweetest thing there is, India. Besides, I come from a country where women like Willie carry guns. *That's* something to be scared of."

I laughed.

"Want me to continue watching Cox today?" Cyclops asked, depositing the bale at the other end of the stables.

Matt shook his head. "There's no point anymore. If Coyle

really did have something on him, it must be so deeply buried that we won't be able to uncover it within the week. Besides, now that we've made our decision to leave, I find I don't care as much." He shot me a small, secret smile.

I returned it as best as I could, despite the lump forming in my throat.

"Go on, Matt," Duke said, rising. "Me and Cyclops will finish up here. You got to clean up and go interrogate Nash and Mrs. Delancey."

Matt passed him the broom. "What about your lunch?"

"This won't take long." He looked around at the almost clean stall. "If you didn't get distracted so easy, you'd be done by now."

Matt clapped him on the shoulder as he passed then held out his hand to me, only to retract it. He headed for the door.

I sprang up and hurried after him. "You're not going without me, are you?"

"I wouldn't dream of it." He wiped his hand on a rag hanging from a hook by the door and smirked.

* * *

"I'M GOING to take Gabe's suggestion and have my aunt assessed by a doctor specializing in the mind," Matt said as we drove to the university.

"You're that worried about her?" I asked.

"I want to know if she's fit to travel."

"Oh. You want to take her with us."

"I've decided I can't leave her here. Even if she lives in my house, my uncle will find a way to make her miserable. He can't be trusted now, but when I abandon Patience, he'll be furious. He'll take out his anger on Aunt Letitia. Besides, even with a companion, she'll be lonely."

He had a point about his uncle's revenge. Miss Glass would make an easy target without Matt's protection. "I agree. We have to take her with us, if she can accept our relationship. But she might not like leaving her friends, her home and everything she knows. It'll be hard to say goodbye." I turned to the window, tears burning my eyes.

"Or she might see it as the adventure she was always meant to have. She regrets not going with my father all those years ago. I want her to have that— India?" He swapped seats to sit beside me and took my hand. "Why are you crying?"

"I'm not." I wasn't crying. My tears hadn't spilled, but he'd seen them welling nevertheless.

"If you really don't want her to come, I won't ask her."

"It's not that. I'm in favor of her coming with us."

He touched my jaw, forcing me to look at him. "Then what is it?"

"It's nothing. Just some nerves. They'll fade once we begin our journey." I sucked in a deep breath and gave him a crooked smile, the best I could manage. "I just want to be with you, Matt. I don't care where that is."

He cupped my cheek and kissed me with an aching tenderness that didn't help banish the tears.

* * *

PROFESSOR NASH'S lecture was attended by ten students, half of whom were female. In a university where most of the students were men, having half an audience of women was quite a feat, even if the total number was small. Indeed, calling the gathering a lecture was a stretch. The large lecture halls we'd passed had been filled with the more popular medical science topics. We'd had to ask for directions from several students and staff members before locating Nash in the drafty room at the back of the campus.

We listened to him for a few moments before he saw us. He spoke eloquently and enthusiastically on the life of a particular French king, capturing the attention of his students. They hung on his every word, as if he were giving them answers to life's eternal questions. He was different in almost every way to the man we'd met in his gloomy room. He became animated as he strode around the room like an actor on the stage, flinging his arms wide to illustrate a point or lowering his voice at a crucial moment, making it necessary for his students to lean closer to hear. They were transfixed, and many jumped when he slapped his hand on the desk to punctuate the end of his story.

They applauded him then gathered their belongings to leave, albeit reluctantly. Three young women remained behind after the others left, but he dismissed them when he spotted Matt and me.

"His enthusiasm is refreshing," one of them gushed as she filed past us.

"He's so passionate," her friend said.

The third glanced back and waved at him. He waved back, smiling.

"Your students seemed to enjoy your lecture, Professor," I said.

"I try to make it interesting. History is fascinating and rich with powerful stories that we can learn from. It's my duty to pass those stories on to the next generation. I'm only glad the current crop of students seem to think history is a worthwhile subject to spend their time learning. I think they take something away from my lectures."

"Going by their blushes, I'd say so," Matt said, closing the door.

"Blushes?"

"Nothing," I cut in. "We're here to ask you about your visit to Mr. Hendry, the paper maker, earlier today."

"How do you know I was there?"

I left that question for Matt to field, but he answered with a question of his own instead. "Did he ask you to call on him?"

"No." Nash sat on one of the front row chairs. "I decided to ask him about his magic." He held up his hands in surrender. "I know, perhaps I shouldn't have, but I couldn't help myself. I wanted to know more about his magic, and I thought he might be curious about the history of the art."

"And how did it go?" Matt asked.

"If you've been spying on me, then you already know. He ordered me to leave. He didn't tell me a single thing about himself or his spells, and he didn't want to know about magic history." He shook his head. "Such a shame. If magicians lose connection with the past, all those wonderful stories will be gone within a generation. Their spells too."

"Some of the stories aren't so wonderful," I said. "Villages flooding after rivers flow off the map, for example."

"On the contrary, Miss Steele. It *is* wonderful in its Biblical grandness. Not to mention that the story itself serves as a warning about the misuse of magic. That alone means it's worth remembering."

He had a point.

"What did you plan to do if he told you about his magic?" Matt asked.

"Make notes," the professor said. "If magic ever becomes accepted by the artless, I plan to write a book. If Hendry had some anecdotes about magic, I would have asked his permission to include them."

"How would he know any stories when magic is all but forgotten except by scholars like yourself?" I asked.

"It's not unreasonable to think some stories have passed down through families."

Such as the story of maps coming to life; Mr. Gibbons, the magician cartographer, had once told it to me. The professor was right, and it was very likely more stories were known. It was only a matter of time before they were dug up and published.

"Hendry was very rude." Nash sounded put out. "I'd hardly told him my reason for being there when he shouted at me and ordered me out."

"He's been under some pressure lately," I said.

"That's no excuse. I could have been a friend to him. We both have an interest in magic, after all."

"No, Professor," Matt said. "*You* have an interest in magic. He is a magician. One does not equal the other."

We left him contemplating that and made our way to the Delanceys' house. We were about to alight from the carriage when we spotted Isaac Barratt hurrying down the front steps.

He pulled his hat low over his eyes and bent his head into the wind. He did not see us.

Matt opened the window to ask the driver to follow him at a distance. When Isaac caught a hansom, Matt urged the driver not to lose it.

I clutched the hand strap by the door and braced myself as we drove at a brisk clip. Our larger coach had difficulty navigating the busy roads where the smaller, lighter hansom easily dodged the mid-afternoon traffic. We managed to keep up, however, at the expense of my nerves, and stopped outside Brown's Hotel in Albermarle Street, Mayfair.

I smiled as Matt assisted me from the carriage.

"This place brings back fond memories," he said, looking up at the impressive colonnaded facade, the gold lettering above the door, and the elegant balconies. "Do you remember?"

"As if it were yesterday."

I'd never tasted tea as refreshing as that served in Brown's restaurant, and never had such interesting company as the stranger sitting opposite me, looking as delicious as the food. The stranger I'd quickly fallen in love with and who now loved me back.

My grip tightened around his arm. "Imagine if I had never agreed to help direct you to London's watchmakers that day."

"It doesn't bear thinking about."

We spotted Isaac entering the hotel. The porter greeted him by name and Isaac walked straight past the front reception desk. He wasn't visiting someone else; he was staying at the hotel.

Matt hailed Isaac before he reached the staircase.

Isaac groaned. "Come to arrest me?"

"We are not the police," Matt said.

"Then I have nothing to say to you."

"We are working closely with them, however."

"I don't have time for this." He went to walk away, but Matt stepped in front of him.

"We are trying to help your brother," I said. "Someone is threatening him. They possibly tried to kill him."

Isaac snorted. "He's being overly dramatic, as usual."

"We've seen the letters," I shot back. "They are very real. Your brother's concern is very real."

He threw his hands in the air. "What did he expect would happen by writing those articles? That people would pat him on the back? That magicians and artless craftsmen alike would congratulate him?"

"Naivety isn't a reason to abandon him now, when he needs you the most."

"You say naivety, I say stupidity and impetuousness." Isaac huffed out a bitter laugh. "It wouldn't surprise me if he wrote those articles purely to spite me. He has detested me ever since... Well, for some time. He'd like nothing more than to ruin me."

His nastiness rendered me speechlessness. I would have loved a sibling, and I couldn't imagine ever clashing with a family member so badly that I wound up hating them. Yet the rift between these two seemed so wide it would be almost impossible to bridge.

Isaac tugged on his cuffs and eyed the staircase behind Matt. "Oscar should have realized this would happen. It's his own fault he attracted such animosity."

"What's done is done," Matt said.

"A retraction could still be printed."

"You know Oscar better than anyone," I said. "Do you think he'd print a retraction?"

Isaac grunted. "No, Miss Steele, I do not. He's far too stubborn to admit he made a mistake."

"Not everyone thinks those articles are a mistake."

Matt's gaze bored into me.

"Not you too," Isaac said on a groan. "Look, Miss Steele, you clearly don't understand the implications because you were not named. My brother told the world what he is, and so everyone now assumes that I am an ink magician too."

"You should be proud that you are."

He tugged on his cuffs again, drawing Matt's attention to them. "My suppliers are abandoning me out of sympathy for artless ink manufacturers. Some customers are canceling their orders, scared of what magic ink will do, as if it will grow tentacles and eat them alive or some such nonsense. More will follow."

"Those who want quality ink will flock to you."

"Will it be enough to replace the publishers who flee? I doubt it. The Stationers' Guild is already running a campaign against me. They have a lot of members here in London. I'll be ruined."

"Is that all you care about? Your business?"

He squared up to me. "Without my business, I lose everything. Think on that for a moment, Miss Steele. You clearly have an alternative way of making a living, as does Oscar. Most magicians do not. I do not."

He was right, and I couldn't blame him for being worried. Oscar and I had no right to dismiss his concerns. "I am not unsympathetic," I said.

"Then don't side with my brother or you soon will be."

"That's enough," Matt said quietly. "We didn't come here to argue with you."

"Then why are you here?"

A couple passed us coming down the stairs, halting our conversation. Matt indicated a cluster of armchairs off to one side in the large foyer, but Isaac refused to move.

"Step aside, please, Glass," he said. "I'm busy."

"Not until you tell us why you were at the Delancey residence," Matt said.

Isaac went very still. "I don't have to tell you that."

"Then we can assume you're guilty of something."

"From a visit?" He moved to the side and paused, expecting Matt to block his way again. When he didn't, Isaac passed him and trotted up the stairs.

"I do not like that man," I said, watching him go.

Matt indicated I should walk with him back through the foyer. "He and his brother make quite the pair."

"Oscar is not so bad."

"You only say that because he flirts with you and Isaac doesn't."

I laughed but he did not.

We drove the short distance back to the Delanceys' house only to be informed by the butler that Mr. Delancey was not at home. Mrs. Delancey was available to receive us in the drawing room, however.

Matt took the opportunity to apply his charms on our hostess. He began by bowing deeper than necessary over her hand. "It's a pleasure to see you again, Mrs. Delancey," he said with a smile.

She pulled her hand free. "Quite."

"Do you have a few moments to assist us with our inquiries?"

"I'm never too busy to meet with Miss Steele. I am always glad to see you, dear girl." She smiled at me and patted the space beside her on the sofa.

Matt blinked hard, and I tried not to laugh. I doubted he'd ever been snubbed so blatantly by a woman before.

"How are you holding up now that it has been made public?" she asked me gently.

"Made public?" I echoed.

She leaned closer and whispered, "The engagement." She jerked her head at Matt.

"I, er... I'm fine."

"It must have come as quite a shock to learn that he was betrothed to another all along."

"I...I was shocked, yes. And quite upset."

Matt's eyebrows arched so high they almost met his hairline. I did my best to ignore him. If I was going to follow this path to get answers from her, then I couldn't afford to be distracted.

She rubbed my arm and alternated between sympathetic pouts directed at me and scowls directed at Matt. Thankfully the butler brought in tea, giving her something else to focus on. While she wasn't looking, Matt indicated I should use her sympathy to my advantage.

I began by taking a leaf out of his book of charm. "It's very kind of you to receive us, Mrs. Delancey."

"Not at all, my dear." She handed me a teacup and saucer. "You are more than welcome to visit any time, to talk about anything you like, or simply to pass the time of day. Do consider coming alone, however. I feel we could be such good friends if we talked freely and without censure."

I bit the inside of my cheek to stop my smile.

She handed a teacup to Matt then promptly presented him with her shoulder. "Since you are here, I have something to ask of you, Miss Steele."

"You want me to infuse a watch with magic?"

"Only if you wish to. Actually, I wanted to invite you to a soiree I'm having this evening. It's all very last minute, but five of my friends have said they will attend. I'm sure the rest will come if I tell them you'll be there."

"These are friends from your magic collector's club?"

"Only the women, or the wives of members. No gentlemen allowed." She patted my arm. "I can see you're nervous, but don't be. All of them know about magic. All of them support it. You'll be among friends."

"I'm not sure," I said. "I think I have other plans tonight."

She pouted. "Do say you'll come. They'll be excited to meet you, Miss Steele. You'll be the toast of the evening. It will be great fun, you'll see." I went to look at Matt but she caught my chin. "No, no, no. Don't look to him for guidance. He is not *your* betrothed, after all, merely your employer. Surely you don't let him have a say in your private life."

I might not be looking at Matt but I sensed him tense, nevertheless.

"Let me think about it," I told her. "Mrs. Delancey, we have some questions for you."

She let my chin go but not before stroking it with her thumb. "What about, dear?"

"Do you recall our last visit when we asked if you knew of Mr. Hendry, the paper magician?"

"Of course, and I told you he supplies us with all our stationery needs."

"We know you visited him this morning."

She lowered her cup to the saucer. A second passed before she laughed. "I remember now. Yes, I did visit him. I needed more calling cards."

"Don't your staff take care of that?"

"Usually, but I decided to take it upon myself this time. I admit to being curious about his magic. I wanted to meet him." She lifted her cup to her lips but didn't sip. "He's an intriguing fellow. Very odd."

"And disagreeable," I said.

"Why do you say that?"

"Oh?" I said innocently. "You argued, didn't you?"

She drank deeply, perhaps giving herself time to think of an answer. "Not at all."

"Come now, Mrs. Delancey," Matt said. "You were seen leaving Hendry's shop. His voice was raised."

"I don't recall that. Perhaps he had to raise his voice to be heard over street noise. Smithfield is rather a boisterous place. Anyway, I don't remember our conversation. I asked him to make more cards, he wrote my order down in a book, and that was it."

"You didn't question him about his magic?" I asked.

"That would be rather forward for a first meeting, don't you think?"

"Did you ask him?" I pressed. "Is that why you argued?"

She smiled. "India. May I call you India? Have you come to a decision about tonight?"

"Not yet."

"You should think very carefully. Perhaps I'll remember what I spoke to Mr. Hendry about by then." She touched her gloved fingers to her temple. "The slight ache in my head is making it difficult to concentrate right now, but I'm sure I'll be better by this evening."

I caught Matt rolling his eyes. "Just one more question before we go," I said. "Why was Mr. Isaac Barratt here?"

She set her teacup and saucer on the table very carefully then folded her hands in her lap. "Mr. Glass, please stop spying on us. My husband will take great offence."

Matt set his own cup down and leaned forward. "Perhaps your husband would be very interested to know that Mr. Isaac Barratt visited you."

Good lord; he couldn't say such a thing to a lady of Mrs. Delancey's status! It was quite inappropriate. She did not look as shocked as I felt, however. She just smiled at him, although it held no humor.

"He already knows," she said. "Mr. Delancey was here and met with Mr. Barratt himself. It was a business matter, Mr. Glass, and confidential in nature."

"Do you know what they spoke about?"

"Are you asking me to break my confidence, Mr. Glass? Betray my husband?"

"The thing is, Mrs. Delancey, if it was a business matter, Mr. Barratt would have gone to your husband's bank and spoken to him there. But he did not. Your husband came home from his work specifically to meet Barratt here, didn't he?"

She leveled her gaze with his. "As I said, it is none of your affair. Not only that, I will not speak out of turn to you."

But she might to me. "What time do you require my presence at your soiree, Mrs. Delancey?"

She smiled slowly, victoriously. "Eight o'clock."

I smiled back. "I'll only attend if you make it worth my while. Is that understood?"

"Quite. There may be a little extra for you too."

"Extra?" I echoed.

"A piece of information I'll give you for free." She smiled into her teacup.

CHAPTER 12

"I don't like it," Matt said. He was watching me choose a dress, but I knew he wasn't referring to the outfits.

"Which do you prefer? The pink or green sage?" I asked, studying each one laid out on the bed. "Or are they both too formal for a soiree? What does one wear to a soiree?"

"I don't know. India, I don't think you should go," he said for the second time since arriving home.

"Of course I'm going," I repeated, also for the second time. "Mrs. Delancey made it clear that if we wanted answers, I had to attend."

"It could be a trap."

"It is a trap—a trap to get me to meet her friends. She only wants to show me off, Matt, not kidnap me and keep me in the attic."

"Don't joke, India."

I joined him by the window where he perched on the sill. "Your nerves are more frayed these days than when your life was in peril from your watch stopping."

"And yours aren't frayed enough. I wish you'd be more careful when it came to your own safety."

I touched his chest over his waistcoat. I could just make out the shape of his magic watch, tucked into the hidden pocket. It pulsed in response. I smiled, more relieved and happy than words could express. *My* magic made it pulse. It recognized *me,* its creator. My magic helped keep Matt alive. How could I fear or resent my art when it had the power to do that?

He smiled back and closed his hand over mine. "Come here," he purred, hooking his arm around my waist.

We kissed until I heard footsteps in the corridor outside my room. "You shouldn't be in here, Matt. If the servants catch us, your uncle might find out."

"The servants know if they tattle I'll dismiss them."

"Even so, I'd feel better if we don't meet like this. You're not a free man yet." I turned back to study the dresses. "The green, I think." I put the other away then hesitated. We might have exchanged several kisses, but I would *not* undress in front of him. I raised my brows at him.

"If you insist on going to the soiree then I'm coming with you," he said, pushing off from the window sill.

"Men are not invited. I'll be fine, Matt. Stop worrying."

He crossed his arms. "She wants something in exchange from you."

"She only wants my presence. She might ask me to speak a spell into a watch or clock, but I'll just tell her I don't know any, if that makes you feel better. I'll fix it or something instead."

His fingers drummed against his thigh. "Allow me to escort you to keep an eye on everything."

"I'm going alone." I stepped around him and opened my dressing table drawer. I wished I hadn't said no to Miss Glass's pearl earrings. They would go nicely with the dress.

"Is this because of the wedding announcement?" he asked.

"What do you mean?"

He sat on the bed and dragged his hand through his hair. Being still, even for a moment, seemed beyond him. "I'm not even sure any more. That announcement coming so soon shocked me. I can only imagine how it affected you. Not to mention the wedding being brought forward, along with our plan to leave. I won't lie to you, India. I hate what we have to do to Patience."

I sat beside him on the bed. "I hate it too. Do you want to delay our departure?"

He shook his head. "That's the one thing I don't want to do."

"Then what can be done?"

"That's the problem. Nothing, and I hate doing nothing."

I pecked his cheek and returned to the dressing table. I unpinned my hair and let it fall around my shoulders. He watched me in the mirror's reflection, his eyes warm. He'd finally gone still.

"Are you sure you don't want me to escort you?" he asked.

I laughed. "No, Matt."

"I know how becoming you are in that dress. All the men will be looking at you, and with the damned announcement now advertising your availability..." He muttered something under his breath that sounded like a slang American word I'd heard Willie say when she stubbed her toe. "I hate this."

I stroked his hair back and kissed his forehead. "There'll only be women there, no gentlemen."

"Footmen may act like they see and hear nothing, but they're men too, and neither blind nor deaf. The Delanceys have a lot of footmen."

I laughed. "Go on, off with you or I'll never be ready in time."

He finally left after another kiss, only to be replaced ten minutes later with Miss Glass. She brought Polly with her and the pearl earrings.

"I know you said you don't want them, but you may want to borrow them for tonight." She thrust the box at me. "Polly will do your hair. She's keen to try the more fashionable styles the young women wear nowadays. I like my hair the way it's always been done, but you ought to try something new, India." She steered me to the dressing table chair and ordered me to sit. "Something that shows off the earrings."

"There won't be any gentlemen there," I said, thinking about the footmen and dismissing them just as quickly. Miss Glass wouldn't consider them potential beaus, even for me. "It's for women only."

"India," she chided, making way for Polly to stand behind me. "I am not playing matchmaker. I know how things are."

Did that mean she accepted my relationship with Matt? I eyed her in the reflection, but her face didn't give away her thoughts. She fussed with the things on my dressing table and acted as assistant to Polly, passing the maid pins and combs when she requested them.

"You look lovely," she declared when Polly finished. "A real beauty. Who would have known when you first arrived here that such a lovely woman hid behind that mousy façade? You were so demure and quiet, and those clothes and hairstyle made you look quite plain."

I chose to take that as a compliment and thanked her.

She dismissed Polly and picked up the earrings box. "Put these on. I have a necklace to go with it, if you like."

"It might be too much," I said, fixing one of the earrings in place.

"Nonsense. In a room full of ladies, no amount of jewelry is too much."

"Why only in the presence of ladies?"

"I have no idea." She plucked at the shoulder of my dress, teasing the stiff silk into a peak. "You do look lovely."

I narrowed my gaze at her. "Miss Glass, is something wrong?"

"May I not admire my pretty young companion?"

I wanted to sigh but kept it in check. "Does calling me your companion mean you've accepted Matt and me?"

Her sharp gaze met mine in the mirror's reflection. "I don't like it, India. What do you call it? Blackmail?"

"We're not blackmailing you. You have a choice."

She sat on the bed and skimmed her hand lightly over the coverlet. "It feels as though my mind has been made up for me."

I joined her on the bed and rested my hand over hers. "Are you worried about what will happen to you when we leave?"

"Matthew has already made it clear that I'll be getting a new companion."

"Is that all you want? A new companion?"

"I want my old companion, India. You know that." She stood with surprising vigor and marched out of the room.

I sighed and finished getting ready before going in search of Matt. I found him in his study. He leaned back in his chair, smiled, and beckoned me to join him. "You look beautiful. I'm jealous."

"Of the footmen?"

"Of anyone who gets to stare at you all evening while I'm tackling this paperwork."

"I'm sure the others will challenge you to a few rounds of poker. Or why not go out to the theater? It might do you all some good."

He nodded. "I'll take my aunt and ask her on the way if she wants to leave with us on Saturday."

"Do you think she should be told yet? She might let it slip to someone in the family—or even to Polly. I don't want anything to go wrong at the eleventh hour."

He pulled me onto his lap and locked me in his arms. "Nothing will go wrong, India. As to my aunt, she can't be kept in the dark any longer. She should know."

I snuggled into him with a sigh. "You're right. But extract a promise from her first that she won't tell. Hopefully she'll manage to keep it."

* * *

I MAY NOT HAVE BEEN to many soirees before—indeed, I'd been to none hosted by the likes of Mrs. Delancey—but I was quite sure the long table set up in the refreshment room should have sandwiches and cakes on it, not watches and clocks.

"Champagne, India?" Mrs. Delancey pressed a glass into my hand. "May I call you India?"

"Please do."

As I sipped, I became aware of the gazes of the other guests on me. I felt like a performer in a show, yet I had no tricks for them, no amazing feats. They would be disappointed when they learned my magic had no visual appeal. It wasn't like Oscar's, where he could make words float from the page, or even when I combined my magic with the medical magic in Matt's watch and made it glow.

"Allow me to introduce you to my friends." Mrs. Delancey did not steer me from one guest to another as I expected, but clapped her hands and called them to attention.

The footmen quietly exited the room, and the butler shut the door as he left. The ladies gave their hostess their full attention. Like Mrs. Delancey, they were dressed in elegant evening gowns and jewelry worth more than the entire stock in my father's store. Thank goodness for Miss Glass's earrings, or I would have felt like a slum dweller by comparison.

"Please extend a warm welcome to our guest of honor, Miss India Steele." Mrs. Delancey waited until the applause ended. "You all know of her, but allow me to remind you of her capabilities. She is the granddaughter of the watch magician who was the first in recent memory to experiment with combining his magic with that of other magicians. Her magic is powerful enough that her devices work independently of any spell to save lives."

"Er, that's not correct," I said.

"Come now, India, don't be modest. Lord Coyle witnessed your watch protect you in his own home."

There was no point denying it anymore, but I could at least make sure her information was accurate. "*My* watch, Mrs. Delancey. It was a device I've owned for years and had worked on hundreds of times. I cannot make other people's watches or clocks do that."

Murmurs of disappointment rippled around the drawing room.

"Can your magic heal the sick when combined with a doctor's magic?" one woman asked.

I had expected the question, but even so, the woman's directness, coming so early in the evening, unsettled me. "That rumor was begun by a murderer and a liar," I said. "I wouldn't trust what he says. He'll do anything in his power to cause problems for my friends and me."

"You haven't answered the question directly, Miss Steele," the woman pressed. "*Can* you heal people by combining your magic with a doctor's, as your grandfather once hoped to do?"

I held her gaze. "No."

More murmurs. The woman arched a sharp brow at Mrs. Delancey.

"India's merely being cautious," Mrs. Delancey said quickly. "In these trying times, can one blame her?"

I shook my head. "That's not—"

"You can trust us, Miss Steele," said an elderly woman dripping in diamonds. "We're all friendly here, and supportive of people like you."

"Your kind are so peculiar," added another. "I admit to being quite intrigued. Tell us, how does magic *feel*?"

"Warm," I said, remembering the heat that surged from Matt's watch as it filled with my magic and Gabe's. I'd never felt anything quite like it.

Another round of murmurs rippled among the semi-circle of women.

"Does it hurt you?" the same woman asked. "Does the sensation tingle?"

"No."

"They say you're powerful."

"Who does?"

She waved a hand to indicate the entire audience. "If you're so powerful, surely you can do more than simply make watches run on time."

"Clocks too," I said.

"We know that's not all."

I didn't answer. Before the silence stretched too thin, Mrs. Delancey pointed to a pretty woman with a serious set to her brow. "You have a question for Miss Steele, Louisa?"

"What do you think about Professor Nash's theories on the history of magic?" Louisa asked.

"I don't know enough about magic's past to form an opinion," I said.

"Surely you must be curious. Don't you think it a shame that all that power has disappeared? That all magicians are left with is a few useless parlor tricks?"

"Louisa," Mrs. Delancey chided. "This is supposed to be a light-hearted evening where Miss Steele is celebrated, not derided. Parlor tricks, indeed!"

"I don't mean to offend, and I certainly am not deriding Miss Steele. She's a fascinating subject. I merely want her opinion on the professor's theories."

"It's all right," I told Mrs. Delancey. "I agree with her, as it happens. My magic is next to useless, particularly since I don't make or repair timepieces anymore. I don't find that a shame at all, however. On the contrary, I find it a comfort. The sort of power that Professor Nash describes is beyond comprehension. For a few magicians to hold such power would be worrying."

Some nodded and others whispered to friends behind their hands.

Louisa merely lifted a shoulder. "Or wondrous. Imagine the possibilities."

I blinked hard. "What possibilities?"

"Oh, you know." She waved a hand and gold rings flashed in the lamplight. "The beautiful things you could create, like flying carpets, or towers that reach to the clouds, or a train that could also float like a ship. And you, Miss Steele, could make that magic last into eternity with your extending spell." She sipped her Champagne and stared at me over the rim of her glass, a curious smile in her eyes.

No one else in the room moved and the only sound came from the loud tick of one of the clocks in the adjoining room. I was about to remind her of the terrible things Professor Nash said that magic caused, like floods and plagues, but another woman spoke first.

"If you're as powerful as they say, Miss Steele, wouldn't you be interested in learning if you have a part to play in the resurrection of such amazing feats?"

"I... That is..." My mouth felt dry so I sipped my Champagne. I ended up drinking the remainder of the glass. It gave me time to think of an answer, and a little courage. "There is no evidence that my magic is that powerful. Even if there were, there are no magicians alive who know how to do what you describe. The knowledge is lost."

"There may be no magicians, but that doesn't mean their teachings are gone," Louisa said, that curious smile still in play.

"What do you mean?"

"Perhaps there are spells, or pieces of spells, that a powerful magician can decipher and complete."

"The language of magic is lost, madam."

"Is it?" she asked lightly.

I turned to Mrs. Delancey. "What is this? What do you know, or think you know?"

Mrs. Delancey put up both her hands. "Nothing, I assure you. Louisa is merely speculating. She likes to stir things up." She glared at Louisa. "She's quite the insurgent."

"I like to speculate," Louisa countered. "The possibilities of magic intrigue me. *You* intrigue me, Miss Steele."

"I am quite ordinary." I set my glass down on a table. "Perhaps I ought to go."

Mrs. Delancey caught my arm. "Don't run off." She leaned closer and whispered, "You promised."

"I promised to come, and I have. You have not yet fulfilled your part in our bargain."

"I will, I will. Come with me." She hooked her arm through mine. "Come and speak a spell into the clocks and watches my friends brought in for you."

"I will work on them, but that's all," I told her as we made our way to the refreshment room. "It should be enough to make them all operate efficiently from now on."

"See," Louisa said in a hushed voice from close behind us. "You're powerful. Other magicians need spells for their magic to work. You do not. You are special, Miss Steele. Never forget that." She peeled away to join her friends as they gathered to watch me.

The next hour must have been quite dull for them, as I simply checked the inner workings of each device, removed parts and reassembled them. It was a task I'd performed my entire life, but it was far from dull for me. I'd not worked on many clocks or watches since Matt's return to full health, and the exercise calmed me in a way few other things did. It allowed me to empty my mind of my troubles, even thoughts of Matt and our future together, and simply drift away as peacefully as a boat on a lake.

It wasn't until I closed the housing on the last clock that I once again became aware of the other guests as they applauded. I dipped my head to hide the flush spreading over my cheeks. It seemed silly to be celebrated for something so ordinary.

Mrs. Delancey put a finger beneath my chin. "Don't be shy, India. You deserve this. You were wonderful."

"I'm afraid there's nothing to see," I said, indicating the devices.

"That's not important. What matters is that you are here and have been more than willing to share your magic with us. We are quite privileged."

"Indeed," the woman named Louisa said. "Do have some more Champagne, Miss Steele."

"Call me India."

She smiled. "And you must call me Louisa." She extended a hand and I shook it. "I believe we will be friends."

I gave her a polite smile before enduring more polite conversation with her and some of the other women. Mrs. Delancey supervised the removal of the timepieces to another room, and upon the arrival of sandwiches and cakes to replace them, she steered me away from the group to a quiet corner.

"Now, your payment," she began. "You wished to know why Isaac Barratt was here."

"You said he spoke with your husband about a business matter."

"I don't know the particulars of that conversation, but I assume it's the same reason Mr. Hendry spoke to my husband privately, too."

"Hendry!"

She nodded. "I do know about *that* meeting. He asked my husband for a loan."

"Why not go to the bank?"

"Not a bank loan, a private one. Mr. Hendry has debts, you see, and his usual bank won't lend him any more to pay them off. It wasn't a problem until recently. You see, his debts are being called in."

"All of them? All at once?"

She nodded. "After Mr. Barratt's articles, the banks decided to stop lending money to known magicians. It's their way to ensure their businesses are hobbled in favor of the artless ones. Despite my husband's attempts to prevent this attitude, his own bank is also refusing to loan money to magicians."

"So Mr. Hendry needs a sum of money now to pay off debts that have suddenly been called in, and he cannot get that money due to new loan constraints."

"Precisely."

"Poor Mr. Hendry, and Mr. Barratt too, if he was indeed here for the same reason. Did Mr. Delancey loan Mr. Hendry the money?"

She nodded. "He is a friend to magicians. Both Mr. Hendry and Isaac Barratt will benefit from my husband's generosity."

"Have any other magicians come calling on your husband at home?"

She shook her head.

"And what about your visit to Mr. Hendry? Why did you call on him?"

"I wanted him to perform magic for me."

"You mean speak a spell into the paper as he made it?"

She crossed her arms and tapped her finger on her sleeve. It should have been a very simple answer to a very simple question, but she gave it deep consideration. "He can do more than speak a single spell to make strong paper," she finally said. "I've heard he can make paper fold itself to form lovely designs."

I stared at her and didn't realize my jaw had dropped until I went to speak. That made three spells Mr. Hendry knew—one to make quality paper, one to fling it as a weapon, and a third to fold it into beautiful shapes. "The paper folds without him touching it?"

She nodded and glanced toward the group of ladies. Only Louisa noticed. "That's what I heard, but don't tell anyone. He wouldn't confirm it, so I wouldn't wish to spread the rumor if it's not true. The poor man seems to have enough on his plate at the moment, without this gaggle descending on him."

"How did you learn that he could fold paper with a spell?"

She hesitated, and I had to prompt her before she would answer. "I am not an eavesdropper, you understand. It is not something I make a habit of doing, but I was simply there at the right time when they were discussing Hendry."

"Who?"

"Lord Coyle and Sir Charles Whittaker. It was at a collector's meeting, a few evenings ago, and I'd retired to a sitting room with a headache. They came in and shut the door. Sir Charles told Coyle what he'd learned about Hendry. They didn't see me."

"How did Sir Charles know about Hendry?"

She shrugged. "I don't know. This is our secret, India. Well, I did tell Mr. Delancey, of course. I'm not proud of my actions. I should have declared myself that night, but..." She shrugged again and looked away.

"Neither man mentioned Hendry's abilities to the rest of the collectors?"

She shook her head.

"Is that odd?" I asked.

"Yes, very. Mr. Delancey wasn't happy to be excluded, but he won't tell them what I overheard. The thing is, India, my husband thinks this is not the first time those two have discussed magical matters between themselves and not passed the information on to the rest of us."

"Why would they do that?"

"I don't know, but I do want you to be aware of it. Neither man can be trusted." She patted my arm. "Now, come and have some more Champagne."

* * *

MATT WAS WAITING up for me when I returned a few minutes

before midnight. He opened the front door himself and asked me to join him in the library. I flopped into one of the deep, comfortable leather armchairs and tossed my reticule onto the side table.

"You look happy," he said with a small smile.

"Why wouldn't I be? I'm running away to be with the man I love. Also, I drank a little too much Champagne. It is rather delicious, though. Have you tried it?"

"I have. Brandy?"

A hiccup escaped at precisely that moment. "I think I'd better abstain."

He put down the decanter and glass and crouched before me. "If I were a gentleman, I'd send you to bed and not take advantage of you." His gaze turned hooded and smoky. "But my intentions toward you are not at all gentlemanly."

I hiccupped again and clapped a hand over my mouth.

He laughed softly and drew my hands away. He kissed me lightly on the lips then settled in the chair opposite. "How did the evening go?"

I shook my head. "You first. Did you go to the theater?"

"We did. My aunt and I arrived home fifteen minutes ago. I sent her and the servants to bed. The others decided to continue with their evening." He glanced at the clock on the mantel. "Hopefully they're not getting into too much trouble."

"Did you tell your aunt our plans?"

"Only that we're leaving on Saturday. I decided not to tell her we want her to join us. Not yet. I'll do it on Friday, at the last possible moment. She'll want to visit her friends and tell them, and we can't risk it. She can write letters, and I'll ask Bristow to post them after we've left."

"*If* she decides to come with us."

His gaze slid away. "I think she will."

"Matt?" I hedged. "What is it?"

He drummed his fingers on the chair arm and for a moment, I thought he'd tell me nothing was wrong. Then he said, "She's upset about us leaving."

"Then perhaps we should tell her she can come after all."

He leaned forward and rested his elbows on his knees. He sighed and scrubbed a hand through his hair. "As upset as she is, I don't want to jeopardize our plans. If she tells someone..." He shook his head. "It's cruel but for the best, and it's only for a few days. She'll be fine, once we tell her."

"On Friday," I said hollowly. Poor Miss Glass. She must feel as though we were abandoning her. "I'll spend some time with her over the next few days between investigating."

"Speaking of which, how did it go tonight? What did Mrs. Delancey want you to do?"

"I worked on the timepieces her friends brought in. I didn't speak any spells," I assured him. "She simply wanted to show me off, I think. It was a little odd but quite harmless. Besides, I learned that Mr. Hendry went to see Mr. Delancey about a loan. Isaac Barratt probably did too."

I told him what Mrs. Delancey had said about Hendry's business problems, as well as the conversation she'd overheard between Lord Coyle and Sir Charles Whittaker. That seemed to concern Matt more, if his frown was an indication, but he made no comment about it.

"What I want to know is," I said, "who told Hendry's creditors and his bank that he was a magician?"

Matt nodded slowly. "Someone must have. Sweeney, perhaps, or one of the other guild masters."

"Abercrombie," I added. "It's precisely the sort of underhanded and cowardly tactic he'd employ. No bloodshed but an awful amount of trouble can be inflicted to Hendry's business this way."

"And that of other magicians."

"Thankfully Oscar didn't name any names aside from himself and my grandfather. I don't owe anyone money, nor do I need a loan, so I am quite safe. Isaac Barratt can't say the same. Mrs. Delancey suspects his financial problems are behind his visits to Mr. Delancey too."

"It's yet another reason for him to be angry with his brother," Matt said.

"As long as it's contained to just Isaac Barratt and Mr. Hendry, there's no reason for concern."

"You have more faith in Abercrombie and his cronies than me. What's to stop them talking to the banks about men they merely *suspect* are magicians?"

"Let's worry about that when it happens. Besides, we'll be far away from London and all these problems after Saturday. None of this will concern us anymore."

He smiled that boyish smile. "You'll be far away, India. Safe."

"Safe," I echoed. Yet I felt as though I was abandoning my fellow magicians at a time when they needed me the most.

* * *

"INDIA! INDIA, WAKE UP!" Matt's shout would have woken the entire household, not just me.

I threw a shawl around my shoulders and opened the door. He stood there dressed only in trousers and a shirt that he had not yet tucked in. Stubble darkened his jaw and his hair was a tumbled mess.

"What is it?" I asked, my heart in my throat.

"Aunt Letitia has gone."

"What do you mean? She can't have vanished."

"She's not in the house, and Polly searched the vicinity before waking me." He scrubbed his hands down his face. "This is all my fault. I should have told her. I should have—"

"Matt." I grabbed his hands and pulled them away. He blinked back at me with tired, worried eyes. "We'll find her. Rouse the others while I dress. She can't have got far. She's probably walking in Hyde Park."

"If she wanted to go for a walk, she wouldn't have taken her case. Polly said some of my aunt's clothes are missing." A muscle in his jaw bunched. "And Peter saw a hansom pull away from the curb outside the house earlier. She's gone, India. She's run away."

CHAPTER 13

Trying to find an elderly lady in a city the size of London was more difficult than the proverbial needle in a haystack. After another check of the surrounding streets and Hyde Park, Matt sent word to Lord and Lady Rycroft, but they sent word back to say Miss Glass had not gone there. Matt's cousins, the three Miss Glasses, arrived with the response. They crowded into the entrance hall just as I was about to leave. Although Matt had asked me not to go out, in case Miss Glass returned, I couldn't stand being idle while he, Willie, Cyclops and Duke conducted a search. Unfortunately, his cousins caught me before I left.

"She'll show up sooner or later," said Hope, the youngest, prettiest and most precocious of the three.

"She'll be calling on a friend," said Charity, glancing toward the staircase.

"We sent messages to all her friends," I told her. "She's not with any of them."

I tried to avoid looking at Patience but couldn't help myself. She, however, kept her gaze focused on the tiled floor.

Hope cleared her throat. "This is rather awkward." Her smile would imply otherwise. Indeed, she seemed to enjoy our discomfort. "In truth, we thought you'd have moved out of

Matt's house by now, India. It is, after all, only fair to my dear sister that you move on. It would be better for everyone."

"Hope," Patience whined. "Don't make trouble."

"I am merely looking out for you. You know how Matt feels about India, and having her here, constantly reminding him of what he's giving up, is too cruel for all involved, including you. Don't you think?"

Patience's shoulders slumped further. Her sister was the cruel one, and I had a mind to tell her so, but I bit my tongue. Patience would get caught in the crossfire, and she had endured enough—and would endure more soon.

"Bristow," I said to the butler who hovered in the shadows near the staircase, "please show the Miss Glasses out. Their business here is concluded."

He opened the front door, but only Patience moved to leave. Charity plucked off her gloves and glanced up the stairs again. "Is Cyclops here?"

"He's out looking for your aunt," I said.

She pouted. "I don't see why he should. It's not as if she cares about him. She's only putting up with him because of Matt."

"She does care," I shot back.

She pulled a pencil from her reticule and wrote on the back of a card that she handed to Bristow. "Give this to Mr. Cyclops. Don't peek." She gave me a pointed look. "It's private."

I refrained from rolling my eyes. Just.

"Patience, you might as well wait here for your fiancé to return," Hope said to her sister. "I'm sure he'd like to see you."

"I'd rather not," Patience mumbled.

"Tosh." Hope thrust her nose into the air. "This will be your home, soon. You should get used to being here. Perhaps introduce yourself to the servants and make them aware of your wishes. They'll be taking orders from you soon enough."

"Hope," Patience whispered. "Please, stop. I can't stay while..."

Both Hope and Charity looked sharply at me. Patience continued to focus on the tiles at her feet.

"Stay if you wish," I told her as I headed for the stairs. "I'm going out to look for your aunt."

Charity snorted again. "That mad old bat could be anywhere by now."

I spun around. "Precisely. She could be confused or hurt or upset. The sooner we find her the better."

"I'll search for her too," Patience said quickly. "You two go home without me."

Hope swanned past her and out the door. "Do as you wish, I don't care. But you know how Aunt Letitia dislikes you, Patience. She'd never go looking for *you,* if you went missing."

Patience's face fell. She bowed her head again but not before I saw the tears well in her eyes. A satisfied look passed between her sisters.

"She doesn't dislike you," I told Patience. "She just didn't know you very well until recently. You've always been in your sisters' shade, so your own light has never had a chance to shine. She does like you now, very much." I didn't wait to see her reaction. I picked up my skirts and headed to my room to fetch my gloves and hat.

I TOOK a hackney to all the main railway stations and asked at the ticketing booth, but none could recall selling a ticket to an elderly, well-to-do lady early that morning. I drove around to the shops I thought Miss Glass might visit, but no one had seen her. I returned home in the late afternoon, deflated and overwhelmed.

It was an immeasurable relief to find her sitting on the sofa, a cup of tea in hand. Matt sat beside her, holding a plate of cream puffs.

"Eat another," he urged her.

"Are you trying to make me fat?" She spotted me and sheepishly took another cream puff off the plate.

"Where have you been?" I asked, embracing her. "We were so worried."

"There was no need." She nibbled on the cream puff.

"Well?" I prompted. "Where did you go?"

"Here and there."

"She's refusing to say," Matt said. "She was here when I got back."

"Tea, India?" Miss Glass asked.

"I need something stronger." I poured myself a glass from the sherry decanter on the tea trolley. Bristow was the perfect butler, knowing in advance what we might need.

"I came home to see if anyone else had any luck," Matt said. "And she was in here, being fussed over by Mrs. Bristow and Polly. I've been trying to find out where she's been all day but with no luck." He glared at his aunt. "It seems she wishes to keep it a secret."

"It's no secret," she told him. "I simply can't recall. There. Are you happy now?"

"No. That's even worse." He sandwiched her hand between both of his. "Aunt, you can't leave without telling anyone where you're going. You had us all worried. I even sent word to my uncle."

She wrinkled her nose. "You shouldn't have bothered him."

"You gave me no choice."

She sniffed. "He wouldn't have cared."

"He sent his daughters here," I said. "That's how concerned he was."

"Don't confuse duty with concern, India," Miss Glass said. "He was only worried about his friends finding out."

"Patience was worried," I said. "She wanted to help look for you."

"*She*, at least, is a good girl."

"Are you implying that I am not?" Perhaps it was a little too forthright, but it had been a trying day. I'd been at the end of my rope on the way home after a fruitless search, only to find her already here, eating cream puffs and unwilling to say where she'd been.

She turned her face away.

"Something is troubling you, Aunt," Matt said. "What is it?"

"You're going away. Both of you. It was horrible enough to find out that India no longer wishes to be my companion, but to have you leave too, Matthew... It's too much." She threw the half-eaten cream puff on the plate. Blobs of cream splattered across the table.

Matt looked to me. I nodded. It was time to tell her. "Aunt—"

She pulled her hand free of his. "I know I'm old and useless, but I'm not a piece of furniture that can be left behind and forgotten." She lifted her wobbling chin and turned her face away.

"We'd like you to come with us," he finished.

She turned huge eyes onto him.

"We were going to tell you on Friday, but since the topic has come up now, I thought you shouldn't be left wondering another moment. You can come with us, if you want, but you must promise not to mention it to anyone. That means no goodbyes in person, only letters that Bristow can deliver after we're long gone."

"Leave?" Her trembling voice was barely above a whisper. "With you?"

"If that's what you want. It will mean leaving your friends and all this behind."

"All this?"

"The house, London, the places you're used to seeing every day. The weather." He smiled.

She simply stared at him then turned to me. She showed not a flicker of emotion. Perhaps her mind had wandered off.

"We're leaving on Saturday," I reminded her. "If you do decide to come, you'll need to choose what to take and what to leave behind."

"Saturday," she repeated dully.

"I know it's not very long, but it should be enough time. But please don't tell anyone else. Understand?"

I dipped my head to look at her better but still couldn't gauge her thoughts.

"Promise you won't betray us, Miss Glass." I didn't think she would, but it wouldn't hurt to elicit a promise from her. "Don't tell Lord or Lady Rycroft about our departure. Don't tell your nieces or your friends. Don't even tell the servants. Miss Glass? Will you promise?"

She clasped her hands to her chest and looked to Matt. "You won't leave me behind this time, Harry?"

My heart lurched. I patted her arm. "It's me, Miss Glass."

"Veronica, yes, I know."

Matt sighed. "Perhaps you should lie down, Aunt."

She stared at his hands as he took hers and helped her to stand. "I do feel tired."

He put an arm around her and steered her to the door. She paused, however, and looked back at me. "I have something to tell you, Veronica. Harry has asked me to leave with him. I didn't want to go last time. I couldn't leave...you know who. But now that business is over, I am finally free. You will come, won't you? You will keep me company?"

"Of course," I said, playing the role of her maid from years past. "Of course."

I went in search of Polly, all the while wondering if it mattered that Miss Glass never actually promised to keep our secret.

Matt returned ten minutes later. He sat in the same spot on the sofa and pressed his fingers to his forehead. "It's been some time since her last episode. I thought she was getting better."

"I don't think she'll ever get better." I sat on the sofa arm and kissed the top of his head. "She can't cope with confrontation or difficult matters. They cause her to lose focus and slip into the past."

He leaned into me and reached around my waist, holding me in place. I stroked his hair, and he sighed deeply. "We did the right thing in telling her," he said. "We couldn't put it off any longer."

"Not if she's going to wander off like that."

"Do you think she did it to punish us because she thought we were leaving her behind?"

"I don't know," was all I said, even though I suspected he was right.

"I wouldn't put it past her," he went on. "She can be as manipulative as her brother when she wants to be."

I fell into his lap and circled him in my arms. "At least she seems keen to come with us. I feel better about going now." Although I was still worried about hurting Patience.

"I think you were right and she sees this as a second chance to escape." He touched his nose to mine then teased me with light, pecking kisses.

I wanted to clasp his face in both my hands to force him to kiss me properly, but the reminder of my earlier encounter with Patience suddenly came to the fore. She'd looked miserable, and I couldn't attribute that to her sisters' company. She was miserable because she knew her marriage would hurt me and because she knew she was marrying a man who could never love her.

The misery she felt now would pale in comparison to what she'd experience when Matt broke off their engagement.

I couldn't think about that. I couldn't think about her, and what we were going to do, or I might abandon our plans.

I pulled away from Matt just as Cyclops entered, holding the card Charity Glass had left for him.

"She's persistent," I said.

"Bloody-minded, as you English say," Cyclops said, passing the card to Matt upon his request.

Matt read it and passed it back. "Will you go?"

"Not even if my life depended on it. She scares me."

Matt chuckled. "If only Catherine Mason had written it."

Cyclops tossed the card onto the tea trolley. "Wouldn't matter. We're leaving Saturday."

"What if we weren't?" I asked. "Would you meet Catherine if she asked you to?"

Matt tilted his head to the side and frowned at me.

"Something I should know about our departure?" Cyclops asked, glancing between us.

"No," I said quickly. "I was just speculating. Don't mind me."

"India," Matt began, only to be interrupted by the blustery arrival of Willie. Duke followed in her wake.

"Where is she?" she said, hands on hips. "Where's the woman who made us walk all over the city only to come back here?"

"So you heard of her return," I said.

"Bristow told me. Where is she? I'd like to tell her how much my feet ache." She threw herself onto the sofa with a groan. "Maybe I'll just show her the blisters." She reached down to remove her boots but was met with a barrage of protests from the four of us.

"Not in the sitting room," I begged her. "Why not have a soak in the bath?"

"I ain't some pampered lady, India."

"No one will pamper you."

"Or mistake you for a lady," Duke added.

"After a drink. That sherry?" she asked, pointing at the decanter on the trolley. "Pour me a glass, Duke. A big one."

He picked up the decanter in one hand and Charity's card in the other. He read it and smirked. "I've got to get an eye patch."

"Why?" Willie asked.

"Ladies like pirates." He handed her the card.

Willie slapped her knee and whooped with laughter. "You have to go, Cyclops."

"No," Cyclops growled.

"Aw, go on. Meet up with her. We're leaving in a few days, so what does it matter? Go and have some fun on your last days in England then leave with no regrets."

Cyclops snatched the card off her and tore it in two. "No regrets? You live in a fantasy world if you think I wouldn't regret meeting Charity at that hotel."

"Hotel?" I asked. "As in the restaurant of a hotel?"

"As in a room," Duke said, grinning. "At a hotel near Kings Cross station."

"And Patience is the one with the reputation in that family," Willie muttered with a shake of her head.

"Patience's mistake was getting caught," I told her.

"And the gentleman was indiscreet about it," Matt added.

Duke passed Willie a glass of sherry. "He weren't no gen'leman then."

Willie took the glass in one hand and Duke's waistcoat front in the other and pulled him down to her eye level. She pecked his cheek and patted it as he stared back at her, unblinking. "Sometimes you say just the right thing and I remember why we're friends," she said.

He flushed and stepped away, flattening a palm down his waistcoat. "And here I thought it was because I'm so handsome."

"You'd be more handsome with an eye patch." Cyclops punched Duke lightly in the arm as he passed. "If you ever want to try it, I've got a spare."

Duke chuckled and returned to the trolley to pour another glass of sherry.

"*You* could meet Charity at the hotel instead of Cyclops," Willie said to Duke. "See if the patch works. Just don't go near Catherine Mason or Cyclops'll get jealous."

Cyclops narrowed his eye at her. "You ain't funny, Willie."

"Then why's Duke laughing?"

Cyclops glanced at Duke, catching him grinning. He quickly sobered beneath Cyclops's withering glare and handed him a glass of sherry. "Drink this and forget about your women troubles. We'll be gone soon so it won't matter." He sat with a sigh and stretched out his legs.

"You don't sound particularly happy about leaving," I said.

Duke shrugged. "I got used to it here. Except for the weather, London ain't so bad. There's lots to do and see, different places to go and ales to try."

"And you like having servants at your beck and call," Willie added.

"So do you."

She lifted her glass in salute. "True, but I can admit it."

"Ain't no one trying to kill us here," Duke added. "Well, not anymore. Back home, your family wants revenge for your grandfather, Matt."

"And Cyclops has his own problems," Willie added.

"Do any of you want to leave?" I asked.

"I do," Cyclops said.

"No you don't," Willie shot back. "You just say you want to, but you really want to be near Catherine." She put her fingers in her ears when he protested. "I can't hear you."

Cyclops rolled his eye. "I do want to go. I do." He focused on the contents of his glass and drank it all in one swallow.

Matt sat forward and eyed each of his friends in turn. "So nobody wants to leave?" he prompted.

Willie lifted a shoulder. "I'd like to stay longer if it were possible, but it ain't, so there ain't no point to this conversation." She finished her drink and set the glass down on the trolley. "I'm going to soak my feet in the bath, right after I tell Mrs. Potter to make me two helpings of whatever she's serving for dinner. I'm half starved."

"And I'm going to check on Miss Glass," I said, rising.

Matt followed me out. "You're having second thoughts about leaving, aren't you?" he murmured in my ear as we walked up the stairs together.

"No."

"India," he purred. "I know you're questioning our decision to leave."

I stopped on the landing and turned to face him. I took his hands in mine and made sure he was looking at me before speaking. "You're right, I don't want to leave London. This is my home, and I'm a little scared that I might never set foot here again. But I want to be with you, Matt. I'd give up anything—everything—so we can be together."

He pressed his forehead to mine. "We will come back one day. I promise you."

I did not mention my concerns for Patience. There was no point. It changed nothing. Of course I worried about hurting her, and I hated that our happiness would cause her humiliation and sorrow, but I couldn't sacrifice myself for her. I just couldn't. I wasn't selfless enough.

Yet even as I told myself that, I knew it would haunt me for some time and would leave a stain on our relationship. The more I tried to ignore thoughts of her, the more I couldn't stop thinking about her. As I lay awake, I kept picturing the way she studied the floor, how she wouldn't look at me, how her sisters bullied her. That bullying would only grow worse after Saturday.

* * *

MATT WENT out to see his lawyer in the morning, giving me the perfect opportunity to pay a call of my own in secret. I'd spent a sleepless night considering what to do and kept coming up with only one solution. I had to speak to Lord Coyle, and I had to do so without Matt's knowledge. As much as I hated lying to him, I would never forgive myself if I didn't do everything in my power to convince Lord Cox to marry Patience. The only way to do that was to use the information Lord Coyle had against him. Matt would never approve.

I told Bristow to inform the others that I had gone shopping and walked to Lord Coyle's Belgrave Square house. I almost stopped and turned back a dozen times, but something convinced me to keep going. Perhaps it was the look on Patience's face when her sisters teased her, or perhaps it was my own desire to remain in London. By the time I reached Lord Coyle's house, I'd convinced myself that I was doing the right thing. If only my stomach would stop churning.

"This is an unexpected pleasure," Lord Coyle said, greeting me in his study. It smelled of cigars and was filled with the smoke from the stub of one wedged between his fingers. He indicated I should sit. "Tea?"

"No, thank you. I can't stay long." I waited until his butler left before I sat.

Lord Coyle's ponderous features softened a little as he regarded me with curiosity. "While I'm always glad to see you, Miss Steele, I doubt you would say the same for me."

I looked down at my hands, clasping my reticule. Inside, my watch lay silent. This man was no physical threat to me. At least, I didn't think so. However, I would have liked to know if this new watch was capable of saving me, if necessary, as my old one had.

"You once told us that you had some information that could be used to convince Lord Cox to marry Matt's cousin."

He sucked on the cigar then blew out the smoke slowly, all the while watching me as if he were trying to decipher my thoughts. It was unnerving, but I managed to hold his gaze.

"The information will convince Cox to do anything," he finally said. "If you want to use it to force him to propose to one of Glass's cousins, then I'm sure it will work."

"How sure?"

"One hundred percent." He plugged the cigar back in his mouth and clasped his hands on the desktop. He leaned forward. "You are aware that the information comes at a price, Miss Steele."

"What price?"

He bit down on the cigar and his lips stretched around it in a distorted smile. "A price that I will determine at a later date."

"That isn't fair."

He removed the cigar and pointed it at the door. "If you don't agree, you're free to leave."

I clutched the reticule tighter. "I'll speak a spell into one of your clocks or watches."

He chuckled a throaty, phlegmy chuckle that ended with a cough. "No, Miss Steele. That won't be enough. Not for this information."

"An extending spell then," I blurted out before I changed my mind.

He considered it. "Perhaps. I'll let you know when the time comes for you to repay me."

"That isn't fair," I said again.

"Those are my terms, Miss Steele. You can choose to take them, and I'll tell you what you want to know about Cox, or you can leave." He put the cigar back in his mouth, crossed his arms and waited.

I drew in a deep breath and coughed as the smoke caught in my throat. If I left now, there would be no returning. We would leave England on Saturday, leaving my grandfather, and the life I knew, behind to start a new one with Matt. We would leave Oscar Barratt alone to battle a war of words with Abercrombie and the other guild masters. We would potentially be handing Abercrombie precisely what he wanted—a London without me in it.

We would also break Patience's spirit. I couldn't have that on my conscience. I couldn't be completely happy knowing we'd caused her to suffer more.

"I won't do anything illegal for you," I said. "And I won't hurt anyone."

He nodded.

"Then I agree to your terms," I said. "Tell me what you know about Lord Cox."

CHAPTER 14

"What did you buy?" Willie asked as I joined her in Miss Glass's room. They sat on the bed together, both propped up against pillows, legs outstretched. Miss Glass wore a robe over a nightgown and was covered from the waist down by blankets, whereas Willie wore her usual masculine clothes and sat on top of the blankets. She had removed her boots, at least.

"Have you been shopping, India?" Miss Glass asked. "Without me?"

"Ain't something she'd ordinarily do, eh, Letty," Willie said, her gaze narrow. She knew me too well. I rarely went shopping, let alone without company.

Thankfully I'd walked home via Piccadilly and stopped in at The Family Confectioner. The longer route had given me time to think about the information Lord Coyle had given me. I still could hardly fathom the shocking news, but his lordship had assured me it was not a joke, and his information was correct. It was so shocking, in fact, that I doubted my ability to use it against Lord Cox. How could I, a nobody, threaten to tell the world what I knew if he didn't marry Patience? What would he do?

After mulling it over, I knew the answer to that question. He'd do precisely what I asked him to do because he would not want the information becoming public. It would ruin him and change the course of his life—and the lives of his children. I wouldn't follow through on the threat lightly, and I needed time to think if it was what I really wanted to do. I couldn't visit him today. Besides, Matt and the others would be suspicious if I went out alone again.

I fished the bag of Bullseyes out of my reticule and handed it to Willie. "I bought these and some marshmallows."

She looked inside the bag and screwed up her nose. "It ain't jewelry."

"Why were you expecting me to buy jewelry?"

"No reason." She nudged Miss Glass with her elbow.

"A lady does not buy her own engagement ring," Miss Glass said stiffly.

"She does if the gen'leman ain't bought one for her."

"Matt is still engaged to Patience," I reminded them. "It would be crass for me to wear one now."

"Precisely," Miss Glass said. "You are quite correct, India." She patted the bed near her. "Off you go, Willemina. India and I need to talk."

Willie shuffled aside and popped a Bullseye in her mouth then settled back against the pillows.

Miss Glass clicked her tongue and eyed the door. Willie sighed and got up. "I'm going," she said. "But I'm taking these with me." She took the bag of sweets, picked her boots up off the floor, and left.

"Sit, India," Miss Glass said, patting the bed again.

"Is this about going away?" I asked. "Do you need advice on what to pack?"

"It's about you and Matthew." She took my hand between both of hers. "I want you to know that I give you my approval."

I stared at her a moment, then threw my arms around her. "Thank you," I whispered. "It means a lot to us."

"Not that you needed my approval."

"No, but it's nice to have." I pulled away and smiled. She smiled back, and I was relieved to see that it was genuine. She was not giving her approval because she was backed into a corner but because she wanted to give it. "Why the sudden change of heart?"

"Hardly sudden, my dear. You have been chipping away at me for some time."

"You don't think me a gold digger?"

"I never thought that, India."

"Your brother and sister-in-law do."

"Ignore them. Richard is a bully, and Beatrice has a cold heart. She wouldn't know love if it presented itself to her on a bed of rose petals. It's no wonder their daughters are all deranged. They've not experienced a moment of love their entire lives."

"I'm worried about how they'll treat me," I said. "For Matt's sake, I don't want them to belittle me or gossip about me."

She patted my hand and smiled. "It doesn't matter though, does it? You won't be here. None of us will. We'll be traveling the world, seeing glorious things, while they can molder away in that damp pile of stones they call Rycroft Hall."

I sighed. She would be most disappointed of all if we decided not to leave. "When did you change your mind about us?" I asked.

"I finally realized you two were meant for one another after Matt told me you're leaving so you can be together. Your sacrifices prove it."

"Sacrifices?"

"You're giving up the only home you've ever known for him, and he's moving away from the doctor who can save his life."

I suddenly felt cold. I hadn't thought of that. Why had I not thought of it? Matt needed to be close to Gabriel Seaford in case the watch slowed down again. My magic wasn't enough. *Why had I not thought of that?*

"India?" Miss Glass's face filled my vision. "India, you did think it through, didn't you? You and Matt must have discussed it."

A knock sounded on the door and it opened a little. Matt saw us and entered. "There you are, India." He kissed my cheek then Miss Glass's. "How are you, Aunt?"

"Well enough to get up, thank you. I don't know why you told Polly to confine me to bed. If it weren't for Willemina, I'd have been quite bored."

Matt looked at me. "You weren't here all morning, India?"

"I went out," I said. "Shopping. I bought sweets but Willie stole them." I swung my legs off the bed and got up. "I'll send Polly to help you dress, Miss Glass. And thank you. For everything."

Matt arched a brow. "What have I missed?"

"Your aunt gave us her blessing," I said.

His smile started slow then quickly broadened. "Thank you, Aunt. I knew you'd come to your senses. I'm just glad it's sooner rather than later." He kissed her forehead and made to leave with me, but she called him back.

"I need to speak with you," she said, patting the space on the bed I'd just vacated.

I left them but did not immediately go in search of Polly. I stood with my back to Miss Glass's door, clutching the handle. She was right. All doubts I had about blackmailing Lord Cox into marrying Patience were banished in the moment she reminded me about Gabe.

As long as he lived here, Matt could not leave London.

* * *

MATT, Duke, Cyclops, Willie and I were in the process of considering our next move in the investigation when Oscar Barratt arrived with news.

"A new editor has been appointed," he said, peering through the library window. "A fellow by the name of Pelham." He glanced up and down the street before finally moving into the room. Instead of sitting, however, he paced from one side of the library to the other. As if the signs weren't telling enough, he also wrung his hands. Poor Oscar was at the end of his tether.

"What do you know of him?" Matt asked.

"This is the interesting part," Oscar said, pausing only long enough to stamp his hands on his hips. "He was the editor of *The Morning Chronicle*. Delancey owns a share of it."

"Delancey!" I cried.

"That's it," Willie said, slapping her hand on the chair arm. "He's the killer. Must be."

Oscar shook his head. "Not necessarily. *I* received the threatening letters, not Baggley. *I* was supposed to die that night." He resumed pacing. "The editor's position shouldn't have become vacant, but when it unexpectedly did, Delancey took advantage of the situation and put in his own man. That's my theory, anyway. Pelham has already told me I can't write any more articles. I'm sure that's Delancey's influence."

"Good," Matt said.

Oscar scowled at him without breaking stride. "I'll publish them somewhere else. Interest in magic is extremely high. Another paper will take them. I'm on my way to meet with an editor now." He paused by the mantel and tapped the clock face.

"It's working perfectly well," I told him. "Why don't you sit down, Oscar? You'll wear the carpet out."

"Not to mention my neck," Duke said, rubbing it.

Oscar perched on the edge of a chair, looking as if he'd spring up at any moment. "So what's next, Glass? Where is your investigation at?"

"It's worth speaking to Delancey in light of what you just told us," Matt said.

Oscar waited, but when Matt said nothing more, he threw his hands in the air. "So you have nothing." He pushed to his feet and once again paced the room. "You don't care, do you? You're happy the new editor is stopping my articles."

"You think I'm happy that Baggley died?" Matt growled. "If I was going to use violence to stop you writing articles, I would have done so by now. My fists don't miss and hit the wrong man."

Oscar finally stopped pacing. He stood by the fireplace and crossed his arms. "Speak to Delancey if you want, but it won't help. Baggley was never meant to die. I was. Delancey merely took advantage of the vacancy to put his puppet in."

"There is something else we know about Delancey, as it happens," I said. "He gave Mr. Hendry a loan after the banks refused to lend him any money because he's a magician. His debts have also been called in, leaving him rather desperate."

Oscar shrugged. "How does that make Delancey guilty of my murder?"

"*You* ain't been murdered," Cyclops said.

"Yet," Willie added with a cool edge to her voice.

Oscar's eyes widened and he took a step away from her.

"Hendry's bankers and creditors somehow learned that he's a magician," Matt said.

"How?"

"We don't know, but if the banks aren't loaning him any more money because he's a magician, it stands to reason that any other known magicians will have a similar problem. And aside from India's grandfather, you only named yourself in your articles—and your brother by association. In light of that, it's interesting to note that Isaac also went to Delancey for a private loan."

Oscar went still. "He did?"

"Perhaps that's why he came to London," I said. "To speak with his bank after they stopped doing business with him."

"When they refused to loan him more money, he went to Delancey," Matt finished.

"He could also have come to kill the source of the articles," Willie said with an apologetic shrug.

Oscar strode up to her, fists clenched at his sides. "My brother is not a killer! For God's sake, he'll hit me but he won't shoot me."

Matt shot to his feet and pulled Oscar away. Willie hadn't looked concerned for her safety but she had also clenched her fists. Oscar jerked free of Matt's grip and rounded his shoulders.

Matt didn't back away. "Find out if your brother's usual bank refused to loan him more money. I want to know by tomorrow."

"Why tomorrow?" Oscar asked.

"This is dragging on too long. Willie, I want you to watch Delancey. Duke and Cyclops, follow the new editor, Pelham. I want to know where he lives, who he associates with, and if he seems to have more money than a newspaper editor ought. Anything that looks suspicious."

The three of them filed out, and Oscar also indicated he had to go.

"I have a meeting in thirty minutes," he said.

"I think you should reconsider trying to sell your articles to other papers," I told him gently. "It's wiser to lie low for a while. At least until we've caught the murderer."

"Or it might flush him out into the open again."

"Are you mad?"

"Why not just paint a target on your back?" Matt said with a shake of his head.

Oscar pointed a finger at Matt's face. "If you were doing your job, I wouldn't have to resort to desperate measures. Find the killer, Glass, before it's too late."

"Stop it, Oscar," I snapped. "We're doing our best."

"Might I remind you that we're doing this gratis?" Matt said

Oscar grunted.

"Consider India's suggestion of lying low," Matt went on. "It's the sensible thing to do."

Oscar squared up to him, puffing out his chest. "You'd like that, wouldn't you? You've never wanted me to write the truth about magic. This has all worked out perfectly for you. Typical. Men like you and my brother always get what they want at the expense of the rest of us."

"You'd better go," Matt said, his jaw hard. "Before I'm tempted to escort you out."

Oscar put his hands in the air in surrender and backed away. "I think I liked you better when you were sick."

Matt opened the library door, and Bristow saw Oscar out of the house. Oscar hesitated on the top step, checking the vicinity, before striding purposefully to the waiting cab.

"He's anxious," Matt said as Bristow shut the front door.

"That's no excuse for the way he spoke to you just now," I said. "Or the way he threatened Willie."

"Agreed." He rubbed my arms. "Are you all right, India?"

"Fine. What do we do now?"

"We wait for Willie, Cyclops or Duke to report back."

"Then let's have an early lunch with your aunt."

* * *

WE DIDN'T HAVE to wait long for the first report. Willie returned as we finished our lunch with details of Delancey's movements. "He met with Hendry at the shop," she said, plucking a sandwich off the platter. "I saw them arguing through the window and then Delancey left. Hendry looked upset." She shoved the entire sandwich in her mouth, much to Miss Glass's disgust.

"Then we'll pay Delancey a visit." Matt rose and held his hand out to me. "Did he go home or to the bank?"

Willie managed to say, "Home," despite a mouth full of sandwich.

It wasn't long before we were once again visiting the Delancey's house. Although we asked to see Mr. Delancey, it was Mrs. Delancey who greeted us in the drawing room.

"India, dearest, how lovely to see you again." She kissed my cheek and greeted Matt politely if not effusively. "Sit, sit. My husband will join us shortly. You just caught him. He came home for luncheon but he must go back to the bank. Ah, here he is. Darling, I was just about to ask India if she'd like to dine with us this evening. You will, won't you, India?"

"I'm afraid I can't," I said. "We have other plans." The lie rolled effortlessly off my tongue, and I didn't feel the least guilty. I'd had quite enough of Mrs. Delancey and her ilk for a while.

"Perhaps next week," she said. "That'll give me more time to ask some friends. Shall we say Tuesday evening?"

I nodded, unsure how to get out of it a second time. Perhaps I could plead ill on the day, assuming I was still in London. I caught Matt watching me closely and turned my attention to Mr. Delancey.

"You were seen arguing with Mr. Hendry, the paper magician, earlier today," I said. "What about?"

He looked taken aback by my direct question. "It's a private matter."

"Please answer Miss Steele," Matt said.

Mr. Delancey bristled. "Why should I?"

"Because you're a suspect in the murder of Mr. Baggley, and not cooperating will make you look guilty."

Mrs. Delancey gasped. "A suspect? India, how *could* you? After everything I've done for you?"

"I rather think I've done more for you than you have for me," I shot back. Her stunned silence gave me a small measure of satisfaction. "Mr. Delancey, I'm sure you'd like to clear your name, so please answer honestly. We know you loaned Mr. Hendry money."

Delancey turned a frosty gaze onto his wife. She swallowed and took great interest in her hands, folded in her lap.

"Have you retracted the loan?" I went on. "Is that why you argued?"

"Yes," he said.

Mrs. Delancey shook her head at her husband. "Oh, you *didn't*, did you? Honestly, Ferdinand."

"Why the change of heart?" I asked.

Mr. Delancey crossed his arms and legs. "That is none of your business."

"That poor man," his wife said. "Just when he needs us the most, we abandon him."

"I don't do private business with that sort of man," her husband hissed at her. "I'm sorry, my dear, but you know my thoughts on that."

"I didn't before," she said with a sniff, "but I do now. If I had known you'd be this horrid about it, I wouldn't have told you."

"Told him what?" Matt asked.

Mrs. Delancey arched her brows at her husband.

He uncrossed then re-crossed his legs. "I don't do business with his sort," he repeated.

"Magicians?" I asked, rather stupidly.

"Murderers?" Matt suggested.

When he didn't answer, Mrs. Delancey spoke instead. "Men who like other men."

Ah. I had wondered if Mr. Hendry preferred men to women, but it seemed irrelevant to the investigation so I had not mentioned it to Matt. He didn't look shocked either, so I suspected he'd also guessed.

"So?" Matt said.

"It's not natural," Mr. Delancey muttered. "Men like that disgust me. I'd rather not have a stake in his business. I'd rather not have anything to do with him. I think we should get our stationery made elsewhere, too."

"No!" Mrs. Delancey cried. "Certainly not. He is the best, and I want only the best paper. Besides, he's a magician. I don't care what else he is."

"Well *I* do."

"Honestly," she muttered. "Where are your priorities? It's not as if he finds *you* attractive."

Her husband's face flushed crimson.

I looked to Matt, catching him trying hard not to smile. "How did you learn about his, er, preference for men?" I asked.

"My wife informed me only this morning," Mr. Delancey grumbled. "Even though she found out some time ago."

"I went to sample some new card stock a little while ago, and I saw Mr. Hendry with another man through his shop window," Mrs. Delancey said. "They weren't doing anything overt, if you understand my meaning. It was simply the way they stood with one another, the way their bodies were angled, their hands close but not touching. Their smiles were secretive, too, and rather sweet. Ordinary men do not smile at each other like that. I could tell they were lovers."

Her husband made a sound of disgust in his throat.

"Can you describe the other man?" Matt asked.

"Slight of build, well dressed, handsome. I passed him as I entered the shop and couldn't help noticing his lovely blue eyes and an unfortunate nervous twitch here." She touched her top lip.

Sweeney.

"Thank you," Matt said, rising and buttoning his jacket.

Mrs. Delancey rang for a footman to show us the way out. "You will come next week for dinner, India dear," she said as we waited.

I nodded and wished I had the nerve to refuse her to her face.

The footman arrived and indicated we should walk ahead of him.

"I wish you'd told me before today about that fellow," Mr. Delancey mumbled to his wife as we were leaving. "You could have saved me the trouble of retracting the loan today. It was a most unpleasant scene. I hope none of his neighbors thought we were arguing over something of a more personal nature."

"No one will think that," his wife bit off. "He prefers handsome young men."

Matt directed our driver to Hendry's shop. "We're not visiting Sweeney?" I asked as we settled into the carriage.

"I think we should check on Hendry, first," Matt said. "The last time we saw him, he was anxious and a little irrational. This setback must be a blow."

I sidled closer to him and took his hand. "It's good of you to worry about him."

"Don't make me out to be a saint, India. I'm also hoping to get some answers."

"To which questions?"

"To the question of Sweeney's guilt in the murder of Baggley."

"You think Sweeney did it?"

He shrugged. "I don't know. Something isn't quite right." He flipped my hand over and drew circles on my palm with his thumb. "For instance, if Hendry and Sweeney were lovers who fell out over Hendry being a magician, what led Sweeney to want to murder Oscar Barratt? Wouldn't he want to murder Hendry?"

"Perhaps they didn't fall out over Hendry being a magician but something more personal. Jealousy, perhaps."

Matt laughed. "Perhaps Oscar Barratt is the other man in the equation."

"He isn't."

Matt's laughter suddenly died. He twisted to see me better. "How can you be so sure?"

"Because Oscar looks at me in a certain way."

His eyes darkened. "What way?"

"In a way that neither Mr. Hendry nor Mr. Sweeney have looked at me."

He grunted. "Fine. So Barratt isn't the reason they fell out. Then why try to kill him?"

"To stop the articles?" I said on a sigh. "But you're right. I don't think Sweeney discovering that Hendry is a magician is a good enough reason to suddenly kill someone else. I also don't think jealousy is behind this. Mr. Sweeney seems quite alone, and I'm not a relationship expert, but I do think Mr. Hendry still cares for him."

Matt considered this with a slow nod. "You might be right. We'll ask him."

"Do you think it wise to simply ask him these things directly? Their relationship is very personal, not to mention illegal."

"Then you must employ your charms on him, India."

"I don't think those will work." I patted his cheek. "You try."

He gave me a lopsided grin. "I suppose I am more his type."

"Matt, you're everybody's type."

* * *

MR. HENDRY LOOKED as if he would cry when he saw us enter his shop. "Why can't you leave me alone?" he whined.

"Because you are our chief suspect in the murder of Mr. Baggley," I told him.

"Me?" He shook his head in rapid, jerky movements. "I didn't murder anyone. Th—the gun." He indicated the shelf behind the counter with a shaking hand. "It was put there by someone else. I gave you his description. You should be looking for him."

"We gave the gun to the police," I said.

His shoulders slumped as he rounded the counter. "Then I suppose I can expect a visit from them soon."

Matt rested a hand on Mr. Hendry's shoulder. "We've come about another matter," he said gently. "A delicate matter."

Mr. Hendry frowned and plucked Matt's hand off. I bit back my smile. "What matter?" Mr. Hendry asked.

"About your private life. With Patrick Sweeney."

Mr. Hendry backed away, bumping into the counter. "I—I don't like your implication."

Matt followed him and stood a little closer than necessary. "Don't be anxious. You can talk to us. We don't care who you're in a relationship with, we only care about solving this crime."

Mr. Hendry swallowed loudly. "Go away."

Matt rested a hand on the counter.

Mr. Hendry slipped along the counter in the opposite direction. "I said *go away*. I've got nothing more to say to you. Go and find the real murderer and leave me alone." He lifted the counter hatch and stepped through, slamming the hatch back into place.

"We know you still care about him," Matt went on.

Tears welled in Mr. Hendry's eyes. "Leave me alone! I've got nothing to say to you."

Matt and I did as asked and left. "Do you call that flirting?" I said as he assisted me into the carriage.

"I'm out of practice. Besides, I only want to flirt with you. It doesn't feel right flirting with someone else."

"You must learn to set aside your principles if you want to get anywhere in this investigation business," I teased.

He ordered the driver to continue on to Sweeney's factory and sat alongside me in the cabin. He kissed the skin below my ear. "I think I need a more thorough lesson in investigative technique," he murmured. "Will you teach me?"

His lips tickled and I giggled and squirmed. Next thing I knew, I was being thoroughly and completely kissed.

* * *

Mr. Sweeney's assistant told us we would find him at the Stationers' Hall. Unfortunately, the porter there not only knew us but had been warned to keep us out. He watched as we retreated to the carriage and slammed the door. Instead of leaving, we waited.

We occupied our time with talk of our plans to leave London. Or rather, Matt talked, and I listened. He told me of all the places on the continent he wanted to take me, and he listed reasons for and against living in each city he'd visited before. I was glad he didn't expect me to contribute more to the conversation than a nod here and there, because I wasn't sure I could lie to him very well. My heart wasn't in the discussion, knowing we wouldn't leave. We couldn't leave.

An hour and eight minutes passed before Mr. Sweeney finally emerged from the hall. He slapped on his hat, spoke to the porter, and headed off up the street. Once the porter closed the door, we followed Sweeney on foot. We waited until we were out of sight of the hall's windows before we hailed him.

He stopped and, upon seeing us, groaned. "What do you want?" he snapped.

"To ask you a few questions," Matt said.

"This is harassment."

"This is nothing compared to how the police will treat you if we tell them what we know."

Mr. Sweeney's throat worked but no words came out.

Matt filled the void. "We know about your relationship with Hendry."

Mr. Sweeney bristled. "You're mistaken, sir, and your implication disgusts me."

"You were seen together," I said.

Mr. Sweeney's eyes widened. Then he turned and marched off. "This is outrageous. Slanderous. I'll be speaking to my lawyer."

"Is your relationship the reason why you were so angry when Mr. Hendry told you he's a magician?" Matt pressed, easily keeping up. I had to lift my skirts and trot a few paces behind them.

"I don't know what you're talking about."

"Were you in love with Mr. Hendry and felt he'd betrayed you by keeping it from you until those articles were printed?"

He stopped again and rounded on Matt. "What does your accusation have to do with the murder? Why would I kill anyone at the newspaper? What has my falling out with Hendry got to do with it? I don't like the articles but I'm no murderer. As to your suggestion of love, it's laughable. There's no such thing as love, particularly of *that* kind." He strode off again, his steps quick, his back straight.

Matt went to follow him but I caught his hand. "Let him go."

We returned to the carriage and asked the driver to take us home. "Interesting reaction," Matt said as we pulled away from the curb. "Very interesting."

"In what way?" I asked.

"I believe him when he says he doesn't believe in love. I don't know why, I just do. I don't think he cares about Hendry at all."

What that might mean for Sweeney's guilt or otherwise in the murder, neither of us could fathom.

* * *

MATT and I were about to sit down to dinner when Detective Inspector Brockwell arrived. He greeted us with his usual briskness then sucked in a deep breath, swelling his chest.

"Something smells good," he said.

"We're about to dine," Matt told him.

"I am sorry. I'll return later."

"Please stay." I indicated to Bristow to take Brockwell's hat and coat. "Join us for dinner. It's only Matt and me, tonight. His aunt is dining in her room and our friends are out."

"Well, that would be a pleasure." His cheeks flushed pink. "Thank you, Miss Steele, you're very kind. I don't get to dine at fine houses like this too often."

"Then you're in for a treat. Mrs. Potter is a marvelous cook."

"If the delicious smells emanating from the kitchen are anything to go by, then I already agree."

I hooked my arm through Brockwell's and escorted him to dinner. "Coming, Matt?" I asked over my shoulder.

"Oh, I'm invited, am I?" he said with a crooked smile.

Bristow answered a knock at the door, and Matt stayed to see who it was. Bristow accepted a note from the messenger and handed it to Matt. Matt's scowl deepened as he read. I resisted the urge to ask, and instead I directed Brockwell to sit at the long table. I sent Peter off to fetch more silverware, to make another place, and sat opposite Brockwell. I had to lean to the side to see past the vase of lovely roses. He stood and moved the vase aside then sat again.

"Better." He smiled at me.

Matt took his seat at the head of the table. The note was nowhere in sight but the scowl was still in place, although he directed it at the roses. "To what do we owe this visit?" he asked Brockwell.

"All in good time," I said. "Let the inspector enjoy his first glass of wine before you demand answers."

Matt's eyes tightened.

Bristow poured the wine and melted away into the background as Peter returned and set another place. Brockwell seemed uncomfortable; no doubt being waited on felt strange. I understood completely.

"Are you working late this evening?" I asked him.

"I do most nights," he said. "If not at the office then at home. It keeps me occupied. A bachelor's life can be rather dull."

"Then you must dine with us more often. Don't you agree, Matt?"

Matt lowered his glass to the table. "Most definitely. India and I are very fortunate to have your company tonight, Inspector. We would have been quite alone otherwise." He lifted his glass in salute and drank.

It was my turn to scowl at him, but unfortunately he wasn't looking at me.

"How is your health?" Brockwell asked Matt.

"Fine."

Brockwell eyed the footman and butler and lifted his brows. Matt gave a slight shake of his head. There would be no conversation about magic until the servants left. Unfortunately, that left us with little in common to talk about. I tried to engage the inspector with other topics, but he admitted to reading few novels and rarely attending the theater. That left us with current events that did not involve magic.

I was rather glad when we retired to the drawing room and Matt finally dismissed the servants.

"I'm afraid we can't smoke in here," Matt said. "My aunt prefers it to be confined to the smoking room.

"That's all right, I'm not much of a smoker anyway." Brockwell eased himself into one of the chairs, looking rather satisfied as he patted his stomach. "Dinner was grand. Your cook is indeed a marvel. Thank you for having me."

I waited for Matt to say something. When he didn't, I said, "Our pleasure."

"So what do you have to report?" Matt asked as he poured brandies. "Any news on the weapon?"

"It was the same type as that used in the murder," Brockwell said.

Matt stopped pouring. "Interesting."

"I spoke to Hendry this afternoon. You two had just been there, as it happens. He was in a state over it and demanded I make you stop pestering him, as he put it."

"We won't stop," Matt said. "Our investigation is a private matter."

"And I have no authority to force you to stop. At least, that's what I told Hendry."

Matt gave him a nod of thanks.

"Do you want to know what we learned?" I asked Brockwell.

"That's why I'm here, Miss Steele, although I will admit the prospect of your pleasant company lured me too." He smiled warmly. "Of course, if Glass weren't engaged to his cousin, I would never dream of intruding on a private dinner. Happily for me, he is."

Matt stepped between us and handed Brockwell the tumbler of brandy. "We learned that Hendry was...very good friends with Sweeney, master of the Stationers' Guild. They are no longer friends."

Brockwell showed no surprise. "I know."

"What did *you* find out from your conversation with Hendry, Inspector?" I asked as Matt handed me a glass.

"Very little. As I said, he was upset about you calling on him incessantly."

"Hardly incessantly," Matt countered.

"He listed the dates and times of all your visits. There were quite a number of them." Brockwell put up his hand to halt Matt's protests. "I agree, it was perhaps necessary, considering the letters to Mr. Barratt were on his paper and the gun was found in his shop. Speaking of which, I questioned him about it this afternoon, and it's my belief that he lied to you about how the gun came to be in his possession. I think he knew who put it there, and it's not Abercrombie."

"Why do you say so?" I asked.

"He acted suspiciously when I confronted him. He wouldn't meet my gaze and he wouldn't stand still. Both are classic signs of a poor liar. When I told him his false description could see an innocent man arrested, he broke down. He didn't admit it, of course, but he changed his story and claimed he couldn't recall what the man looked like."

"Blast," I muttered. "I thought we had proof of Abercrombie's involvement, although I did doubt that he pulled the trigger himself. He's too cowardly to do that."

Matt pulled out a piece of paper from his inside jacket pocket and handed it to me. "This arrived before dinner. It proves Brockwell's theory about Abercrombie's innocence."

The note was from the clockmaker in Abercrombie's workshop who'd told us his master had received Mr. Sweeney on Friday, the day the gun had been placed in Hendry's shop. According to the clockmaker, he'd remembered incorrectly and the day had in fact been Thursday, not Friday. He went on to explain why he'd made the mistake.

"Do you think this is the truth or has Abercrombie learned that we spoke to him?" I asked Matt as I passed the note to Brockwell.

"Impossible to know for sure, but if the inspector believes

Hendry lied and gave a false description, I'm inclined to believe the note."

Brockwell passed the note back to Matt. "So if it wasn't Abercrombie who left the gun in Hendry's shop, who did?"

"Sweeney?" I offered. "Perhaps Hendry realized it was him and wanted to protect him from our inquiries. If he still has feelings for Sweeney, he wouldn't want to make trouble for him."

"Or it could be Hendry himself," Matt said.

"Either way," Brockwell said, "I owe you an apology, Glass. And Miss Steele, too. I believe now that this crime *is* related to magic. Hendry is in up to his neck, and he's a magician, and Barratt is the author of those articles. That makes it a sensitive case." He sighed. "My superiors will not like it."

"Then tell Commissioner Munro to speak with me," Matt said. "We'll find a way to word it so that the press can't link the murder to magic."

"I can do that myself." Brockwell finished his drink and stood. "I must go. Thank you again for a delicious dinner. Miss Steele." He bent over my hand, lightly brushing his lips against my knuckles. "It has been delightful, as always. If I may be so bold, may I ask if I can call on you soon? In a personal capacity. And without your employer here."

I tried to think of the best answer in order to be polite yet not encouraging and found my tongue wouldn't work.

Matt came to my rescue. "Stop by any day after Saturday."

I pressed my lips together to suppress my smile.

Bristow escorted Brockwell out, and Matt rejoined me. He plucked the glass from my fingers and pulled me out of the chair. He pressed close, assuming a waltzing position, and swayed with me. I leaned into him and breathed deeply, relaxing into the rhythm, relishing the feel of being so close.

"That was torturous," he murmured into my hair.

"It wasn't too bad," I said. "And we did learn something."

"Even if he told us who the killer was, I would still rather he hadn't stayed for dinner." He let go of my hand and circled both arms around my waist. I tilted my head up so I could see him better. "Tonight was supposed to be just you and me."

"Oh. Is that why your aunt stayed in her room?"

"I asked her to."

"And the flowers on the table. Oh, Matt, they were lovely. I'm sorry, I didn't realize. You should have told me, and I wouldn't have asked Brockwell to stay."

"It doesn't matter." From his heavy tone, it sounded like it mattered very much.

We danced slowly together in the silence until Duke and Cyclops interrupted us. They had nothing of interest to report and happily tucked into the left over food. Willie arrived twenty minutes later and helped herself to the cold meat and salads from the tray Bristow brought in for her.

"How was your evening?" Willie asked brightly. "Did we miss anything?"

Matt sat quietly and stared into the fireplace. He managed to give me a wan smile when I squeezed his arm but he didn't answer her.

"Brockwell dined with us," I said.

She pulled a face. "So your night was as exciting as mine."

"What did he want?" Duke asked.

"To tell us the gun we found in Hendry's shop was the same type as that used in the murder."

"So Hendry's the killer?" Cyclops asked.

"Perhaps," I said. "Or someone really did hide it in his shop, perhaps even to implicate him."

"Abercrombie," Duke said, shoveling lettuce into his mouth.

I shook my head. "It wasn't him."

"So now what?" Willie asked. "Confront Hendry and accuse him?"

"Or ask him who he's protecting," Matt said. "My money's on Sweeney."

"He won't admit it, if he is," I said. "Not if he still cares for Sweeney."

One side of Matt's mouth lifted. "He'll admit it. Just leave the questioning to me."

CHAPTER 15

Mr. Hendry's shop was closed, and despite our knocks, he did not answer.

"I wonder why he's not open today," I said as we drove off. "It's mid-week."

"Wait!" Matt thumped on the cabin ceiling and the driver pulled to a stop. "I saw the upstairs curtain flutter. He's home."

"He won't open the door to us," I said, following him back to the shop.

"Then we won't go through the door. Not the front one, anyway."

"We can't break into his shop!"

"We can if we're concerned for his wellbeing. Indeed, we should. It's our duty as his acquaintances." He took my hand and we raced to the laneway.

"No wonder you got into so much trouble in America," I said, pressing my hand to my hat to stop it falling off.

"Excepting Payne, the law loves me in America."

"As much as our police do here?"

"Brockwell only dislikes me because I'm in his way to get to you." He pushed open a gate off the back lane to reveal a courtyard filled with potato sacks and crates.

I kicked one of the sacks. It wasn't filled with potatoes. More likely it carried the rags that Hendry used to make his paper.

Matt went to work on the lock and had the back door open before I even joined him. He entered but I didn't dare.

"Hendry!" he called out. "Hendry, it's us, Miss Steele and Matthew Glass. We've come to check on you."

Well, since he announced himself, I supposed it was all right to enter. I followed him into the workshop. "We're worried about you and thought you might need company," I called out. I wished I'd brought a pie or some of Mrs. Potter's cakes. Food would lend more authenticity to our visit.

Mr. Hendry was not at all quiet and we heard his footsteps coming down the steps well before he appeared in the workshop. "How dare you!" he shouted. "I'm fetching a constable."

"Don't do that," Matt urged. "We only want to talk."

"I'm not interested in talking to you. That detective was here yesterday, and he assured me he'd warn you to stay away."

"So we heard. Detective Inspector Brockwell dined with us last night."

Mr. Hendry's face fell. I understood how hopeless he must feel, how powerless and alone. If Brockwell was on our side, he really had no way of getting rid of us.

I pushed past Matt and approached Mr. Hendry. It was dull in the workroom without any lamps lit, but I could clearly see his red, swollen eyes. "You haven't slept well, have you?"

He turned his face away. "Please leave."

"I don't think that's wise. Let's have a cup of tea and talk. We need to tell you something."

His gaze snapped back to mine. "What is it? What's happened?"

"We know you lied about the man who left the gun here," Matt said.

Mr. Hendry's face went blank. He stared straight ahead, his face expressionless. Then he burst into tears.

I glared at Matt. He blinked back, looking somewhat lost.

I steered Mr. Hendry to the chair by the bench and urged him to sit. He followed my instructions as if he were an automaton winding down. His crying eased and stopped altogether when Matt held out his handkerchief. Mr. Hendry paused before taking it and dabbing at his eyes.

"Was Mr. Abercrombie even here that day?" I asked gently.

Mr. Hendry studied the handkerchief, his head lowered. "No."

"So why implicate him?"

"I don't like him. He turned Patrick against me."

"Patrick Sweeney?"

He nodded. "If it weren't for him..." He lifted one shoulder and didn't finish.

"While I certainly understand why you dislike Mr. Abercrombie enough to implicate him in the murder, it hasn't helped our investigation."

"I'm sorry." He wiped his eyes again then offered the handkerchief to Matt.

"Keep it," Matt said.

Mr. Hendry gave him a watery smile. "Thank you."

Matt moved a wooden box mold aside and sat on the bench near Hendry. "Who put the gun on your shelf?"

"I don't know."

"You have a suspicion, though."

Mr. Hendry shook his head.

"It was Sweeney, wasn't it?"

Mr. Hendry swallowed. "I don't know."

"But you suspect him," I said. "As do we."

He looked away. "I've told you everything I know."

"That may be the case," Matt said, "but you haven't told us everything. So let me encourage you."

Mr. Hendry grunted. "Impossible."

Matt stretched out his legs and crossed them at the ankles. He leaned forward, close to Mr. Hendry, and said, "Sweeney told the banks about your magical abilities."

Mr. Hendry looked away.

"He also informed your creditors," Matt went on. "He's the reason your debts were called in. He's the reason the bank won't lend you more money."

Mr. Hendry nibbled his lower lip but didn't seem shocked by the news.

"You have the power to make life difficult for him," Matt went on. "We know you suspect him of the murder. We know you're protecting him. We just want to know why you think he tried to kill Oscar Barratt. We can't find a motive."

Mr. Hendry swallowed. "Do you have proof he told my creditors?"

"Indirectly."

I didn't like that Matt made it seem as if we did indeed have some proof when we only had our suspicions. I changed my mind, however, when Mr. Hendry gave a faint nod. In this instance, the ends justified the means. We would get nowhere in our investigation if Hendry continued to protect Sweeney.

"You're right," he said as fresh tears filled his eyes. "I do think he's guilty, and I have been protecting him." He huffed out a humorless laugh. "Or I was trying to. I did a poor job of it. You knew I lied; the detective inspector knew I lied."

"Had you seen the gun before the day we found it?" I asked.

He shook his head. "That was the first time, but I remembered Patrick coming here soon after the murder. I caught him near those shelves. He was empty handed. I just assumed he wanted to talk, but he made up some excuse and left."

"He set you up to take the blame."

He nodded, and his face crumpled. I rubbed his shoulder and waited for his tears to abate.

"I'd told him about the letters I wrote to Barratt," he went on, his chin wobbling. "I made it easy for him."

"So you did send the letters."

He nodded. "But I didn't try to kill him—or anyone else."

"We never thought you did," I assured him.

He sniffed. "Thank you, Miss Steele."

"But you believe Sweeney is the killer," Matt said. "Why are you protecting him?"

"Why do you think?"

"Love," I said on a sigh. "It makes us do mad things."

Matt frowned at me.

"I thought Patrick loved me," Mr. Hendry said. "But now... How could he betray me? He's trying to ruin me financially."

"And get you arrested for the murder," Matt added.

Mr. Hendry sobbed into the handkerchief. "He's conflicted over his feelings for me. I know he's had difficulty accepting our relationship. He despised himself for having feelings for me. Perhaps that self-loathing is making him want to hurt me. He wants to punish me, to blame me. I'm not mad at him. How can I be when...?" He broke down and deposited more tears into Matt's handkerchief.

Matt looked at me and indicated I should do something. I mouthed, "What?" and he merely shrugged.

I crouched beside Mr. Hendry and patted his arm. When his tears finally subsided again, I asked, "Why does Mr. Sweeney want to kill Mr. Barratt? To stop him writing the articles?"

Mr. Hendry nodded.

"Then that's something," I said hopefully. "He's worried about how the public will treat magicians. He's worried about you."

"I would like to think so, but..." His face fell. "I think it has more to do with his investments."

"Investments?" Matt echoed, leaning forward. "What investments?"

"Patrick invested heavily in a paper manufacturer after he learned that I was a magician. The company is my closest competitor, producing high quality paper and card stock but without magic. He made a point of coming here and telling me, and he said he'll make sure the company flourishes while I fail."

That certainly wasn't the act of a man in love, not even one who couldn't come to terms with his emotions. That was an act of pure spite.

"He was so angry when I told him I was a magician," Mr. Hendry went on. "If he loved me, he would accept me for what I am." He lifted his watery gaze to Matt. "Wouldn't he, Mr. Glass?"

"Yes," Matt said. "He would."

We escorted Mr. Hendry up to his rooms above the shop, and I made him a cup of tea. Clutching the cup in both hands, he seemed calmer, although misery was etched into every line on his face.

"What happens now?" he asked in a small voice.

"We warn Oscar Barratt to be careful of any man matching Sweeney's description," I said.

"And inform the police," Matt added.

Mr. Hendry clutched the cup to his chest and stared at the tea. "I've sent Patrick to his death."

"You mustn't think like that," I said. "He would have been caught anyway. It was only a matter of time."

"We'll make sure he never finds out that you spoke to us," Matt said. "We'll look for other evidence to give to Detective Inspector Brockwell that won't involve informing him of your relationship."

"Thank you," Mr. Hendry mumbled. "But it's on my conscience now, and I must learn to live with it."

We left him to his troubled thoughts and returned to the carriage. Matt gave the driver instructions to take us to *The Weekly Gazette's* office.

"Sweeney told us he had no stake in this matter," Matt said as we took off at a brisk pace. "He led us to believe he didn't care what was written about magic, since the publishing industry doesn't have any magicians."

"He didn't mention his investment," I said. "He must have thoroughly hated Hendry to want to use his investment to ruin him."

Matt's fingers drummed on the windowsill. "What I still don't understand is how Sweeney thought killing *Barratt* would stop the articles and save his investment. Baggley could simply assign another journalist to take over."

"What if Baggley was the intended target after all?"

His gaze locked with mine and his fingers stilled. He considered my question for a moment then his fingers started up again. "He couldn't have known the replacement editor would be against the articles."

"Are you suggesting Sweeney didn't do it? That stopping the articles isn't the killer's motive?"

"No, I think he did it, but we're missing something. If we can't uncover what it is, we'll have to break our promise to Hendry and tell Brockwell he convinced us of Sweeney's guilt."

That would devastate Mr. Hendry. He was at his wits' end, and I didn't want to cause him any more suffering. "Sweeney is horrid. He's full of spite. I cannot believe he'd hate poor Mr. Hendry so much that he tried to have him blamed for the murder, as well as trying to ruin him financially."

"I tend to agree with Hendry. Sweeney hates himself for his involvement with Hendry. He thinks getting rid of Hendry will cure him or absolve him in some way. Self-loathing can make a person do terrible things to others. I've seen it before."

We spent most of the remainder of the journey in silence, but just before we arrived, Matt said, "I think you're right, India."

"About everything or something in particular?"

"I'd be a fool to say everything this early in our relationship."

"But a happy fool."

His lips twitched but he didn't break into a smile. "I was referring to Barratt not being the intended victim after all. Considering there have been no more attempts on his life, I think it's safe to say Baggley was meant to die that night."

"And perhaps Pelham was meant to replace him. That points to Delancey being the killer, though, not Sweeney." I rubbed my forehead. "Perhaps we're wrong about him, Matt. We can't accuse Sweeney without more evidence."

The carriage pulled to a stop outside the *Gazette's* office and he opened the door. "So let's find it."

We found Oscar at his desk, head lowered, his fingers buried in his hair. He'd re-arranged the furniture to ensure he wasn't sitting with his back to the window. From his position against the far wall, he could see both window and door if he looked up.

Matt's knock on the open door made Oscar jump.

"Oh, it's just you two. Come in." He looked like he hadn't slept a wink.

"Is everything all right?" I asked as I sat.

"Fine. Everything's fine. My brother wants to punch me every time he sees me, someone wants to kill me, and no newspapers will touch my articles on magic. So yes, everything's perfect, India, thanks for asking."

"Don't speak to her that way," Matt growled.

Oscar slumped back in the chair with a heavy sigh. "I'm sorry. I'm not at my best, at the moment."

"Then allow us to take one of your troubles away," I said. "We don't think you were the intended victim after all."

His brows shot up. "Truly?"

I nodded. "There have been no more attempts on your life."

His sighed again. "The killer may be lying low for a while."

"Or Baggley had to be removed so that another editor could replace him, someone who doesn't want to publish articles about magic. Someone you can't persuade."

"Then…Delancey is the killer? Pelham worked for one of his other papers." Oscar sprang up. "It must be him!"

"Sit down," Matt said. "It might not be Delancey. He was dining with us when the murder occurred."

"He could have paid someone."

"Or he's not the murderer."

Oscar sat again and pulled the inkstand closer. He dipped the pen in the ink pot and wrote Delancey's name on a notepad. "Writing in ink helps me think," he said, making notes beside the name. "Do you know, all the other newspapers I approached are refusing to even talk to me? My meeting yesterday was canceled. My letters are being returned unopened. It's a concerted effort to block me and my articles." He no longer spoke in harried, angry tones, and sounded calmer. Working with his magical element must soothe him as working with timepieces soothed me.

"Who do you think is orchestrating the campaign against you?" Matt asked.

"Delancey, in light of what you've just told me."

I opened my mouth to tell him our thoughts on Sweeney, but Matt spoke first. "Might I remind you that your brother was seen visiting Delancey."

Oscar's head jerked up. "I've told you, my brother wouldn't try to kill me."

"But we've just told you we don't think you were the intended victim."

Oscar's pen formed a blob of ink on the paper. "He's not a murderer."

"Did you ask him if he got a loan from Delancey?" I asked.

Oscar nodded. "Delancey helped him out of a bind."

"Then perhaps he also enlisted Delancey's help to—"

"He's not a murderer!"

"I was going to say that he enlisted Delancey's help to turn other newspapers against you. Neither man wants magic to become a topic for public debate. They both want it to remain hidden, albeit for different reasons. Is it unreasonable to think Delancey contacted other newspapers and asked them not to publish your articles if you approached them? He has influence with several owners."

"Delancey has that kind of influence; my brother doesn't. Nor is he a murderer."

"We tend to agree," Matt said. "We think it's Sweeney."

"The Stationers' Guild master? Why?"

"We're still gathering evidence, but we wanted to warn you to be careful."

"But you just said that I wasn't the intended victim. Baggley was."

"We can't be certain," Matt said. "Not until we have the final piece of the puzzle. In the meantime, it's best to be careful."

Oscar looked down at the paper and saw the mess he'd made with the ink. He returned the pen to the inkstand. "And what are you going to do to find this puzzle piece?"

"Speak with your new editor," I said.

"He's not in."

"Then we'll wait."

We waited in Oscar's office for fifteen minutes before Mr. Pelham finally arrived. Oscar signaled for him to join us, but Mr. Pelham refused to enter.

"I'm busy, Barratt," he said. "Something you should be too. We have an edition to get out." He hung his hat and jacket on the coat stand outside Oscar's office and proceeded to roll up his shirtsleeves. He might be past middle age but he was strongly built, with muscular forearms and a thick neck. He looked more like a bruiser than a newspaper editor.

"Before you go," Matt said, "I need a word, Mr. Pelham."

Mr. Pelham eyed Matt up and down. "Who're you?"

"Matthew Glass, and this is Miss Steele. Mr. Barratt engaged us to find the author of the threatening letters."

Mr. Pelham grunted. "Nothing to do with me. Before my time here. Good day."

"It'll just take a moment."

Mr. Pelham walked off without a backward glance.

"Let me try," I said.

Before I could, a staff member approached and addressed Matt. "There's a man named Duke here for you, sir. He's waiting outside."

We found Duke patting Matt's horses and talking to our coachman. Cyclops was nowhere in sight. Duke indicated we should walk with him, away from the coach and the *Gazette's* office, up a narrow side alley where it was quieter. A strong breeze whipped my skirts and caught the edge of a discarded newspaper. It flipped over and over until it joined other newspapers piled against a stack of crates at the alley's end.

"You learned something?" Matt asked Duke.

Duke nodded. "Cyclops and me followed Pelham when he left here an hour ago." He checked his watch then slipped it back inside his waistcoat pocket. "We followed him to one of the suspects' homes. Cyclops went back to Park Street to report to you, and I followed Pelham back here. I saw your brougham." He grinned. "Cyclops'll curse me when he finds out he had a wasted trip."

"Don't keep us in suspense," I said. "Where did Pelham go?"

"To Sweeney's."

I looked to Matt. He smiled back at me. "That's it," he said. "That's the link we were missing. They know each other."

"You say Pelham went to Sweeney's home, not his office?" I asked.

Duke nodded. "I saw Sweeney answer the door and let him in."

"It's a working day, and he's not at his place of work or the guild hall. Interesting."

Matt nodded slowly, thinking. "Pelham's appointment to the *Gazette* may have nothing to do with Delancey. He could have applied for the position off his own bat, at Sweeney's urging."

"Let's ask him." I turned and walked quickly down the alley.

"Thanks, Duke," Matt said. "You may as well go home. You're no longer needed here."

Matt caught up to me at the *Gazette's* door. We greeted the man at the reception desk and asked to see Mr. Pelham.

"He's not receiving visitors unless they have an appointment," he said.

"Then tell Oscar Barratt we wish to see him again," Matt said.

The man looked dubious but went to fetch Oscar anyway. He returned a moment later with both Oscar and Mr. Pelham.

"What do you want with my journalist?" Mr. Pelham snapped. "He's busy."

"It's you we wish to see," Matt said. "We know you've just come from Patrick Sweeney's home. Can you tell us why you visited him there?"

Mr. Pelham glanced out the window. Fortunately Duke had gone. "That's none of your business, Glass."

"It is when Sweeney is a murderer."

Mr. Pelham blinked hard. "You think he killed my predecessor? For God's sake, don't be absurd."

"Not only do we think he killed him, the police do too. They're on their way to arrest him now. When we tell Detective Inspector Brockwell that Sweeney is known to you, he'll come to the same conclusion we did—that you and Sweeney conspired to kill Baggley so you could take his place."

"What?" Mr. Pelham exploded. "No! I had nothing to do with the murder! Patrick came to me and suggested I apply for the position, that's all."

"Was that before or after the murder?" I asked.

"Well, he, er..." Mr. Pelham swallowed. "He first mentioned it before the murder, but that doesn't mean I had anything to do with it." For a big man, his voice had become remarkably high pitched. "You must believe me. I had nothing to do with Baggley's murder. I'm innocent. Ask Sweeney, he'll tell you."

I smiled. "Thank you, Mr. Pelham. We'll do that."

Matt stopped me before I exited. "You're going home," he whispered in my ear. "I'll take a hack to the police station."

"Why can't I come to the police station with you and *then* go home?"

"Because..." He rolled his eyes. "Fine. Let's both go. But neither of us is going with Brockwell to arrest Sweeney. His men—"

The door crashed back and Sweeney strode through, a gun pointed at us. "Don't move!"

Matt stepped in front of me before I could react. "Don't shoot. You don't want more deaths on your conscience."

"One death, two, three... What does it matter?" Sweeney's voice shook. "I'm going to hang for murder, anyway. Aren't I?"

In my mind's eye, I undid Matt's waistcoat buttons and fished out his watch. I'd saved his life before when he was in danger of bleeding to death. If Sweeney's shot didn't kill him instantly, I could do so again.

If...

"Oh God," I whispered.

Matt half turned then froze on Sweeney's barked order. "Don't move or I'll shoot."

"What do you want?" Oscar said. "Are you going to shoot everyone? What will that achieve?"

"A measure of satisfaction," Sweeney's voice shook even more.

I peeked past Matt and saw that Sweeney was crying. Tears streamed down his cheeks and dripped off his chin. He reminded me of Mr. Hendry, a lonely, miserable figure forced to live his life in hiding because he loved men. Unlike Sweeney, however, Hendry had a chance of shaking off his misery when this was all over and finding happiness, because he had accepted who he was.

Mr. Sweeney couldn't accept it. Even if he had never committed the murder, he could never be happy because he wanted to bury that part of himself. Mr. Hendry was right—Patrick Sweeney despised himself.

"We made a promise to Mr. Hendry today," I told him.

"Stop talking," he snapped. "Don't mention that name to me."

"You'll want to hear what I have to say," I said.

"India," Matt warned.

"Mr. Sweeney," I said, "if you don't let me tell you what we promised him, your good name will be ruined." His reputation was all he had left now. He may not have a future, but he still cared how he would be remembered. In his eyes, being a murderer was not the worst thing he could be.

He understood me. His gaze flicked to Oscar and Pelham. "You two, leave," he said. "No one is to disturb us or I shoot Mr. Glass."

Pelham opened the door to the office and hurried out. Oscar hesitated before following him.

"I'm listening, Miss Steele," Mr. Sweeney said. "Tell me about the promise you made to…that creature."

"First of all, you need to tell us how you knew we were here."

"Because *he* told me. That nasty little snake sent me a message to say he was no longer going to protect me and that he knew what I'd done. He told me you knew too."

"You tried to blame him for the murder," I said. "After everything you two—"

"Stop!" He aimed the gun at me.

Matt pushed me back behind again. "You truly hate him, don't you?" Matt asked.

"More than you can ever know. He ruined my life! He ruined *me*! Killing him wouldn't be enough; I had to ruin him too." I could no longer see his face but I could hear the sneer in his voice. "Two birds, one stone, Mr. Glass. I remove Baggley, replace him with my friend, Pelham, who won't stand for Barratt's nonsense, and I lay the blame at Hendry's door. I knew he'd sent those letters to Barratt, and I knew it was only a matter of time before someone traced the paper to him. I also knew he'd been here, asking after Barratt that day. If everyone assumed Barratt was the intended victim, my plan would work."

"You placed the gun in Mr. Hendry's shop, just to make sure," I said, stepping out from Matt's shadow.

"Correct, Miss Steele."

"And in case your plan didn't work, you went about destroying Hendry financially. You spoke with his bank and creditors. You bought a stake in his rival's company."

His grin was macabre. "He won't swing for the murder, but he'll never come back from this."

"You destroyed his spirit, Mr. Sweeney. Your rejection and betrayal are what buried him, not his financial problems."

His lips stretched thin. "I hope he stays buried. Now, if you don't mind, I have unfinished business." He aimed the gun at Matt's chest.

"No!" I screamed, trying to push Matt out of the way but failing. "I told you, if you kill anyone today, your reputation will be destroyed. Everyone will know about your relationship with Mr. Hendry."

He glanced quickly at the door through which Oscar and Pelham had exited. "Keep your voice down."

"Stay calm," Matt said, eyeing the gun and grasping me tightly, preparing to push me out of harm's way. "Listen to what India has to say."

He would not be fast enough if the gun went off. We couldn't both be saved.

I felt sick but pushed on. "We promised Mr. Hendry we would keep his name out of this investigation," I said, my voice trembling. "There's enough evidence from Mr. Pelham to convict you without Mr. Hendry getting involved. But the police don't know that yet. Brockwell's only evidence is what Mr. Hendry has told him about the gun and…and your relationship."

Mr. Sweeney's nostrils flared. He flexed his grip around the gun handle but he let me continue.

"Brockwell knows you set up Mr. Hendry to take the blame for the murder because you're upset over the…private affairs you two conducted. If you kill someone here today, those affairs will come to light at your trial. Everyone will know. Is that what you want?"

"What do you think?"

"If you let us go," I said with as much levelness as I could muster, "we'll keep our promise to Mr. Hendry—and to you. No one will ever find out."

"The detective is an acquaintance," Matt said. "He'll co-operate. You have my word as a gentleman that your relationship with Hendry will remain a secret." He inched forward. "Hand me the weapon. This is over."

Mr. Sweeney flexed his grip again and swallowed hard. His hands began to shake. I eyed the gun. How sensitive was the trigger?

Matt took another small step. I grasped his sleeve in an attempt to halt him. "No," I whispered.

He stretched out his hand, palm up. "The gun please, Mr. Sweeney."

The door through which Pelham and Oscar had exited opened a fraction. With a yelp, Mr. Sweeney swung toward it.

The gun went off.

CHAPTER 16

Mr. Pelham, peering through the open doorway, swore loudly. Mr. Sweeney stared at him, his face white, his hands shaking violently.

Matt lunged and snatched the gun off him. "Is everyone all right?" he asked without taking his gaze off Mr. Sweeney.

"Fine," Mr. Pelham said. "The bullet missed."

I closed my eyes and pressed a hand to my stomach. Fingers grasped my shoulder and squeezed. When I opened my eyes, I saw that it was Oscar. Matt was giving orders, directing Mr. Pelham to find something to use to tie Mr. Sweeney up.

"Are you all right, India?" Oscar asked.

I nodded. "A little shaken. You?"

"Unharmed and grateful." He looked to Mr. Sweeney. "Did he admit that I was the intended target?"

"Baggley was. Sweeney wanted Baggley gone so he could replace him with Pelham and stop the articles. Killing you wouldn't have been enough. Baggley would have found another journalist to write them instead."

"Nice to know I'm replaceable," he muttered.

"At least this way, the *Gazette* could no longer be your mouthpiece. It wouldn't surprise me if other editors in the city were given incentives by Sweeney, and perhaps Mr. Delancey too, to ignore you if you approached them."

"That explains a lot. But why?"

"Money and revenge. After a falling out with Hendry, the paper magician, Sweeney invested in a rival business. He hoped that stopping the articles would see the end of the rise of magicians like Hendry, while also making it look as if Hendry were to blame for the murder. He also used his influence to cause Hendry financial problems."

"They must have fallen out over something serious for there to be so much hatred between them. Not even my brother and I would hurt one another on such a scale."

I almost told him he had gravely hurt his brother through the articles but bit my tongue. I didn't want to get involved in his family squabble.

Pelham returned with some rope and tied Sweeney's hands behind his back.

Matt removed the remaining bullets from the gun and pocketed them. "I'll deliver him to Scotland Yard and speak to Brockwell. India, take a cab home."

"You can't go alone," I said.

"I'll go with him," Oscar said.

Matt touched his thumb to my cheek and met my gaze. "Will you be all right to return home alone?"

I gave him a wry smile. "Of course. I'm not a delicate flower, Matt. This was nothing compared to the last time someone wielded a gun in my presence."

"You're the most composed woman I know when it comes to facing danger." He kissed my forehead. "I'll see you soon."

* * *

I SPENT much of the evening taking my watch apart and putting it back together. It hadn't chimed when Sweeney aimed the gun at me. My old watch would have. Perhaps I simply needed to work on the new one more. I tuned out Matt and the others, as they discussed plans for our future, until one by one they retired for the evening, leaving only Matt and me alone in the sitting room.

He sat in silence as I replaced the final pieces and closed the watch housing. I looked up to see him looking at me.

"Sorry," I said. "I've ignored you all evening."

He crouched in front me and closed his hand over mine. "You're upset about today's events."

"It didn't chime." I indicated the watch.

"It probably will after tonight. You've been working on it for hours."

"That long? Sorry, I lost track of time."

His mouth kicked up on one side. "That's a first." He placed both hands on the chair arms, trapping me, and rose to kiss me. "Are you also worried about leaving?"

I couldn't lie to his face so looked away then nodded. Not that it was entirely a lie. I was worried, though not about our departure. I was worried that I wouldn't find a moment to get away to speak with Lord Cox. I was worried that he wouldn't listen to me. I was worried that my information wouldn't be enough to convince him. So many things could go wrong.

We were leaving in two days' time unless I could convince Lord Cox to marry Patience.

"Aunt Beatrice sent word that she's coming tomorrow morning to speak with me about the wedding preparations," Matt said heavily. "Patience is also coming. I have to go along with it, but it'll be the last time. I'm sorry to put you through it. I'm sorry to put her through it too, when I know the wedding won't go ahead."

I cupped his face in my hands and stroked his cheeks, hoping to stroke away the anguish. "I'll go for a walk when they come. Matt, are you sure you don't want to ask Coyle what he knows about Cox?"

"Definitely not. Being beholden to Coyle is too big a price to pay. I don't trust him." He took one of my hands and kissed the wrist. "When you get home tomorrow from your walk, you'd better start packing. Time's running out."

I allowed him to escort me to my room and kiss me good-night. It wasn't until I lay in bed and thought it through that I knew I'd done the right thing in not telling Matt my real plans for the morning. He wouldn't let me use Coyle's information against Cox.

But I couldn't let Matt carry the burden of hurting his cousin. It would eat at him forever, and he didn't deserve that guilt. Neither of us did. And, of course, we couldn't move far from Gabe and his medical magic.

* * *

LORD COYLE HAD GIVEN me Lord Cox's London address. Thankfully, the townhouse was only a ten minute walk from Park Street, because the day had begun wet and, from the endlessly gray sky, it didn't look like it would dry up soon.

It was also a blessing to find Lord Cox at home. He met me in the drawing room, where the footman had bade me to sit and wait.

"My name is India Steele," I said. "I am Matthew Glass's assistant."

"You're the woman he wants to marry." Lord Cox had not taken a seat and, with his hands clasped behind his back, he possessed all the bearing of a man born to wealth and privilege.

"He told you?" I said.

"He did when he explained why he didn't want to marry his cousin. I see from the announcement that the wedding is going ahead, after all. I am sorry for you, Miss Steele, but I don't see what this has to do with me, anymore."

"Patience is a lovely person," I began. "She's kind, modest, and would make an excellent mother and wife. Any man ought to be pleased to marry her."

"You are not fully aware of the situation, Miss Steele, so kindly don't ask me what I think you're going to ask me."

"I am aware of it. I know everything. Please understand, sir, that Patience regrets what happened in her past. She was young and did something foolish, and she has been punished by her family for it in the most cruel way."

His brow creased momentarily then cleared. "It doesn't matter if she regrets it. It happened. A man in my position cannot risk news of it getting out. My reputation is everything to me."

In that case, I had him on my hook. Now I just needed to reel him in. I smiled a slow, easy smile. "It is of paramount importance to you, isn't it? Your reputation, I mean. It would be a terrible shame if an even bigger secret should come to light and taint that reputation you've so carefully cultivated."

He stilled. For a moment, I thought he'd explode in anger. But this wasn't a man used to revealing such a base emotion. He'd spent his entire life suppressing strong feelings, and he wasn't about to let them rise to the surface now. "What is this about? Why have you come here?"

I was relieved to get to the point so quickly. Drawing this meeting out would have been painful. "You may wish to shut the door and make sure no servants are listening."

He cocked his head to the side and regarded me with a severe frown before shutting the door. "Go on," he barked.

"Before your father married your mother, he had another wife."

"I beg your pardon! This is outrageous!"

"It is, I agree. But it's not a lie. Please, hear the rest of what I have to say. It's in your best interests that you know precisely how much I know."

"What you *think* you know."

"Everything I am telling you is the truth." Dear lord, I hoped it was. "They married in secret, without anyone but God and the necessary witnesses—strangers—knowing. Your father's first wife was still alive when he married your mother." He protested again, but I continued over the top of him. "She was a governess, and poor, whereas your mother was a woman more worthy of the title Lady Cox. The governess gave birth to a son before you were born. He is the legitimate heir to the Cox title and estate, because his parents' marriage was legitimate. You are not. Your parents' marriage is not legal. You should not have inherited."

"You have no proof."

The breath left my body. It was as good as an admission that Lord Coyle's information was correct and that Cox knew about his half-brother. "The parish records in which the first marriage took place are readily available, if anyone knew to look, as are birth and death records." It was a logical assumption and a safe bet.

Lord Cox suddenly sat. He scrubbed a hand over his jaw as he shook his head, over and over. "You're blackmailing me."

"At present, your half-brother is not aware of his noble lineage. Both of his parents are now dead, and I have been informed that he was never told about his father. But I will make him aware. If you don't convince Patience Glass to marry you by four o'clock this afternoon, I will tell your half-brother everything. Indeed, I've even left a letter with a lawyer to send to him if something happens to me here today."

His eyes widened even further. "What kind of person do you think I am, Miss Steele?"

"You're a good man, my lord. Patience has often told me so. She was devastated when you ended your engagement, because she wanted to spend her life with you. She wanted to be a mother to your children and to love them—and you. She is a sweet and loving person and will make you very happy. Your marriage is my only demand in exchange for my silence."

He passed his hand over his eyes, down his face. My stomach tied itself in knots as I waited for him to respond, but he simply stared at the carpet. He reminded me of how Mr. Sweeney had looked after he shot the bullet that nearly hit Mr. Pelham. His hands shook, his face was deathly white, and he looked as if he wanted to sink into the floor and disappear. Matt had taken the moment to disarm Sweeney; I must use the lull to disarm Cox.

"The thing is," I said, "the man who threatened to expose Patience's past is now in jail awaiting trial. He'll be executed soon. Even if it does cross his mind to expose Patience's indiscretion now, who will he tell? His guards?" I shrugged. "You have a choice, my lord. You can worry about Sheriff Payne, a liar and murderer, or you can worry about me. I *will* keep my word. If you marry Patience, I will not tell anyone what I know about your brother." I stood. "I want to hear of your happy union by four o'clock today or the letter to your half-brother will be sent."

I strode off, not at all sure if I should leave without his agreement.

I walked for another hour, in an attempt to settle my nerves, before returning to number sixteen Park Street. Once inside, I went straight to my room, closed the door, and withdrew my watch from my reticule. I stroked the case with my thumb and removed the back. A sense of calmness slowly washed over me, soothing me so deeply that I didn't jump when someone knocked on my door. I opened it to Matt, who looked somewhat harried.

"I would ask how your meeting went but I can see it's rather a stupid question," I said.

He sat on the bed and lowered his head. "Patience hardly spoke a word. Aunt Beatrice carried the entire discussion, informing me of the plans. I hated every second of it."

I shut the door and leaned back against it. I wanted to hold him, stroke his hair and tell him what I'd done, but I didn't dare. While I knew he would forgive me for going behind his back, in time, he would only worry about what Lord Coyle wanted from me in return for the information. If I could spare him the worry, I would.

"You're still working on your watch," he said, indicating the timepiece on the dressing table. "Are you still upset that it didn't chime yesterday, or is something else the matter?"

"Everything's fine, Matt. It's just habit, and something to fill in the day."

"You haven't started packing."

"I'll start after luncheon."

"I can help you. Most of mine is done."

I smiled. "It would be highly inappropriate for you to see my underthings."

He chuckled. "I long for the day when you will let me see and do inappropriate things with you." His smile faded and he settled his dark gaze on me. "I know you're worried. I know you don't really want to leave your home, your grandfather and friends. But we will return one day. I promise you."

I took him in my arms and rested my chin on the top of his

head. I felt horrible for not telling him what I'd done. I wished I could reassure him that I wasn't afraid to leave, but I couldn't tell him that my real fear was that Lord Cox wouldn't do as I asked.

* * *

IT WAS the longest afternoon of my life. My nerves stretched thin, and I couldn't sit still, not even to work on my watch. What if Lord Cox didn't believe that I'd inform his half-brother? Had I sounded convincing? Perhaps I should have been more threatening.

What if he told Matt?

"India!" Miss Glass barked from where she sat on the sofa. "Stop pacing. You're hurting my head."

"Sorry, Miss Glass," I mumbled. "I'll sit down now." I glanced at the clock on the mantel. It was three forty-five. I got up again and looked out the window to the street. Then I summoned Bristow.

"Has the afternoon mail arrived?" I asked him.

"Not yet, Miss Steele."

"Thank you, Bristow. Please inform me when it's delivered."

He left and I began pacing again, earning me a narrowed glare from Miss Glass.

"What are you expecting?" she asked.

"Nothing," I said.

"Nonsense. You're a hopeless liar, India. Tell me, what are you expecting?"

"Just a letter from a friend."

"Catherine Mason?"

"No. Actually, it's not from a friend, it's from Chronos."

She sighed. "India—"

"Have you packed yet, Miss Glass?"

"I did it this morning."

"Perhaps I should check it for you. Come on, let's see."

She rose, frowning. "India, you're acting very oddly. What's wrong?"

"Nothing."

"You're nervous about leaving, aren't you?" She patted my arm. "It's all right, dear. It's understandable that leaving London makes you anxious. It makes me anxious, too."

"I thought you wanted to go."

"I do, but one must be aware that at my age, I might not return." She tucked her arm through mine and led me to the door.

Matt entered, cutting off our exit, followed by Duke, Cyclops and Willie. He'd been meeting his lawyer, and the others had been enjoying their last day in London, visiting all the sights they had not yet seen.

"What are you two up to?" he asked, a suspicious smile curving his lips.

"India wants to oversee my packing," Miss Glass said. "She thinks I may have missed something."

"Have you packed, India?" Matt asked.

I nodded. I had thrown some things into a trunk, but if no message arrived in the next few minutes, I was going to have to do it properly. I glanced at the clock again.

"What about the three of you?" Matt asked his friends.

"All done," Duke said. "It didn't take long."

"That's because you ain't got many clothes," Willie said, swaying a little.

"And you have?"

"I got more than you."

"Aye, but you don't wear the dresses and petticoats."

"Or corsets," she agreed with a chuckle that was promptly followed by a hiccup.

Miss Glass wrinkled her nose. "Do stop talking of vulgar things. Cyclops, dear, why the long face?"

Willie nudged her with her elbow. "You know why, Letty. He's love sick."

"Shut it, Willie," Cyclops growled.

Willie tilted her head back, drew in a deep breath, and shouted, "He's in love with Catherine M—"

Cyclops clamped a hand over her mouth. "She's drunk," he told us. "Don't listen to her."

"You've been out drinking?" Matt asked. "Is that wise, the day before a long boat ride?"

"We were wise," Duke said, pointing at himself and Cyclops. "She drank as if it were her last."

"I thought you were going sightseeing," I said as Willie plucked Cyclops's hand from her mouth.

"We did," she said. "We saw lots of sights at lots of saloons around the city." She hiccupped and swayed again.

"Come with us," I told her. "I'll help you to your room." I glanced one more time at the clock on the mantel. Two minutes to four.

I gave Matt a grim smile. He frowned back. "India?"

A knock on the front door sent my heart leaping. I pushed past them all to see if the mail had finally arrived, only to see Bristow greet Lord Cox and Patience. They were smiling, although his was cautious, wary. His gaze met mine.

I pressed a hand to my rapidly beating heart.

Everything suddenly felt very strange, as if I were watching the scene from afar. Matt greeted his guests and invited them in, but they politely refused to move beyond the entrance hall.

"We have several other people we wish to call on," Lord Cox began. "Because of your…unique relationship with Patience, we thought you should be the first to know that we are getting married."

Silence.

"Who's getting married?" Willie asked, her nose screwed up.

"We are," Patience said, clinging to Lord Cox's arm.

"To each other?"

Duke smacked her shoulder. "Of course, idiot. Look at 'em."

Cyclops was the first to remember his manners. He shook Lord Cox's hand and then Patience's. Duke followed suit.

"Patience?" Miss Glass whispered. "Is this true?"

"Yes!" Patience said, bouncing on her toes. "Isn't it wonderful? He asked me just an hour ago and insisted we come here immediately to tell you."

"Does your father know?"

"Of course. He was shocked, but he gave us his blessing after

I begged him. As much as I would have been content to be your wife, Matt, I do prefer my dear Byron. We are more suited to one another than you and I."

Matt nodded, somewhat automatically.

"You look shocked, Glass," Lord Cox said carefully.

It was as if his words triggered Matt into action. He stepped forward to shake Cox's hand and kiss Patience's cheek. "I am, but I had thought—" He winced as Willie pinched the back of his hand. "Never mind."

"Byron told me he couldn't bear the thought of me marrying you," Patience said with childlike happiness that made her seem so young and innocent. "I'm sorry I didn't break off our engagement with you first, but Byron insisted I agree then and there, and well, I knew you'd be pleased, Matt." Her voice softened. "You and India."

Matt grinned and kissed her cheek again. "I am very pleased, Patience," he said gently. "Pleased beyond words. Congratulations. You will both be very happy together."

Despite his insistence that they join us for a drink, they refused and left. The door had hardly closed when Willie let out a *whoop*. She hooked her arm through mine and danced me around the entrance hall.

Duke drew Matt into a hug and Cyclops clapped him on the back. "You're free," Duke said.

Matt extracted himself from their embraces and ran up the stairs, taking two at a time. "Wait here!" he called down.

I stopped dancing and watched him go. That was it? That was his response to the news?

"India?" Miss Glass asked. "Does this mean we're not leaving London?"

"We're staying," I said. "There's no reason to go now."

"Oh." She toyed with the lace at her collar. "Pity."

"Perhaps we'll go on a holiday to the seaside," I said, taking her hands.

"You could go to France for your honeymoon," Duke said. "It ain't far. We could come with you and take care of your aunt while you two, er..."

Willie smacked his arm. "They don't want us on their honeymoon."

"Your honeymoon," Miss Glass murmured. "Yes. I see. Of course."

I clasped her hands, but Matt returned, commanding everyone's attention with his sheer presence. He sported an oddly serious expression that had me worried. Shouldn't he be pleased? Was he concerned about what his uncle thought of the business of Patience's changed mind? Did he think Lord Rycroft would follow through on his threat to expose me now that Matt wasn't marrying Patience?

"Matt," I began, but I was cut off when he picked me up and swung me around.

He broke into a grin. It was a magnificent sight, and relief flooded me.

He set me down on the bottom step so that we were the same height. Then he dropped to one knee. My heart leapt into my throat. He was going to do it here? In front of everyone?

But the others faded into the background of my awareness. It was just Matt and me. Time itself no longer mattered. Only now. Only us.

He removed a box from his pocket and opened it to reveal a diamond ring. "India Steele," he said in that rich, velvety voice of his, "will you do me the honor of being my wife?"

"Yes!"

He slipped the ring on my finger and picked me up. He kissed me to the sound of applause from his friends and family, even Miss Glass.

They hugged us and congratulated us. Bristow appeared with Champagne, as if he always kept some on hand for impromptu celebrations. He ushered us into the drawing room and asked me if I wanted to give Mrs. Potter instructions to make something special for dinner.

"Nothing in particular," I said, "but I'd like to invite two more guests." I glanced at Matt and he only smiled.

"It's your house, India," he said. "You're the hostess. Ask whomever you want."

"Please send invitations to Miss Catherine Mason and my grandfather," I said to Bristow. I glanced at Cyclops, but he gave me a flat lipped smile in return. "Will you be all right if she comes?" I asked him.

"Don't mind me," he said, hugging me. "This is your night. Yours and Matt's."

Willie snorted. "And he'll make sure he sits at the other end of the table to her."

We toasted our engagement with Champagne and everyone began to talk at once, discussing dates and the menu and guest lists. Neither Matt nor I contributed. We would listen to their thoughts and then do as we pleased, but the time for planning would come later. Tonight, I wanted to enjoy being engaged to him.

He seemed to have the same idea. He pulled me aside and kissed me lightly on the lips. "Happy?" he asked.

"Very. I feel so lucky."

"I'm not sure luck had anything to do with it."

My heart thudded to a halt. "Oh?"

"Something changed Lord Cox's mind. I don't know what, but I am grateful he had a change of heart."

I blew out a measured breath. "So am I."

"I'm also glad that you accepted me without hesitation. I would have looked a fool today if you hadn't." He gave me a rare shy smile that I wanted to capture. I cupped his jaw and stroked his lower lip with my thumb.

"Matt, of course I want to marry you. Why wouldn't I?"

"It doesn't matter."

I clasped his hand hard, holding him to my side. "Matt?"

He glanced at his friends or perhaps at his aunt. She didn't notice. She was too busy arguing with Willie over what Willie should wear to the wedding.

"A little while ago, you said marriage would smother you," Matt said quietly. "That you've just found out what it's like to have independence but marriage to me, to anyone, would take that away from you."

I remembered saying that. Remembered how he'd looked

when I'd said it, and I remembered how much I regretted my words later. "I no longer think that way, Matt. Not with you. I know you won't be that sort of husband, and I will always be my own person. I'm sorry I didn't clear it up at the time."

His chest expanded and his smile returned, more confident. "As long as you understand I won't stifle you. You've become a strong, vibrant, and independent thinker, and that's the woman I want to spend my life with."

"So we'll stay in London?"

"For as long as you want." He looked at his aunt again. "She doesn't seem too disappointed."

"That's because she thinks she's coming on our honeymoon with us. Apparently we're going to France."

He laughed softly. "I know this is all so new, but I want to set the date soon. I don't want my uncle to change his mind and decide to marry me off to Charity or Hope."

I pulled a face. "That would be a tragedy worthy of Shakespeare. I agree, we should marry soon." I rested my forearms on his shoulders and admired my diamond ring. "When did you buy it?"

"A few weeks ago. I wanted to have it with me in case the moment arose."

"I recall that day. You refused to tell us where you'd been."

He smirked. "I have to keep some mystery in our relationship or you'd grow bored of me."

"Not too much mystery, please. My poor heart can't cope with it."

He stepped closer until he crushed my skirt against my legs. I could smell the spicy soap he used, feel his heat, and see the throb of his pulse at his throat.

"Let me worry about your heart from now on," he murmured in my ear. "I'll take good care of it."

"I know you will, Matt. I know you will."

THE END

Now Available:

THE CHEATER'S GAME

The 7th Glass and Steele novel by C.J. Archer

As Matt and India prepare for their wedding, trouble arrives in the form of a Wild West show. Meanwhile, India finds herself in demand - and Matt doesn't like it.

Read on for an excerpt from THE PALACE OF LOST MEMORIES, the 1st book in C.J.'s new series.

EXCERPT: THE PALACE OF LOST MEMORIES

About THE PALACE OF LOST MEMORIES

The new king's magnificent palace is built in a matter of weeks. No one saw the builders, no villagers are allowed beyond the gilded gate, and only one servant has ever left. She was recaptured by the palace guards, but the haunted look in her eyes is not forgotten by Josie, daughter of the village doctor.

For Josie, the palace is a mystery that becomes more intriguing after she meets the captain of the guards, a man known only as Hammer, as mysterious and captivating as the palace itself. Whispers of magic fuel Josie's desire to uncover the truth, but an ordinary girl can only dream of getting close enough to find answers.

When the king decides to take a wife from among the eligible daughters of the noble families, the palace gates are finally thrown open and the kingdom's elite pour in. In a court where old rivalries and new jealousies collide, the king's favorite is poisoned and the doctor is summoned. Finally Josie sees inside the lavish walls, but she soon learns the palace won't give up its secrets easily, for not a single resident, from the lowest servant to the king himself, has a memory from before the palace existed.

In the search for the truth, the very foundations of the kingdom will be shaken.

Author's Note: To view the map of the Fist Peninsula go to C.J's website. Read on for an excerpt.

CHAPTER 1

Whispers of sorcery began when the palace's foundations appeared overnight. One frost-bitten day, the broad plain five miles from Mull contained nothing but grass and muddy puddles; the next solid walls took shape as if they'd sprouted from the ground like daffodils at the first hint of spring. Looking at the completed building now, surrounded by mature formal gardens, I could see why those whispers had grown louder. Despite the distance between the palace and the clearing on Lookout Hill, where I stood, I could tell it was enormous. It must be four times as long as the street on which I lived, and it was certainly higher than the temple in the center of Mull. According to my father, it was even bigger than the main temple in Tilting, Glancia's capital city, where the last king had ruled from a crumbling old castle. That structure had taken three years to build. The palace had taken less than three months.

Three months in which not a single builder had been seen coming or going. No locals had been tasked with the labor, and according to the travelers and traders who now filled Mull's taverns to bursting, they hadn't come from elsewhere in Glancia or any of the neighboring kingdoms, either. It was as if they'd been conjured from the air and returned there after the palace's completion.

Magic.

Even I, a practical woman who believed in what she could see, hear and touch, couldn't explain the sudden appearance of the palace. It wasn't simply the speed of its erection but also the secrecy that shrouded it. Only a handful of delivery carts from the village and nearby farms had been to the palace to supply its kitchens, and guards hadn't allowed them beyond the gate. Palace servants unloaded the goods and retreated inside. They did not engage in conversation, they did not make eye contact, and they certainly didn't come to the village on their days off.

Except for that one time a maid wandered into Mull early one morning, asking passersby if they knew her. When no one could offer answers, she fell to her knees and sobbed until four palace guards collected her. She went with them meekly enough, but her haunted eyes stayed with me. Not just hers but theirs, too.

With a last look at the dazzling building, glinting in the late spring sunshine like a jewel, I picked up my battered old pack, as well as the new one given to me by the patient I'd called on, and turned to go.

The thundering of hooves along the forest path warned me to remain in the clearing. By the sound of it, more than one rider was heading my way and they were traveling fast. To move onto the path would be folly, so I waited until the reckless youths passed. No doubt it was Lord Deerhorn's sons, come to see the palace for themselves. Lookout Hill afforded the best view, after all. Either that or they'd decided to hunt here. They were supposed to keep to their own estate, but they were arrogant enough to shoot their arrows on common land whenever they pleased.

I'd learned a long time ago to stay away from the Deerhorn lordlings, but I didn't want them to think I was an animal worth hunting. I made myself visible in the middle of the clearing, facing the area of dense forest where the path briefly emerged before disappearing again on the other side. They couldn't mistake me for a fox or rabbit. Then again, they were as thick as the tree foliage in this part of the forest and fond of loosing their arrows.

The dull *thud thud* of the hooves came closer then the first rider burst into the clearing. His head jerked toward me and I caught a glimpse of a short dark beard but little else, thanks to the hooded cloak he wore. He disappeared into the forest again, his horse's stride not even slowing.

A few moments later, the forest spat out another rider, this one wearing black leather with gold trim at the shoulder of his doublet, and long black boots. He sat tall in the saddle, looking comfortable despite his horse's ferocious pace. I got a good look at his face as he slowed to study me in return. Short dark hair framed hard planes and a cleanly shaven jaw. It was his eyes that commanded attention, however. They were the blue of the shallows in Half Moon Cove on a sunny day. Those eyes made a quick assessment of me before focusing forward again.

"Question her!" he barked before urging his horse into the forest ahead.

He'd hardly disappeared when another rider emerged. He wore a crimson doublet with gold braiding. Crimson and gold—palace uniforms.

I clutched my bag to my chest.

The rider stopped and swore. He looked at me, swore again, and stared into the forest after the other riders. He swore a third time as his horse circled. Clearly good manners weren't a requirement for palace servants. Good looks, however, must be. This rider was dark like the one who preceded him, but with brown eyes and a bow mouth that turned down severely as he scowled at me.

"You there," he hailed me.

Branches and brush rustled and a fourth rider emerged into the clearing. This one also wore a palace uniform but he was younger than his companion. My theory about handsome servants was dashed by the newcomer. Though he was also dark, he had a nose like a horse and a spotty forehead and chin. His narrow chest rose and fell with his heavy breathing. He couldn't be more than eighteen.

"Who're you?" he asked me, as bold as could be.

I bristled but forced my spine to relax. I would usually treat such rudeness with silent disdain, but these were the king's men and must be obeyed. Besides, if I was nice, I might find out something about the palace and King Leon.

"Joselyn Cully," I said, still holding my pack in front of me. The new, empty one, remained slung over my shoulder. "Everyone calls me Josie. Are you from the palace?" I indicated the view behind me.

The lad sat higher in the saddle. "Huh. It looks tiny from up here, Max. Come take a look."

The man addressed as Max did not move. "Did you see him?" he demanded of me.

"Who?" I said.

"The rider in the hood."

"A little. The other man followed him." I pointed to the gap in the trees where the path led.

"The captain," the young man told me. "Captain Hammer."

Hammer? I managed to contain my snort of derision before it escaped.

"What did he look like?" Max asked. "The man in the hood?"

I shrugged. "I didn't see much. He had a short, dark brown beard."

"What shade of brown?" asked the younger man, leaning forward on the pommel. "Chestnut? Mud? Dung?"

Was he making fun of me? He didn't laugh. Not even a hint of a smile touched his lips. "Medium brown," I said.

"Anything else?" Max pressed, glancing toward the path again. Unlike the younger man, he seemed restless and eager to follow the two riders. The younger man still looked like he hadn't quite caught his breath.

"No," I said. "It was very—"

Thwack.

Max grunted and lost his balance, half falling, half staggering off his horse. An arrow protruded from his arm. *Merdu, be merciful.*

"Get down!" Max shouted as he fell to his knees. "Find cover!"

I dashed behind a row of shrubs on the opposite side of the clearing from where the arrow had been shot. I was safe but the men were not.

I swallowed hard and dared to peek through a gap in the bushes. The two men were still alone with their horses in the clearing. Max lay flat on the ground. Blood seeped through his clothes, darkening the crimson fabric. He must have pulled the arrow out, the fool. The younger man knelt beside him, his body over Max's, protecting him and making a target of himself in the process.

"Get off me, you little prick," Max snapped, easily shoving off the skinnier lad. "Do you want to get shot in the arse?"

The youth glanced behind him in the direction of the forest then angled himself behind a horse for protection. "Max," he hissed. "Take cover."

"He'd have shot again by now if he was still here." Max sat up and inspected his arm.

He was probably right and it was safe to emerge from my hiding spot. "Let me see," I said, crouching beside him. I reached for him but he leaned away. "I'm a… I have some medical skill."

"You can't," the lad blurted out.

"Because I'm a woman." It wasn't a question, but he answered as if it were.

"No. That is, I can see you're a woman." His gaze dipped to my breasts and his face turned as red as his clothes. "But you can't be a doctor. You're too pretty. Pretty women aren't smart and doctors have to be smart."

"Shut up, Quentin," Max growled. He got to his feet, only to sway a little. He was shorter than me with a wide set of shoulders and a barrel chest. If he toppled onto me, I would not be able to hold him up.

"Please, let me look at the wound," I said, eyeing him carefully. "I assure you I know what I'm doing. I've been studying at my father's knee ever since I could read. He taught me everything he knows, and he's a brilliant doctor. The best in Glancia, perhaps the entire Fist Peninsula. Even so, I've taken my learning upon myself this last year or so. My patients have seen the benefit, too." Of course all my patients were childbearing women, although I was perfectly capable of treating ailments and injuries too. Unfortunately, the lawmakers disagreed. "I'm perfectly capable," I finished.

Max put up his hand. "Be quiet. You're as annoying as he is."

Quentin beamed as if he'd been paid a compliment. I kept my mouth shut. I did tend to chatter too much when I was nervous.

The pounding of horses' hooves had us all turning toward

the path again, but it was only the second rider returning, the one who'd given these men orders to question me. Captain Hammer. "I lost him," he bit off with a shake of his head. He glanced at me and looked as if he were about to speak when Quentin got in first.

"If you'd been riding Lightning, you'd have caught him."

"He doubled back," Max told the captain.

Hammer glanced sharply at the injured man and his gaze dropped to the arrow lying on the leaf litter at the edge of the clearing. "How bad is it?"

"I can't tell," I said before Max answered. "He won't let me inspect it. I'm Joselyn Cully, from Mull. It's my professional opinion that the wound needs to be bound before he loses too much blood. It may also require suturing." I held up my bag. "I have the necessary equipment right here." I was always prepared with surgical thread, a fine needle and small doses of Mother's Milk for painful births. "It's some distance to the village, and I'm your best option."

It was perhaps a little reckless, considering they were the king's men, but I was prepared to take the risk. This man needed immediate medical attention, and surely I'd only incur a fine and slap on the wrist. Perhaps not even that, if the captain chose to overlook the fact I wasn't qualified. I was, after all, doing his man a service.

I went to open my bag but the captain jumped down from his horse and snatched it from me. He was much taller than me, with a powerful frame. His shoulders were as broad as Max's, but due to his height, he didn't look blocky.

He checked inside the bag.

"It contains medical equipment," I said hotly, "not weapons."

The captain handed the bag back after a thorough inspection. "Let her see the wound, Sergeant."

"I'm fine," Max growled. "I don't need a healer."

I focused on the forest behind him and gasped. All the men spun to look, but only Max swayed and fell to one knee. He swore then sighed and sat.

Quentin snickered. "I like her."

Max glared at him, but even I could see there was no animosity in it. He tried to remove his doublet but Quentin had to help him. By the time he'd removed his shirt, Max was sweating and breathing heavily. Quentin and I both helped while the captain kept watch on the surrounding forest. He seemed oblivious to his sergeant's pain.

I tied Max's shirt around his upper arm to stem the blood flow. His veins soon bulged nicely.

"His fingers are going purple," Quentin said. "Is that good?"

"For now." I rummaged through my bag, tossing aside forceps, vials and a suction pump until I found the bottle of Mother's Milk. "Swallow a mouthful of this," I said to Max.

"You trying to get him drunk?" Quentin asked.

"It's a soothing medicine. It numbs pain and will keep him calm while I stitch him up."

"Just like ale, eh?"

"Better than ale. He won't need as much to feel the effects, although too much has the same symptoms felt the morning after a night spent drinking."

Max shook his head. "I don't need it."

"It'll hurt," I warned.

"I can cope with a little pain."

"I'll leave the bottle here. Grab it if you change your mind." I set the bottle down beside him and pushed aside the equipment in my bag again until I found the jar. It would be wonderful to move all of my things into the new bag the leather seller's wife had given me as payment after the safe delivery of her baby. It had internal compartments, pockets and straps to organize all my tools and medicines.

I removed the lid on the small jar and extracted the needle and thread stored within. "Ready?" I asked, threading the needle.

"Ready," Quentin said, crouching beside me, watching closely.

"Get on with it," Max snapped.

I stuck the needle into his flesh.

"Fuck!" he blurted out.

"Mind your tongue in front of Miss Cully," the captain said without turning around. He stood rigid, his shoulders tense.

"Doctor, not Mistress," Quentin told him. "Doctor Cully. How deep does the needle have to go in?"

Max paled. "Quentin!" he gasped. "Bring that ugly face of yours closer."

Quentin leaned in. "Why?"

"So I can shut your mouth for you."

The captain whipped around and intercepted Max's fist before it made contact with Quentin's face. "Maybe you should take the Mother's Milk," he said.

"You going soft, Hammer?" One side of Max's mouth hooked into a wry smile.

I pushed the needle in again. Max grunted and squeezed his eyes shut.

The captain snatched up the bottle of Mother's Milk. "Drink!"

Max accepted the bottle.

"Two mouthfuls," I reminded him. "You're a solid man but three will have you throwing it up."

I waited for the medicine to take effect before continuing with the suturing. The captain returned to watching the forest, his arms crossed over his chest, but his stance was a little more relaxed. I'd thought he was tense from alertness, but now I suspected it was partly due to concern for his sergeant.

"So your friends call you Josie, eh?" Quentin asked me. "Can I call you Josie?"

"If you like."

"You can call me Quentin. He's Sergeant Max and that's Captain Hammer."

"Are those first names or last?" I asked.

The captain half turned and glared at Quentin over his shoulder. The sergeant glared too. Quentin swallowed. "Is he ready now?" he asked. "He looks ready. You ready, Max?"

The sergeant sighed and closed his eyes. He finally relaxed. "The Mother's Milk isn't working. I can still hear him."

I laughed softly. "It only numbs the pain."

"Listening to him *is* painful."

I went to work, finishing what I'd begun. The task wasn't difficult, particularly with Max now calm and pain free. I'd stitched far more delicate areas than a big man's arm. It gave me time to think about the strangeness of the situation I'd found myself in. Aside from the mad servant and the guards who'd collected her from the village, these were the first people from the palace I'd ever seen. No one in Mull had been presented with such a good opportunity to learn more.

"Are you palace guards?" I asked as I stitched.

To my surprise, Quentin didn't respond. He looked to Hammer.

"Yes," the captain said without turning around.

"Who was that man you were chasing? Does he work at the palace too?"

"That's not something I can divulge."

"Have you worked at the palace long?"

The captain shifted his stance. "The entire time."

"So you saw it being built? Where did the builders come from?"

"Here and there."

"Can you be more specific?"

"No."

This wasn't going well. "Where are you originally from?"

He didn't answer.

"Why can't you tell me?" I pressed. "It's a simple question."

"You'd think so," Quentin muttered.

"You and Sergeant Max are short with dark hair," I said to Quentin. "So you must be originally from Freedland."

Quentin turned huge eyes to me. "You've been there?" he whispered. "You've been to Freedland?"

"No. My father has, and he told me stories of all the kingdoms and the republic. He traveled all over The Fist before marrying my mother and settling here in Mull. But everyone knows the sand people of Freedland are short with dark hair. You don't need to go there to know."

"Right," Quentin said. "Of course."

"Captain Hammer is different," I said, glancing at his broad back. "He's tall, like those of us native to Glancia, but he's dark like you. Glancia folk are naturally fair."

"And pretty." Quentin blushed. "Real pretty."

I smiled. "I suspect the captain doesn't like to be called pretty."

Hammer shifted his stance again. "The captain doesn't like people talking about him behind his back." He glanced over his shoulder and those eyes, so blue against his tanned skin, drilled into me. "Are you done, Doctor?"

It was a little embarrassing to be called the title I hadn't earned officially through the college—and never would. Women weren't allowed to study doctoring. Midwifery and how to make medicines, yes, but not surgery or other medical disciplines. The college system was archaic; not only for entry into the college of surgery, but into all the colleges. The rules ought to be changed, but I couldn't foresee women being allowed in any time soon. None of that was a secret. It was common knowledge. Why did these men not know it?

I finished stitching and tied the end of the thread. I asked Quentin to cut off the excess and he looked more than pleased to contribute. After removing the shirt from around Max's arm, I told the sergeant he could sit up.

He answered me with a soft snore.

"How will we get him back to the palace?" Quentin asked.

Captain Hammer tapped Max's cheek. "Wake up."

Max cracked open an eye. "The doctor's not finished." He closed his eye again.

"She is." The captain pulled Max into a sitting position. "Come on. We must go." He scanned the forest again. Did he think the archer was still there, watching?

I handed the doublet to Max. He slung it around his injured side but needed help with the other. The captain and I managed to arrange it equally on both shoulders before assisting him to stand.

Max groaned but slumped against Hammer. The captain looped his arm around Max and guided him to the horse.

Quentin gathered the horse's reins. "You can do it, Max. Upsy daisy."

The sergeant pushed off from Hammer. "I'm not a child," he growled.

He tried to mount alone but couldn't. The captain wordlessly stepped in and helped. He managed to get Max on the horse easily, even though the broad-set man must be heavy. From what I'd witnessed, Max was a barrel of solid muscle.

"Where's your horse?" Quentin asked me as he mounted.

"I don't have a horse," I said. "I walked."

"It's a long way back to Mull," the captain said. He remained standing, his hand resting lightly on his horse's neck. "What were you doing up here?"

"Passing through."

"It's a hill. No one climbs a hill if they're just passing through."

"She was looking at the view," Quentin said. "There's a nice one of the palace from over there." He pointed to the edge of the clearing where the hill dropped away too steeply for trees to grow.

The captain walked to the edge and studied the palace in the distance. He stayed there for some time, his back to us. Only the ends of his hair fluttered in the light breeze, but otherwise he didn't move. The silence stretched.

Quentin cleared his throat. "Captain? Max is falling asleep again."

The captain turned away from the view and my breath caught in my throat. He had the same haunted look in his eyes as the mad maidservant and the guards who'd collected her that day.

"Are you all right?" I asked in a rush of breath.

He halted and blinked rapidly at me. "We'll take you back to the village."

"It's all right," I said. "I can walk. I had a patient to visit at the base of the hill and decided to come up and have a look at the palace. It's such a pleasant day and the sun is shining. The palace is so pretty in the sunshine with all those glass windows sparkling like gems. Is it made of gold? It looks like gold from up here, but perhaps its something else. I imagine gold is too expensive to use as a building material." I bit my tongue to stop my rambling.

"We'll take you home," the captain said again. "You can't stay here alone."

"Why not?"

He hesitated before saying, "You saw the man we were chasing?"

"Only a little. Just his beard really."

"He might think you saw more. That's why he doubled back."

My heart skipped a beat. "You think he was shooting at *me*?"

"It's possible."

"Then why not try again after missing?"

"Perhaps he couldn't get a clear second shot before I returned."

"She hid in the bushes," Quentin told his captain.

I swallowed hard. Someone had tried to…to kill *me*?

The captain touched my elbow. "Doctor? Are you all right?"

"I… Yes. I'm fine."

"It's doubtful he'll come back for you. If you didn't recognize him then he doesn't know you either, or where to find you. If he's clever, he'll be far away by now. Even so, I'd prefer it if you allowed us to escort you home."

Quentin shifted back on the saddle and patted the front. "Climb on."

"She'll ride with me," Hammer said.

Quentin sighed. "Don't you have enough?"

"You're a terrible rider. If Doctor Cully wants to get home safely, she rides with me."

"I fell off *once*."

"Once *today*," Max piped up from where he sat slumped in his saddle.

"A ride back to the village is the least we can do," the captain said to me. "I'll send payment for your service. I have no coin on me. We left in a hurry."

I gathered up both my packs and helped myself onto the

saddle, sitting aside rather than astride as I'd seen Lady Deerhorn do. The captain mounted behind me in one fluid movement. I felt small and delicate next to him. He smelled of horse and leather, and his hard thigh bumped against mine. Like Max, I suspected he was all muscle too.

We headed slowly through the forest, back down the hill. Little light reached through the canopy, making it feel like twilight, despite being just after noon. The air felt damper too, denser, as if rain wasn't far away. If I hadn't been out in the bright sunshine moments before, I would have thought the weather entirely different.

The captain remained alert and silent as we rode. His reassurance that the hooded archer wasn't a local and would be far away by now offered little comfort. I held my packs close to my chest and watched the forest too. I'd wager the archer was a burglar or poacher who thought to try his luck on palace grounds.

Or perhaps he was an escaped servant who needed to be retrieved.

CHAPTER 2

We emerged from the forest at the base of Lookout Hill and rode into the village. The familiar salty scent of the sea hit me along with an undertone of gutted fish thanks to the northerly breeze. We passed the leather seller's hut, where his wife convalesced with their third born, and the clutch of other buildings built of the same warm yellow stone.

"You said your father traveled." The captain had been quiet for so long that his voice startled me. It wasn't so much the sound of it, but the way it rumbled through my body. He sat very close. "Where has he traveled to?"

"Everywhere on The Fist Peninsula," I said. "Freedland, Dreen, Vytill of course, and even into The Margin and across the sea to Zemaya. Not beyond Widowmaker Peaks, though."

"How long was he gone?"

"Years. He studied in Logios, and after graduation, he took

his new education and traveled. He says he learned more in Zemaya than he ever learned in college, particularly about medicines and poisons."

"What do you know about the other nations on The Fist Peninsula?" the captain asked.

What a strange question. I turned more fully to see him properly. At such close proximity, he filled my view. "You don't have Zemayan coloring, yet you can't be from the Margin, either."

Those blue eyes lowered to mine. "Why not?"

"Because you're too sophisticated. Margin folk are simple tribespeople. You're clearly not a barbarian."

Quentin nodded sagely, proving he was listening. He did not look around, however, preferring to concentrate on the road ahead. His white-knuckled grip on the reins and stiff back were at odds with the other two, who both sat comfortably in their saddles. Max had straightened a little and seemed more alert. The fresh sea air had woken him up, and the effects of the Mother's Milk were wearing off.

"Tell me more about the Margin," the captain said.

"It's mostly plains and then the foothills of the Peaks." I shrugged. "Nomadic tribes live there. They fight amongst themselves and don't venture into Glancia. There's not much more to tell."

"What about Dreen? The college city of Logios is in Dreen, is it not? What else is it known for? What are the people like?"

We passed the Bramm sisters walking back from the main street, their baskets full. They stepped out of our path then stopped altogether and gawped at us. "Josie?" asked one.

"Good afternoon, " I said.

"What are you doing with those...?"

"Palace guards?" I filled in for her. "I'll explain later."

They glanced at each other then rushed off, their strides long and purposeful. The entire village would know I'd ridden with palace guards by nightfall.

"Dreen is large in area but smaller than Vytill and Glancia in population," I said, answering the captain. "Most of it is sparsely populated farmland. There are two cities—Upway, the capital, and Logios, the college city."

"And Vytill? What are the folk there like?"

I huffed out a laugh. "The most intelligent, beautiful, and wealthy. Just ask them. Did I mention they're arrogant too? According to the king of Vytill, it's the most important nation on The Fist. Not anymore, though. Not since the Rift. Have you heard of the Rift?"

"I have."

That was something, at least. I was beginning to think he was completely ignorant about everything to do with the peninsula.

"Tell me about Glancia," he said. "You've lived in this kingdom your entire life?"

I nodded. "In Mull. That probably makes me quite dull to you."

"Why?"

I waved at Yolanda and her three children, each carrying a package. None waved back. They were too busy staring. "You must be from somewhere very far away," I said to Hammer. "Otherwise you wouldn't be asking me all these questions about the Fist nations. So where *are* you from?"

"The palace," was all he said. "Glancia is a pleasant country with nice scenery. Is it mostly made up of fishing villages?"

It would seem he wasn't prepared to give too much of himself away to a stranger. I wondered if he was following king's orders or whether it was a personal choice. "It is, except for the capital, Tilting. It's on the River Upway, near the borders of Dreen and Vytill. Apparently being close to our wealthier neighbors makes it more strategic and affords better communication, although I don't think the kings of either Dreen or Vytill cared overmuch about communicating with Glancia until now. We were nothing to them, just a poor dog they had to throw a bone to every now and again to stop us starving over winter. Before the Rift, that is. Everything changed after that. Why did King Leon decide to build his palace near Mull and not Tilting? The capital was good enough for the old king."

"The old king kept to the old ways. The new king wanted to do something new and different."

"The palace certainly is different," I said. "For one thing, it's not a crumbling old relic of a castle."

He smirked. "No, it's not."

I directed the captain to move off Mull's main road with its shops and bustling market that now opened every day instead of twice a week. I knew far too many shopkeepers, and I was already growing tired of the stares and gasps. Soon the sheltered harbor with its two jutting piers were in view. The smell of the sea was strongest here, and the noise was incessant. Dock-workers shouted at one another, sometimes in anger but mostly barking orders. Crane ropes groaned and the machinery whirred as barrels and crates were lifted from boats onto the piers. Carts, drays and passenger vehicles came and went, jostling for space on the concourse. Everywhere foundations for new warehouses and shipping company offices sprang up. The customs building was already two-thirds built, with another level to go on soon. It looked very grand already, commanding the best view over Tovey Harbor.

Large ships anchored in deeper waters at the harbor's mouth while their smaller rowboats navigated Tovey's shallows, waiting for their turn to unload and reload at the piers. Timbers creaked and oars bumped as crews maneuvered through the crowded harbor and vied for the best positions.

The sooner the harbor was dredged and bigger docks built, the better. Perhaps. Mull was bursting at the seams with the influx of trade since the Rift, and I didn't particularly like the way my sleepy village was being swamped. I hated to think what it would be like if it grew to the size of Tilting.

"Mull is changing quickly." When he didn't respond, I added, "Because of the Rift."

"I see," he said blandly.

"I'm sorry, I'm boring you. You must already know this."

He hesitated then said, "I would like to hear about Mull from the perspective of someone who lives here."

"Very well." I indicated the busy harbor. "The Rift cut off The

Thumb from the rest of the continent." I waited for a reaction. He gave none so I thought it best to begin at the beginning. "A series of earthquakes, one after the other, tore the headland known as The Thumb from the mainland. Seawater flooded the gap, now known as the Rift. The quake event is also called the Rift, for want of a better word. The Thumb was—and still is, administratively if not physically—part of Vytill. Before the Rift, Port Haven on The Thumb was the eastern most port on The Fist Peninsula, making it a trading hub. It's also on the River Mer so it was doubly strategic. Port Haven is the reason Vytill became the richest and most important kingdom on The Fist. Now that's all changing."

"Because the Rift severed The Thumb."

"Nice pun."

Once again he did not react. Not much of a sense of humor then.

"With The Thumb cut off from the peninsula, Vytill no longer has the easternmost port on The Fist. Glancia does." I stretched out my hand to encompass the activity. "My sleepy fishing village has woken up. The population has already trebled, and market prices have risen quickly. On the one hand, it's good for everyone's business, but on the other…" I sighed. "I liked it the way it was."

I directed the captain into a street to take us away from the harbor. It was quieter but we still passed people I knew. Considering I knew everyone in the village, except for those who'd settled since the Rift, it wasn't surprising.

"Is that why King Leon built his palace nearby?" I asked. "To be closer to Mull and the trading activity?"

"I don't know what's behind his thinking."

"It did seem strange to us that he'd move away from Tilting and its administrative offices. The ministers can't be too happy to travel here."

"They haven't come yet. They arrive next week for the first time."

"Will they stay at the palace? Every spare room in Mull is already taken."

"There are rooms prepared for them at the palace."

"Many, many rooms," Quentin piped up.

Captain Hammer asked me a few more questions about Glancia, mostly about its history and the various lords. I could answer many but not all. Aside from Lord Deerhorn, who lived north east of Mull on an estate that overlooked the village and harbor, the other powerful families of Glancia were a mystery to me. There wouldn't have been enough time to answer questions about them, anyway. We turned into the narrow street where I lived, and I told the captain to stop outside my cottage just as old Bessie Tailor emerged. She squinted at me.

"Who's that?" she asked.

"It's just me, Bessie," I said. "Josie. Are you here for your eyes? Could Father help?"

"Josie? Are you on a horse? Who're you with?" She squinted harder.

"Josie?" my father said, peering over Bessie's head. "What in Merdu's name…?" He took in Quentin and Max's crimson and gold uniforms, and my position on the horse in front of the captain. "Get down, Josie! Come away from them!"

"It's all right," I said. "They're palace guards. They—"

"I know what they are."

I hadn't seen him look this furious since I came home late one night after celebrating a friend's betrothal at The Anchor tavern. He'd had good cause then, but his anger didn't make sense this time. I was twenty-four, for Goddess's sake, and hardly a naive girl anymore. The captain and his men may be strangers, but it was broad daylight. Father was overreacting, as usual.

The captain dismounted and assisted me to the ground, his hands on my waist. Our gazes connected but I couldn't read his. Or perhaps I might have if I hadn't been transfixed by his eyes. Their color really was quite beautiful.

"My name is Captain Hammer, sir," he said to my father. "These are my men. You're Doctor Cully?"

My father lifted his chin in a nod. "What are you doing with my daughter?"

"Doctor Cully—Doctor Joselyn Cully, that is—assisted my sergeant after he was shot by an arrow on Lookout Hill."

I groaned silently. I'd have a devil of a time convincing Father there was no cause to worry now. It was difficult to know which was worse—the fact I hadn't come straight home after seeing to the leather seller's wife, the fact that I rode on a horse with a strange man, that he was from the palace, or that his sergeant had been shot by an arrow and called me doctor. I could see my father grappling with the overwhelming number of possibilities too. Thankfully, it rendered him speechless. For now.

It did not have the same effect on Bessie. "*Doctor* Joselyn?" She chuckled. "Very amusing."

Captain Hammer turned a frosty glare to me.

I sidled off to join the sergeant. He sat well on his horse and looked much better. "I sutured the wound," I told my father. "We were on top of Lookout Hill and he was losing blood. There was no time to bring him down here, and since I had everything I needed..." I stopped as my father's face darkened.

"Get inside, Josie," he said coolly.

"In a moment."

He arched a brow but did not scold me.

"Those stitches will need to be removed in ten days," I said to Max. "I can come to the palace—"

"No," both my father and the captain said.

"Max will come to you," the captain clarified.

"To *me*," Father added. "My daughter would make an excellent doctor, but an unqualified girl cannot attend to a servant of the palace. Or to anyone," he added.

"But he's *my* patient," I said. "What's the worst that could happen? They're the king's men."

"Thank you for bringing my daughter home safely," Father said to the captain. "Good day to you, sir. Josie, inside."

I slipped past Bessie and Father, dumped my bags on the floor, found what I wanted in my father's surgery and returned just as the captain remounted. I handed him the roll of bandage but addressed the sergeant. "Cover the wound with a thick layer of bandage so that it doesn't rub on your clothes. If it pains you, ask the kitchen staff to grind up some hollyroot. They probably grow it in the kitchen gardens. It's not as strong as Mother's Milk but it's good for mild aches and pains. You look like a man who only needs mild pain relief."

He puffed out his chest and gave me a nod. "Thank you Doc — er, miss."

"Josie will do."

"And I want to apologize for my language earlier. I was...not myself."

They rode off amid stares from our neighbors. I waved at Meg across the street, and she signaled me to join her. I glanced at my father. His deeply furrowed brow gave me my answer.

"Later," I called out to Meg.

"Josie," Father snapped as Bessie made her way carefully along the street. He shut the door behind me. "What do you think you were doing accepting a ride from those men?"

The childish part of me wanted to storm up to my attic bedchamber, but I was too old for petulance. I bypassed the front room that Father used as his surgery and workroom and entered the kitchen instead. I took my time filling the pot with water and mildwood leaves and nestled it amid the burning embers. I saw no reason to make it easy for Father. He was over reacting, as usual, and I was heartily sick of it. He'd been very close to creating a scene out there, and in front of the neighbors and palace guards too.

"The sergeant needed help," I told him. "So I helped."

"I understand that," he said, strained patience tightening his voice. "You're a healer and wanted to assist an injured man. You can't help your kind nature."

"And we were too far away from here."

"I don't disagree with your decision to suture his wound. If the captain gave you permission, you won't get into trouble, even if the sheriff hears of it. You were simply in the wrong place at the wrong time."

"Or at the right place at the right time."

"Don't mock me, Josie. This is serious. Those men could have been dangerous."

"They weren't."

"You don't know that."

I threw up my hands. "I helped one of them! Why would they hurt me?"

"Any number of reasons, none of which you're foolish enough to dismiss so easily. You're a young, attractive woman on your own in the forest on top of Lookout Hill. They're young, virile men. Do I need to spell it out to you? You're not a child anymore, Josie."

"Precisely," I spat. "I am not a child. I'm capable of assessing whether three men are a threat to me. I am well aware of what can happen to a woman alone, but you should *not* assume every man is after *that*."

"I don't," he said, sounding put out. "But they're strangers," he added, gentler. "You can't trust strangers, particularly after the prison escape."

"The prison escape! Oh Merdu. Not only did that happen a long time ago and those escapees are probably rounded up by now, but the prison was miles away! Miles and miles!"

"I've heard that they have *not* been rounded up, and nor is it a stretch to assume they would be in Mull by now. We have so many strangers in the village these days that they could easily blend in, find employment or attempt to leave The Fist on one of the trading vessels."

"These men wore palace uniforms. If I can't trust palace guards, who can I trust?"

He removed two cups from the shelf and placed them on the table. "Their authority does not make them trustworthy." He sat heavily, all the bluster knocked out of him. He looked every bit his age of sixty-five, with the deep lines across his forehead and the last remnants of his hair clinging to his head like a summer cloud.

I kissed his cheek to show him I wasn't too mad. I knew his anger was born from worry. It had been just the two of us for so long that he was afraid I'd either leave him voluntarily through marriage, or reluctantly if something awful befell me. "You think the king employs bad men?" I asked.

"Not on purpose. Besides, it's not just that. There's something odd about the palace and its servants."

I sighed. "Don't say magic. Those men are real." So real that I could still feel the captain's thigh against mine, his hands on my waist. "Magic doesn't exist outside of children's stories."

He said nothing and I poured the brewed mildwood into the cups. "Have you eaten today, Father?"

"Not yet. Do we have any eggs for breakfast?"

I smiled. "It's well past breakfast time, but I'll cook you some eggs if you like. Tell me about Bessie's eyes."

"You first. Tell me how the birth went."

***

Tamworth Tao, the Zemayan born spice merchant, sported a knowing little smile; he had gossip to impart. Meg noticed it too and dragged me by my arm through the crowded marketplace to his stall. We'd been heading there eventually anyway, preferring to leave it to the end of our marketing, but she couldn't wait and it became our first stop.

"Josie, Meg, my two favorite Mullians." Tam flicked his long black braid off his shoulder with a jerk of his head. The bells attached to the strip of white leather threaded through the hair tinkled musically before falling silent at his back. "You are a wonderful sight for my world-weary eyes." Tamworth's face-full of wrinkles deepened with his grin, but there were no signs of weariness in his eyes or elsewhere. The spice merchant was of indeterminate age. Despite the wrinkles, he sported no gray in his black hair and his slender shoulders and arms were all wiry muscle. He could be forty, seventy, or anywhere in between.

I inhaled deeply, drawing the chaotic blend of sweetness and tartness, tanginess and sharp heat into my lungs. According to Father, Zemaya smelled like the spices sold in Tam's stall, but rarely all together like this.

"What news from your travels, Tam?" Meg asked, not bothering to hide her enthusiasm. She was the same age as me, but sometimes she seemed much younger, when her eagerness got the better of her or if she became overly shy about the birthmark discoloring one side of her face.

"I will tell you," Tam said, still smiling, "but first Josie must tell me about the palace guards she rode with last week."

"There's nothing to tell," I said.

"There must be. No one else has been as close to them as you, Josie, so you must forgive our curiosity."

Meg regarded me with mischievous blue eyes. "Go on, Josie. Tell Tam how you rode with the *very* handsome captain of the guards."

Tam leaned forward, rising off his stool. He bumped his head on the string of reek roots hanging from the bar. His eyes widened, their whites so bright within the dark skin. "What did he look like? What was he wearing?"

I described Hammer's looks and clothing and those of his men. Tam listened intently, and I realized his curious little smile that enticed us over to the stall wasn't as a result of *his* gossip but because he saw the opportunity to gather tidbits about the palace from *me*.

"How did he seem to you?" Tam asked.

"Seem?"

"Aye. Did he seem…solid?"

Oh yes, Captain Hammer was certainly solid in the thighs and chest. Being close to him on the horse had given me the perfect opportunity to feel just how solid. I said none of that to Tam, although I'd already described Hammer in detail to Meg, at her insistence. "Solid enough."

"Was there anything unusual about him?" Tam asked.

"Such as?"

He shrugged. "Such as fading in and out. Or shimmering, perhaps. I don't know. Anything?"

"Oh," Meg murmured. "Are you referring to…" She lowered her voice. "To magic?"

Tam winked.

I sighed. "He was real and solid and alive. They all were. His sergeant even bled red blood. Come now, Tam, I expect a well traveled man like you wouldn't believe in superstition and magic."

"Perhaps that's why I *do* believe. Did the men tell you

anything about the palace? Anything at all about its origins—or King Leon?"

"Nothing. Now, may we conduct our business? I'd like a bulb of fire breath, some reek root and one scoop each of amani, tumini and borrodi spices please."

As he packaged up my purchases, he finally imparted his own gossip to us. I was right he didn't have much to tell. He'd just come from Port Haven on The Thumb where houses lay empty and shops had closed.

"The downriver section of the Mer has been cut off from its source and dried up," he said. "It's now just rocks, sand and stagnant pools. The surrounding farms are struggling to irrigate their crops. The harbor is no longer bringing in any trade, and the king of Vytill isn't doing anything to help The Thumb folk. I heard the ministers have advised him to no longer consider it part of Vytill but rather an island nation that must administer itself. The population has been given a choice to resettle on the mainland or stay."

"They'll starve if they stay," I said with a shake of my head.

"They may starve on the mainland," Tam went on. "There's little work elsewhere in Vytill, particularly for those experienced only as dock workers."

"What about their mines?" The Fist Peninsula mined most of the stone, iron and other materials the various nations needed, but all those mines were concentrated in Freedland and in the south of Vytill and Dreen. There were none in Glancia or The Margin to the north.

"Dock workers aren't miners," Tam said.

"They can find work here," Meg said in all her good-hearted innocence. "There's plenty to do now that Tovey Harbor has become so important."

"Mull isn't ready for such a rapid increase in population," I told her. "We're not coping as it is."

"There's a rumor that Glancia may close its borders to migrants. They must already pay a fee to cross," Tam went on. "You're right, Josie, and Mull can't cope with rapid expansion.

Glancia can't cope. The villages are small and disparate, and quite primitive."

Meg bristled. "We are *not* primitive."

"Glancia is nothing but a handful of fishing villages." Tam handed me my purchases and I paid him. "Few people are educated, the roads are poor, and the ministers are too busy fighting amongst themselves to make the quick decisions that are necessary at a time like this. It didn't matter if they sat on their fat arses and twiddled their thumbs before, but it matters now. Perhaps the new king will whip them into action."

"Let's hope so," Meg said, thoughtfully. "I wish we knew more about him and his intentions."

All of Glancia wished that.

We thanked Tam and finished the rest of our marketing. Despite having told my story about the palace guards numerous times in the last week, I found I had to re-tell it again and again at each stall. Ultimately, my listeners were disappointed. I had so little to pass on, and I refused to embellish the tale as Meg suggested.

We did learn one more interesting piece of news. A farmer from outside Mull told of a procession of ministers arriving at the palace. The cavalcade of carriages, carts and wagons had stretched for a full mile along the road to Tilting, where the ministers and previous king had lived. It seemed the new palace was finally allowing in outsiders. It was a positive sign that King Leon might whip the ministers into action, as Tam had put it.

Meg and I parted in the street between our houses, and I found my father in the larder, reading labels on jars with his eyes screwed up so tightly it was a wonder he could see at all.

"Why is the Mother's Milk now stored in these pottery jars?" he asked. "We used to keep them in glass ones."

"Because the glass ones are too expensive," I said. "I told you that at the time. Why do you need Mother's Milk? What's happened? You're not scheduled for any surgeries today." Mother's Milk was used to relieve only the strongest pain because of its expense and the difficulty in sourcing ingredients. We made it ourselves to our own formula, but the ingredients came from my foraging expeditions and traders like Tamworth Tao, and they didn't always have what we needed. We only used it for surgeries, births where the mother had torn, and deep wounds. I probably shouldn't have used it on Sergeant Max, but the decision had been made and it was too late for regrets.

"Have you got the forceps?" Father asked.

"Someone's giving birth?" There weren't many pregnant women close to term that I knew of, and I thought I knew them all.

Father shooed me out of the larder. "Fetch the forceps. In fact, just give me your pack."

"Who's having a baby?"

"A woman."

I stepped in front of him and crossed my arms. "Why are you avoiding the question?"

He looked away.

"Father!"

He sighed. "A woman in The Row. Her waters broke overnight but the baby is stuck. Her sister came here and begged me to come. The expectant mother is fading."

"I'll go."

"You most certainly will not! Not to The Row."

"When I explain I'm the midwife—"

"They won't believe you. The fact is, Josie, you are a woman, and the only women in The Row are...you know."

"Whores," I finished for him since he seemed to have trouble with the word.

The Row had begun as a single street in the north of Mull, but over the years, it became synonymous with the entire area where the prostitutes eked out a living—if it could be called living. The buildings were little more than lean-tos, built from whatever materials had drifted onto the beaches. There were no proper gutters so the slops accumulated on the streets until the stench became too much and the residents themselves organized a cleanup. I'd never been into The Row, but I'd smelled it in summer and heard of the cramped conditions where the makeshift buildings couldn't keep the rain out let alone the wintry cold.

As much as I hated admitting it, Father was right. The women of The Row might trust me and accept me as a midwife, but the men would think of me as something they could purchase for a few minutes. It was too dangerous.

"Take Meg's brother with you," I said.

He shook his head. "Having a guard is as good as putting a target on my forehead. It'll make me look well off and in need of protection. I'll be safer alone."

He pushed past me and picked up my pack, the new one given to me by the leather seller. He placed the jar of Mother's Milk inside.

"You can't take the pack," I told him. "For the same reasons that having a guard will be a danger, so will carrying a bag."

"I have to take it."

I took it off him and removed the tools he'd need. "Place these in your pockets. I'll siphon enough Mother's Milk into a smaller jar."

He followed me into his surgery where I found an empty vial. "I had an unscheduled patient come this morning," he said. "Well, sort of unscheduled. Sergeant Max came to have his stitches out."

I turned suddenly, spilling a drop of the Mother's Milk. "Was he alone?"

"Yes. Why?"

"Just curious." I turned back to my task. "How is his wound?"

"Healing nicely. Your stitching was very fine. I couldn't have done better myself. Your mother would be pleased."

I laughed at that. We often joked how Mother would have liked me to be a normal girl with an interest in needlepoint, not surgery and medicine. She'd died when I was six but I'd already shown more enthusiasm for my father's books than embroidery at that age. The fact that we did laugh about it meant she hadn't really minded at all. According to Father, if she were still alive she would have been active in petitioning the authorities to change the laws so female students could study at the Logios colleges. Apparently I got my independent streak from her.

"What else did Max say?" I asked, careful not to sound too interested. "Did he mention Quentin? Or the captain?"

"Not specifically. He said everyone at the palace is busy with the arrival of the ministers and also preparing for more visitors."

"More?"

"Here's some gossip for you that no one else in Mull will have, I'd wager."

That got my full attention. I placed the stopper in the vial and regarded him. He was grinning. "Tell me!"

He chuckled. "You never did have much patience. He said the new visitors are the lords and ladies of Glancia, along with their daughters. Eligible ones, that is. The king wants a wife."

I quickly calculated numbers in my head. "Will they all stay in the palace?" There must be two hundred at least.

"They can't be put up at The Anchor, can they?" He laughed. "They're arriving in two weeks. Now, is that vial ready? I must hurry."

"I'll tell your afternoon patients to come back later."

"I wish you didn't have to," he said, pocketing the vial. "But it's for the best." He tossed me a smile and left.

A half hour later, I was inspecting Perri Ferrier's infected toe after he refused to leave. According to Perri, his pain was so intense that he required immediate attention. I cleaned up the toe, applied a salve, and bandaged it. When he left, he paid me the fee and an extra amount to buy "something pretty." I took that to mean he was satisfied with my service yet felt I ought to be more feminine. I'd never win with the Perri Ferriers of the world.

Father returned at dusk unharmed but disheartened. The baby had died; the mother, too. "The conditions in that place are appalling," he said, nursing his ale at the kitchen table. "It's a miracle anyone lives to adulthood. Someone should do something about it."

***

Two weeks later, Mull was abuzz with the news that several

of the country's best families had passed by the village on their way to the palace. I'd caught a glimpse of one of the processions and was surprised by how many vehicles one family of four needed. Apparently they required a carriage to transport themselves plus another six wagons for luggage and servants.

Lady Deerhorn pranced around Mull for days too, boasting how she and the other Deerhorns were staying at the palace, despite living so close. She insisted on seeing every bolt of silk and satin that arrived from Zemaya first, and bought several different colors, as well as beads, ribbons, lace, feathers and even gemstones.

Mull felt different since the arrival of the first families of Glancia at the palace. Anticipation and excitement hung in the air and gossip was rife, although how anyone could possibly know that Lady Laxley padded her bodice was a mystery. Some villagers ventured to the palace gates and were pleasantly surprised to find they were not ordered to go away. They were allowed to gaze upon the spectacle, but could not enter. Some of the visiting servants came into the village on their afternoons off and told tales of the dazzling palace and its inhabitants, but none had seen the king in person, and no matter how many I asked, none had met Captain Hammer, although they'd heard of him. His guards were omnipresent, apparently, yet he was confined to the king's side most of the time and out of view of the lower staff.

Another two weeks after the arrival of the nobles, in the final days of spring, the captain himself arrived at our house, alone.

"Josie," he said, greeting me as I opened the door on his urgent knock.

"Captain! What a surprise. Is Sergeant Max all right? Is it his arm?"

"He's fine." He glanced over my head. "Is your father home?"

"He's with a patient. He won't be long. Is someone at the palace injured? Ill?"

He nodded and once again glanced over my head toward Father's surgery, where low voices could be heard through the closed door. "I need Doctor Cully urgently."

"Perhaps I can help. What are the symptoms?"

A flicker passed through his eyes but I couldn't determine what it meant. "You said your father is an expert on poisons. Are you?"

"Poison! I, er, have some knowledge, but there isn't much call for poison expertise in Mull. Has someone ingested something noxious?"

"I believe so."

"Is it the king?"

"A lady." He eyed the closed door again. "He needs to come with me now. She's very ill."

He strode off but I rushed past him and knocked on the door. "Father! Father, we have an urgent situation," I called out. "It's the palace."

The door jerked open and Father stood there. He took one look at Hammer and slipped past me. "Josie, see to Peter while I gather what I need."

I glanced at Peter, a regular patient with a bad back. He usually only needed to replenish his ointment supply. I tucked a bottle into his hand.

"You have to go," I said to Peter. "This emergency requires us both." I caught a glimpse of the captain, standing just beyond the doorway, his brows raised at me.

He turned away when my father called out some questions about the patient's symptoms from the depths of the larder where we stored more medicines than food.

"What about a massage?" Peter asked me.

"Not today," I said. "The ointment is free."

I saw him out then assisted my father. Based on Hammer's answers, he'd gathered what he hoped would be the right ingredients to ease the pain.

"Cancel the rest of my appointments for the day, Josie," he said as he strode for the front door. He never looked more in command, more energetic, than when he was racing off to a medical emergency.

I grabbed the sign hanging from the nail on the outside of the door and flipped it over. GONE FISHING it read. Everyone in the village knew my father didn't fish, and that it was his way of telling them we were both out.

"Done," I said. When he gave me a stern look, I added, "I'm coming with you. What if you don't have the right medicine? You'll need an assistant to fetch ingredients for you. This job is far too important for just one."

"You get more and more like your mother every day."

"Thank you. Oh, look, it seems we're going to the palace in style."

A carriage blocked the street. The coachman and footman both wore crimson and gold livery. Another footman held a horse's reins which he handed to the captain. He opened the carriage door and I climbed in, followed by my father. We were away the moment the door closed.

I smoothed my hand over the crimson velvet covered seat and matching door with gold embroidered LL, the king's initials, repeated in a regular pattern. I blew out a breath and watched the streets of Mull whisk past, the people I'd known all my life staring with open mouths. And suddenly the reason for their shock hit me too.

I was going to the palace of King Leon, a man whose origins were as mysterious as those of the captain of his guards and the palace itself.

CHAPTER 3

I caught my first glimpse of the palace as we drove along the tree-lined avenue that led to the main gate. The symmetrical building was built from the same warm pale stone as much of Mull, but that was where the resemblance ended. The palace was three levels high with one wing stretching south and the other north. The entire length of gray slate roof was capped with gold, and gilded balustrades edged the roofline in an opulent statement. It was so bright in the sun that I couldn't stare at it for more than a moment. There was more to see, anyway. Much more.

The trees lining both sides of the avenue suddenly gave way

to buildings fronted by columns and arches. Servants dressed in royal crimson and gold lead horses in and out of the right building, while a carriage drawn by two black horses rolled through an arched entrance of the building to our left. These grand structures must be the coach house and stables.

"The horses live better than we do," I murmured.

Father didn't answer. He was too busy peering through the front window. The overwhelming sight of the palace up close was almost too much to take in. I didn't know where to look first. The gold-capped roof? The pink marble columns? Or the vast forecourt beyond the gate with its towering central fountain? Quentin was right. The palace did look tiny from Lookout Hill. Up close, it was enormous. The entire village of Mull could fit in it, with space to spare.

The captain rode ahead, and the guards manning the gate opened it for him. The gate itself was painted gold and topped by a golden statue of a warrior riding a chariot, brandishing a sword with a shield strapped to his arm. The House of Lockhart's coat of arms, featuring a key and a prancing deer, were picked out in gold relief on the shield, while the king's initials of LL made an impressive centerpiece on the gate.

My father gazed up at the statue and snorted. "He didn't win the kingdom through battle. I'd wager he's never lifted a sword in his life."

"Don't say that out loud around here," I warned. "Besides, we don't know if he has fought or not. We know nothing about him."

"Precisely."

We passed through the gate at a slower speed and into the expansive paved forecourt. Two identical long pavilions, fronted by high colonnades, faced each other across the area. They were not attached to the palace, but they seemed to guide visitors ever closer to it. Steps from the forecourt led to a smaller one paved in red, white and black marble. Water sprinkled from the fountain in the court's center. Beyond, the palace's main entrance was set back behind more pale pink marble colonnades.

It was not the only door, however. Others were dotted along

the central part of the palace, between the statues set into the façade and the high windows of sparklingly clean glass. The upper levels sported more doors opening onto balconies.

I was so stunned by the palace that I almost missed the lady dressed in lustrous sage green silk climbing into a sedan chair carried by two burly men. An attendant closed the door and off she went across the larger forecourt toward the palace. It was quite some distance from the gate to the palace door, but surely she could walk?

Instead of heading toward the palace, we drove past one of the pavilions. It was bigger than the new customs house would be and just as grand. We did not stop there, however, but continued to a square building south of the pavilion, hidden from the forecourts. Smoke billowed from the chimney pots high above us and cooking smells blended into a miasmic stew in the air. Servants bustled in and out of the building, some dressed in palace uniforms, others in the colors associated with their house, and again others in maids' uniforms, kitchen garb or gardening clothing. I even recognized two Deerhorn servants.

We'd hardly stopped when a palace footman opened the carriage door. "This way," Captain Hammer said as his horse was led away by a groom.

Ogling servants stepped aside to allow him to pass. Father and I trailed behind, despite walking quickly to keep up. The servants watched the captain in eerie silence then turned those curious gazes upon us. One of the Deerhorn servants whispered to the other, nodding at Father and me. They knew who we were, and if the rest of the servants didn't, they soon would.

The captain led us along the breezeway separating the square servants' building and the pavilion. We entered the palace through a service door and wove our way down dimly lit corridors before ascending a flight of stairs. We emerged into another corridor through a door that, when closed, blended into the wall so well that one had to know it was there to find it. This must be part of the palace seen by the lords and ladies. Where the walls in the servants' stairwell and corridors had been unadorned stone, these were plastered and painted in a vivid shade of green. Vases on pedestals filled with white lilies flanked each of the doors along the corridor. I counted five doors, separated by long expanses of paneled walls. We finally stopped at the sixth, manned by two guards holding long pikes.

They stepped aside and Captain Hammer held the door open for us. The room beyond wasn't a bedroom, as I expected, but a sitting room with elegant furniture arranged around a black marble fireplace and gold leaf gilding the cornices. A portrait of a man dressed in furs hung above the mantel, one hand resting on his hip, the other holding a scepter. His dark eyes seemed to follow me as we hurried across the thick carpet to a door on the far side that led to the bedroom.

Hammer nodded at Sergeant Max, who stood by the wall, trying and failing to look inconspicuous between a spindly-legged chest of drawers and a dressing table topped with small bottles, a jar of cream, and hair combs.

I smiled at him. He gave me a nod then flicked his gaze toward the four post bed where my father now stood, inspecting the patient. He was more professional than me. Where I'd been distracted by the awe-inspiring palace, and the men I'd met some weeks ago, Father had immediately focused on the deathly pale woman throwing up into the porcelain bowl held by a maid. Another man and woman had moved aside to allow my father closer to the bed. Both were in middle age and looked on anxiously. They wore long richly brocaded gowns and slippers, and the man held one of the woman's hands between both of his. These must be the patient's parents.

Father placed the palm of his hand to the girl's forehead then checked the pulse at her wrist. I dipped my fingers into the basin of water on the bedside table. I touched the back of the patient's neck and she sighed from the coolness.

It wasn't a hot day but the room felt stifling, thanks to being higher up in the palace. Sweat dampened the woman's blonde hair and her nightdress clung to her curves.

"Open the windows," I said. The captain nodded at Sergeant Max to follow my orders. "Do you have a fan?" I asked the maid.

The patient had finished throwing up but the maid still held the bowl ready. I took it from her and she disappeared into the sitting room. She returned a moment later with a large fan. Under my direction, she stood on the other side of the bed and flapped it at her mistress.

"How long ago did the vomiting start?" my father asked the patient.

"Last night," the woman whispered through cracked, colorless lips. "I went to bed after midnight and woke up with terrible cramps." Her hand fluttered weakly at her stomach. "I thought it would pass."

"Did you raise the alarm?" I asked the maid.

She nodded quickly. "My lady was like this when I brought in her breakfast. I fetched Lady Claypool straight away."

Claypool. I knew that name. The Claypools were a noble family with an estate near Coldstream. Lord Claypool had come to Mull once, years ago, to inspect a fishing vessel. I'd not met him but had heard about him from those who had. Looking at him now, anxious about his ill daughter, he did not seem like the same man that Meg had called both masculine and graceful in the same awed breath.

"She has been like this all morning," Lady Claypool said.

Going by the contents of the bowl, the patient had long since thrown up her last meal and now discharged only liquid. Someone had emptied the bowl.

Father asked the patient questions as he peered into her eyes, down her throat, and at her fingers. I didn't know what he was looking for, but I would certainly ask later and make notes. I hated having gaps in my knowledge.

I did know one thing he would need, and while he was tied up investigating the patient's symptoms, I could be of use elsewhere. "Have you disposed of the other contents?" I asked the maid and indicated the bowl.

She chewed on the inside of her lip. "I emptied it into the bathtub."

"And where is the bathtub now?"

"The bathroom."

The palace had a bathroom! What a luxury.

I followed her through another door near the back of the bedchamber into a large room painted yellow with a pink marble tiled floor. An unlit furnace squatted in the middle of the room beside a bathtub raised on a dais. The tub was large enough for me to stretch my legs out if I sat in it. Not that I would want to sit in it with the remnants of the patient's stomach pooled at one end. There didn't seem very much, however, and I realized the rest had disappeared through a hole in the bottom of the tub.

"Is that a drain?" I asked, looking closer. "Where does it go?"

"I don't know." The maid held up a plug then peered into the bath. She pulled a face. "I didn't know it hadn't all gone down. I didn't look. I just wanted to get back to Lady Miranda. Will she be all right?" She blinked back tears. "She's been so good to me. She's such a lovely lady, so beautiful and kind. It's no wonder the king has fallen in love with her already. I wouldn't be surprised if they wed before the summer is out. If she... If she doesn't..." Her lower lip wobbled but she managed to keep control of her tears.

I squeezed her shoulder. "You're a good maid to her. She's very lucky to have you. Don't worry. My father is the best doctor in Glancia, and he's an expert on poisons."

"Poison! You think she's been poisoned? Oh, dear Hailia, no."

"I—er...that is, we're not sure. She probably just ate something that didn't agree with her." Damn. The captain hadn't told her he suspected poison, and I'd just blabbed as if it were common knowledge. I hoped the Claypools didn't know.

The maid gasped. "Do you think someone fed her the poison deliberately?"

"No! Of course not. She most likely ate the wrong kind of salad leaf."

"But she didn't eat anything that the rest of them didn't. And she had no late night snack before bed, just the food at dinner that the others also ate. Even the king ate the same as my lady." She gasped again. "Do you think it was meant for him?"

Merdu, she had a macabre imagination. I had to reel it in

before she accused someone of murder. "Do all the bedchambers in the palace have their own bathroom?"

She blinked rapidly at my sudden change of topic. "Not all. Most of the nobles have to share. We servants have a communal bathroom. Only the king's apartments and these ones are grand enough to have their own. Lady Miranda and her parents only moved down here two days ago from the attic rooms allotted to them when we first arrived." She drew in a breath and her chest swelled. "*These* apartments are supposed to be for dukes and duchesses, not for the lower nobles like Lord Claypool. He's only a baron, so the family shouldn't be here at all. But King Leon insisted on them moving out of the attic once he took a shine to Lady Miranda, even though Lord and Lady Claypool insisted they were comfortable where they were." She leaned closer and lowered her voice. "The higher up families are so jealous. You ought to hear what they say about my lady. Vile things." She shook her head. "Seems jealousy isn't just for the likes of you and me, miss."

I asked her for a towel and used it to pluck up partially-digested remains of Lady Miranda's last meal. Back in the bedchamber, I stuffed the towel into one of our empty jars.

It was then that I noticed a newcomer in the room. Another guard wearing a uniform with identical gold braiding on his shoulder and chest to Max's. He was of medium build with brown hair and the sharp cheekbones of a Vytill native. He stood by the door, his hands at his back, and stared straight ahead.

I turned to my father as he spoke, but not before I noticed Hammer watching me.

"Note the color of the fingernails, Josie," Father said, indicating the dark half moons on Lady Miranda's fingernails. "And tell me what you see in her eyes."

"The whites are milky," I said. "And the pupils are dilated. Her breathing is erratic too. Does your stomach still hurt?" I asked her.

My father nodded his approval of my question, but I guessed

he'd already asked it while I was in the bathroom. He began to pack away his things.

Lady Miranda nodded and winced. She was putting on a brave face, but I could see by the way her jaw tensed that she was in pain. I touched her arm and gave her a reassuring smile.

"Don't worry," I said. "You're in the best hands now."

"Do you know what ails her?" Lady Claypool asked.

"Direweed mixed with traitor's ease," Father said. "Two poisons blended—"

"Poison!" Lord Claypool cried.

"Dear Hailia," Lady Claypool whispered, clasping her daughter's hand. Tears slipped down her cheeks. Lady Miranda lifted a hand to wipe them away but it fell to her side. She was too weak.

"Is there an antidote?" Captain Hammer asked.

My father nodded. "I'll make one up."

"Will it take long?"

"An hour once I get back to my surgery." An hour for an antidote was too long. He was holding something back, but I couldn't fathom what.

"Then go!" Lady Claypool said through her tears. "Go now, Doctor, please. Hurry back."

"Captain..." Lord Claypool began, casting a look toward Hammer.

The captain nodded. "He'll have an escort the whole way and our fastest horses."

"Continue to give her liquids," Father told the maid. "We need to flush it out of her system as much as we can before I give her the antidote." He had hardly finished speaking before he was out the door.

I hurried after him, the captain and the Vytill sergeant on my heels. Max remained behind. We caught up to my father.

"Does she have an hour, Doctor?" the captain asked.

"She has two," Father said without breaking his long strides. "If she's strong and healthy."

"She seemed to be, before this."

"Are you a god-fearing man, Captain?"

The sergeant grunted a harsh laugh.

"Pray to the goddess Hailia that she lives. Come. We must hurry."

***

Captain Hammer's silent presence was a distraction. He stood inside the front door, his arms crossed, legs slightly apart, and watched us through the open door of Father's workroom as we tested and re-tested the contents of Lady Miranda's stomach. Without a sample of the poisoned food or liquid, we had only the evidence of her discharge to go by. It should be enough.

Father clicked his tongue. "Too much riverwart." He used the tongs to remove the small dish from the grill over the low fire and threw both dish and liquid into the pail near his feet. It was a terrible waste but we couldn't risk reusing a dish the poison had touched. "Damnation." He pressed a hand to his lower back and stretched. "Another, Josie."

I handed him a clean dish and scooped a coin-sized chunk of Lady Miranda's regurgitated meal onto it with a spoon. We had precious little left. "Should I halve the quantity of riverwart this time?"

"Try one third. Going by the speed at which it burned, I grossly overestimated the amount."

I handed him the bowl of ground riverwart but he shook his head. "You do it. My hands are shaking."

I'd noticed them trembling a while ago but hadn't pointed it out. He could be sensitive about his age on occasion, but I knew he'd ask me to take over if the trembling interfered with his ability to work. He might be somewhat vain about his age, but never to the detriment of a patient's wellbeing.

I added the requisite quantities of the six other ingredients that we'd identified for the antidote based on Father's old notes from a book I'd never seen him refer to before. We only had the riverwart to go. The painstaking process of testing and re-testing to find the right quantities of each ingredient had meant we'd taken longer than the hour. Father told me upon our arrival at the cottage that he'd only said that to give the patient hope. If she had hope, she might find the strength to fight and we needed her to fight. We'd be cutting it very fine to get back to her on time. It all depended on how much riverwart needed to be added to the other ingredients to neutralize the poison left in Lady Miranda's vomit.

I heard the front door open but did not turn around as I measured out the powder.

"Aren't they ready yet?" came the voice of the other sergeant, the one named Brant. "The hour has long passed."

"Go back outside," the captain growled.

My father left the workroom to speak to them. "It's a complicated process," I heard him hiss. "It's not a combination of poisons I've come across before and the ratios used are unknown. Traitor's ease is rare. Very rare. I've only seen it once in its raw form—years ago, in Zemaya. If you want us to work faster, you'll shut up so we can think."

I smiled. Father might seem like a meek professorial type of man, but two things stirred his passionate nature—the wellbeing of his patients, and when someone disparaged me.

"Shouldn't you be in there making the antidote?" Sergeant Brant said to him.

"My daughter is more than capable."

"Is she qualified?"

"She has a lot of experience."

"I'm sure the king would like to hear how the unqualified daughter of the local healer was left to create the antidote to save one of the most important ladies in the realm. We should have used the finance minister's doctor, as he offered."

"The king will receive a full report," was all the captain said. "Return to your post outside, Sergeant."

I heard the front door close. I added a lump of peat to the fire contained within the heatproof box set up on the desk and tipped the riverwart into the dish. Father rejoined me and watched as I mixed the powder with the other ingredients until it was fully dissolved then set the dish on the grill over the fire.

The liquid quickly heated to simmering point but seemed to take forever to boil. The other experiments hadn't taken this long. I looked to Father.

His lips twitched into a smile. "I think this is it."

The liquid in the dish bubbled and turned a yellowish-green color.

"Take it off the heat," Father said, handing me the tongs. "Quickly now. We don't want it to burn away."

I set the bowl down carefully on the tray. "That's the right color?"

He handed me a ceramic jar. "It is. Commit it to memory, Josie. I hope you'll never need to make this antidote again, but one never knows, particularly now that the palace has sprung up nearby."

"What has that got to do with poisons?"

"It's the favorite method of murder at courts all over The Fist and beyond. Has been for centuries." He pressed the jar into my hand with a grim smile. "There's no time to wait for it to cool. Pour it in now. Don't spill any."

The dish had cooled enough for me to touch it with my bare hands. With a steadying breath, I poured the medicine into the jar. Father fixed the cork stopper in place.

"Remind me to update my notes later," he said, tucking the jar into the pocket of his loose doublet.

Without a word of instruction, Hammer opened the door and followed us out.

"About time," Sergeant Brant muttered under his breath.

I hadn't thought it possible to go any faster, but we drove at such a speed on the return to the palace that we did not slow for bumps or dips. Father and I got tossed around inside the cabin but it didn't seem to bother him in the least.

He didn't wait for the footman to open the door upon our arrival at the palace. He strode on ahead, joined by the captain. I picked up my skirts and ran after them, the sergeant behind me. The hairs on the back of my neck prickled and I turned quickly on the service stairs, catching him watching me.

"I hope I didn't offend you earlier," he said. "It's not personal. It's just that the king's mistress should have the best doctor."

"And you believe the finance minister's doctor is the best?" I asked.

"So I hear."

"You hear wrong. My father is the best, and if he lived in Tilting, he'd have the sort of reputation that would satisfy you. But he prefers to be in Mull, where the people are in dire need of excellent medical attention. That's just the sort of person he is."

"I can see why Max and Quentin like you," he muttered.

I forged ahead and met the glare of Captain Hammer, holding the door open for me. His eyes had a way of making me feel as though he was rummaging around inside me, searching for my secrets. I pushed past him and followed my father along the corridor to Lady Miranda's sitting room.

A man dressed in black with gold braid at the shoulder, like Captain Hammer's uniform, stood just inside the door. He nodded gravely at Hammer, who nodded back.

Another man paced across the carpet near the hearth. He stopped abruptly and fixed dark eyes on my father. He was short and slender with black hair that fell to his white lace collar in gentle waves. He couldn't have been more than mid-twenties, and his face looked vaguely familiar but I couldn't place it. He wore a doublet of deep blue with silver leaves and vines embroidered over the sleeves and down the front. The white lace cuffs of his shirt fell to his knuckles. He tipped his head back and peered down his nose at us; quite a feat considering he was shorter.

"Are you the doctor?" he demanded.

"This is Doctor Cully and his daughter Joselyn Cully, sire," Captain Hammer announced.

Sire? So this was Glancia's new king? I hurriedly performed a curtsy that almost ended in my humiliation, since I hadn't a clue how to curtsy properly. Thankfully the king was too busy ushering my father through to the bedroom to notice.

"Hurry then!" he said. "There is not a moment to delay."

I caught a glimpse of the painting hanging above the mantel as I passed and realized why the king looked familiar. It was his portrait hanging there, although he seemed more imposing in the picture as he looked down on the painter with disdain. The real monarch was far less regal. Indeed, he looked quite ordinary.

I nodded at Sergeant Max, still standing where we'd left him, and joined Father at the bed. Lord and Lady Claypool had stood upon our entry and peppered Father with questions about the antidote.

He put up his hand for silence as he bent over Lady Miranda, who lay almost unmoving in the bed. She looked little better than a corpse. Sweat dripped from her brow onto the pillow, and her face was as white as the sheets on which she lay. Her breathing labored in shallow rasps and her eyelids fluttered. She was barely conscious, but at least she was alive.

Father removed the jar from his pocket and asked the maid to assist Lady Miranda to sit up. She struggled, and Max came to her aid. The maid settled behind her mistress to support her, and I tipped her head back and opened her mouth. Father poured a little of the liquid down her throat. She instinctively swallowed and he poured more. He continued the process slowly until the entire contents of the jar were gone.

The maid laid Lady Miranda down again, and everyone, including the king but not the guards, crowded close to the bed. The room fell silent. Father and I exchanged glances and small smiles. Lady Miranda's breathing was returning to normal. It was an excellent sign.

"She'll sleep now," Father whispered, backing away from the bed. "May I respectfully suggest that she be left in peace for the rest of the day? Only her maid is to be allowed to check on her from time to time, but not wake her."

"And me," Lady Claypool murmured without taking her eyes off her daughter.

"Yes, of course. It's imperative that Lady Miranda sleeps as long as she needs. Her body must rest to allow the antidote to work as efficiently as possible. I expect her to sleep through the night to the morning. It's vitally important she isn't disturbed. Is that clear?"

Everyone nodded. The maid looked terrified, particularly when Father signaled for her to follow him into the sitting room.

"She may grow restless in a few hours," he said quietly. "This is normal and expected. Make sure Lady Claypool is aware when it happens and does not try to wake her daughter. I don't expect Lady Miranda to purge any more. If her color hasn't returned by dawn, send for me. If she doesn't wake by midday the day after, send for me. I'll return after then to check on her anyway."

"You will stay until she is well, Doctor," the king commanded. He signaled to his man standing by the door to the corridor, and the servant approached.

"I regret that I cannot," my father said.

Merdu. Was he mad? He was certainly behaving irrationally. He might not be all that respectful when he had to tend to one of the Deerhorns, but they were only lords. This was the king, and kings' wishes were not refused.

King Leon bristled. "Lady Miranda is very dear to me. If she dies—"

"She won't if she's left alone to rest."

The king's nostrils flared at the interruption. He slapped one hand against the palm of the other behind his back. "Nevertheless, the village is too far away. If you're needed urgently, it will take too long for you to be fetched."

"I have an afternoon schedule full of patients who need me, sire." Father bowed. "I am sorry, but the people of Mull are important too."

The king puffed out his chest and lifted his chin. His manservant winced, as if he expected an explosion of temper from his master.

"I'll stay," I said quickly.

"Josie," my father scolded.

"I know the danger signs," I added. "I can answer any questions His Majesty or Lady Miranda's family may have, and I'll know how to keep her comfortable."

The king glanced at me, away, and back again. Those deep, dark eyes scanned me from head to toe with cool assessment. "You're a woman."

"Yes," I said, biting back the sarcasm that came naturally to my lips.

"My daughter would be a doctor if the college allowed it," Father said proudly. "She would graduate top of her class."

"But they don't allow it."

A small frown creased the captain's forehead as he followed the exchange.

"Please, Your Majesty," I said. "I know it's unusual, but I also know my father will not give up his Mull patients, and I am more than capable of tending to Lady Miranda as she recovers. Besides, there'll be little to do except observe her." The more I thought about it, the more I wanted to stay. Not for Lady Miranda, who seemed to be out of danger, but because the palace and its inhabitants fascinated me. It was an opportunity to learn more.

"I prefer you to come home with me, Josie," Father said. "I need your help. My eyes are bad now and my hands..." He held up his hands. They trembled too much for it to be a natural shake.

I gave him a glare that told him I knew it. He looked a little sheepish for lying, at least.

"She stays." The king turned to his manservant, a slender fellow of about thirty with the flat face and straight hair of the Dreen. "Send someone to go with Doctor Cully and bring back the things Miss Cully will need overnight."

"Yes, sire." He turned to go.

"And Theodore?"

"Yes, sire?"

"Make sure the court knows that no noise is to reach Lady Miranda's rooms. There will be no revelries tonight, no musicales, and no games. If they complain, tell them to use the time to reflect."

"Yes, sire." Theodore hurried out of the room.

Captain Hammer directed Sergeant Brant to escort my father home. Sergeant Brant looked as if he'd question the order, but a glare from Hammer silenced him.

My father didn't immediately follow him out. "May I have a word in private with my daughter?"

"Of course," the king said, stepping toward the captain.

"Hammer, you *must* find out who did this before he strikes again."

My father grabbed my elbow before I could stumble through a curtsy and steered me away from them. "Josie, I forbid you to leave these rooms."

"Why?"

"Because..." He indicated the sitting room, the window, the door, but I had no idea why. "Because this place is strange. Its very existence is strange. The sooner you leave here, the happier I'll be."

"Father," I chided. "This place may be odd, but it's not sinister. And it's certainly real, not a magic palace."

One white eyebrow crept up his forehead. "It seems there is a poisoner within these walls. Is that sinister enough for you?"

"I won't eat anything intended for the Lady Miranda."

"Don't be glib." He looked toward Captain Hammer who stood with Sergeant Brant, the king having left. "I don't like you being exposed to these people, Josie. There's something about them..."

"Something odd, yes, we've established that." I kissed his cheek. "Go. They're waiting."

Father gave me a flat smile and joined the captain and sergeant. "Where can direweed and traitor's ease be purchased in Mull?" I heard the captain ask as they exited the sitting room.

"Direweed is sold by two traders that I know of," Father said. "Traitor's ease is another matter. I've never seen it in Mull's market."

I re-entered the sickroom. Lord and Lady Claypool seemed to take my presence as a signal for them to leave. They excused themselves and hurried from the room. I sat with the maid, Hilda, but almost fell asleep in the chair. The return of Lady Claypool roused me some time later. She looked much fresher and extraordinarily elegant in a dove-gray gown trimmed with pink lace, her golden hair fixed into an elaborate arrangement that must have required at least two maids to do in the time she'd been absent.

I signaled to Max to join me in the sitting room and shut the door behind him. "You won't be needed," I said. "She'll sleep for a while."

"I don't require rest, and the captain ordered me to remain here." He checked the corridor outside then rejoined me. After a moment, he sighed and sat on a chair. He rubbed his knee. "Will she really be all right?"

"There is always some lingering concern until the patient is fully recovered, but she should be fine. My father wouldn't have left if he thought otherwise."

"The captain said Doctor Cully is an expert in poisons."

"He is, from his travels."

"Would he know who supplied the poisoner?"

"No. He can guess, as I can, and he will pass those guesses onto your captain."

He blew out a breath. "Of course. My apologies, Josie, I didn't express myself very well."

"It's all right. I can see that you're troubled. Do you know Lady Miranda well?"

He shifted forward in the chair and rubbed his hand over his jaw. "Not at all. I've seen her from afar, walking with the king, playing cards with the other ladies, laughing." A ghostly smile touched his lips before setting into a serious line again. "She laughs a lot. It's obvious she enjoys the king's company and he hers."

"You think they'll marry?"

"Not if the ministers have their way."

"Why don't they want him to marry her?"

"Because her family isn't important enough. They want him to make a strategic marriage, not a love match."

"Will he bow to their wishes?"

He lifted one shoulder. "Who know what the king thinks? He keeps his own counsel."

"He doesn't confide in his ministers? Or his trusted servants?"

He hesitated and shifted his feet before finally answering. "He trusts Theodore, Hammer and Balthazar with his life, but not with his secrets. He prefers to meditate on problems of state in his own rooms, alone."

"Who is Theodore? I noticed he wears a similar black uniform to the captain's."

"That's because he's the highest servant in the palace, along with Hammer and the Master of the Palace, Balthazar. Theodore is the king's chief valet. He organizes all personal matters for the king, from his wardrobe to his food, who gets to see him and when. Hammer takes care of the king's personal security, and Balthazar oversees the staff who don't fall under Hammer's or Theodore's jurisdiction, as well as the day to day running of the household. Between the three of them, they have utmost authority."

"The king must have known them a long time to entrust them with such important roles."

"It would seem so." He stood and turned toward the bedroom but stopped. "Quentin will want to know you're here. He's been driving everyone in the garrison mad with talk of you these last few weeks."

"He's sweet."

"He's a fool but a harmless one. I'll tell him you're here when I'm relieved of duty. He'll want to take over but I doubt the captain will let him. He's too..." He waved a hand, as if that explained Quentin's inadequacy.

"Tell Quentin I'll visit later. Where's the garrison?"

Max hesitated before answering, "Ground floor, almost at the end of the northern wing."

I followed him into the bedchamber and checked on the patient. She slept peacefully so I decided to go for a short walk along the corridor. I was surprised to see more guards on duty. Two had been stationed at each end. I asked one of them who occupied the other rooms and he said that aside from Lord and Lady Claypool's apartments, only the duke and duchess of Gladstow had permission to use that corridor to access their rooms. Captain Hammer had instructed the guards not to allow anyone else in until Lady Miranda was better.

I sat with the patient and checked her pulse on the hour simply to keep her mother and maid happy. I could tell by looking at Lady Miranda that she was better. She wasn't quite so pale anymore and she slept peacefully.

The maid left to have her supper and brought some bread and cheese back for me. She whispered something in Lady Claypool's ear then her ladyship rose and left. I ate in the sitting room. By the time I'd finished, Lady Claypool returned. She smiled warmly at me and entered her daughter's bedchamber.

After another hour, I could no longer stand the boredom. I signaled that I was going out then slipped into the corridor. Someone had lit the torches in the wall sconces and the flames danced merrily in the drafts.

I found the hidden door that opened up to the service stairs by running my palm along the wall. Thankfully the torches had been lit in the service corridors too. I headed downstairs then in the direction that I hoped was north, although I couldn't be certain. The windowless passages used by the servants played havoc with my usually good sense of direction. I asked a passing footman dressed in palace livery which way to go but I didn't like the way he licked his lips as he looked at me, so hurried on. Thankfully he didn't follow. I came across two maids moments later, talking quietly.

"Can you point me in the direction of the guards' garrison?" I asked them.

"Who do you work for?" asked the larger one.

"No one. I came to tend to Lady Miranda Claypool."

"You're that woman doctor!" the thin one cried. "Is she all right? Will she die?"

"She'll be fine."

"Good. I liked her."

The big woman grunted. "I know a few what will be disappointed with that news. Some around here want her dead. Some would rather the king looked at them the way he looks at her."

"Well some ain't as pretty or as kind as her and ought to just piss off back to where they came from," the thin maid said. "I'll be glad when they're all gone again. They're lazy and rude. Fetch this, empty that...it's all they ever say, and me not even their own maid. That's just the ladies too. The men are worse. My arse still hurts from where that Deerhorn prick slapped it when I was trying to make his bed."

"You should have slapped him back," the big woman said.

"I would have but he looked like he could smack me from here to the other end of the palace."

"He can," I warned her. "Stay away from the Deerhorns, especially the sons."

"Thanks. I will." She pointed along the corridor. "Take this all the way. Turn right, then left, then right again. Go down the steps, through the arched doorway—"

"The second one," the thin maid said.

"No, the third. Then it's right, right again and left. Why?" she asked with a crooked grin. "Who're you meeting there?"

"Quentin, and it's not like that."

Both women chuckled. "We believe you," the bigger woman said. "If it were the captain, I'd have my suspicions."

"He has a lot of lovers?" I dared ask.

"Don't know. I meant you ain't the first one who's tried to find her way to his room in the night. Problem is, his chambers are next to the king's. It's impossible to sneak in without a dozen servants seeing."

"You tried, eh?" The thin woman chuckled and nudged her companion in the ribs with her elbow.

I continued on my way but became hopelessly lost when the corridor darkened. The torches in this part were not lit. I was surrounded by cool stone walls, a flagstone floor and wooden ceiling that creaked as someone walked above me. That's it! I'd forgotten to go down the steps.

I was about to retreat when I heard someone speaking. "How did he know, Hammer?" the man asked. "How did he know women aren't allowed into the medical college in...where is it again?"

"Logios." I recognized Captain Hammer's voice, drifting to me from along the corridor. He was still far enough away, however, that I couldn't see him. "It's an old city in Dreen where all the colleges are located, and the libraries. Perhaps he read about it. There's a book on the history of The Fist Peninsula in the palace library. More than one, in fact."

Why would the king need to read up on Logios? Everyone on The Fist knew of the colleges and how they didn't allow women. I could believe that these men, who may not be native to the peninsula, would need to read a historical text on the area to know such a thing, but it struck me as odd that they thought their king in the same boat.

"He doesn't read books. I know that for a fact." I now recognized the voice as belonging to Theodore, the king's valet. "He's worried the poisoner meant to target him and not the Lady Miranda. Can you reassure him?"

"Not yet."

The voices became more distant and I realized they weren't coming toward me after all. I went in search of them. I thought I almost had them but as I rounded a corner, I saw Theodore's back as he walked alone through a doorway. There was no sign of Hammer.

I took the other door. A faint keening echoed along the narrow space. I couldn't tell if it was human or animal, but it was certainly disturbing. My heart raced and every part of me wanted to turn back. But I was a healer and that sound could have come from an injured or ill person. It was my duty to check. Besides, Captain Hammer must be up ahead and he was no danger.

I crept along the dark corridor, feeling my way with a hand pressed against the stone. The keening sounded again. At first it seemed as if it was all around me, but as it faded, I could tell that it came from ahead. I sucked in a deep breath in the hope it would calm my rapidly beating heart, then pushed on.

Soon the pitch dark lightened to a dull gray and finally the flames of a lit torch banished the darkness to the shadowy edges on either side of a closed door. A padlock as big as my hand hung from the bolt. It was open.

Beyond the door, wood scraped and a metal chain clanked, but the keening had stopped. There were no other sounds. The silence closed in, as thick as a winter fog.

I reached out but the handle turned. My heart leapt into my throat. I don't know why, but I ran off back up the corridor.

I got as far as the corner when someone grabbed me from behind. I tried to scream but a hand slapped over my mouth. A strong arm wrapped around my waist and pulled me back against a solid chest.

"You shouldn't be here, Josie," Captain Hammer said in a low voice that stretched my nerves to breaking point. "You shouldn't be anywhere near here."

Get **THE PALACE OF LOST MEMORIES** now.

GET A FREE SHORT STORY

I wrote a short story for the Glass and Steele series that is set before THE WATCHMAKER'S DAUGHTER. Titled THE TRAITOR'S GAMBLE it features Matt and his friends in the Wild West town of Broken Creek. It contains spoilers from THE WATCHMAKER'S DAUGHTER, so you must read that first. The best part is, the short story is FREE, but only to my newsletter subscribers. So subscribe now via my website if you haven't already.

A MESSAGE FROM THE AUTHOR

I hope you enjoyed reading THE INK MASTER'S SILENCE as much as I enjoyed writing it. As an independent author, getting the word out about my book is vital to its success, so if you liked this book please consider telling your friends and writing a review at the store where you purchased it. If you would like to be contacted when I release a new book, subscribe to my newsletter at http://cjarcher.com/contact-cj/newsletter/. You will only be contacted when I have a new book out.

ALSO BY C.J. ARCHER

SERIES WITH 2 OR MORE BOOKS

After The Rift

Glass and Steele

The Ministry of Curiosities Series

The Emily Chambers Spirit Medium Trilogy

The 1st Freak House Trilogy

The 2nd Freak House Trilogy

The 3rd Freak House Trilogy

The Assassins Guild Series

Lord Hawkesbury's Players Series

The Witchblade Chronicles

SINGLE TITLES NOT IN A SERIES

Courting His Countess

Surrender

Redemption

The Mercenary's Price

ABOUT THE AUTHOR

C.J. Archer has loved history and books for as long as she can remember and feels fortunate that she found a way to combine the two. She spent her early childhood in the dramatic beauty of outback Queensland, Australia, but now lives in suburban Melbourne with her husband, two children and a mischievous black & white cat named Coco.

Subscribe to C.J.'s newsletter through her website to be notified when she releases a new book, as well as get access to exclusive content and subscriber-only giveaways. Her website also contains up to date details on all her books: http://cjarcher.com She loves to hear from readers. You can contact her through email cj@cjarcher.com or follow her on social media to get the latest updates on her books: